BEAUTIFUL THINGS

ALSO BY EMILY RATH

JACKSONVILLE RAYS SERIES
SPICY HOCKEY ROMANCE
That One Night (#.0.5)
Pucking Around (#1)
Pucking Ever After: Vol I (#1.5)
Pucking Wild (#2)
Pucking Ever After: Vol. 2 (#2.5)
Pucking Sweet (#3)

SECOND SONS SERIES
SPICY 'WHY CHOOSE' REGENCY ROMANCE
Beautiful Things (#1)
His Grace, The Duke (#2)
Alcott Hall (#3)

STANDALONES
CONTEMPORARY MM OMEGAVERSE
Whiskey & Sin

THE TUONELA DUET
North is the Night

BEAUTIFUL THINGS

EMILY RATH

KENSINGTON
PUBLISHING CORP.

kensingtonbooks.com

KENSINGTON BOOKS are published by:
Kensington Publishing Corp.
900 Third Avenue
New York, NY 10022

kensingtonbooks.com

All Kensington titles, imprints, and distributed lines are available at special quantity discounts for bulk purchases for sales promotions, premiums, fundraising, educational, or institutional use.

Special book excerpts or customized printings can also be created to fit specific needs. For details, write or phone the office of the Kensington sales manager: Kensington Publishing Corp., 900 Third Avenue, New York, NY 10022, attn: Sales Department; phone 1-800-221-2647.

The K with book logo Reg US Pat. & TM Off.

ISBN 978-1-4967-5679-4 (trade paperback)

First Kensington trade paperback printing: August 2025

10 9 8 7 6 5 4 3 2 1

Printed in China

Electronic edition: ISBN 978-1-4967-5615-2

Interior art by Lucy Rose
Interior design by Kelsy Thompson
Author photograph by Jennifer Catherine Photography

The authorized representative in the EU for product safety and compliance
is eucomply OU, Parnu mnt 139b-14, Apt 123
Tallinn, Berlin 11317, hello@eucompliancepartner.com

To Darcy and Wentworth and
Knightly . . . collectively.
And more especially to Jane, the saucy
minx who created them.

AUTHOR'S NOTE

MAYBE YOU SAW the cover of this book or read the blurb, and thought, "I loved Bridgerton, let's give this a try!" But be forewarned, dear readers, this is a Regency-era polyamorous romance. What does that mean? Glad you asked.

This story is first and foremost a Regency romance. So be ready for a deliciously slow burn. We're talking prolonged eye contact, subtle hand touches, and soooo much sexual tension. We all know that Darcy hand flex scene. BUT this is also a "why choose" polyamorous romance. That means the female main character will have multiple male suitors (Austen approved) and she won't choose just one in the end (Emily approved).

Not only is everyone ultimately happy with this arrangement, they wouldn't have it any other way. That's not to say there won't be some tears, heartache, and more than a few dramatic surprises to enjoy between page one and our long-awaited happily ever after.

If you love the humor and heart of Jane Austen and the sexy vibes of Bridgerton and you've ever felt like screaming "Christ Almighty, just pick them both!" while watching an episode of Poldark, this series might just be for you. Grab your smelling salts and get ready to clutch your pearls—this is not your grandmother's Regency romance.

XO,

E Roth

THE LORDS AND LADIES AT ALCOTT HALL

In the British social hierarchy, the order of rank is as follows:
- King/Queen
- Duke/Duchess
- Marquess/Marchioness
- Earl/Countess
- Viscount/Viscountess
- Baron/Baroness
- Baronet/Lady
- Knight/Lady

Names and titles can be confusing, but I tried to keep it as true to the time period as possible. The following are characters with titles, presented in order of rank (high to low):

The Corbins (Dukes):
- George Corbin, The Duke of Norland
- Harriet Wakefield Corbin, The Dowager Duchess of Norland, George's mother
- Lord James Corbin, The Viscount Finchley, George's younger brother

The Rutledges (Marquesses):
- Constance Rutledge, The Marchioness of Deal
- Lady Olivia Rutledge, daughter

The Swindons (Earls):
- Mary Swindon, The Countess of Waverley
- Lady Elizabeth Swindon, eldest daughter
- Lady Mariah Swindon, youngest daughter

The Blaires (Viscounts):
- Diana Blaire, The Viscountess of Raleigh
- Lady Madeline Blaire, daughter

The Oswalds (Knights):
- Sir Andrew Oswald, esq.
- Lady Anne Oswald, wife of Sir Andrew
- Miss Blanche Oswald, daughter

1

Rosalie

THE CARRIAGE RATTLED down the rain-soaked road, hitting each puddle and bump with a vengeance. Rosalie groaned, holding tight to her seat with both hands. Three days of rain with no reprieve, but she couldn't risk delaying her journey any longer. When a duchess requests your immediate presence, you don't question it. You pack your bags and get on the first coach.

Which is how Rosalie found herself wedged in the corner of a public coach bound for Carrington. She'd been trapped in this miserable box all day, windows shut tight against the gale. Six hours with no air, forced to endure the overly informal touch of the country solicitor seated next to her. Across from her, a tradesman was asleep, his knees knocking against hers as he snored, hat tipped down over his eyes.

When she couldn't take the stifling air for another second, she used her handkerchief to wipe the foggy window, peering out through the glass.

"Stopped raining?" the solicitor murmured, leaning against her until she felt his hot breath fan over her cheek.

She clenched her teeth as she fought down the urge to

elbow him in the gut. "Mhmm." She unlatched the window and pushed open the pane of glass.

"Do you know how much longer to Carrington, sir?" the old lady on the far side of the carriage asked.

"Can't be much farther, ma'am," the solicitor replied.

"How I long to freshen up," the lady sighed.

Rosalie couldn't agree more. Disheveled was a nice word for how she felt. She would have preferred to meet the Dowager Duchess of Norland looking less like a duck waddling in from the pond. Her dark curls were flat, her dress sticky against her legs, sweat beaded uncomfortably between her breasts. Such ghastly summer heat was most unusual for September.

The solicitor groaned, stretching his legs. "It will be so nice to—*aghh*—"

CRACK.

One moment Rosalie was peering out the window. The next she was crashing into the tradesman. The whole group flopped in a tangle of twisted arms and legs.

"*Ouch*—"

"Gerroffme—"

Outside, the horses squealed.

"Easy on! Whoa, whoa, *whoa!*" came the coachman's cries. The carriage tilted at a wild angle as he reined the team to a halt. After a few panicked moments, all was still. A heavy fist rapped on the roof. "Everyone all right in there?"

The tradesman groaned under Rosalie.

"Get—*off*—me," she panted, jabbing the solicitor with both elbows as his arms wrapped needlessly around her.

He moved off, helping the elderly lady right herself.

"Everyone all right?" the coachman called again.

"Ye-yes," Rosalie replied.

"What happened?" the tradesman growled, dabbing at his cut lip.

"Broken wheel," the coachman replied. "Damn it!"

"Stay within," said the footman, his head popping in view of the foggy window. "It's quite slick out here."

"Oh, I knew we would crash," the old lady whined. "All this rain . . . foolish to travel in such conditions . . . should have delayed."

Rosalie held back a smile. The poor lady sounded just like her Aunt Thorpe, who was prone to nervous fits. She could only imagine how her aunt would shriek at a broken wheel. "Don't worry, ma'am," she said. "Nothing so broken that can't be mended—"

Just then, the coachman rattled the door open, stuffing his face within. "Sorry ladies and gents, but it looks like this break can't be easily mended."

The group stared daggers at Rosalie, as if this were somehow her fault for being optimistic.

"I've sent the lad on ahead," the coachman continued. "We're not but a mile from Carrington. He'll get us a new wheel, and we can be on our way in no time."

"I'm sure you'll do your best," said the tradesman with an irritated grunt.

The carriage door rattled shut and Rosalie was left wedged next to the solicitor.

"Well," he said with a grin. "Looks like my luck is improving leaps and bounds."

"What can you mean, sir?" cried the old lady.

He flashed Rosalie a smile. "Only that I get to spend more time with this divine creature, eh Miss Rose?"

Rosalie stiffened. She told them all her name, as was only fitting when one shared a coach for hours on end, but he certainly had not earned the right to drop the use of her surname . . . or shorten her Christian name. Perhaps if Aunt Thorpe were here, Rosalie would have smiled and ignored his advances. But Rosalie was blessedly, *brazenly* alone.

And she would suffer fools no longer.

She snatched up her travel case and wrenched open the door, pushing her way out of the coach. Her feet sank with a squelch into the mud, and she grimaced, trying to hold her skirts out of the mess. The air smelled of wet earth, but the surrounding countryside was lovely as a painting. The rain was little more than a fine mist now. All around sat rolling hills. Off to the left, a tree line glowed in the mist, the changing autumn leaves glistening like gold and rubies.

The solicitor ducked his head out the open door. "Get back in here, you silly girl."

"No," she replied through clenched teeth. "The coachman says it's barely a mile to Carrington. I'll walk."

She heard three confused murmurs from within the carriage.

"In all that mud?" came the old lady's voice. "Child, what can you be thinking?"

Rosalie just squelched over to the coachman. "Sir, I will walk on to Carrington. But I'll leave my case, if you don't mind. Can I retrieve it when you get to the village?"

"'Course, miss," he said with a tip of his hat. "We'll settle up out back o' the Whispering Willow."

She nodded her thanks and lifted her skirts, squelching over to the wet grass.

"Miss Rose, do you require a chaperone?" called the solicitor.

Rosalie turned, eyes flashing. "Sir, if you attempt to follow me, I shall have to find a stick and whack you about the shins until you can follow no more!"

It took nearly an hour to reach Carrington, which assured Rosalie the distance was most certainly greater than one mile. By the time she shuffled down the high street towards the glowing lights of the Whispering Willow, her dress and pelisse were slick with mud up to her knees. Her every step squelched.

"Good evening, welcome to—*heavens*—" The innkeeper gasped as she eyed Rosalie. "Did you fall from a horse, dear?"

"Something like that," Rosalie replied, doing her best to wipe her feet on the mat. "I was on the morning coach from Town. We broke a wheel about a mile out on the north road."

"Aye, we heard about that," the innkeeper replied. "And you . . . walked here?"

"Trust me, a little mud was preferable to the alternative," Rosalie muttered, still feeling the whisper of the solicitor's hot breath on her neck.

"Well . . . you'll be needing a cup o' tea," the innkeeper said. "You best come with me."

Rosalie followed the lady down a dark, narrow hall that connected to a small pub.

"Are you looking for a room?"

"I haven't money for a room," Rosalie replied. "My aunt only gave me enough to cover the coach fare. I'm supposed to be going to Alcott Hall. I was told a coach would meet me here to take me the rest of the way—"

The innkeeper turned. "Oh dear, Mr. Henry came already. He picked up a few high-society types and left . . . oh, two hours ago now."

"Perfect," Rosalie muttered. Could this day get any worse? "How far is it to Alcott?"

"About five miles," the innkeeper replied, showing her to a little table in the corner.

Dark wood paneling gave the public house a closed-in, cozy feel. A few crowded booths sat along one wall, a bar along the other, and a man stood in the corner tuning a violin.

"Rest yourself here, and I'll get you set up with some tea. I'll have my cook bring you a spot of stew too. On the house, dear, while you wait."

"Thank you," Rosalie murmured, taking the offered seat.

In moments, she was served a cup of tea. She sat alone, holding the cup with both hands, loving the feel of the heat sinking into her palms.

It felt daring to sit alone in a pub. Her aunt would surely disapprove. Rosalie just smiled, taking another sip of her tea. She watched as the men in the room laughed and told jokes, patting each other on the back, lighting pipes, taking swigs from their mugs of ale. It was a picture of country life. She longed to fish the sketchbook out of her travel case and capture the scene.

"Hello, darlin'," a burly man said, dropping into the seat across from her. He spilled a bit of the frothy beer from his mug on the table. "Well, yer a pretty lass, aren't ya! You remind me of me daughter, Bessie!"

Rosalie leaned back as the man spittled. Was she to be accosted by every unscrupulous man in England?

"Oh, leave the lady alone, Alfie," a man called from the bar. Others chuckled, but none seemed interested in coming to her aid.

Alfie wasn't deterred. "What's a beauty like you doin' alone in a pub, sweetness?"

She grasped around for something to say to make him leave. "I'm not alone, sir."

He leaned across the table, eyes glassy with drink. He even had the audacity to reach across, trying to snatch her hand. "'Course not. I'm here, ain't I?"

She lifted her cup out of his reach, lest he spill it in her lap. Suddenly, a hand closed on her shoulder, and she jolted. The hand was firm, and far too large to belong to the innkeeper.

Then a deep voice spoke. "Sorry to keep you waiting."

2

Rosalie

ROSALIE STIFFENED AS Alfie's mouth opened in a comical *O*, displaying his wide set of yellowing teeth. The masculine voice behind her was smooth as honeyed tea.

Heart in her throat, she lowered her eyes and followed the line of a leather-gloved hand up the crisp cut of a wet slicker to the man's face, half hidden in the shadow of his hat brim. He was tall and handsome, with the bearing of a gentleman.

He doffed his hat, and a spill of black hair swept across his forehead. His grey eyes narrowed under dark brows. "Have you been waiting long, *sister*?"

She blushed. "I—"

"This ain't never yer sister," Alfie barked.

The man's face lost what little warmth it had. "Do you mean to say you know the members of my family better than me, sir?"

Alfie sputtered, eyes darting from her to the gentleman.

In moments, the man from the bar tugged on Alfie's sleeve. "He didn'a mean nothin' by it, sir," he said, dragging Alfie away. Only when Alfie was forced out the door with complaints of not having finished his ale did the stranger release his hold on her shoulder.

"Terribly sorry about all that," he said. "The rabble are usually better behaved. In the future, if you're dining alone, I suggest taking meals in your room, Miss . . ." He raised a dark brow, waiting for her name.

"Harrow," she supplied. "Rosalie Harrow."

"Miss Harrow," he repeated.

"And you are . . ."

His stoic countenance gave way to a smirk. "Happy to have helped."

Rosalie noted how every eye in the room watched him with a combination of stolen glances and open stares. A few murmured behind their hands. Surely, he must be someone of great importance. No doubt a lord.

Before she could ask another question, he tipped his hat. "Good evening, Miss Harrow." Then he turned and left.

Rosalie finished her meal in silence, thanking the innkeeper for her generosity. With her travel case in hand, she found her way outside, determined to wait at the back of the inn for the delayed coach. Perhaps she could persuade the coachman to take her all the way to Alcott. What was five more miles to him?

She slipped into the alley between the inn and the milliner's shop. As she passed a stack of barrels, she heard a pained groan. In the dark, she could just make out the silhouette of a man hunched in the shadows. She held tighter to her case as she tried to slip past.

"S'that you, black beauty?"

Heaven's sake. It was the drunk from the bar.

Alfie stumbled to his feet, holding onto a barrel for support. "Gimme yer arm. I'm in need o' help."

"You're in need of sleep." She'd dealt with the drunken fits of worthless men all her life. She was in no mood to deal with another. "Go home to your wife, sir. She is surely wondering where you are."

Alfie stumbled forward, trying to grab her shoulder.

She darted away, ready to sling her travel case in his face. "Do not touch me—"

"I wanna feel yeh . . . feel yer curls . . . such a black beau'y," he mumbled.

"You're drunk. Go home, before I scream and bring a constable down on you."

"Yeh rotten drab," he growled. "Come 'ere!"

He pressed forward and Rosalie shrieked. On instinct, she balled her left hand into a fist and swung with all her might. Her knuckles cracked across his nose and they both let out yelps of pain. He dropped to his knees, hands covering his bleeding nose.

"I think ye broke it, yeh bitch!"

Heavy footfalls from just behind Rosalie had her turning sharply on her heel. She felt quite feral as she swung her travel case with another shriek.

"Whoa, *easy!*" The handsome gentleman from the pub slid to a halt. "I'm not going to hurt you," he said, throwing both hands up. He looked down at the prone figure at her feet. She could barely make out his eyes under his hat brim, but he simmered with tension. If Alfie tried anything again, this man would stop him.

Her arms sagged to her sides as she stifled a sob.

"Are you hurt?"

"I'm fine," she said, shaking out her left hand. That wasn't entirely true. She was a mess—filthy and exhausted, penniless, trunkless, and she probably just broke her hand punching a drunk square on the nose.

Alfie moaned on the ground between them. "The bitch clocked meh nose!"

The gentleman snatched Alfie up by his untidy necktie. He lowered his face inches from the drunk man's bleeding nose. "Call the lady that again, and I'll give you two eyes to match your worthless fucking nose. Now get the hell out of here!" He shoved the drunk away, aiming a kick for him when he didn't move fast enough.

Alfie squealed and crawled off into the shadows like a stray dog.

Rosalie was breathless as she watched the gentleman right himself. "You didn't have to do that."

She could feel his smile, even if she couldn't see it. "Clearly not. You seemed to have things well in hand. You have a powerful left hook, Miss Harrow."

She gave him a sheepish look. "I didn't mean to break his nose."

"Oh yes, you did. And the lout deserved it. Let's see your hand then."

She stilled, her stomach doing another flip as he took a half step closer.

He paused. "Perhaps . . . let's go round back towards the light, eh?"

She breathed a sigh of relief and nodded, following him as he led the way to the carriage yard. It glowed amber, lit by a few lanterns. The gentleman turned and she could better see his features in the light.

He held out his gloved hand. "Now, let's see it."

She hesitated only a moment before she placed her left hand in his. He looked at her reddening knuckles, touching each with a gentle stroke. She winced but moved each finger as he bent them.

"Nothing broken," he murmured. "I told you it would be best to stay to your room, did I not?"

She bristled at being chastised by a stranger and jerked her hand away. "I have no room, sir. I am not staying at the inn."

His eyes narrowed. "Then where are you staying? Clearly you have no need of a bodyguard, but I'd like to offer my services all the same and see you safely home."

"That's not necessary."

"It's a matter of honor," he said. "You rendered me useless back there. I must redeem myself."

"I'm waiting here, sir," she replied. "My hired coach broke a wheel about a mile north of the village. It still has my trunk."

"That explains the mud," he said with a murmur. His steely gaze bore into her. "It has your trunk . . . but you're not staying at the inn. You must have some destination in mind. Or do you intend to sleep up a tree like a squirrel?"

She huffed. "Fine, if you must know, I am expected at Alcott Hall. There was supposed to be another coach waiting to take me, but it came and went, and I'm stranded here." She gestured around the empty carriage yard. "I've no money for a room, and I'm waiting for the coach to arrive to beg their mercy to bring me the rest of the way."

"You're going to Alcott Hall?"

"Yes, sir."

He gave her another appraising look. "Are you a new maid there?"

"No, sir. I am a guest of the dowager," she replied.

A frown tipped his lips. "*You* are a guest of the duchess?"

She bristled. "Not that it's any of your business, sir, but yes.

I am the personal guest of the Dowager Duchess of Norland. Do you want to see my invitation? I didn't know you were a person of authority entitled to verify my credentials."

That damnable smirk again. "Well, Miss Harrow, you're in luck. I'm on my way to Alcott Hall and would be happy to deliver you there. I'm on horseback, mind you, so we'll be snug. But it's only a couple miles."

She blinked. "You're going to Alcott Hall? Now? Tonight?"

"I am," he replied, then leaned in. "Would you like to see *my* credentials?"

Her heart raced as she considered her options. One, wait for the coach and beg them to take her. Two, find a cozy spot in the barn next to the mice in the hay. Three, trudge there herself in the dark, dragging her trunk through the mud. Or four, accept the help of this handsome stranger, who refused to offer so much as his name.

"I . . ."

He sighed, checking his pocket watch. "While you pretend to think about it, let me just pop in and tell Mary to have your trunk delivered as soon as it arrives. We can't have you sleeping naked tonight for want of a clean shift," he added with a wink.

Her mouth opened on a gasp of indignation as he walked away. The man was insufferable, downright irksome . . . and so handsome it made her want to laugh . . . or cry. And now he was offering to take her to Alcott Hall. Quite a turn of events from how the day started. She'd already suffered the attentions of two horrible men. Perhaps she owed it to herself to let mankind offer redemption in the form of Mr. Grey Eyes. She had the sense she wouldn't be quite so perturbed by feeling the warmth of *his* breath on her neck . . .

He emerged from the back of the inn and offered out his gloved hand again. "Well, Miss Harrow? Are you coming with me?"

Taking a deep breath, she placed her hand in his. Before his fingers could close around hers, she jerked back. "But I insist on carrying the whip, sir. And you will tell me your name."

He blinked. "Why should you want to hold the whip?"

She squared her shoulders at him. "Because you men have not been at your best today, and I reserve the right to strike you with it should your hands begin to wander anywhere I don't want them."

His eyes flashed with some unreadable emotion, but he gave a curt nod. "Done. You shall hold the whip. Hell, hold the reins if you want. Leave me to run alongside you. I'm sure the exercise would do me good."

She fought her own smile, giving him a level stare. "And your name, sir?"

"My name is Burke," he replied. "Pleasure to meet you."

3
Burke

OF ALL THE ways Burke thought a trip to town might end, riding double through the dark with a gorgeous woman pressed against his chest had been nowhere in his imagination. Miss Harrow sat astride in front of him, her muddy skirts riding up to show off her ruined stockings.

The sound of crickets buzzed in the air as his horse trotted down the lane. True to his word, Burke gave Miss Harrow full command of the riding crop. Christ, he nearly got a cockstand when she made that demand, her dark eyes blazing with a fire set to consume him. He cooled when he realized her full meaning. Whatever happened today beyond that scum in the alley, she was feeling vulnerable. He fought his every instinct to hunt that drunk down and pummel him bloody.

Well . . . *bloodier.*

This lady could clearly take care of herself. Even as part of him loved to think of a beautiful, confident woman fighting her own battles, it gave him serious pause. Who was she that she knew how to throw a punch? Why was that a skill she had to learn? And why the hell was she traveling alone with no money on direct invitation from the duchess?

Whoever she was, she didn't know *him* . . . which meant she couldn't be a very close acquaintance of Harriet Wakefield Corbin, Dowager Duchess of Norland. Anyone close to the Corbin family knew everything about Burke—the details he was proud of and the details he wished they'd forget. And Burke had never heard of Rosalie Harrow. This meant she was either lying, which they would soon uncover . . . or the duchess really *did* have a secret interest in the girl, which made her a mystery he was desperate to solve.

He cleared his throat, reining the horse to a walk. It felt strange to have the cage of his arms around her so intimately. "So . . . where are you from, Miss Harrow?"

"Town," she replied. "My aunt keeps a place in Cheapside."

He liked the sound of her voice. It wasn't high and nasally, or falsely sweet. It was just . . . *her*. She had the accent of a refined lady, but her clothes were a bit worn, and he couldn't forget that left hook.

"And where is your family from?"

She shifted, catching his gaze with one eye. "Are you trying to place me, Mr. Burke? Running through your list of gentry families to see where and how you might measure a Harrow against yourself?"

He chuckled, the sound dying in his throat as he felt her shift again, her rounded arse rubbing against his cock. Christ, this was a mistake. "Once you get to know me better, you'll find I am the last person to measure someone's worth by their family name," he replied, jaw tight.

She was quiet for a moment. "My family is from Richmond . . . or at least my mother's family. I know nothing of the Harrows beyond that I had an uncle who immigrated to India nearly thirty years ago. My father never heard from him again."

She was from Richmond? This was a useful clue. Burke was well-versed in Corbin family affairs. Before the duchess married the fifth duke, she was a gentleman's daughter from Richmond.

"So . . . you know the Wakefields, then?"

"Not personally, sir," she replied. "I'm told my mother and the dowager were childhood friends. It is on her behalf that the dowager sent for me."

"The duchess," he corrected.

"Hmm?"

"She may be announced formally as the Dowager Duchess of Norland," he explained, "But she prefers the title of duchess, especially since her son remains unmarried. And she thinks being called 'dowager' makes her sound old. I wouldn't want you starting off on the wrong foot," he added, his breath fanning over her ear. "And who are your mother's people?"

"My mother was—*oh*—" She fell silent as they made the last turn towards home.

The trees gave way to Burke's favorite view of the house. He reined his horse to a halt, its hooves crunching on the pea gravel. Alcott Hall was a three-story structure of grey stone perched on a low hill. The lower floors were lit from within, their glow shining out over a vast expanse of gardens, which gave way to a lake glistening in the moonlight.

"Well? What do you think of the house?"

"It's incomparable," she whispered. "I don't know that I've ever seen a place so perfectly situated."

"Wait till you see her in the daylight," he replied, prodding the horse back into a trot.

"Do you live here?"

He laughed. "Are we done asking questions about you, then?"

"My life is an open book," she replied. "I have no secrets, sir."

He very much doubted that, but he wasn't sure if he trusted himself to know her better. Her beauty was arresting, even being covered in mud. If anything, the wildness of her countenance endeared her to him even more. Give him one woman like this over a drawing room full of high-society twits who only ever talked about dresses and dancing.

He groaned, for that was exactly what awaited him at the house. Christ, but this was going to be a long month. He'd almost considered going away, for there was no world in which three weeks spent rubbing shoulders with a marchioness would be to his benefit.

She went stiff in his arms. "Mr. Burke? Are you unwell?"

Damn, she heard him groan. "Quite well, just ready to be out of the saddle."

"Me too," she admitted. "I'm not used to riding astride." She wiggled a bit and he wanted to die.

They rode in silence, following the sweeping lane around the back of the house to the stable yard. Johnny, the tired groom, stumbled out at Burke's call, pulling a wool cap down over his ears. His eyes went wide as he took in Miss Harrow sitting astride in front of Burke.

Burke swung his leg back and dropped down to the cobblestones. Then he reached up with both hands, holding her at the waist, as she slid down. He caught her, pulling her close against him. She felt so small in his arms. He felt a sudden urge to protect her, to pick her up and carry her inside. He wanted to wash away the mud and wrap her in silk.

"Mr. Burke," she whispered, suddenly stiff.

Her eyes were open wide, her lips parted as she tried to control her breathing. He tensed with realization: She felt it too, whatever this was between them. Christ, she was beauti-ful. That fair skin and those dark eyes. He wanted to brush his fingers over her mouth. He wanted—

"Please let me go."

He blinked twice, the soft plea of her words making him drop his hands away as if she'd burned him. She might want him, but she didn't trust him. Hell, she didn't even *know* him. And he didn't know her. What was happening to him?

He cleared his throat and took a step back. "Let's get you inside."

He untied her travel case from the back of his saddle and gave Johnny a nod. The lad led the mount away. Taking a deep breath, Burke turned and offered his arm. Miss Harrow hes-itated before she looped her arm in his and let herself be led towards the great house.

As they walked in silence, he could almost feel her build-ing strong walls with brick and mortar, determined to keep him out. He smiled. If that feisty woman in the alley was the prize waiting within, there was quite possibly nothing he'd like better than planning a prolonged siege.

"Where will you take me?" she murmured.

"To see the man in charge."

4

Rosalie

Rosalie walked at Mr. Burke's side into the great house, eyes wide as she took in every detail. They were in a long hall with a beautiful parquet floor. One side boasted floor-to-ceilingwindows set every six feet along the wall. Rosalie was sure that in daylight each must offer an incomparable view of the back gardens. The other side contained a series of closed doors. Artwork adorned the space between each door—landscapes in gilded frames, a spindly legged table set with a china vase full of blooming flowers, a carved wooden chair that looked more like a throne . . . in fact, it probably *was* a throne.

She'd never felt so out of place. Her muddy dress slapped awkwardly against her legs and her poor toes squished inside her stockings. She was desperate to take off these ruined clothes. But as Mr. Burke said, she had nothing else to wear.

"Wait," she slid to a stop, tugging on his arm.

He turned, dark brow raised in question.

"You can't take me to the duke looking like *this*," she cried.

He chuckled. "He's seen stranger sights than this, I assure you."

"But—"

"Look, it's late. I don't want to wake staff if I don't have to. James is sure to still be awake, and he'll take care of it. Just trust me."

Damn him and that devilish smile. Each time the corner of his mouth tipped up, she felt it tug at her. This man was dangerous. He was beautiful and confident, and he looked at her with open want in his eyes, as if he'd seen her and determined she was exactly what he'd been waiting for. It was enough to have her gasping for breath . . . and he'd noticed. In the stable yard just now, she was sure of it. There was a reckoning in his gaze, a promise of more.

But Rosalie Harrow would not be tied to any man. Forget the fact that she didn't believe marriage could ever bring out the best in two people trapped within the bars of such a cage. She was also quite possibly the *worst* prospect for a wife. She had no family living, aside from her desperately poor widowed aunt. She didn't have two shillings to rub together. In fact, she had nothing to her name but mounting debts. Her wastrel of a father saw to that, leaving her and her mother to fend for themselves when he stumbled drunk into the Thames.

That was seven years ago. Seven long years of fighting off the creditors, selling everything they owned. Then her mother got sick . . . or just gave up. Rosalie wasn't sure which truth hurt her more, so she put all the details of her mother's death in a little box on a shelf in the back of her mind.

That was eight months ago. Now here she was, covered in mud, wandering the halls of a duke's house late at night. Mr. Burke led her a bit farther down the hall to where a door stood open. Rosalie heard the unmistakable *whack* of billiard balls. Mr. Burke pushed open the door and stepped inside, leading her through by the hand.

It was a masculine room, with dark leather furniture and deep green walls. A billiards table sat under a half-lit chandelier. A handsome man in evening clothes stood at the table's edge, bending over with a cue to take his shot.

"Don't miss," Mr. Burke barked.

The man whacked the ball, sending it careening the wrong direction. "*Damn*—Burke!" His anger faded immediately to relief. "Good god man, I thought you got lost in a ditch."

This must be the duke. He had a natural air of authority that oozed aristocracy. Heavens, but he was handsome too. Narrower in the shoulders, and not quite so tall, but he had shocking green eyes and auburn hair that curled around his ears. A dusting of freckles spotted his cheeks.

"And yet, I didn't spot a search party on the road," Mr. Burke replied.

"What did you—" The duke's smile slipped off his face as he saw Rosalie. He glanced from her to Mr. Burke. "Who is this?"

"Picking up strays now, Burke?" came a deep voice.

She turned to see another man step out of the corner, glass of brandy in hand. If she thought the others were handsome, this man was . . . words failed her. He was like something out of a painting, a sculpted David come to life. He had a halo of golden curls and skin so tan he looked almost foreign. She felt sure he must be a sailor. His jaw was chiseled, his shoulders broad, and he had the most devastating blue eyes.

Mr. Burke set her travel case on a chair. "Bloody hell . . . Renley, is that you?"

"Of course, it's me," the other man said. "Burke, how are you?" He crossed the space in three strides and the two embraced like brothers, slapping each other's backs.

"I think you've gotten taller since I last saw you," Mr. Burke laughed, pretending to measure his friend. He was the tallest of the three by several inches.

"Damn, it does me good to see you," said Mr. Renley, still holding his friend by the shoulders. "You haven't changed a hair."

"In foul temper or manner," Mr. Burke joked.

"Enough," the duke barked over both men. "Burke, who the hell is this?" His finger was pointed straight at Rosalie.

She shrank under the heat of his gaze.

"Oh, right," Mr. Burke said, as if he suddenly remembered she was still in the room. "I found her tonight in Carrington in a bit of a desperate situation."

"And you brought her home with you?" The duke's voice dripped with derision. "What the hell were you thinking?"

"I was thinking she was a guest here," Burke replied. "This is Miss Rosalie Harrow. She has an invitation from your dear mama to join the house party," he added with a wink.

Rosalie took in the surprised looks of both gentlemen.

"Would you have preferred me to leave her stranded outside the inn?" said Mr. Burke.

The duke rounded on her. "You have an invitation from my mother?"

Rosalie blinked at his rudeness. Why did no one believe her? Did she have to pin the letter to her pelisse? She dipped into a curtsy. "Yes, Your Grace."

As soon as the words were spoken, she knew something was wrong. The man called Renley stifled a laugh. The duke's eyes flashed with some heated emotion, as the muscle in his jaw ticked. Next to her, Mr. Burke snorted.

The duke rounded on Mr. Burke. "Goddamn it, you know

how George hates it when you do that. The last thing I need is for him to be in a mood."

Mr. Burke raised both hands in mock surrender. "I never said you were the duke. Any implication was a total slip of the tongue."

Rosalie gasped, eyes narrowing on Mr. Burke. Had he tricked her? She fought the urge to use her uninjured fist to punch him square in the nose too.

"Oh, and this is Tom Renley," Mr. Burke added, gesturing to his friend.

"Lieutenant Tom Renley," the handsome sailor added, confirming her theory. "Pleased to meet you."

The false duke stepped forward. "Please excuse my worthless friend," he said. "I am not the Duke of Norland. I'm his younger brother, James Corbin."

She looked from Mr. Burke to the lord. "I'm sorry if I'm a nuisance, my lord. I was meant to arrive three days ago, but the rain—"

"Aye, it's delayed half the house party," he replied. "But why did you not come with the group this afternoon?"

"My coach broke down, sir. I walked into Carrington, which is where Mr. Burke found me. As he said, I had a spot of bother at the inn, and then he offered to—"

"Whoa, wait." Lord James held up a hand. "What happened?"

Mr. Burke looked down at her with a smile. "A drunk made the mistake of trying to have his way. Miss Harrow here put him in his place."

Lord James puffed out his chest in anger as Lieutenant Renley's brows lowered in concern over those beautiful blue eyes. "What happened?"

"Tom, you should have seen it," Mr. Burke said with a grin. "She broke the lout's nose with a mean left hook. It was poetry."

Both gentlemen watched her with wide eyes. The lieutenant looked impressed; Lord James wary.

"I think she's had enough excitement for one night, though," said Mr. Burke. "James, can we get a room sorted? Her trunk should be arriving soon. A bath is probably in order too," he added.

"Right, come with me. I'll wake the housekeeper." The lord moved towards the door and snatched a candle off a side table, waiting for her with one brow raised.

Mr. Burke gave her a half smile and held out her travel case. "Welcome to Alcott, Miss Harrow."

Rosalie followed closely behind Lord James as he swept down the hall, heels of his shoes clicking on the polished wooden floor. He took a sharp right and the space opened into a hall three times as large. Rosalie stifled a gasp.

It was still a hallway . . . but the grandest hallway she'd ever seen. It was broad, with a vaulted, Baroque painted ceiling. Four massive chandeliers floated in the air. Their crystals appeared eerily muted in the dark. The walls were festooned with works of art. Some of the frames were larger than life— portraits, still-lifes, hunting scenes, landscapes. The artist in her couldn't wait for the daylight to see them to better effect.

The lord turned, raising his candle high, and she nearly stumbled into him. "So, who are you, then?" he said with that imperiously arched brow.

"I'm Rosalie Harrow," she repeated. "Look, I get the distinct impression no one knew to expect me. But I promise, my intentions are honest. I *was* invited by the duchess. I have her letter here if you—"

"That won't be necessary," he said. "I know my mother is expecting you. What I don't know is *why*. What does she want with you?"

By the look on his face, Lord James must be used to people answering any question he asked with alacrity. The trouble was, she wasn't sure of the answer. "All I know is that our mothers were childhood friends. My mother died recently, and that's the first I heard mention of the dowager duchess. My invitation here is as much a mystery to me as it is to you, sir."

He considered her words with a deepening frown. "How old are you, Miss Harrow?"

It was rather a rude question to ask, but she was beyond propriety standing in this grand space half dipped in mud. "I'm twenty-two, sir."

"And your father?"

"Dead, sir."

"Your family?"

"I have but one aunt living."

"Your fortune?"

Now she laughed. "Is this an interrogation, my lord? If I pass your test, will you do the gentlemanly thing and show me to a room?"

His nostrils flared like a dragon without fire. Before he could respond, hurried footsteps echoed down the gallery. They both turned to see a footman trotting towards them, candle flickering in his hand.

"My lord," the footman said, sliding to a halt, wig askew.

"What is it, Parker?"

"A carriage arrived, my lord, delivering a trunk for the lady."

She heaved a sigh of relief. At least she wouldn't have to sleep naked tonight.

"Mr. Burke promised the coachman payment, my lord," the footman added. "But Mr. Reed has already gone up to bed—"

"I'll handle it," said Lord James. "Please go find Mrs. Davies." He turned, thrusting out his candle. "Take this, Miss Harrow, and wait here. The housekeeper will be along shortly." Their fingertips brushed as he handed it over and she pulled back from his touch.

Without another word, the lord turned on his heel and stormed away. The footman gave her a little nod before he too ran off, the orb of his candle bobbing away down the grand gallery. Rosalie stood alone, candle in one hand, travel case in the other, waiting for the housekeeper . . . and praying for a bath.

5

Tom

As soon as James left with the young lady, Burke breathed a deep sigh and sank into one of the leather smoking chairs. Tom stepped forward and extended his glass of brandy. "Here, I think you need this more than me."

Burke took the glass and drained it, setting it down with a clatter.

Tom sank into the opposite chair, loosening his cravat with a sharp tug.

"When did you arrive?" Burke asked.

"Just this afternoon," he replied. "I didn't know I'd be interrupting a house party. I feel I should take my leave, but James said I could stay . . ."

"Yes, well you can't possibly expect a restful time at your brother's house. How many hellions does he have now, four?"

"Six," Tom replied.

"Hell on earth," Burke said with a groan, stretching out his long legs. "I'm sure I speak for His Graceless when I say you can stay here as long as you like."

Both men were quiet for a moment as Tom watched Burke with a growing grin. "So . . . are we going to talk about it?"

Burke glanced up. "Talk about what?"

"The *girl*," Tom said with a laugh. "What the hell happened with that girl?"

"She already told you," Burke said evasively. "A drunk was pawing at her in the pub and I stepped in. Then she was outside, and he came at her again. She socked him right in the nose, dropped him like a stone before I could lift a finger."

Tom leaned forward, elbows on his knees. "I meant between *you* and her."

"Nothing happened," he said quickly.

Tom grinned. "Right . . . so the sexual tension you could cut with a knife was . . ."

Burke smirked, not looking up.

"Oh, you are in *so* much trouble," Tom laughed, slapping his knee as he flopped back in the chair. He knew his friend well. Granted, they hadn't seen each other in nigh on two years, but Burke's taste in women could hardly have shifted so greatly in their time apart. "James is going to have kittens over it, you know."

"James can mind his own bloody business," Burke said with a scowl. "Nothing happened."

"Right . . . and now that she's here, I imagine you're hatching no plans . . . making no designs on her," he teased.

Burke dragged a hand through his hair. "She's a guest of the duchess, Tom."

"When has that ever stopped you before?"

"I'm a work in progress," Burke muttered.

"She's gorgeous . . . feisty too."

"Don't," he groaned.

Tom laughed, loving how easy it was to goad him.

Burke got to his feet, snatching the empty glass off the

table. He went over to the corner and filled it, bringing a fresh one over for Tom. Before Tom could take a sip, the door snapped open, and James swept in like an angry storm front. Burke handed out his glass. James snatched it, taking a deep sip. Burke went and made himself a fresh one, while James sank into one of the other empty chairs.

"Well? Is Miss Harrow settled?" asked Tom.

James nodded, leaning back with a tired sigh. "I don't know what the hell my mother was thinking bringing her here. The other ladies are going to eat her alive."

Burke returned to his chair. "You can't possibly think she means to throw her at George, do you?"

Tom sensed the hint of anxiety in his tone, the simmering note of possession.

James glowered, setting his glass down with a clink. "Burke, I don't know what happened—"

"Don't start," Burke replied. "I can see a pretty girl and not touch her. Your gentility lessons have not been in vain."

Tom decided it was safest to change the subject. "So . . . what's the deal with this house party?"

Both men groaned.

"My mother is determined to see George settled," James explained. "She's invited a horde of high-society ladies and their chaperones to fill the house for the next month. I guess she imagines if George can't escape them, he'll eventually break down and propose to one."

"That seems . . . foolproof?" Tom offered with a shrug.

"It's idiotic," James snapped.

"It's a goddamn nightmare," echoed Burke. "We've already got a viscountess and her mousey daughter, the Swindon sisters, even Sir Andrew and Lady Oswald are here chasing Blanche around with a butterfly net."

Tom couldn't help but laugh. Blanche Oswald grew up with them. She was one of the silliest women breathing. "That's the duchess' idea of a good match for George?"

"I think it's less about her manners and more about the fact that Sir Andrew now owns half of Carrington. We're told her dowry is pushing thirty thousand," James said.

"Surely you don't need to be fortune hunting," Tom said with a raised brow. "Is the estate in crisis?"

"Not currently," Burke replied. "All thanks to James, here."

"But capital is capital," James added. "No lord can afford to settle for a penniless bride. George is too eccentric to get brains, beauty, and a dowry. At this point, mother is putting all her chips on a dowry. She means to have him announcing his engagement by the Michaelmas ball."

Tom was well familiar with the Corbins' annual ball. They'd been hosting a Michaelmas soiree every year for nigh on four generations. Navy life meant Tom had missed quite a few, but it was always a smashing good time. The Corbin punch was legendary.

"How long are you on leave this time?" Burke asked.

James snorted into his drink and Tom shot him an annoyed look. "I have a somewhat open order," he told Burke. "It may last until Christmas . . ."

Burke raised a dark brow in question and Tom groaned.

"He's in the same situation as my dear brother," James explained.

Tom rubbed the back of his neck with a weathered hand, wishing he could sink through the floor. God, it was so infuriating. But naval politics meant that sometimes an officer had to make sacrifices in the name of his career. In Tom's case that meant—

"Wait," Burke said on a gasp. "You never . . . oh, Tom, are you only home to bag a wife?" At Tom's look of solemn resignation, Burke let out a laugh. "What a romantic you are. Like Poseidon in search of Amphitrite, you come in from the sea."

"I'm First Lieutenant now," Tom argued. "A captaincy is next, so long as I can rank up. And my captain believes the surest way I rank within the year is to take a wife who can help me pay for it."

Burke leaned forward. "So, young Poseidon, the plot thickens. The duchess plans to parade eligible ladies in front of George for the next month, and you figured you'll what? Pick one off the end with a title and a reticule full of diamonds and hope George doesn't notice? Do you really think you can fall in love in a fortnight?"

Tom scowled. "It's not like that. You both know I have no interest in marriage. Not after . . ." He fell silent and, for once, Burke tactfully made no comment. "This isn't about love. I'm through with all that. This is a career move, plain and simple."

Burke set his glass aside. "Well, Lieutenant, you have your mission, and now we have ours. The duchess has kindly arranged for a bouquet of eligible ladies to stay in the house for the next three weeks. That's plenty of time for us to find you a suitable wife with a thick pair of lips to kiss and deep pockets to caress."

"You're both going to stay out of this," Tom growled.

"Nonsense," said James. "Between the three of us, we'll find you a lady so perfect you'll forget all about . . ." He cleared his throat and drained his glass. "Just leave it to us. We'll have you walking down the aisle by Christmas."

The prospect made Tom positively miserable.

Burke raised his glass in mocking salute. "Glad to have you home, Tom."

6

James

JAMES WOKE WITH a start as his valet jerked back the curtains, letting a bright stream of sunlight cascade across the bed. He untangled himself from his sheets. Another odd series of dreams last night had him feeling just as tired as when he laid down his head.

"Sorry, my lord. You asked me to wake you promptly at seven. Shall you take a tray here, or go down?"

James rubbed his face with both hands. "What? No, I'll dress and go down. Is my brother awake? Or my mother?"

"Her Grace's bell rang at half six, my lord." William set out a blue morning coat, red brocade waistcoat, and tan breeches.

"And my brother? He didn't abscond in the night back to Town?"

"I believe His Grace is still here, my lord," William replied.

"Be sure his valet wakes him soon and remind him that his guests will expect to see him for breakfast."

"Very good, my lord."

William helped him dress in silence. James took one last look in the mirror, noting the dark circles under his eyes.

Perhaps his mother might know of a tonic to aid with sleeplessness. Leaving that problem aside for now, he donned the mask of a Corbin and left the serenity of his bedchamber.

The breakfast room was already occupied by multiple early risers. As James entered, everyone jumped to their feet, no doubt expecting him to be the duke.

"Only me," he said with a smile. "Please, let's not stand on ceremony while you're all guests here. Think of Alcott as your home."

"Too kind, Lord James," one of the ladies murmured.

Burke was the first to resume his seat. Sir Andrew returned to eagerly salting his poached egg. Next to him, Lady Oswald and Blanche twittered about every feature of the room, from the flowers to the china patterns. Across the table, the Viscountess Raleigh and her daughter Madeline spoke in hushed tones.

James took his seat, leaving the end chair open for his brother. As he was served a plate, he noticed the subtle glances cast his way. The ladies waited for him to offer up something . . . *anything*. Plans for the day's entertainment, a delightful anecdote about George, history of the house. Instead, he focused on his breakfast.

"His Grace?" he muttered, as a footman poured him a second cup of tea.

"Not yet awake, m'lord."

James folded his newspaper and shot Burke a look to tell him where he was going.

Burke lifted the corner of his mouth, his expression clearly saying, *Better you than me.*

James cleared his throat and stood. "After breakfast, I

thought we might walk in the gardens . . . now that the rain has eased. I'm sure His Grace will be happy to join us. He's quite proud of his fruit trees."

"Capital idea," replied Sir Andrew.

"What a lovely thought," chimed his wife.

"And of course, the ladies will take tea with the duchess," he added, nodding to the two younger ladies. "And more of our house party arrives today."

The table murmured their excitement as James leaned down, one hand on Burke's shoulder. He spoke only loud enough for his friend to hear. "If I'm not back in half an hour, it's because I'm burying George under those damned trees."

Burke took a sip of his coffee. "Shall I instruct the tour guide to avoid the side gardens?"

With a scowl, James nodded and left.

James crossed half the house and scaled three flights of stairs to reach his brother's bedchamber. A footman waited outside the door with a sleepy look on his face. James didn't envy him. He couldn't imagine a worse job than being forced to stand outside a door and wait endlessly until someone chanced to need it opened.

"Open it," James said.

The footman scrambled for the handle and gave it a tug.

James swept into the room, making no noise on the plush blue carpets. His eyes adjusted to the darkness, the fire in the hearth having gone out hours ago. He sighed as he saw the state of his brother—spread-eagle in the middle of his massive four-poster bed, bare arse on display. To either side of him, a girl was curled, not a stitch of clothing to cover their nakedness. One still wore a belted contraption around her waist that gave her . . . the anatomy of a man.

James looked pointedly away. This was one of the less compromising states he'd found his brother in recently. His brother, who—on top of being a virulent breed of fornicator—was also prone to drinking, smoking, gambling, and all other forms of vice.

"Christ, man, get up," James barked. He crossed over to the window and jerked open the curtains, letting the room flood with blinding sunlight.

"Wha—whashappen?" George grunted, face still deep in his pillow.

James grabbed the ewer of water from the side table and tossed the contents over the bed. The maids squealed and bolted out either side, their wet tits bouncing. The girl wearing the cock harness blushed crimson as she noted James standing at the end of the bed. She shimmied out of the device, which left the dark curls of her sex on full display.

"Get out," he said, pointing towards the concealed servant's door in the corner.

Both women rushed to leave with their clothes bundled in their arms.

"Killjoy," George groaned, rolling over to give James an unwanted view of his half-hardened cock. "I wanted to enjoy them again when I woke up."

"You've had more than enough fun for now," James said, tossing his brother a robe. "Get dressed. You have a house full of guests and I *need* you. They're here to see the Duke of Norland, not his little brother."

George stuffed his arms through the sleeves of his robe

and snatched the ewer from James' hands, using it as a piss pot. He tried to hand it back to James, but James stepped away. There were many roles James would serve in his quest to protect the family and the county from George's influence, but piss pot attendant was not one of them.

George set the ewer aside and stood, stretching his arms high over his head. His half-masted cock was still on display and James had to fight the urge to smack it.

"I'll call Robert in to help you dress."

"I'm famished," George said, dropping into a chair by the bed.

"Well, you missed breakfast," James replied. "Robert will bring a tray."

"You really are an insufferable little fuck, James."

"Coming from you, I'll take that as a compliment," James said, wholly unfazed by his brother's rudeness. Seeing as they were eight years apart in age, they had never been close. "I will not have you ruin this for mother," he said. "She's invited several prominent families, and they will be your guests for the next three weeks. Not mine, George. *Yours*. If you want to see just how insufferable I can be, try and weasel your way out of this."

"You are absolutely no fun." George rubbed at his temples. "Christ, I need a cure for this headache."

"The perfect cure is fresh air and sunlight," James replied. "You'll find both in the gardens when you take your guests on a tour in half an hour."

George groaned again. If the brothers had one singular thing in common, it was how much they detested playing tour guide. "What do I get if I play your little game and behave as the benevolent duke for the morning?"

"Not just this morning. You need to be on form for the next *three* weeks—"

"Impossible—"

"Mother expects you to announce your engagement by Michaelmas. I've never seen her so determined, George. Your options at this point are either the altar or the grave."

George muttered under his breath something about fleeing to the continent.

James just gave his brother a bitter laugh. "You're not going anywhere. The coachmen are under strict instructions not to remove you from this house."

George puffed himself up. "So, I'm to be a prisoner in my own home?"

"If that's what it takes," James replied. "As long as we have guests here, I'll be riding your arse at every moment . . . and you won't like it nearly as much as you did last night when whoever she is did whatever it was with that filthy wooden cock."

George grinned. "If you knew the pleasures that little toy could bring, you'd not be trying to use it as a threat."

"Yes, but I won't use a cock," James growled. "It will be my booted foot up your arse, and I'll keep kicking until I knock out your goddamn teeth."

Before another barb could be uttered, there was a soft knock at the door.

"Enter," James called.

The door swung open to admit the young valet. Behind him, a footman carried a breakfast tray piled with boiled eggs, sausages, toast, and a small cup of piping hot cocoa.

James turned to the valet. "You have exactly twenty minutes to get His Grace fed, clothed, and downstairs. If I don't find him there in twenty minutes, I'll be docking a shilling from your pay."

The young valet swallowed and nodded.

"Killjoy!" George called again as James took his leave.

"Do your fucking job!" James shouted back from the doorway, closing it with a snap.

7

Rosalie

IT STILL DIDN'T feel quite real when Rosalie woke in the middle of a comfortable four-poster bed in her own room. She slipped out of the bed and pulled back the curtains, blinking as bright morning light flooded the room. The view out her window was lovely—a sweep of manicured garden leading to a tree line, with rolling farm hills stretching beyond. The trees were awash in a bright array of autumn colors.

She faced the room, a soft smile playing on her lips. The large bed took up most of the space, with two chairs and a tea table situated before the fireplace. A dressing table sat in one corner, a changing screen in the other, and a narrow closet in the third.

She was so grateful to the maids for preparing her a bath last night. The floral smell of the soap still lingered on her skin. She changed into her best blue morning dress and arranged her dark curls in a symmetrical spray around her face, pulling the rest up into a looped bun. Arranging her hair each morning had become a sacred ritual, like putting on armor. With her hair in place, she felt ready to brave the high-society lords and ladies that waited below.

Alcott Hall was even more opulent in the daylight. All the curtains were open wide, letting morning sunshine cascade in. It made the blues deeper, the reds brighter, and the golds shine even more golden. Everywhere was comfort and wealth: artwork and fine suits of armor, sculptures, Ottoman carpets, delicately carved furniture, woven tapestries.

It was almost . . . *too* much.

Rosalie paused at the sixth massive floral arrangement she passed. Who used peonies beyond May? The floral bill alone must be enough to feed a small village.

"Good morning, Miss Ha—oly hell."

As she turned, she found Lieutenant Renley standing not five feet away. His eyes went wide as he took in her appearance. Scrubbed free of mud, her hair no longer a mess of sodden curls wedged under a bonnet, she knew she looked good. He looked delicious too. He wore a brown morning coat with a red waistcoat. His breeches fit snug against his thick thighs, and his riding boots were polished to shine.

"Good morning, Lieutenant."

He cleared his throat. "Good morning, Miss Harrow. Are you going down to breakfast?"

"I am," she replied. "Though I'm afraid I don't know the way . . ."

"Well, let me show you." He stepped forward, offering out his arm.

She took it, walking in step beside him. In the entry hall, a double staircase led from the top floor down to a second-floor landing. From there, the stairs merged to form one massive staircase that led down to a black and white checkered floor. Works of art adorned every inch of the walls, ending in yet

42

another painted ceiling. She nearly made herself dizzy trying to look up into the dome as she walked down the stairs.

"It's quite something, isn't it," the lieutenant said with a smile.

"The whole house is a masterpiece," she murmured, pulling her eyes away from a massive, framed portrait of a former duke in full military regalia. "It's all a bit intimidating for someone like me; I'm not ashamed to admit it."

"Aye, me too," he said with an easy smile. "My family house is nothing near so grand as this. Give me a comfortable parlor and a family dinner table and I'm content."

"I assume if you chose navy life, you must have an older brother?" she asked. "Does he run the family estate, or your father, or . . ."

"My father passed a few years ago," he replied. "It's Colin's house now."

"But you choose to stay here?"

He gave a chuckle. "My brother has a brood of six children, Miss Harrow. Five of them are boisterous, bad-tempered boys. If I tried to stay there, I'd not get a moment's rest."

Rosalie came from such a small family, and none of her years were happy ones. She could only imagine what it might be like to feel wanted. "You are lucky, sir. I imagine they must love you very much and miss you when you're away."

"Don't think me heartless," he added. "I aim to split my time between Alcott and Foxhill. If I don't, my brother's wife will send out the hounds."

They both laughed.

"What's so funny?" came a new voice.

Rosalie turned to see Mr. Burke striding down the stairs.

Heavens, had he gotten more handsome overnight? His coat was a soft olive green, with a navy brocade waistcoat. His black hair fell in a sweep across his forehead. She found herself wanting to brush it back with her fingers.

Rosalie Harrow, don't you dare.

Mr. Burke's stormy grey eyes settled on her. "I can't decide which version of you I prefer," he said with that smirk. "There was something feral about your countenance last night, like you were a forest fairy set to bewitch us all . . . but now I see you this morning, and you are more beautiful than Aphrodite."

"That is quite enough, Mr. Burke," she replied. "I refuse to indulge your flirtations until after I've had some breakfast."

Both men laughed.

"Puts you in your place," said the lieutenant. "You heard the lady. No flirting, Burke."

Rosalie let herself be carried along on his arm.

Mr. Burke walked at her other side. "And you heard the lady *wrong*, Tom. I am free to flirt to my heart's content . . . she just demands breakfast first."

Rosalie liked their easy way of teasing each other. "The lady will amend her statement to say no flirting of any kind will be permitted," she said, drawing both their gazes to her. She almost had to contain a shiver.

"Does our flirting offend, Miss Harrow?" said Mr. Burke.

"Not at all," she replied. "It's been ages since I've had such a pair of agreeable men pay me polite attention . . . but we can hardly expect Lord James to approve . . ."

Both men stiffened, and she had her answer. Yes, of course they gossiped about her last night. Did she really expect any less after the strange manner of her arrival?

She paused in her steps, looking from one man to the

other. "You both must know by now that I am a wholly worthless prize. No money, no connections, not a relation in the world save my poor, widowed aunt. There are far better fish in the sea to . . . fish for . . ." she finished lamely.

The gentlemen exchanged a look. The lieutenant lifted a shoulder in a sort of shrug and Mr. Burke just shook his head.

"Sorry, darling, you won't escape our nets that easy," said Mr. Burke.

On the other side of her, the lieutenant barked another deep laugh.

"Flirting with beautiful ladies is too much fun," Mr. Burke went on. "And poor Tom lives on a boat with only salty men for company. Would you deny him this chance to indulge in feminine conversation?"

Rosalie raised a brow at the lieutenant. "Feminine conversation? Shall we discuss embroidering cushions then, sir? Or did you wish to exchange ideas on the best arrangement for a table?"

"I will talk embroidery until I am blue in the face if it means you keep your hand on my arm," he said with a wink.

"Oh, you are both beasts," she said, pulling her hand away. "You're teasing me again. And what have I done to deserve it?"

Both men laughed again.

She faked storming off with a small smile on her lips.

Mr. Burke caught up easily on those long legs. "I'm sorry, Miss Harrow. No—*we're* sorry," he said, gesturing to the lieutenant.

"You may laugh with me, sirs, but not at me," she said, giving them each a level look. "I don't take kindly to bullies. Mr. Burke here knows I can and will stand up for myself."

Mr. Burke's face lost some of its mirth. "Speaking of, let me see your hand again."

"Are you a doctor, sir, that you would examine me?"

"No," he replied. "But you happen to be in the presence of two prize-winning fighters. We both know a little something about swinging a left hook."

She smiled. At least their devastating physiques made a little more sense. You didn't get shoulders like that by lounging on a chaise all day. She hesitantly lifted her left hand. Mr. Burke was the first to reach out. She felt a shiver shoot down her arm at his touch. Did he feel it too? This connection between them?

He inspected her swollen knuckles. "Hmm . . . they might bruise a bit. Do they hurt overmuch?" The fingers of his right hand brushed the top of her knuckles. It raised gooseflesh down her arm, and she was eternally thankful for her long sleeves.

"No," she said on a breath. "The pain is a trifle."

Lieutenant Renley stepped closer, those golden curls falling forward. This felt inappropriate. True, nothing was happening. The men were even an arm's length away from her . . . but still . . . she pulled her hand gently out of Mr. Burke's grasp.

"I've seen worse," the lieutenant muttered. "You're lucky you didn't break any fingers. Punching the nose hurts like hell—*damn*—sorry . . ." He blushed. "And sorry about saying damn—"

Mr. Burke clapped him on the shoulder. "Excuse my friend. As I said, he's not been in mixed company much of late."

It was quite possibly the most endearing thing she'd ever seen. The man was blushing about cursing, as if he could upset her feminine sensibilities. That would be hard to do, for she had none. "Lieutenant, when I tell you I've heard worse—heavens, I've had worse directed *at* me. Hazard of having a mean drunk for a father," she added.

Before either man could reply, a new voice called. "Mr. Burke, sir!"

All three of them turned to see a footman approach, his heels clicking on the marble.

"What is it, Wes?" said Mr. Burke.

"The duchess is asking for Miss Harrow."

8

Rosalie

THE LIEUTENANT AND Mr. Burke stayed by Rosalie's side as the footman led the way through the house. She soon found herself in a handsome room with wine red walls. A pair of Italian silk sofas were centered in the room, framed by two sets of striped chairs.

"This is the morning room," said Mr. Burke. "Good light for reading." He gestured to the wide windows.

"Of course, the library gets even better light," Lieutenant Renley added.

Rosalie stifled a snort. "Does the family never use this room unless it's morning?"

"Not especially," Mr. Burke replied. "They use the drawing room for after dinner. And there's the library, of course . . . and each member of the family has a private study. The duchess has her own parlor, which is where we're going."

"The late duke always preferred the small library," said the lieutenant. "He had a rather fine collection of books on astral navigation. He let me borrow one when I joined the navy."

Rosalie's senses were spinning. To think of a house having so many rooms with a singular use—a room for sitting in the morning, a room for dining, a room for billiards, a room for reading. It felt extravagant to the point of wasteful.

The footman opened the door on the far side of the room. Lieutenant Renley gestured for her to pass through first. She stepped into a canary-yellow room with ivory and gold accents. She didn't need Mr. Burke's muttered "this is the music room" to know its purpose. A handsome pianoforte sat before the windows, and a harp stood in the corner.

The footman walked to the other door and knocked with two raps of his fist. He stepped back, gesturing for Rosalie to step past him. As she did, his booming voice called out, making her jump. "Miss Rosalie Harrow, Your Grace. And Mr. Burke and Lieutenant Renley."

Rosalie blinked, trying to take it all in. The duchess' parlor was easily three times the size of her aunt's modest drawing room. Two separate seating areas of sofas and patterned chairs were arranged to either side of a massive fireplace. The walls were finished in a beautiful indigo wallpaper.

Rosalie stepped fully into the room, the two gentlemen just behind. Her slippered feet moved soundlessly over the plush carpet. The occupants of the room all turned to watch her approach. Two older ladies sat on the nearer couch, their necks craning to get a look at her. They oozed opulence. One wore a fashionable turban while the other had a painted face framed in rigid grey curls.

On the farthest couch, seated alone, was the woman sure to be the dowager duchess. "At last, you've arrived," she said in a low voice.

She was quite possibly the most beautiful woman Rosalie had ever seen. She had to be over fifty, but she still had a pile of blonde curls artfully arranged. Her dress was red striped

EMILY RATH

satin. Beading along the bodice put Rosalie greatly in mind of pomegranate seeds. Diamonds sparkled at her ears and neck. She sat alone and apart, as if she were Persephone triumphant, holding court over mere mortals.

"Burke, dear, what are you doing in here? Should you not be out with the others in the garden?" Her voice had a musical lilt to it.

He smiled, stepping past Rosalie to bow and kiss the hand she extended to him. "I was on my way, Duchess, but met Miss Harrow on the stairs. I thought I'd show her to you. We wouldn't want her getting lost."

The duchess pursed her lips in annoyance. "Should I consider this an audition for the role of footman? Poor Wesley . . . you'll put him out of a job."

"I will serve Alcott in any way you need, Duchess," Mr. Burke replied.

"*Hmph.* Be gone with you." She swatted him away with a small smile. "Put your charms to work and go help George tend to the ladies."

Mr. Burke bowed. As he turned, he gave Rosalie a little wink and walked out.

"Step forward, Tom Renley," the duchess called.

The lieutenant took two steps forward.

"James told me you arrived. Not in time for dinner," she added with a narrowed look. "Just like a Renley to slip in with the night. How's your family?"

"Well, Your Grace. My brother sends his regards."

"You'll be staying in the house while you're in the country?"

"Only if it's not too much trouble, Your Grace," the lieutenant replied. "James assured me I was welcome, but—"

50

"Of course, you will stay. Do your best to influence Burke and James. Second sons are always in need of a useful occupation, as I'm constantly telling them both. You at least seem to understand what is owed to your family."

"Yes, Your Grace," he said with a slight bow.

"When will you make captain, Renley? I'm quite desirous to say I have a bright, young naval captain amongst my intimate acquaintance."

Rosalie watched his shoulders stiffen.

"I hope to rank up by the end of the year, Your Grace," he replied.

The duchess leaned forward. "And you can afford your promotion?"

The lieutenant was quiet for a moment. Rosalie knew he was considering his words. Would he make known his plans to poach an eligible lady from this house party? For that must surely be his design. Rosalie had brushed shoulders with sailors far more often than dukes and duchesses. She knew military politics. The lieutenant was looking for a rich wife to rank up, for all low-born officers had two ladders they must climb at once: the military ladder *and* the social ladder. It was the way of this world.

He settled for saying, "I intend to do all that is required to advance my career."

Rosalie didn't understand why, but she felt an odd sort of fluttering at his admittance. The last thing she wanted was to be a sea captain's wife. Let a woman born and bred to the life be content to watch from the window as he sailed off on adventures without her. The most she allowed herself was a half smile to consider how very fine he'd look wearing those golden shoulder lapels on his coat.

"Well then, be off with you," said the duchess. "All of you can go," she added, nodding to the two ladies on the opposite couch. "I wish to speak with Miss Harrow alone."

Like Mr. Burke, the lieutenant turned, giving her a little nod of encouragement.

Rosalie waited anxiously as the rest of the room departed.

"You too, Wesley," the duchess called to the footman. "I shall ring the bell when you're needed again."

Rosalie heard the door shut softly behind her.

"Step forward, Miss Harrow."

Rosalie mirrored the lieutenant and took two steps forward. She kept her eyes downcast. You weren't supposed to look at a duchess, right? Or was that only for royalty . . .

As if in answer to her question, the duchess tsked. "Look at me, child. I'll not turn you to stone."

Rosalie met the duchess' piercing blue gaze.

"Turn," she said.

Rosalie blinked. "Your Grace?"

"Turn," she repeated, with a swirl of her finger. "I want to see all your angles. Chin up, that's it."

Rosalie did a little turn on the carpet. She faced the duchess again, a faint bloom warming her cheeks.

"Yes, I see you must be Elinor's girl. I can almost imagine her standing here," the duchess finished in a whisper. For a moment, it looked as if she might shed a tear. "All except those eyes," she added with a frown.

It was true, Rosalie's mother had distinctive icy blue eyes, while hers were brown as a walnut. Thankfully, they were the only thing she inherited from her father. Not knowing what else to say, she murmured, "Thank you, Your Grace."

The duchess gestured to the other sofa. "Sit over there."

Rosalie sat and folded her hands demurely on her knee.

"I'm so glad you accepted my offer," the duchess began. "I've long had a desire to meet you."

"Your offer was so kind. How could I refuse?"

"How, indeed." The duchess narrowed her eyes. "You're no doubt wondering why I invited you."

"Yes, Your Grace."

Silence stretched between them, punctuated by the *tick, tick, tick* of the mantle clock.

"Tell me, did your mother never mention me?"

Rosalie wished she had something to do with her hands. "No, Your Grace."

The duchess shrugged, as if she already knew the answer. "I'm not surprised."

Rosalie waited. When the duchess offered nothing more by way of explanation, she changed the subject. "How did you hear of her passing?"

"It was in the papers," the duchess replied. "And I have other sources. One cannot have too many eyes and ears in a place as rife with gossip as the *ton*."

"The death of my mother was deemed worthy of *ton* gossip?"

"In certain circles," the duchess replied. "In my circle certainly, for she was my oldest friend . . . even if time and distance tore us apart."

"I'm sorry you couldn't be reunited before her death," Rosalie murmured. "It would have relieved her to know she still had friends."

The duchess gave her a wary look. "Was it very bad?"

Rosalie cleared her throat. "Yes, quite. By the end, I could carry her from the bed to the chair as if she weighed no more than a leaf."

"Enough," the duchess whispered, placing a hand over her heart. "Don't tell me. I think I'd rather hold on to my memories. She was so full of life, such a beauty . . . as are you." Her piercing gaze rooted Rosalie to the sofa. "You are her mirror, child."

"We were often told as much," she murmured.

"Tell me about yourself, Miss Harrow."

Rosalie shifted. "There's not much to tell, Your Grace. I am plain Rosalie Harrow. I live with my widowed aunt in a little flat on Reeve Street in Cheapside."

"What of your education?"

"My mother did the best she could. We could never afford a governess, but I suppose we took advantage of living in Town."

"And are you accomplished?"

Heavens, why was everyone set on interrogating her? "If you're asking if I can sew and trim a bonnet and plink out a few tunes on a piano, then yes. My father may have been a worthless lout, but he was a gentleman, and I see myself as a lady."

Some flash of feeling flickered in the duchess' eyes. "Do you have a head for figures? Surely, given your aunt's position, you must be used to economizing."

This was a highly inappropriate conversation, but she assumed a duchess could ask whatever question she wanted. "Yes, of course, we economize. My father has been dead for nigh on seven years, and he left us with nothing but debts. With my mother's illness, it is not a matter of economizing any money I have left, but rather an exercise in holding off creditors with the force of will of the Spartans at Thermopylae."

"Do you dare joke about it, child?"

Rosalie's smile fell. "I suppose I'd say I laugh to keep from weeping, Your Grace."

The duchess cleared her throat. "Well, I'll not beat about the bush, Miss Harrow. When your mother died, I had my man at the bank investigate." She met Rosalie's eye. "I know about your father's debts. I know about the medical expenses. You may make light of it, but your situation is dire." Those blue eyes searched Rosalie, peering into her soul. "You strike me as a clever girl. I'd expect no less from Elinor's daughter. You must have a plan."

"A plan, Your Grace?"

"Yes, of course. Are you angling to bag a rich husband? Is that why you accepted my invitation? You're certainly beautiful enough to get a proposal. Don't think I didn't notice the way my Burke was eyeing you."

Rosalie fought the urge to blush. "My mother's illness was a full-time job. Now that she's gone, I mean to take work. I must earn a wage, and I'm not above hard work."

The duchess frowned. "What kind of work would you seek?"

"I could be a governess in a grand house like this . . . or an art teacher."

"Do you paint, then?"

"I prefer sketching to painting, but yes," Rosalie replied. "It is the one accomplishment I claim with any amount of hubris."

"But surely, to seek a wealthy husband would be a more fitting solution for a lady. Why work your fingers to the bone teaching unruly girls how to foreground a landscape when you could marry and solve all your problems?"

Rosalie never expected her first conversation with a duchess to take such a turn. "I have no interest in marriage," she admitted. "It is not an option I'm considering."

"This is a highly unladylike position to take, Miss Harrow."

"I said I was a lady," Rosalie replied. "I never said I was a very good one."

"I don't know how someone in your position can afford to be so bullheaded."

Rosalie smiled. "If Your Grace will allow it, I'll speak with equal frankness."

The duchess pursed her lips but gave a little nod.

"In my limited experience, marriage is a convention that takes all the best of love, affection, and friendship, and twists it into something cruel. I am convinced marriage would take a soul such as mine and clip her wings, leaving her beating against the bars of a cage, desperate to escape."

"Heavens, but that is a bleak outlook," the duchess said on a breath. "You must speak of your mother's marriage . . ."

"My father was neither good nor kind," Rosalie admitted. "Any love they shared quickly withered on the vine. In truth, it was a blessing to us when he died."

The duchess made no response to this shocking statement.

"Their marriage was a case study in what not to do . . . but then, I think I've never known a good marriage," Rosalie went on. "How can it be anything less than a tragedy, so long as we women are treated as the property of the men we marry? Can you dare say your marriage to the duke was a happy one?"

The duchess pursed her lips again. "Careful, Miss Harrow. I want to like you. I'll allow for a certain degree of impertinence, but your unguarded tongue will get you into trouble."

"It wouldn't be the first time," Rosalie said with a shrug.

The duchess wasn't impressed. "Well, you seem quite determined."

"I am," Rosalie replied. "I know it will look like I'm coming down in the world to take work. And you may think it will cost me my pride to do it, but I am free. I will make my way in the world, and no matter where I end up, I will get there on my own two feet . . . and there is pride in that."

"Stubborn pride," the duchess added.

Rosalie tipped her chin up in defiance. "I will do what I must to protect my aunt from my father's shadow, which seeks to haunt me even in death—"

"Enough." The duchess raised a tired hand to her brow. "It is the worst kind of cruelty, is it not?"

"Your Grace?"

"That a worthless man can waste all his good chances in life, and then ruin those of all his family with his death. Sins of the father, indeed," she muttered with disdain.

Rosalie couldn't agree more.

"I thank you for your candor, as it makes what I have to say rather straightforward. I wanted to meet you and get the measure of you before I revealed my purpose."

Rosalie stifled a laugh. "And you have measured me in the span of this conversation?"

"I am an excellent judge of character," the duchess replied with a haughty sniff. "So, I'd say yes, I imagine I have you exact."

Rosalie waited, holding her breath.

The duchess held her gaze. "First, I shall have you know I've settled all your father's debts. His wretched ghost will haunt you no more."

9

Rosalie

"What did you say?" Rosalie whispered.

"I said I've settled all your father's outstanding debts," the duchess repeated. She leaned over towards the edge of the sofa and picked up a stack of envelopes from the side table wrapped in a blue ribbon. "I have a full accounting here. Everything my agent could find. I'll leave it with you to review, and if anything is missing, tell me and I will settle it." She held out the stack.

Rosalie was suddenly standing before the duchess, the proof of her father's wastefulness in her hands, burning her cheeks with hot, bubbling shame. "You didn't have to do this," she whispered.

"Well, it's done now," the duchess replied. "And I've also settled all your mother's medical expenses. I sent the cheque to your aunt a few days ago. I imagine you crossed paths with it in transit here."

This was too much. Rosalie sank back onto her sofa. The bundle of sins dropped from her hands to the carpet as she covered her face. Rosalie had resigned herself to the idea that her father's debts would follow her into her own grave. How was she ever to repay such a kindness? She took a steadying breath and lifted her head, eyes shining with tears.

"I don't understand . . . please tell me why. I must know what I have done to deserve you as a benefactress."

"As I said, your mother and I were friends. Our lives drifted apart when I became duchess. But I'd like to think, if our situations were reversed, she would offer me the same help. I only regret I was too late to help her while she lived."

"But this is too much—"

"For you, maybe. For me, it is little more than pin money. I am not a heroine, Miss Rose. Remove that notion from your mind," she added with a stern look. "I am a duchess with an expense account that rivals that of some kingdoms. That being said, I'd appreciate it if you would say nothing about this in front of my son. He likes to think he controls my spending, silly dear."

Rosalie didn't like the sound of that. Keep secrets from the duke? It wasn't her way to indulge in secrets, but she somehow found herself saying, "I would never presume to speak out of turn in front of His Grace—"

"No, not George," the duchess corrected with a soft laugh. "He wouldn't care a fig if I bought all of Jerusalem. I'm talking about James. You are not to speak to him about this. I will handle him in my own way. And if there are any additional debts to settle, you will do it through me. Understand?"

Rosalie nodded, reaching for the envelopes. "Would you at least let me try to work off the debt? I could work here, Your Grace. I'd gladly work here."

The duchess snorted. "My youngest child is five and twenty, and already graduated from Eton and Oxford. I doubt very much James would take kindly to gaining you as his governess."

"Please, Your Grace, I cannot just accept this gift without any attempt at repayment. There must be something—"

"Oh, there is," the duchess replied. "I'm not sure how much you already know about the house party I've planned . . ."

"I only know you invited some of your friends to stay."

"True enough, but this is not just any house party," the duchess replied. "You must know my son needs a wife." At Rosalie's look of shock, she laughed again and said, "Oh no, dear, of course I don't mean *you*. No, despite my canceling your debts, you remain penniless. You've no connections, no hope of advancement, no breeding. You're quite possibly the worst possible choice I could imagine." She arched a brow. "Does my bluntness pain you?"

"Not at all, Your Grace. I find it refreshing."

The duchess held her gaze a moment longer before saying, "I brought you here to serve a dual purpose. First, I'd like you as my spy. Meet the other girls, learn about them, feel them out for vice or foul temper . . . and report directly to me."

Rosalie's breath caught in her throat. "But . . . why can't you just ask them your questions like you are doing with me now?"

"You think I can so easily corner the daughter of the Marquess of Deal and press her to reveal her secrets? She was born and bred to be a veritable vault of scheming and social climbing. We cannot all be as unguarded in tongue and manner as you, Miss Harrow," she added. It wasn't meant to be a compliment.

"No," the duchess went on, "I want someone they will not see as a threat. Someone who can watch them interact with my son and help me determine which will make the best fit. For this will not be any ordinary marriage, Miss Harrow. The woman George picks will be the next Duchess of Norland. I want him married and settled, but not at the expense of the Corbin family's honor. Certainly not at the expense of Alcott Hall."

Rosalie saw the sense in this, even if she disliked the idea of herself playing the role of informant. "Can I tell no one my task? Your sons, or Mr. Burke, or—"

"Absolutely not," the duchess said. "I imagine they will guess soon enough, but for now you are to stick to the story that you are Elinor's daughter, here to spend time with me as my guest. And you will attend the ball, of course."

Rosalie swallowed. "I . . . I'd not thought . . . I didn't actually bring a ball gown, Your Grace. I have an evening dress I could wear—"

"Heaven's no. I'll ring down to the modiste in Carrington and get something started. Leave your measurements with your maid."

Rosalie was in too deep at this point. What was a ball gown on top of her other debts? She just nodded. After a moment, she glanced up. "You mentioned a dual purpose, Your Grace. Acting as your spy was one service. What is the other?"

The duchess smiled. "We can't go revealing all our cards in the first hand, Miss Harrow. Let's start with my first request and see where that gets us. I shall expect a report in a few days, after you've had a chance to meet the ladies."

Rosalie nodded again, at a complete loss for words.

"I think we've left the rest of the party in suspense for long enough. It will shortly be time for tea, and you can meet the other ladies. I will warn you: They have sharp claws and sharper tongues, Miss Harrow."

"Don't worry, Your Grace," Rosalie said with her own

smile. "As Mr. Burke can attest, I am well able to fight my own corner. A marquess' daughter doesn't scare me."

"Good girl," the duchess replied with a smile.

Rosalie got to her feet, envelopes in hand. She turned to leave.

"Oh, and Miss Harrow . . ."

Rosalie turned back around.

The duchess' face was now mirthless. "I'll not presume to speak for Tom Renley. He is not my child; his affairs are his own. But I *do* speak for George and James, and I also speak for Burke. Know yourself, Miss Harrow. Know your place. There is nothing I like less than a devious social climber."

Rosalie's heart pounded, but she found enough strength in her voice to say, "You direct your threat at the wrong person, Your Grace. As I've already said, I have no interest in marriage. If any of the gentlemen under your charge seek to claim me as a wife, it will be their hearts that break . . . not mine."

10

James

IF JAMES HAD to spend one more minute in the company of Blanche Oswald, he was going to climb to the top of the house and leap off the side. George and their mother would just have to manage affairs without him. Burke would mourn, of course, but after a few months George would tire of his moping and get him a new hunting dog. They would name it "James" and all try to move on. Corbins always kept a stiff upper lip.

These were the thoughts swirling in his head as Blanche prattled away, hand curled possessively around his arm, as she told him everything he didn't want to know about why Scottish reels were superior to English ones.

"And of course, I like 'Maxwell's Rant' better than 'Hamilton House,' but my favorite must be 'Moneymusk.' Do you like to dance, Lord James?"

"Undoubtedly." That was the third time she'd asked him.

She scarcely paused for breath as they took their third turn around the garden, still chattering away. Burke seemed to intuit he needed saving. "Miss Blanche," he called. "Won't you join me in a game of lawn bowls?"

"Oh yes, let's," Blanche cooed, holding tighter to James' arm.

Burke let out a laugh. "Trust me when I say, you want James watching. He can't bowl for anything. He's as likely to sling it straight into the hedge. Eh, James?" He jabbed James playfully in the ribs.

"Quite," James replied, forcing a smile.

"And his dancing is worse," Burke added with a feigned sigh of disappointment. "It's tragic, really. The lord was born with two left feet."

Blanche gave James an appraising look, as if not being able to dance was a cardinal sin. She let go of his arm and flitted away as she called on the Swindon sisters to join her.

"You owe me," Burke muttered, still wearing his fake smile.

"Hmm, I let you live here rent free, so . . ."

"Fine, we'll call it even. Now get out of here, before I tell the whole party you're the best bowler for three counties."

James took his chance, not offering a word to Renley or George before he slipped away. He trotted up the sweeping stone steps towards the new wing. Not that it was especially "new," for it dated back to the reign of William of Orange. But it was the newest part of the house in terms of construction, so the name stuck.

He only got three steps inside the hall before he paused. Miss Harrow was curled up in the nearest window seat, her face streaming with tears. Something in his chest squeezed tight as his pulse raced. Had someone hurt her?

"Oh," she said on a gasp, wiping at her eyes. "Forgive me, I shouldn't . . . I'll go—" She slipped out of the window seat, clutching a stack of letters in her hand. He noticed the way she tried to conceal them on the side of her skirts as she stood.

"What happened?" His voice came out like a low growl.

Why was he being so rude? He was sure he sounded angry. Her answering flinch confirmed it.

"Nothing, my lord. I . . . it's nothing." She wiped at her eyes again.

Christ's sake. Burke told him she was called in to see his mother. He took a step closer. "What did my mother say to you?"

She swallowed, shoulders tense as she fought the urge to back away from him. "She . . . we . . . we discussed my mother, my lord. I wasn't quite prepared for . . . I haven't let myself mourn, and with everything . . ." She gestured at nothing with her empty hand. The hand holding the letters was still angled behind her.

If this were Burke or George trying to be evasive, he'd lunge forward and snatch the letters away, but this was a lady. As badly as he wanted to know what she was hiding, he couldn't dare ask her to hand over a possession. Perhaps they were merely old letters exchanged between his mother and hers. That would certainly explain the tears . . .

"Did my mother say why you're here?" He took another step closer, and she stiffened. He ignored the sting of her rejection. Why should he care what she wanted? This was *his* house. It would be his mess to clean up when whatever scheme his mother was plotting inevitably fell apart.

"She just wanted to meet me, sir. To condole with me for my mother's passing."

It felt like a lie . . . or if not a lie, certainly an obfuscation of the whole truth. James fought the urge to press her harder. She didn't owe him answers, and he felt instinctively that a firm hand wasn't the way to get what he wanted from her. He checked his pocket watch. "It's almost ten o'clock. Tea will be

served in the drawing room. Why don't I take you and introduce you to the other ladies?"

She stiffened again. "I need . . . I'd like to go to my room
first."

He frowned. Ahh, of course. She needed to hide her letters.

"But I got turned around when I left the duchess' study,"
she admitted. "I don't know the way."

He pointed past her. "Go down the hall and turn left.
There's a back stair. It will take you up to the guest corridor on
the third floor."

She nodded and gave an odd little curtsy. If he wasn't so
annoyed with his mother, he might just find it charming.
Miss Harrow clearly had no idea how to act in the presence
of a lord. How refreshing to know there was one person in
this house besides Burke who wasn't ruled by high-society
conventions.

"Thank you, my lord," she murmured.

He watched the soft sway of her hips as she moved away.
The bundle of letters was now carefully concealed in front of
her as she disappeared around the corner.

James fought the urge to grind his teeth.

Mother, what the hell kind of game are you playing now?

11
Rosalie

WITH THE HELP of a footman, Rosalie found her way to the drawing room just in time for tea. She hated that Lord James had caught her weeping like a fountain. It wasn't like her to cry. She'd just been so overwhelmed. Whatever motives the duchess had for her interference, Rosalie had her to thank for her freedom. If the price Rosalie had to pay was three weeks of spying on a few high-society ladies, she would do it.

As she stepped into the drawing room, the footman inside the door called out, "Miss Rosalie Harrow!"

Every head in the room turned her way, and Rosalie had the sudden urge to step right back out. A dozen sets of eyes watched her. She was saved the embarrassment of going to stand alone in the corner when Mr. Burke swept forward. He was all warm smiles as he crossed to her side.

"Miss Harrow, Renley and I were just about to send out a search party. He was sure you took a wrong turn and ended up in the greenhouse."

A few people chuckled.

He offered out his hand. "Come, let me introduce you

around. Renley you've met, of course," he said. "And these are the delightful Swindon sisters, daughters to the Earl of Waverley. This here is Lady Elizabeth Swindon," he said, gesturing to the taller of the two. "And the younger is Lady Mariah."

The sisters boasted matching heads of fiery red hair, freckled faces, and bright green eyes. They looked like forest nymphs from the pages of a fairy-tale book. Rosalie longed to sketch them. "Pleased to meet you," she murmured.

"Miss Harrow," Elizabeth said with a stately nod.

"But . . . I don't know any Harrows," said her sister, head cocked to the side as she took in Rosalie from head to toe. "Sister, do you know the Harrows?"

"I don't think there's much to know," her sister replied with a faint scoff.

"Well, now you both know one," said the lieutenant.

Rosalie wasn't bothered by their rudeness. There *was* nothing to know. Before she could say as much, Mr. Burke was steering her away.

"Over here we have Sir Andrew Oswald, Lady Oswald, and the Countess of Waverley," he said, gesturing to the trio sitting on the closest set of sofas, cups of tea in hand.

Sir Andrew was a portly man, with beady eyes and a thick mustache. His wife was the austere woman from the duchess' parlor. The countess had the same red hair as her daughters, if not quite so brilliant in its sheen.

"You're a pretty little thing," said the countess. "Her Grace has been so cagey about you. Pray tell, are you to be her newest charity case?" She said this with a glance at Mr. Burke, who still held Rosalie's arm.

Rosalie stilled, noting the way Mr. Burke continued to force a smile. She spoke before he could. "My mother was a close friend of the duchess, Lady Waverley. She's invited me here to enliven my spirits now that my period of mourning is done."

"Oh . . . oh, I am sorry," the countess muttered.

"You are quite welcome, I'm sure," said Lady Oswald, giving her a nod.

Sir Andrew had already resumed reading his paper.

Mr. Burke steered her away to the other collection of sofas. "And this is the Viscountess Raleigh, and her daughter Lady Madeline Blaire," he said, gesturing to a kindly looking blonde lady in a beautiful green dress. Next to her sat a frail little thing that couldn't have been more than sixteen or seventeen. She had white-blonde curls and big doe eyes.

"My lady," Rosalie said with a nod to the viscountess. "Lady Madeline."

She glanced around to see that two of the faces at least were known to her: the duchess and Lord James. They stood at the farthest window to either side of a buxom woman with raven black hair tucked under a fashionable turban. This was the other woman from earlier. Rosalie could not soon forget that hawkish nose.

"That's the Marchioness of Deal," Mr. Burke muttered in her ear, noting the direction of her gaze. "And a nastier woman you'll never meet. Her daughter Olivia sits just there," he added, pointing to where a woman sat with her back turned. Rosalie could only make out the shape of her neck and the artful pile of curls on her head.

"I shall never remember all these names," she murmured. "How will I avoid making a fool of myself with their mix of ranks."

"I'll write you a list," he replied. "And as far as titles go, just refer to everyone as 'my lord' and 'my lady' and that will about cover it."

She stifled a laugh.

"Now, to avoid the appearance of monopolizing your time, I'm going to leave you with the silliest girl in England. You can thrash me for it later," he added under his breath before saying, "Dear Blanche, have you met Miss Harrow?"

12

Tom

TOM PACED HIS room like a caged animal, wearing out the carpet as he made each turn from wall to door. He was dreading every minute that ticked by, waiting for the gong to signal dinner. Coming to Alcott was a mistake. He was in no right mind to seriously consider securing himself a wife. Was such a thing even possible in three short weeks?

If Tom ever learned the identity of the first man who thought up the idea of buying military ranks, he'd drag him out in the yard and shoot him. Advancement should be *earned*, not bought. And Tom had earned it. Eight long years in the service, steadily ranking up. He'd seen quite a bit of action; he'd earned the respect of his men. He should be in Town celebrating his promotion, not pacing in his dress uniform, readying himself for another round in the ring with a pack of ravenous ladies.

The sound of the gong echoed down the bachelors' wing, and he groaned. He checked himself over in the mirror, righting the knot of his black cravat. This dress jacket was too tight in the shoulders. He dragged his fingers twice through his hair, trying to tame his unruly curls, before leaving it as a lost cause.

Burke met him in the hall, and they went downstairs

together. Most of the guests were already below. For a moment, Tom was taken aback by the bright display of silks and feathers. The neck of each lady glittered with jewels. Being so accustomed to seeing only men—and only men in uniform, at that—he imagined a flock of exotic birds fluttering before him. The ladies all cast eager smiles with rouged cheeks, eyes twinkling with excitement.

He quickly followed Burke's lead and offered his arm to one of the passing girls. It was Blanche.

She accepted his arm with a smile. "Oh Tom, did you hear daddy is a knight now?" Her falsely high voice set his teeth on edge.

"I did," he replied, but she barely heard it, for she was already talking about the cost and style of her gown.

"—and the lace was imported from France, you know. Have you ever been to France? We could speak French if you like, for I am practically fluent. Just listen to this: *Où est mon parapluie?*" She giggled. "Well, what do you think? Do I not sound positively Parisienne?"

Entering the dining room felt like stepping into a forest scene from *A Midsummer Night's Dream*. There was a fairy-like quality to the sweeping floral arrangements. It was as if a garden was growing all around them. Potted trees festooned with glittering orbs framed the room, while vines were draped over the massive hearth. A harpist played softly in the corner. Candlelight shimmered off all the crystal and glassware.

Blanche cooed with delight. "Oh look, Tom. Isn't it just like a fairy land?"

The seating was arranged, so Tom helped Blanche find her place, then he found his own at the opposite end of the table. Thank God for small mercies. He was seated between Miss

Harrow and a resplendently dressed young woman wearing a feathered turban. He glanced down to note her name card: Lady Olivia Rutledge. Christ, this was the daughter of the Marquess of Deal. After the Corbins and the marchioness, Lady Olivia was the highest-ranking person in the room.

He glanced again at Miss Harrow, noting those beautiful dark eyes. This girl was trouble. Tom might be able to resist, but he doubted very much Burke could do the same.

She smiled at him. "Good evening, Lieutenant."

"Good evening," he replied.

Before he could say another word, the butler's voice rang out through the room. "His Grace, the Duke of Norland, and Her Grace, the Dowager Duchess of Norland!"

George swept in with his mother on his arm. The duchess looked like an ocean goddess, draped in layers of blue silk. Brilliant sapphires glittered at her neck. The table bowed as one, while George helped his mother to her chair. Then he moved down the length of the table and took up his place at the other end. A footman pulled out his chair, and he sat. The table followed suit, with the gentlemen helping the ladies before all were settled.

Miss Harrow turned away to speak with the gentleman to her right. Tom recognized him immediately as old Mr. Selby, the curate of Finchley, the little village that sat in the shadow of Alcott Hall. In the noise of the room, he couldn't hear what she said, but she drew a smile from Selby almost at once, and a moment later they were both laughing.

Tom waited for the footmen to serve the first course before he dutifully turned to speak to Lady Olivia.

"Did you have a difficult journey?"

"It rained," she said dispassionately, sipping her leek soup.

"Yes, well . . . it's the season for it," he replied lamely.

When Lady Olivia made no effort to ask him a question in return, he let himself take a few sips of his soup. He was saved having to think of another question when Miss Harrow reached for the salt, accidentally bumping his wine glass. He caught it with a quick hand.

"Oh, I'm sorry," she cried, her hand brushing his as she too tried to catch the glass.

He flinched at the touch. She had her gloves off, folded in her lap for the dinner, so her bare hand wrapped around his and the glass, steadying both. His eye traced a line up her arm to her elbow.

"Heavens, that was a near thing," she said with a soft laugh. "Thank goodness for your fast reflexes."

He blinked. Was she flirting with him? Or was it just something to say? Christ, she was looking at him. She said something else and he missed it. "Beg pardon?" he said.

"I asked how long you've been in the country, sir," she repeated.

"My ship put in at Portsmouth at the end of May."

Her eyes flashed with interest. "Oh, I only meant the countryside . . . but you've been out of England, sir?"

He nodded. "I spent a little over two years stationed in the West Indies. Jamaica, Barbados, British Honduras . . . a few other places."

"You make me quite envious, sir. I have never left England. What was it like?"

He considered for a moment. He wasn't used to talking to ladies about his misadventures. "It was . . . hot," he replied.

A silent moment stretched between them, and he wanted to kick himself. *Damn it all. Tom, get it together.*

Her lips quirked. "Well, it must not be so very foreign. England is hot too."

He didn't know her well enough to determine if she was teasing him. Her countenance was open, and she was relaxed, willing to listen if he had something to say. If not, he was sure she'd engage with Mr. Selby instead. He didn't want to lose her attention yet.

"Aye, but you've never known a heat like this," he said. "Months of cloudless skies, the sun sitting low like a golden orb. Your skin burns, turning pink and freckled before it bronzes. You've no doubt noticed my horrible complexion," he said, pointing at his deeply tanned face.

"I had noticed, sir," she replied with a smile.

"We deserve hazard pay for the suffering our poor hides endure," he said, drawing a laugh from her. This was easy. Was this flirting? Or were they just talking? Tom was so out of practice. Either way, wasn't he supposed to be focusing his attention on a lady of wealth and consequence? Miss Harrow had neither . . . but he wasn't ready to turn away.

"And what did you like best about your time in the West Indies?" she asked.

He considered, rubbing his thumb up the stem of his wine glass. "The water," he murmured. He could almost smell it, feel the movement of the waves, hear it lapping against the sand. It was a rhythm as known to him as his own heartbeat.

"Is water in Jamaica so very different from England?"

He turned to catch her dark eyes, noting the way the candles reflected in them. "Imagine the deepest shade of sapphire," he began. "So dark it appears almost black. Then, as you near the shore, it changes to the most alluring shade of blue, sparkling in the sunlight. Best of all is when you come right up on land, and the blues turn jade green, before a glittering stretch of aquamarine carpets the sand with each rolling tide."

Her mouth opened slightly, and his eye settled on her pink lips. When she noticed, she reached distractedly for her own wine glass. "Heavens, Lieutenant. You should have no problem securing yourself a wealthy wife, so long as you paint her such a pretty picture—"

He registered her words at the same time she did. While he frowned, she blushed, setting down her glass.

"I'm sorry, that was unpardonably rude. I should never presume to know you, sir."

He recovered first. "Am I so transparent?"

She was still flustered. "I . . . well, that is to say . . ."

He leaned in. "Be at ease, Miss Harrow. I'm on leave, it's true. And it is the hope of my captain that I follow the path of other officers and marry to rank up. You do not speak out of turn to admit you know my plans."

She sighed with relief. "Surely you will find a lady well worthy of you amongst this glittering assemblage. But I should consider myself quite safe," she added.

He raised a brow in question.

"If I am to call you out so brazenly before they serve the fish course, should you not take the measure of me as well?" She leaned in. "You already know I have no title, no family, and not a shilling to my name. I shall add that I have exactly three morning dresses and two evening dresses . . . oh, and these pearls are fake," she added, gesturing to the single strand of pearls around her neck. "There, we can be friends again."

They both laughed. Burke wasn't the only one in trouble.

"I fear we must turn now," she said. "But when it is my turn to have you again, you shall tell me more about the waters of

Jamaica." With a smile, she turned and immediately fell into conversation with the curate.

Tom sat for a moment, eyes on his plate. Miss Harrow was . . . odd. No, that wasn't the right word. Curious? Unique. *Special.* He smiled. Yes, that word would do nicely.

He felt eyes on him and glanced up, gazing across the table. James wore half a scowl as he cast a pointed look at Lady Olivia. Christ, Tom had a duty to perform. He couldn't leave the lady to sit alone all evening.

Think of a question, Tom.

"Do you spend much time in Deal? Or are you more accustomed to Town?"

"I prefer Town," she replied. "But we will winter in Deal."

"And . . . how do you choose to occupy yourself? Do you sketch or sew or—"

"No."

He lowered his fork. "No, you don't sew or . . ."

"No, we're not going to make small talk," she replied, without a shred of shame at her remarkable rudeness. "I would make you a terrible wife, sir, and you'd be a sorry excuse for a husband."

He felt sure he must have heard her wrong. "Excuse me?"

She gave him a level look, that pinched expression and the spray of feathers in her turban putting him in mind of an angry peacock. "I am the daughter of a marquess. Did you know that?"

He kept his face carefully expressionless. "I was aware, yes."

"Good, well then you'll no doubt be aware that the man I marry will claim a barony and thirty thousand pounds."

"I—"

"I'm six and twenty, sir. I don't have the time or the patience

EMILY RATH

to offer attention to inconsequential suitors. You are a middling level officer in His Majesty's Navy, yes?"

"Yes, but—"

"You have no title or prospects beyond maybe a captaincy, am I correct?"

Why did he suddenly feel like his tongue was tied in his mouth? "Well—"

"Let me use language you'll be sure to understand," she said with a sneer. "I'm angling for a much bigger fish, Lieutenant." She shot a pointed look down the table at George. "Now smile, and eat your soup," she said dismissively. "We'll be able to turn again soon."

At a complete loss to register any emotion but shock, Tom stuck out a hand and snatched up his glass of wine. He drained it and held it aloft for the footman to refill it. He couldn't help the grin that played on his face as he fought the urge to reach down and cup his manhood right there at the table. For he was quite sure, if he had the ill manner to check, he'd find it was missing.

13
Burke

BURKE GROANED AS the gentlemen rejoined the ladies in the drawing room after dinner. The room was set for cards, and the ladies had two tables waiting. He loathed cards, especially in mixed company where he might have to make small talk with a marchioness. The duchess and Lady Oswald immediately called on Sir Andrew and James to complete their set, while the Swindon sisters batted their lashes at poor Tom.

"Escape while you can," Tom muttered as he passed.

Wasting no time, Burke snagged a decanter of port and ducked through the door that led into the small library. He closed it as softly as possible and turned. It was a handsome, dark-paneled room, bound by bookcases on three sides, with a wall of windows along the fourth that was perfect for late afternoon reading. The windows were all closed now, hidden behind thick yellow curtains. A few candles burned on side tables, but the best light came from the fireplace.

He heaved a sigh of relief at being alone at last. The sound caught in his throat as he realized he was not, in fact, alone. Miss Harrow sat in his favorite chair, bathing in the warmth of the fire. She had her legs curled under her, book open in her lap. Damn, but she was beautiful. He traced the line of her neck, held at an angle by her cupped hand as she smiled, lost to her book.

She jerked herself upright. "Oh, forgive me sir, have the gentlemen come through already?"

"Please don't bother on my account."

"I confess, I slipped away," she said, not listening as she adjusted herself to sit properly, hands folded in her lap, back straight. "I've never been much of a card player," she admitted with a tired smile.

He watched the tension mount in her shoulders. She was nervous . . . and he knew why. Their stolen moment was on his mind too. Her warm body pressed against him, holding her in his arms. Was she afraid of him, or afraid of herself? He was eager to find out.

"Right now, you are contemplating fleeing like a startled fawn," he mused. "Is it *my* presence that so discomfits you . . . or would the presence of any man here do the same?"

Her eyes darted for the door. "I should rejoin the ladies . . ."

"Do so at your own peril," he said, moving around the back of the other chair. "The tables haven't settled. I'm sure you'll make a fine fourth at whist." He poured himself a glass of port and took a sip, knowing he had her cornered. Was her fear of being alone with him greater than her annoyance at being trapped at a card table?

"I should . . . I'll . . . just wait another moment," she muttered, turning her attention back to her book.

He smirked, victorious. "Glass of port?"

"No, thank you," she replied, not raising her eyes from her book.

Silence suited him just fine. He stretched out his legs,

angling them towards the fire. Laughter and chatter filtered through the wall, followed by the telltale sound of shuffling cards.

After a few minutes, Miss Harrow snapped her book shut with a huff. "How long have you lived in the country then, Mr. Burke?"

His hand paused with his glass halfway to his lips. "Pardon?"

"Well, we can't very well sit here making no conversation when we aren't acquainted," she argued. "It feels . . . intimate . . . and I refuse to share an intimate moment with a stranger, so please, will you tell me how long you've lived in the countryside?"

But she wanted to share intimate moments with a man she knew well? How did Burke get himself on that list? "So, you'd rather ask me mindless questions, interrupting my port and your book? That's more preferable to you than silence?"

For a moment her eyes flashed, and he saw the fire she kept hidden deep inside. "You only assume the questions will be mindless, sir. Perhaps you'll find that I am a wit. Perhaps it will be only your answers that are mindless."

There she is. Oh, this was a delightful turn of events. Much more entertaining than a bloody game of cards or even his own company. "And are you a wit, Miss Harrow?"

"I—don't—"

Yes, there was that blush he was coming to know so well. Perhaps when she knew him better, she'd let him press his lips to each cheek, tasting that warmth for himself. "Come now, don't be shy. You want to parry words with me, and I'm more than happy to oblige."

"I never meant to imply this was a fencing match," she replied. "I meant for us to make small talk."

"How long have I lived in the country? Oh yes, very small talk indeed. I've watched you since that first moment in the pub. I see how those dark eyes of yours survey every scene like a hawk on the hunt. You miss nothing, do you? You must have questions more probing than the length of my tenure residing in the country."

Her eyes narrowed again. "One minute you call me a scared little fawn . . . now I am a queenly hawk, surveying all the land. Which is it, Mr. Burke? Am I predator or prey?"

Fuck, he liked the way she said his name. The sound was low and throaty. She put music in it. He wanted her to say it again. "Perhaps you are a shapeshifting goddess," he mused. "Did not Artemis change form at will?"

This comparison made her laugh. "Please, Mr. Burke. Between you and the lieutenant, I won't get a moment's peace. No more references to goddesses, or I shall know I'm being teased and take offense."

His name on her lips again. She wasn't a goddess; she was a witch, and this was some spell. Worse, she was a siren, for the very sound of her voice was luring him in. He found himself wanting to slip from his chair and drop to his knees before her. The vision of it made his cock twitch. Christ, what was happening to him?

"As you wish," he muttered. "Shall we steer this ship to safer waters? Stick to questions of the mindless variety?"

Her head tilted to the side, those brown eyes holding him captive. "How is it, sir, that you seem so at ease here? You seem more like a master of this house than a guest."

Well, that wasn't a mindless question. He met her steady gaze. Her cheeks bloomed again, but she didn't shift away. She seemed genuinely curious to know him better. Could he ever allow such a thing? He promised James he'd keep his distance . . .

"I was raised in this house, or near enough to it," he explained. "My late father was steward to the late duke. I'm the same age as James, so we were always together as lads—hunting, fishing, climbing trees." He leaned back in his chair. "I imagine I know the forests and hills of Alcott better than any man living . . . except for maybe James."

"And the duke, surely," she added.

He snorted. "George was never much for outdoor sports."

"Does he prefer indoor sports, then? Fencing, boxing, and the like?"

To own the truth aloud about George's hobbies would be indecorous. He said the only thing that could pass as neither truth nor lie. "And the like . . ."

"The Corbins clearly adore you," she murmured. "And yet most of the other house guests seem to only tolerate you. What am I missing?"

He met her gaze, unable to control his frown. This was most certainly not a mindless question. "If I tell you, Miss Harrow, we will be acquainted. To use your own word, it would spark an 'intimacy' between us. Are you sure you want to know?"

He watched her breath catch in her throat. For a moment, he thought she would say no and flee for the safety of the drawing room. Instead, she leaned forward and whispered, "Yes."

He sighed and spilled the worst kept secret in England. "Miss Harrow, I am quite literally the bastard son of a whore."

14

Rosalie

ROSALIE FOUGHT TO contain her gasp. She didn't know what she was expecting Mr. Burke to say, but it certainly wasn't that.

"I shock you."

"No," she quickly replied. "Well . . . yes. Perhaps a little," she added.

"Are you disgusted, Miss Harrow?"

"Not in the least," she replied, meaning every word. "I am the last person to judge someone for the sins of their father. But I have questions . . . if you don't mind me asking . . ."

She'd hardly been able to look away from him since the moment he entered the room. This was dangerous. Her feelings for this man felt too volatile. She'd never felt such an instant attraction to someone before. Why did it have to be *this* man—a man the duchess expressly wished her to avoid?

"Ask your questions, Miss Harrow. I have nothing to hide."

She swallowed. "When you say . . ."

"I mean that my mother is quite literally a whore . . . or at least she was. She exchanged sex for payment, Miss Harrow. My father kept her as a mistress for a time, and that's when she had me."

Rosalie nodded. It all made sense—the odd behavior of the other guests, their subtly snide and dismissive comments. Mr. Burke was illegitimate. It wasn't the worst kind of scandal—not for a man, anyway. If Mr. Burke were a daughter, it would be ruinous. But if he were born into the Corbin family, he'd weather it easily. No, it was the combination of being both illegitimate and of lower rank that meant he must exist in a state of limbo . . . neither gentleman nor common, claimed nor unclaimed.

"But you were raised here at Alcott . . ."

"No, when I was born my mother handed me over to my father and his wife. She thought my best chance at respectability would be if she disappeared from my life. She prayed for the mercy of my father's wife to care for me and raise me as her own."

"And did she?"

His scowl deepened and she watched a flicker of violence spark in his eyes.

"I'm sorry, I don't mean to pry. Your business is your own."

He took another sip of his port. "My father's wife didn't even care for her own son, let alone her husband's bastard. She hated me and wanted me neither seen nor heard. That's why I spent most of my time with James. Don't pity me, Miss Harrow," he added. "There are few who can boast living as comfortably as I do."

"I don't pity you, sir," she replied honestly. "I can only imagine you have committed sins in your life that may require atonement, but being born is not one of them. None of us can choose who brings us into this world."

For the briefest of moments, the armor he so carefully wore seemed to slip. She caught a glimpse of the Mr. Burke behind the mask—kind and gentle, longing to belong. He soaked in her praise and gave her a weak smile. "Thank you, Miss Harrow. Am I right in guessing that perhaps you speak from experience?"

Before she could reply, the door snapped open. Not the door that adjoined the drawing room, but the one that led to the hall. Rosalie nearly jumped out of her skin as Lieutenant Renley popped his head into the room. He took in the scene of them sitting alone together and frowned.

"The duchess sent me to track you down," he said to Mr. Burke. "Get in there and play a round before she sets loose the hounds." Without another word, he shut the door.

Rosalie took a shaky breath. Of all the people to catch her and Mr. Burke together, it was perhaps best it was the lieutenant. But still, she had to ask. "Will he . . . he won't . . ."

"What, say anything?" Mr. Burke laughed. "Not a chance. But I don't think we should push our luck," he added, draining his glass and setting it aside. He stood, glancing towards the door.

She stood too. She didn't trust herself to stay close to him. "I'm too tired for cards. I think I'll retire now," she murmured. "Good night, Mr. Burke."

"Good night, Miss Harrow."

She slipped past him and left without looking back.

15

Rosalie

ROSALIE WOKE EARLY and found her own way to the sunny breakfast room. Breakfast was set as a buffet, and some of the guests had formed a line to help themselves. Rosalie murmured "good morning" to those she passed. She joined the line behind Lady Madeline. Quite to her surprise, Rosalie realized she felt bad for Madeline. She didn't seem to fit in with this pack of preening peacocks.

Speaking of peacocks . . .

The marquess' daughter floated into the room, the tail of her blood red dress fluttering as she walked. She swept down the length of the table, offering salutations to no one. Rosalie thought she must have imagined the way Lady Olivia spoke to poor Lieutenant Renley last night. She tried not to listen, but it couldn't be helped.

Rosalie felt the way Olivia's eyes traced her from head to toe, taking in the simple cut and style of her muslin walking dress. There was no way Rosalie could relate to a woman who opted to wear diamonds to breakfast.

"This is ridiculous," Olivia muttered loud enough for Rosalie to hear.

She glanced over her shoulder to see the marchioness had joined her daughter.

"Forced to fetch our own food like servants," the marchioness huffed.

"And apparently there is no assigned seating at breakfast," Olivia added. "Just wait and see how those awful Swindons will monopolize His Grace. Some people don't understand the importance of rank."

Rosalie shut out their elitist chatter and helped herself to a plate of food. Then she found an empty seat at the far end of the long dining table. Much to her annoyance, Olivia claimed the seat to her immediate left. Across the table, Lieutenant Renley glowered at the odious woman from over the top of his newspaper.

Rosalie tucked into her breakfast, determined to make no talk of any kind—large or small—with her neighbor. She nearly lost her composure when Olivia snapped open a newspaper of her own. Her hand flicked into Rosalie's face as she spread it open, nearly making Rosalie tip her tea into her lap. Rosalie set her cup down with a rattle, giving the horrible creature an incredulous look, which of course Olivia could not see through her paper.

This gave Rosalie a devilish idea . . . an idea that had her reaching for the salt. Her childish prank was rewarded when the lady next sipped her tea.

"*Blegh*!" Olivia nearly cracked her cup with the force of slamming it down.

Everyone at the table started. Rosalie's eye darted to where the salt sifter was now carefully concealed in the closest floral arrangement.

"Olivia, dearest? What is it?" said the marchioness.

"My tea was salted!" She snatched up the cup and stared into it, swirling its contents. "Someone has played a cruel and vicious joke and poured salt in my tea!"

"Perhaps you simply mistook the salt for sugar?" Rosalie said sweetly.

Olivia snarled at her before jerking around in her chair to face the wide-eyed footman. "*You* did this, didn't you, you little weasel."

"Olivia, dear, temper," the marchioness warned.

The poor footman mouthed silently like a fish. "My lady, I would never—"

"Do you think it a clever joke?" she shrieked.

A rush of embarrassment sank into Rosalie's stomach. How could she have been so impetuous? Of course, Olivia would blame the servants. Oh heavens, what if this silly joke cost the poor man his position? Rosalie would never forgive herself.

From down the table, Lord James called out, his voice ringing with calm and authority. "Phillip, did you accidentally salt Lady Olivia's tea?"

All eyes in the room were on him, and Rosalie wanted to die of mortification.

"My lord, I would never. I swear it on my life," the footman pleaded.

"I don't take kindly to being made to look a fool by a *servant*," Olivia snapped.

Lord James was out of his chair in moments, sweeping down the length of the table. Rosalie wanted to cower under the table with shame. Instead, she sat perfectly still, hands folded in her lap. Lord James muttered something to the footman, and he darted away.

EMILY RATH

"There's no place for such behavior in a civilized house," Olivia shrieked after him.

"You have my apologies, Lady Olivia, Marchioness," Lord James said. "Please allow Reed to clear this away, and let us serve you some hot cocoa instead." He nodded to the butler, who immediately began to clear away Olivia's ruined tea.

"I will be telling His Grace how I was treated," Olivia said. "And if I were mistress here," she dared to go on, "that man would be dismissed without a reference!"

"That's presuming a lot," Lieutenant Renley muttered. He said the words so quietly, Rosalie could have almost imagined they went unsaid . . . had she not seen his lips move. Mr. Burke jabbed him in the ribs with a feigned movement of adjusting his napkin in his lap.

Lord James forced a smile and a nod for the lady and her mother, then retreated down the table. Everyone settled back into some state of calm. Unable to sit still for a moment longer, Rosalie slipped out of her chair and fled the room.

It took nearly an hour before Rosalie worked up the courage to execute her plan. Sharing her shame with the duke was out of the question. She had yet to meet the man one-on-one. She was too intimidated by the duchess—and too reliant on staying in her good graces—to dare approach her directly either.

For several agonizing minutes, pacing alone in her room, she considered going to Lord James. He seemed ready enough to handle the situation. Perhaps, having seen Lady Olivia's officious behavior for himself, he would be more understanding of why Rosalie thought it warranted to play such a simple practical joke.

In the end, her courage failed her. Lord James intimidated

her. Their every interaction so far had been stilted as he questioned her and challenged her. She got the distinct impression that he didn't like her. No, there was only one person she could think to go to who might be willing to make it known unequivocally that the footman wasn't at fault. With a sigh, Rosalie slipped out of the room and went in search of Mr. Burke.

16

Rosalie

A FOOTMAN DIRECTED Rosalie to the library. Her eyes went wide as she took in the sheer scale and beauty of the room. It was a two-story space with shelves stretching around three walls, packed with more books than she'd ever seen in a private collection. The windows, framed in deep blue curtains, were open wide, catching the best of the morning sunlight. Here and there around the room, large potted plants provided greenery.

Remembering her mission, she stepped fully into the room. A deep laugh echoed from the corner, then another. Mr. Burke lounged across from the lieutenant in a set of wing-backed chairs by the farthest window. There was a chessboard balanced on the table between them, but the game sat ignored as the men laughed together.

"You cannot be serious," Mr. Burke said, wiping his eyes.

"My hand to God," the lieutenant replied, raising one hand in mock oath.

"Christ, I knew something must have happened by the look on your face. I had no idea—what did you say in return?"

"Nothing," the lieutenant replied, still laughing. "I just sat there, trying not to reach for my cock under the table."

Mr. Burke sputtered. "What?"

"I had to make sure it was still there. I thought the bitch might've snapped it off!"

Both men nearly fell out of their chairs laughing.

Rosalie liked the sound of their laughter, so free and easy compared to the reserved, almost forlorn Lieutenant Renley of last night. Not for the first time, she wished gentlemen didn't have such a Janus-like quality in their relations with men and women. Give her a man full of curious opinions and crude manners if it meant he actually behaved as himself, and not as some manicured version deemed palatable for tender ladies.

Steeling herself, she called out. "Hello there? Mr. Burke?"

Both men pivoted in their chairs.

"Damn," Lieutenant Renley muttered, jolting to his feet.

"Can we help you, Miss Harrow?" Mr. Burke asked. "Were you hoping to borrow a book?"

"No, I was . . . well, I was looking for you."

Mr. Burke glanced at the lieutenant, then back at her. She understood why this was awkward. After their chance moment alone together last night, to seek him out again so soon . . . she was sending the wrong message. But it couldn't be helped.

"Looking for me?" Mr. Burke muttered. "Whatever for?"

Lieutenant Renley was clearly curious as well, but he said, "I shall leave you to it."

"No, stay," Rosalie said. "Please."

Part of her suddenly felt it was right that he stay. She wanted him to know what happened at breakfast. And a secret part of her felt anxious about being alone with Mr. Burke again.

"Well, Miss Harrow, how can I assist?" Mr. Burke said,

stepping out of the alcove to join her in the middle of the room. The lieutenant followed close behind.

They were both so tall and handsome. It was quite arresting to see them standing together, giving her their undivided attention. How wrong-minded must someone like Olivia be to slight a man with the looks, manners, and easy temper of the lieutenant? Especially when that slight was done in favor of an eccentric duke who seemed to care little for company or conversation.

"It's about what happened this morning, sir . . . and last night."

"I'm afraid I don't follow," Mr. Burke said, grey eyes narrowed.

She turned to Lieutenant Renley. "I hope it's not too forward of me, sir, to admit that I heard your conversation last night with Lady Olivia . . ."

He clenched his jaw.

Mr. Burke frowned. "What does that have to do with—"

"It was me," she said on a breath. "The footman didn't salt Lady Olivia's tea this morning . . . I did."

The men exchanged a look.

"You're joking," Mr. Burke said with a broad smile.

But Lieutenant Renley's brows lowered over those deep blue eyes. "Why would you do that?"

"Because she was rude to you," Rosalie admitted.

Her heart fluttered as both men took a half step forward. She swallowed and their eyes tracked the motion. Perhaps this was a mistake. She thought speaking to both of them together might cool the fire in her blood, but now her senses swam with their proximity. She'd never been so sure of anything in her life: They both wanted her.

"You don't even know me, Miss Harrow," the lieutenant replied, his voice low.

"I don't need to know you to know that *she* is vile," Rosalie said without hesitation. "She treats everyone as objects. She was rude to you, to Lord James, and perhaps most importantly, to the footman."

Mr. Burke let out a slow breath, his eyes still locked on her as he considered her words. "Why should you care how a marquess' daughter treats a footman?"

She squared her shoulders. "Because I don't like seeing people treat those beneath them in rank as beneath them in dignity."

The men exchanged another look full of shared meaning she couldn't read.

"I salted her tea, Mr. Burke, but she blamed the footman." She took a half step forward. "It is very important to me that Lord James know he was *not* to blame. I would hate for him to lose his position."

Mr. Burke's mouth tipped into another smile. "Ahh . . . I see. You want me to speak to James on your behalf."

"On the footman's behalf," she corrected. "Let him keep his position."

"And keep your name out of it in the process," he added.

She swallowed, knowing he was trying to provoke her. "I will gladly admit what I did if it keeps the footman in his job."

Mr. Burke considered for a moment. "Very well, you have earned my respect with the care you've shown for the poor footman. Not to mention your gallantry towards Renley. Who knew there was such a Lancelot in our midst, eh Tom?"

The lieutenant cast him a warning look.

But Mr. Burke faced Rosalie, those grey eyes dancing with

interest as he gave her another smile. "I shall speak to Lord James personally. I will save the footman the indignity of dismissal. And we'll keep your naughty trick between the three of us, shan't we Tom?"

Lieutenant Renley nodded.

"I thank you," she replied.

It was the best possible outcome she could have imagined. Mr. Burke was showing himself to be a true gentleman. She bobbed a slight curtsy and turned to leave.

"But I shall expect something in return . . ."

She turned slowly. "Sir?'

"Let it go, Burke," the lieutenant muttered.

But Mr. Burke had eyes only for her. "You're asking me to guarantee that the footman gets a three-week paid vacation. He can't possibly be seen in the house while Lady Gorgon is still here," he reasoned. "If I save the footman, and your reputation . . . you will owe me."

She crossed her arms over her chest. "Owe you what, sir?"

Mr. Burke mirrored her stance, his brows knitting together.

"Burke . . ." The lieutenant warned again, putting a hand on his friend's shoulder.

"You will owe me one favor, redeemable by me at a time and place of my choosing," Mr. Burke said at last.

She couldn't help the laugh that escaped her lips. "I have little enough reputation as it is, sir. Why should I ever agree to make such a Faustian deal?"

He smirked. "You paint me as the devil in this bargain. Not very flattering, is it Tom?" He looked to his friend. "Do you agree with her? Am I devilish to ask for a quid pro quo?"

The lieutenant just shrugged, his own smile turning predatory.

Rosalie wasn't frightened. Instead, she felt warmth pooling in her core. Whatever was happening between the three of them right now, she wasn't going anywhere. But she had to find a way to right this course. "Mr. Burke, I never meant to imply—"

"One favor, Miss Harrow," Mr. Burke repeated. "A favor that shall not compromise you in any way," he added. "There, is that still Faustian in your estimation? Or can it be an accord between friends?"

It was her turn to raise a brow. "You wish us to be friends now?"

"I thought we crossed that bridge last night," Mr. Burke teased. "I told you that to learn the truth about me would make you my intimate friend."

"Everyone in this house knows your truth, sir," she rejoined. "Would you call all of them your intimate friends?"

"Not a chance," he replied, storms swirling in his grey eyes. "Just you, Miss Harrow."

"But to be friends requires a mutual knowing," said Rosalie. "And you don't know me, sir . . . except that I'm the type of person who will salt your tea if you rub me wrong."

"Hear that, Tom?" he replied, eyes flashing. "We must make it a point never to rub her wrong. I'd hate to get a mouth full of salt with my morning tea."

She raised her chin. "Are you teasing me again, sir?"

"Wouldn't dream of it."

The lieutenant shifted his weight as Mr. Burke continued to watch her, waiting for her to make the next move.

She took a deep breath. "You are sincere that we shall be friends? You'll help me?"

"Any friend of the duchess is a friend of mine." Slowly,

he held out his hand. "Come, Miss Harrow. If you agree, let us shake on it. Your footman shall be saved the indignity of wrongful removal, and the secret of the salt shall die buried in my heart. Renley's too."

Heart in her throat, she shook his hand. Just like the times before, the moment their skin touched, she felt a jolt up her arm. His fingers closed around hers as he tugged on her ever so slightly, drawing her closer. Standing so close to him, she could sense his warmth and the faint scent of something spiced yet sweet, like brandy or a mulled wine. She pulled her hand free.

"Renley too," he said. "We are all in this bargain together. You now have two devils at your command. Shake his hand to seal our deal."

The lieutenant held out his hand. With a swallow, she took it. The same rush of feeling filled her, leaving her fluttering all over.

"You've already given me my favor," he murmured. "And I thank you for it. Watching her choke on salty tea was like Christmas come early."

Rosalie couldn't help the laugh that escaped her as she fought the urge to step forward. Unlike Mr. Burke's spiced sweetness, the lieutenant smelled like salt and sunshine, a warm summer's day. How was it possible that even here in the English countryside, he could remind her so viscerally of the sea? Before she could do something as utterly brazen as press her face against his coat, wrapping herself in that sunny warmth, the door to the library swung open. She jumped back as Lieutenant Renley dropped her hand.

"James, just the man I was looking for," Mr. Burke called, stepping around her.

She turned as Lord James took in the room. His smile fell. "Miss Harrow, the ladies are all taking a tour of the green-houses. You won't want to miss it."

"Of course, my lord." She turned slightly to glance back at Lieutenant Renley. "Lieutenant, thank you for the advice on the books." With a slight dip, she turned on her heel and walked towards the door. "Mr. Burke," she added as she passed him.

"Good day, Miss Harrow," Mr. Burke called to her fleeing form.

Lord James stepped aside, allowing her to slip past.

"Good day, my lord."

The door shut behind her and she paused. She didn't care that a footman now stood to either side of the door, watching her. She needed to catch her breath before her knees buckled.

What just happened in that room? She felt drunk, weak, buzzing . . . *alive*. Alone in a room with two men . . . two unmarried, desperately attractive men. Two men who wanted her and were making no attempts to conceal it. Making a deal with these men, sharing secrets with them, agreeing to a favor. Touching them, taking in their intoxicating scents, their hands in hers . . . so comforting, so safe—

No. Not safe. Not comforting. *Dangerous.* To any lady, the most dangerous animal in England was not the wolf or the boar. It was the entitled English gentleman with an excess of charm and nothing to lose.

17
Tom

TOM WATCHED JAMES close the door behind the fleeing form of Miss Harrow, his last glimpse of her the bouncing dark curl at the nape of her neck. The door snapped shut and he blinked, her spell breaking. Christ, was the woman a witch? Twice in twelve hours, his head felt fuzzy, as if he were hungover . . . and he jolted to realize his traitorous cock was at half-mast. He took a breath as he registered James was speaking directly to him.

"What?" He raised his hand and dragged it through his curls.

James glowered at him. "I said what the hell was that?"

Tom said the only words that filled his muddled mouth. "I have no bloody idea . . ."

Thank God for Burke. "Oh, Miss Harrow? Turns out she's into astronomy," he said, moving back over to their corner. "Tom gave her some recommendations for books on astral navigation."

Tom was still winded. "Yeah . . . navigation."

James just frowned. It was so clearly a lie, and a weak one at that.

Tom waited, casting a wary look over to Burke.

"Fine," James sighed. He crossed the room after Burke and dropped into the other chair. "Don't tell me if it means that much to you."

Tom joined them in the corner, standing near the window.

James frowned at him. "I thought you were looking for a lady with money and status, not some torrid tryst with a penniless ward."

"Oh, but torrid trysts are my favorite," Burke said, earning him a scowl from James.

Tom bristled. He would never impugn the lady's honor, and for James to imagine otherwise was unpardonable . . . though he *was* holding her hand . . . and standing a bit too close. And Christ if she didn't smell like sweet violets and rosemary. He wanted to bury his face in her hair and breathe her in. His cock was getting hard again just thinking about it.

Perhaps James had a point . . .

He shifted uncomfortably, leaning against the window. "Miss Harrow is perfectly safe, James. Yes, Burke lied. We weren't talking about navigation"—Burke shot him an affronted look—"but trust us when we say nothing happened."

James raised his brow, every inch the imperious lord, but huffed out another "fine."

"Where are your guests?" Burke asked, one eye cast lazily over the chessboard.

"You mean George's guests?" James moved a pawn and flicked Burke's king-side castle off the board. "Most of the ladies are with Mother taking a tour of the greenhouses. I set Sir Andrew up with George. They've gone fishing. I begged off so I could actually get some work done." He rubbed a tired hand over his face.

"What would you have us do today?" Burke asked.

James leaned back with a wave of his hand. "Whatever the hell you want. Renley, feel free to join the ladies . . . *in company* this time," he added with a glare.

Tom blinked. "Whyever would I join the ladies on a greenhouse tour?"

"To *court* them, you great blundering idiot," Burke said with a laugh.

Bloody hell. He was meant to be courting these women and trying to woo one into becoming Mrs. Tom Renley. He was too distracted by the sweet smile of the only unsuitable girl in the house.

"Christ, man," James said with a laugh. "Burke, please stay with him and see that he makes some small effort today."

Tom groaned. The last thing he wanted was to be coddled by Burke as he was forced to make infinitely small talk with the likes of Olivia Rutledge.

As if reading his thoughts, Burke said, "Never fear, Tom. I know you got your cock handed to you by that harpy last night, but—"

"What?" James cried, eyes darting from one to the other.

Oh hell, James hadn't heard the story yet. Tom didn't have it in him to tell it again.

"Don't worry about it," Burke said with a wave of his hand. "Lady Gorgon was in rare form last night, but it's fine. We'll just scratch her name off the list."

"Lady Gorgon?" James repeated. "Who—"

"Olivia Rutledge," Burke provided.

"Oh . . . Christ," James breathed. "That shoe fits."

"Does it ever," Burke said with a knowing nod. "But it doesn't matter, because she's off Tom's list."

Tom grunted his approval. "We should move her to the top of George's list."

Burke beamed at him. "And just like that, Tom's back in the game."

Tom couldn't help but laugh.

"Speaking of the Gorgon," Burke said. "Don't dismiss that footman."

James blinked, confused for a moment. "What . . . oh, of course not. He said he didn't do it. She probably mixed up the salt and the sugar like Miss Harrow said. I gave the lad time off until the Gorgon leaves."

Tom shared a smile with Burke over James' head. It turned out all Miss Harrow's dealmaking was for naught, as James had already done the gentlemanly thing.

"I'm leaving you two now," James said, rising from his chair. "Some of us have actual work to do. Renley, keep Burke out of trouble as best you can."

"That is not possible for anyone," Tom replied.

At the same time, Burke said, "I highly resent the implication that finding Tom a wife is not work. When I'm successful," he called after James' retreating form, "this will surely be my crowning achievement!"

James paused at the door. "I'm going to let you spend the morning contemplating those words, and we'll revisit them later to see if you'll finally admit you're setting rather low standards for yourself."

"I despise introspection of any variety," Burke replied.

James got the last word as he shut the door. "Don't I know it."

As soon as James was gone, Tom took his chair. "Do you really want to join the ladies in a greenhouse tour?" He prayed Burke would say no.

"Of course, I do," Burke replied. "Ladies love a man who can pretend to know anything about flowers. I'd be happy to give you some pointers . . . show you how it's done."

Tom dropped his head in his hands. "It must be so easy to flirt when you've got nothing to offer and nothing to lose—" The words hung in the air between them, and he immediately wished them unsaid. "Burke . . . I'm . . . I didn't mean it—"

"No, you're right," Burke said. "I think you've stumbled on it precisely. Look at you . . . and look at me. Look how easy flirting is for me."

"I don't follow," Tom replied.

"Perhaps you should stop thinking about what you *have* to do and start thinking about what you *want* to do."

"What do you—"

"Flirt because it's *fun*," Burke said with a laugh.

Tom sighed. Once, in his youth, he too loved the thrill of the chase . . . until he let himself get caught. Now he was like a fox wary of traps. "Flirting is not fun."

A glint flashed in Burke's eye. "Liar." His look was suddenly all mischief. "James was right, you know . . . what the hell was that with Miss Harrow?"

Tom met Burke's gaze. "I don't know."

"But it *was* fun. Don't think I didn't see the effect she had on you." He laughed. "Fuck, she's a siren. She's luring me in like I don't know what."

Tom groaned again. It was true. Whatever was happening with Miss Harrow, it was excessively diverting. For a wild moment, he'd been contemplating tracing the tip of his nose up her neck and chasing that sweet scent of violets with his tongue . . .

Oh, hell, Burke was watching him. "James already said it: Miss Harrow is penniless. I can't set my cap at—"

"Who said anything about setting your cap at her?" Burke replied. "I was just pointing out the fact that you are, most assuredly, a liar. You *liked* flirting with Miss Harrow. Hell, you were ready to pounce on her just now. You would have taken her against the bookcase if I wasn't here—"

"Stop," he groaned.

"Miss Harrow proves you've not forgotten how to flirt. So, just treat all your interactions with the other ladies like that. Show them you're a lion ready to pounce—"

Tom choked on a distressed laugh. "God, you are the *worst*—"

"And you'll surely have one curled around your little finger in no time," Burke finished with a confident smile. "Now, get up. You've got to work fast if you want to snag the best one away from George while he's not looking."

18
Rosalie

THE INTERIOR OF the Alcott greenhouses was, if possible, even more beautiful than the outside gardens. Rosalie lost herself in the intoxicating scent of oleander and hibiscus, lily of the valley, *Amaryllis.* The smaller of the two houses was dedicated to growing exotic flowers, while the larger contained a dizzying array of fruiting trees and succulent vegetables.

The moisture in the air curled the fine hairs at the nape of her neck.

"And of course, in winter we move the oranges back indoors," the duchess said, gesturing through the glass.

Rosalie spied a row of potted orange trees happily soaking in the autumn sun.

"Do you grow no pineapples, Your Grace?" said the marchioness.

"I've discussed plans with my son to build an addition which would serve as a pinery," the duchess replied. "They're sourcing a new style of glass from Florence."

Rosalie stifled a groan. Imagine a world where good people worked their backs to the breaking in the pursuit of farming, and here stood a group of ladies in their morning diamonds discussing the construction of a building that would exclusively grow pineapples for one family to consume.

"What makes you frown, Miss Harrow?" Lady Elizabeth was watching her with a catlike grin. She smiled, her pink lips parting around tiny, straight teeth. "Oh, I hope it's something scandalous, for I do believe you are blushing."

"I'm just a bit overheated—"

"*Ugh*, and is it any wonder? I hope this abominable tour ends soon." Elizabeth looped her arm in with Rosalie's and slowed their steps, letting the group move down the row of ornamental lemon trees. Then she leaned in, lowering her voice to a conspiratorial whisper. "Tell me what you think of the gentlemen, Miss Harrow."

Now Rosalie *was* blushing. "I . . . don't know them well enough to make out a character," she replied.

"You coy thing," Elizabeth laughed. "You sat next to the lieutenant at dinner last night. And the maids say you arrived at Alcott with Mr. Burke."

Rosalie fought the urge to scowl. So, the servants were gossiping about her? She should have known. The walls had eyes and ears here; she had to remember that. "I don't—"

The younger sister suddenly pressed in on Rosalie's other side. "Did you ask her?"

"She was just answering, Mariah," Elizabeth replied with a huff.

Both girls turned their bright green eyes back to Rosalie.

"I don't know the lieutenant," Rosalie admitted. "Not after one dinner. I spent more of the evening conversing with the curate—"

"I don't give a fig about a married old curate," Elizabeth huffed again, pulling on Rosalie's arm to lead her away from the main group back down the row of lemon trees. "What about His Grace? Or Lord James?"

Rosalie couldn't help but laugh. "I haven't spoken two words to His Grace—"

"Our maid said you swooned, and Mr. Burke caught you," Mariah pressed. "What can you say of him?"

"I most certainly did not." She was about to ask for the name of the maid, but Elizabeth dragged her down onto the bench and spoke across her with a glare at her sister.

"No, Mariah, not him. Mama said he's quite out of the question."

"Oh, right," Mariah giggled.

This had Rosalie's frustration rising even higher. It was one thing to know Mr. Burke might be treated differently, but it was quite another to see it for herself. Why should *he* be the social pariah?

Elizabeth let out a coo of delight. "*Ohhh*, speak of the devil, and he shall appear."

Two of the gentlemen in question were striding toward them. Rosalie swallowed her flutter of excitement as Lieutenant Renley and Mr. Burke locked eyes on her first. It was too soon since the library to see them again. She wasn't ready. Their narrowed gazes had heat pooling inside her.

Elizabeth and Mariah shot to their feet, smoothing down their skirts.

"Good morning, ladies," Mr. Burke said.

"Good morning, Mr. Burke, Lieutenant Renley," Elizabeth replied, her voice inexplicably breathier than moments before.

Her sister echoed her curtsy, a blush warming her freckled cheeks.

Mr. Burke glanced over his shoulder at the lieutenant. "Tom, didn't you have something for . . ."

Lieutenant Renley stepped forward. "Ah, yes. Miss Harrow, we spoke of those books on astral navigation. I thought you might find this one diverting." He held out a small, leather-bound book.

Two sets of envious eyes bored into the back of Rosalie's head. She had quite literally no idea what he was on about, for she'd never spoken the words "astral" or "navigation" aloud in her life. "Thank you, Lieutenant," she murmured, her fingers brushing his as they closed around the book.

"How very thoughtful of you, Lieutenant," Elizabeth said, standing so close to Rosalie that their shoulders rubbed. "Isn't it thoughtful, Mariah?"

"So thoughtful," Mariah parroted.

"You three seem to be lost little lambs," said Mr. Burke. "The rest of the flock has quite gotten away from you."

The Swindon sisters both smiled.

"Was it by accident or design? Are we interrupting some secret meeting?"

"Of course not," Elizabeth cried.

"Pity," Mr. Burke replied. "Only the lemons shall know if you've been confiding secrets of the heart. I won't let Renley pry any further on the subject."

The Swindons both giggled.

Rosalie glanced at the lieutenant. His mouth was set in a firm line and his ocean-blue eyes held little mirth. Prying into the sisters' secrets seemed to be the last desire of his heart.

"Miss Harrow," Mr. Burke said, "shall we rejoin the others?"

She nodded, looping her hand around the arm he offered. Elizabeth preened as Lieutenant Renley took her arm, forcing Mariah to walk behind.

"Sorry about that," Mr. Burke murmured, lowering his head slightly to speak in Rosalie's confidence. "I needed to test a theory. Thanks for being a good sport."

"I don't know what you mean, sir," she replied, trying to let her hand relax on the soft wool of his morning coat.

"Your footman is safe," he whispered. "I've already spoken with James."

Rosalie heaved a sigh of relief. "You're sure?"

He nodded, his mouth tipping into a grin. "And now that I've held up my end of our bargain, it is time for you to hold up yours."

So soon? Surely, he couldn't have thought of an appropriate favor in the span of a single hour. She tried to swallow her anxiety. "What would you have me do, sir?"

He chuckled. "First, I think we'll have you dispense with calling me 'sir.' If we are to be intimate friends, I think we can drop the honorifics."

She groaned. "Please stop placing the word 'intimate' before each utterance of 'friend' . . . or I shall start to think you have the wrong idea about me, *sir*."

He laughed. "I am only using your word, Miss Harrow—"

"Well, stop it," she hissed.

He chuckled again. "I said I'd not compromise your unimpeachable honor, and I meant it. But I really would prefer you to address me more informally."

"What do you wish me to call you? I don't know your Christian name . . ."

"No, you wouldn't know it, would you? I hate my Christian name and never use it. It's become my most closely guarded secret," he mused. "Everyone in my acquaintance just calls me 'Burke.'"

She chanced to look up at him, wanting to see his expression. It was playful but guarded. He'd clearly donned a full suit of armor since leaving the library. Could she blame him when a duchess, a marchioness, and a countess stood not fifteen feet away? And all their daughters flitted about, desperate to ignore him while throwing themselves at his friends. It was enough to have any man seeking a place to stand well out of the fray.

"Now, about that favor you owe me . . ."

"What can you possibly need of me that you cannot accomplish on your own?"

"You've hit the target with your first arrow. I cannot do it myself because your favor to me is to convincingly flirt with Tom."

She stopped in the middle of the path. She was torn between jerking her hand away or digging her claws into his arm. "You said you'd not compromise me."

"I only mean I want you to flirt with him in front of the others . . . and let him flirt with you," he explained. "You know as well as I what Tom is looking for in a wife. He needs to bag one of these ladies with a fortune. Now, he's a bit out of practice with flirting—hazard of the sailor life—but he clearly enjoys flirting with you."

She had to fight the urge to react. It was one thing to think something in her head . . . it was quite another to get confirmation of it. Tom Renley *was* flirting with her.

"So, let Tom flirt with you where the others can see it," Mr. Burke went on. "If the others *think* you've caught his eye, it will spur them into action."

She understood his logic. She was to be bait, luring the other more desirable ladies in. What she didn't understand was why her first reaction was to be offended. Sure, he was gorgeous and charming, and she felt a natural sense of ease in his presence . . . nothing like the fire and frustration so quickly fueled by Mr. Burke. But Rosalie didn't want Lieutenant Renley for herself. May he marry Elizabeth and be very happy with his new fortune.

She did *not* want him for herself.

Absolutely not.

Still . . . she gave herself a moment to feel the sharp sting of rejection.

They were coming upon the rest of the group. The duchess turned to take them in, arched brows raised. The other noble ladies flanked behind her, watching them approach with a mix of excitement, curiosity, and open suspicion. Rosalie had not thought of that difficulty. Mr. Burke was asking rather a lot. Flirting openly with the lieutenant would put Rosalie into the line of fire of these monstrous mamas and their desperate daughters. Did she have the strength to withstand them? Was the security of one footman worth all this trouble?

And what of her promise to the duchess to spy on the ladies? How could she possibly help both the duchess and the lieutenant? The mission of one party would put her at odds with the other . . .

"Well, Miss Harrow?" Mr. Burke said. "Will you hold to our deal and help me?"

Just then, Lady Olivia sneered at her from behind her plumed feather fan, and Rosalie's resolve hardened into stone.

"Very well," she murmured. "I will help you . . . Burke," she added with a smile. It felt daring to take such a liberty, but his echoing smile pleased her. A secret part of her felt excited to lead these ladies on a merry chase. "I'll help you help the lieutenant."

"Excellent," he replied. "With you at my side, we'll have Tom batting away the other ladies with a stick."

19

James

AFTER A TEDIOUS morning spent poring over the details of a land dispute, James was famished. On a typical day, the butler might bring a tray of sandwiches to the office. More commonly, James was to be found out on the estate, meeting with tenants and addressing various management concerns, skipping the midday meal altogether.

He got to his feet and stretched, watching through the window as George and Sir Andrew caught up with the rest of the group returning from the greenhouses. He frowned as he took in his brother's easy laugh. James was stuck inside all morning, while George spent the morning fishing under the September sun with nary a care in the world.

For four years now, James had played the role of silent duke. He contained the worst of George's impulses while fostering new economic opportunities for the estate, securing it for the unknowable future. But recently, James felt a growing restlessness. He was tired, there was no doubt. Hell, in the past month it felt like he had only managed two to three hours of sleep each night. He was overworked and under-appreciated . . . but that had always been the case, and he'd quite made his peace with it. He never expected George to recognize or value his contributions to the family.

So, what changed that James now felt so dissatisfied? Or perhaps the better question might be: what *needed* to change?

"My lord?" the butler said. "Luncheon will be ready in ten minutes."

"Thank you, Reed," he replied, smoothing down his waistcoat as he moved towards the door. "Once lunch is over, I'll be out all afternoon. Do let my mother and brother know?"

"Of course, my lord," Reed said with a slight bow.

Steeling himself, James went in search of his house guests.

The dining room was empty when James entered, save for two footmen busily setting up the last of the chafing dishes. Reed followed him into the room and quietly went about making sure all was in order.

"Where is everyone—"

Before James could finish the question, the plinking sound of a merry tune on the piano floated through the open door. A burst of laughter echoed over the music. James followed the sound towards the music room. Several ladies laughed and clapped as someone continued to plink a fast tune on the pianoforte.

James crossed the sunny morning room and stepped into the music room to find the group in various states of sitting and standing, the older ladies all fanning themselves while sipping on small glasses of fresh lemonade. The elder Swindon girl was at the piano playing the jolly tune, while there, in the middle of the carpet, stood George . . . juggling three silver candlesticks. The younger ladies laughed and clapped as he sent them twirling through the air, nearly hitting the chandelier.

James slipped into the room, taking the empty place next to Renley. "What the hell is going on?"

Renley just shrugged. "Damned if I know," he replied. "George said we were all being a dreary lot and demanded someone play. Then he just . . . started juggling."

James glanced across the room to where Burke stood behind the duchess. Burke met his eye with a scowl. James gave a heavy sigh. "Is he drunk?"

"I don't know . . . I don't *think* so. It's always so hard to tell with George," Renley replied.

Just as George dropped one of the candlesticks, sending them all thunking to the carpet, Reed slipped into the doorway and gave James a subtle nod.

"And that's the end of the morning's entertainment, I'm afraid," James called to the room, stepping over to place a firm hand on George's shoulder. "Lunch is served. Ladies, please feel free to take your refreshments with you."

He nodded to Burke and Sir Andrew, who did their duty and took the arm of the duchess and the marchioness. Behind him, Renley already had an arm out in invitation for the countess. The ladies filtered out, with most of the young maidens casting blushing smiles up at George. Even Madeline gave him a smile, though she looked like she might faint from the effort.

Only the oddity Miss Harrow seemed content to slip away. James frowned watching her leave. He was still furious at Burke and Renley for cornering her alone this morning. He wasn't an idiot. He saw the way she was looking up at Renley . . . the way he was devouring her with his eyes . . . their clasped hands.

If they said nothing happened, he believed them, but the

lady ought to know better. What could she have possibly had to say that would need to be held in secret? More importantly, if she was in trouble, why did she trust them and not him? Was it a failure of his duties if people in his own house couldn't come to him with their problems?

Perhaps she just preferred their company to his . . .

She was just the sort of distraction none of them could afford. Her complexion and ready wit would need to be tempered by frequent reminders of her status as a social anchor, not a sail. James should have a quiet word with Burke soon. Between the two, he was the greater risk. James knew Burke's type all too well. He would put money on it: Miss Harrow was going to cause trouble before the end.

He pushed all thoughts of her from his mind, turning his attention to his brother. "What the hell are you doing, George?"

George just chuckled as he replaced the candlesticks on the mantel. "Entertaining my guests. Which, as you'll remember, was the threat you made to me yesterday. It's either I entertain them, or you'll shove your booted foot up my arse, right, little brother?"

"I meant entertain them as a duke, not as a medieval court jester."

George laughed again. "You are so uptight. I seriously must wonder whether it is *you* with the boot lodged in your arse." In a fit of boyish exuberance, he snatched at James, grabbing for the waist of his breeches, and made like he was going to wrestle James to the ground and check.

"George—*fuck*—" James wrestled himself away and stumbled back, adjusting his waistcoat with a sharp tug. Then he smoothed back his hair and took a deep breath. "Just . . . don't embarrass us."

"It was just a bit of fun, James," George said with an annoyed frown. "You wouldn't know the word 'fun' if it danced before you wearing nothing but father's monocle."

James refused to concede whether his brother had a point. When *was* the last time James had a little fun? He pushed the thought away. George got to have more than enough fun for the both of them. "After lunch, I'll be out for most of the afternoon, but I'll return in time for dinner."

George walked away with a shrug, for he couldn't care less. He asked no questions about the business that pulled James away. *His* business. Duke business. He paused at the door and tossed over his shoulder, "Come home early enough and you'll catch my evening show. I might just be sporting that monocle . . . and nothing else."

20

Rosalie

AS HER SECOND day at Alcott Hall unfolded, Rosalie found herself falling into a sort of rhythm with the other house guests. After a few quiet words and smiles, Lady Madeline was warming to her. The Swindon sisters hadn't quite forgiven her for receiving a book from Lieutenant Renley . . . and she avoided Lady Olivia and her mother at all costs.

The only other young lady in attendance was Blanche Oswald. From what Rosalie had gathered, her father Sir Andrew only recently received his knighthood. While some in society might look down their noses at a tradesman, Rosalie appreciated the ability of a man who could rise based on the merit of his work, rather than the polish of his family name.

Rosalie wanted desperately to like Blanche for it too . . . but she couldn't. Blanche was, if possible, even sillier than Mariah. The party was terribly short of men, so when Rosalie found herself seated between the girls at dinner, she wanted to choke on the bones of her guinea fowl and expire right there at the table. Anything to avoid engaging in one more debate about quartered versus capped sleeves.

By the time dinner ended, a headache throbbed just behind

her eyes. The ladies left the gentlemen to their port and made their way over to the drawing room. Rosalie slipped away from the others, seeking the blessedly awkward silence of Madeline, who sat in the far corner of the room.

"May I join you?"

The girl jumped slightly at being addressed but nodded and scooted over to the far end of the small sofa.

Rosalie didn't know why her first impulse to pity the girl still held true. Madeline was a viscount's daughter. But there was something sweet about the girl. It made Rosalie feel protective. She reminded Rosalie of a rabbit, all quivering nose and blinking eyes. Rosalie couldn't imagine a worse match for George Corbin.

"How do you like Alcott?" Rosalie said, taking the small glass of sherry offered to her by a passing footman.

Madeline declined hers with a shake of her head. "I find it's all rather grand," she replied as soon as the footman was safely out of earshot.

Rosalie smiled. "My aunt and I have a small flat in Town. Our drawing room is the size of an Alcott water closet." She took a sip of her sweet sherry, grasping for a topic of conversation more appropriate than water closets. She ought to ask at least one more question so as not to appear rude. "Do you have any hobbies, Lady Madeline?"

"Violin," the girl murmured. "And I sew . . . and draw."

Rosalie sat forward. At last, a topic worth discussing! "I sketch too. What do you like to draw?"

Madeline blushed. "Flowers and landscapes and . . . sometimes animals."

"Did you bring your sketchbook?"

Madeline nodded.

"We should sketch together one morning," Rosalie offered.

Before Madeline could reply, the drawing room door opened, and the men entered to coos of welcome. His Grace and Lord James were the first through, followed by Sir Andrew. Burke and Lieutenant Renley brought up the rear. It felt strange to call him "Burke," even in her own head. Rosalie pushed past the awkwardness as he caught her eye, dragging the lieutenant behind him.

She realized with a start that Burke had set Madeline as their target for the evening. The protective feelings the girl stirred in her began to boil over. Shamelessly flirting with the lieutenant in front of Madeline was bound to go disastrously wrong. Madeline was no such game player. She wouldn't recognize Rosalie's flirtations as a call to battle. Instead, she'd move into immediate retreat, white flag billowing behind her.

Another dangerous thought crept in: Rosalie didn't want to watch the lieutenant fall for Madeline. She swallowed that thought and the accompanying jealousy deep down into the pit of her stomach. This was the game she'd agreed to play. She didn't seek him for herself, so she couldn't bat an eye when he pursued another. The last thing she wanted to become was a modern-day Circe, luring this charming Odysseus into her arms, only to see all his hopes dashed upon the rocks of her unsuitable shores.

"And what makes you smile, Miss Harrow?" Burke said, coming to stand at her side.

Her smile widened as she took in his broad shoulders, cut so fine in that black evening coat. If she was the Lieutenant's Circe, Burke was hers. "A lady cannot be expected to reveal all her secrets," she said, taking another sip of her sherry. She turned her attention to Lieutenant Renley. "Lieutenant, have you met Lady Madeline?"

"Aye," he said with a tip of his head. "We met yesterday."

The gentlemen sat in the empty chairs to either side of the sofa, Burke nearest to Rosalie. Across the room, the young ladies howled with laughter as the duke said something funny involving vigorous hand motions. Lord James stood beside him, hand clenched around his glass of port. Rosalie had so far struggled to puzzle the man out. By all accounts, he was quite possibly the most amiable man here. He was the wealthy son and brother of a duke, a viscount in his own right, handsome and clever, and somehow still unmarried.

And yet, none of the ladies seemed to be flirting with him in the same way they did the duke, or even Lieutenant Renley. He was always holding himself apart. Even now, he stood amidst a group of people, yet no one sought out his smiles or shared laugh. He was as much above them as he was invisible to their eyes.

Rosalie suddenly had an urge to know him better, to learn why he felt he must keep his walls so high. For if Burke was a man walking through life in armor, Lord James was a fortress with thick stone walls. A handsome knight and his imposing castle. They were made for each other. Where did the lieutenant fit into this fairy tale?

Her thoughts were distracted by Burke, who watched her with open curiosity, those grey eyes focused on her. "What do the two of you discuss so quietly here in the corner?"

"We were just comparing our many accomplishments," Rosalie replied. In her musings on Lord James, she'd settled on a plan of action for Madeline too. Making her jealous was a fool's errand. Rosalie's time would be much better spent showing the lieutenant her merits. Rosalie's very presence near him was enough to earn the jealousy of the others. To test her theory, she leaned closer and smiled, casting an eye over Burke's shoulder. Both Blanche and Elizabeth gave her disapproving looks.

What was the saying? *Two birds, one stone.*

She spoke directly to the lieutenant. "Lady Madeline is a veritable virtuoso on the violin, and she can sew and draw." Madeline shot her a look of horror at being called a "virtuoso," which Rosalie ignored. "We were just making plans to do some sketching. Alcott's grounds are spectacular. I believe you were often here as a boy, Lieutenant. Perhaps you can recommend some locations for the best views?"

He considered for a moment. "I'd never claim to have an artist's eye, but Finchley Hill provides a nice view of the house with the river foregrounded. And perhaps the view from the far side of the lake. But Burke would know better than I."

Burke crossed one leg as he leaned back in his chair. "My favorite view has always been from the roof," he said. "You get no pretty views of the house to sketch, but the countryside seen an hour before sunset from that vantage point is nothing short of heavenly."

Rosalie envied him his sense of belonging. She'd never felt at home anywhere.

"Do you do portraits, Lady Madeline?" Burke asked.

"Only of animals, sir," Madeline replied.

Burke's eyes took on a teasing glint. "Well, we shall have to snoop about the stables for a stray cat for Renley to hold. Then you may sketch them both."

Rosalie hid her smile by taking a sip of her sherry. She dared to look at the lieutenant, which was a mistake. He too was trying to hide a laugh. She was relieved to see it. Those blue eyes caught and held hers. She narrowed hers in challenge. "Don't tease her, Mr. Burke," she said. "If Lady Madeline prefers only scenes of nature, we shall oblige her. I'm sure if the lieutenant requires a portrait of himself to gaze at in wonder, one of the Swindon sisters would be vastly happy to serve as the artiste."

Both men barked out a laugh.

"Shall I arrange it, Tom?"

"I have not now, nor do I ever intend to sit for a portrait," Lieutenant Renley replied.

"You lie," Burke said. "Why, you used to let Marianne sketch you by the hour—"

The mood between the men shifted so fast, Rosalie was left blinking in surprise. All Burke's joviality was quite dissipated by his friend's waring glare.

"Sorry," Burke murmured.

"Leave it be."

Burke turned to Lady Madeline. "So . . . when should you like for us to arrange your sketching party?"

Rosalie tried to listen as the other three made plans for a morning of sketching by the lake's edge. She was too distracted to do more than nod and smile.

That odd exchange made her desperate to learn the identity of the mysterious "Marianne" who so clearly haunted the lieutenant. All his melancholic moods and terrible attempts at flirting now made sense. He wasn't determined to seek out a wife from amongst the ladies in this crowd, for his heart was clearly already set on another. Rosalie could only speculate as to whether the object of his affection was alive or dead. If alive, where could she be? For who could deny such a man her love if he ever dared to offer it?

21
Tom

TOM LEFT ALCOTT early in the morning, before anyone in the house was awake, and rode the five miles to Foxhill House, his family estate on the edge of Carrington. He'd been promising the family a visit, and his nephew's birthday seemed like an unavoidable event.

It was barely lunchtime, but his sister-in-law had already made three veiled threats about how he ought to stay. She mentioned his ready room, how his nephews missed him, how his brother relied on him. It would take all his strength to break away and return to Alcott in time for dinner. He wanted to be annoyed by her smothering, but he was well loved, so it had to be forgiven.

His nephews were in rare form today. Tom did his duty and chased them about, letting the two younger lads ride him like a horse, but he was now thoroughly done in. Dear little Caroline was the youngest and the only girl. She sat curled up in his lap with her favorite doll as he took a much-needed breather. The boys still charged about like an angry swarm of bees.

Tom's brother Colin sat next to him in a comfortable chair, the sun blocked by a large awning set up for the party.

"Hmm," he said, glancing up from his paper. "I'd quite forgotten to ask you. Did you hear the news out of Yew Warren?"

Tom looked up sharply. Yew Warren was the family seat of the Edgecombes. The age gap between Tom and his brother meant that Colin was away at Cambridge when Tom had his affair with Marianne Edgecombe. It was a secret known only to Tom and the lady . . . and Burke and James, of course.

Tom never spoke of her now. His friends did their best to honor his wishes. He chose to think of her as dead. More accurately, he chose to think of her as the ghost that might haunt him if she were ever summoned by name.

"I've had no news from Yew Warren," he replied, readying himself for the worst.

"You'll remember that daughter of old Sir John's . . . Miss Marianne?"

Tom quietly groaned, the dull echoing beat of his heart slowing in his chest. "It's Mrs. Young now," he replied flatly.

"Aye, Mrs. Young," Colin echoed. "Well, that's just the thing. I heard it from Sir John last Sunday that Mr. Young died. Quite unexpected it was . . . though he was a bit older from what I remember. Did we attend her wedding?"

Tom shook his head. "No, I was out on my first tour to the West Indies." The truth was, he'd volunteered for that tour *because* of Marianne's wedding.

"Oh, that's right . . . I could have sworn we attended that wedding together." Colin shrugged. "Well, in any event, Mrs. Young is now a wealthy widow, and at the tender age of twenty-six." He set aside his paper and stretched his legs. "Mother had an idea that you were sweet on the girl once . . ."

Tom wasn't listening—he was too busy imagining Marianne's porcelain face covered in a black veil. As much as he hated her, he was also loath to picture her in black bomba-zine, haunting her London townhouse like a beautiful, lonely raven.

Marianne was a widow. Her marriage hadn't even lasted eight years. For Tom, it was eight years of mourning. Well, perhaps only *two* years of full mourning. Then another two of debauchery and distraction . . . followed by four much more peaceful years of denial.

"I say, were you sweet on her?" Colin repeated.

"Hmm?" Caroline wiggled on Tom's lap, tucking her head into his shoulder. "I . . . that was a long time ago," he replied noncommittally.

"Well, it could be a possible answer to your current pre-dicament," Colin said with a smile. "You need to marry a lady of some wealth, and Marianne just inherited her husband's fortune. If she was sweet on you once, she might be sweet on you again. Could be worth a call up to London to offer your condolences and . . . test the waters, as they say."

Tom was in a daze. How, after eight long years, could he still not have this woman out of his life? Was this meant to be some kind of sign? He was at last ready to look for a wife, and his first love was once again available . . .

He shrugged Caroline out of his lap and into the lawn chair as he stood. "I need to go."

Colin blinked. "Go? But Agatha said you were staying for dinner—"

"No. I was planning such but . . . can't stay . . . already made a commitment."

Colin rose from his chair with a frown. "Surely you can stay *one* night with your family. Rejoin the house party tomor-row. Are you so desperate to be rid of us?"

"It's not that," Tom replied. "I need . . . this is . . . I need to see James. I need to speak with him about this."

"Can you not speak to me? Christ, man. I'm your brother—"

"And I love you, Colin, but I must go." He clapped him on the shoulder. "I'm sorry. Tell Agatha thank you for the hospitality."

"Tom—"

He gave his brother a weak smile. "I'll be fine. I'll see you all in church on Sunday, if not before."

With that, he left in search of the groom to order his horse saddled. He couldn't stay here another second. He needed his friends, needed their advice. It didn't settle him one bit to admit that he wasn't actually sure whether they would talk him off this ledge . . . or give him an almighty push.

22

Rosalie

IT WAS BEASTLY hot for an afternoon of berry picking, so unusual for mid-September, but at least they had plenty of shade. A picnic spot was arranged in the middle of a clearing near the river's edge. The towering trees ringing the clearing offered some protection from the sun. Additional shade was provided by two large, striped umbrellas. An arrangement of tea tables was scattered about, towering with delicacies—tea cakes with fresh preserves, cucumber sandwiches, colorful jellies, scones with clotted cream, ham, and fruit salads. Two footmen served lemonade off silver trays, while two more wielded large fans to stir the air.

Rosalie stood at the water's edge, watching the rippling of the water as it flowed on its way. She dabbed at her brow with her handkerchief. Behind her, the other ladies lounged on cushions playing a boisterous game of charades. She glanced over her shoulder to see Mariah miming something with great feeling. The duke sat like a spider in the middle of this frilly web, directing all the ladies in the game.

Rosalie longed for the balancing presence of the other gentlemen. Where had they all gone today? She found she missed Burke's smiles and the lieutenant's deep laugh. Even Lord James brought a calming presence to the group, a sense of order.

"*The Lady of the Lake*," shrieked Blanche.

"Yes!" Mariah said with a laugh, her red curls bouncing as she bobbed up and down.

"Well done, Red," the duke called. "Who shall go next?"

Mariah glanced about the group, her smile turning from bright to calculating as her gaze landed on Madeline. "Lady Madeline, it is your turn," she said in a singsong voice.

Madeline was already flushed from the heat, her cheeks matching the pink of her dress. The color deepened as her eyes went wide. "Oh no, please—"

"Come now," Mariah called. "Everyone must take a turn. 'Tis only fair!"

"Yes, play," cooed Elizabeth.

"It's such good fun," Blanche echoed. "I'll pick an easy one for you." She dug her hand into the little cup of folder papers and began opening them to find an easy prompt.

"Please . . ." Madeline murmured.

"What shall His Grace think if you're unwilling to play his game?" Mariah challenged, hands on hips.

"Who wants to be married to a toad's lump?" Lady Olivia sneered. Of course, she was seated closest to the servant wielding a fan. More than once during lunch Rosalie heard her tell the man to hurry his strokes.

"Now, now, ladies," said the duke, raising a hand for calm. "It is not a cardinal sin if my future bride should be unwilling to play parlor games . . . but it's not a ringing endorsement of your merits," he added with a pointed look at Madeline.

The poor girl was on the verge of tears as the other ladies

silently crowed. He was all but dismissing her right in front of them.

Rosalie felt her ire rise. "Was there not talk of more berry picking?" she called. "I've spent quite long enough in a recumbent pose. Does anyone wish to join me . . . Lady Madeline?"

"Thank you," Madeline breathed, reaching for her parasol.

"But we're still playing our game," Mariah cried.

"Let them go," the duke said with a wave of his hand. "We shall have more fun without them."

Rosalie snatched up a basket and looped her arm in with Madeline's, leading her away to the sound of snickering.

"If Lady Madeline is too dull to play our game," called Mariah to their retreating forms, "then I choose . . . *you,* Your Grace!"

All the ladies clapped and cheered.

Ten minutes later, Rosalie slowed her pace. She'd kept Madeline's arm looped in hers and walked her right past the strawberry patches. The basket on her arm hung forgotten as she focused on putting distance between themselves and those pretty little vultures.

"I'm sorry about all that," she murmured, breaking their silence.

"It's nothing."

Rosalie could see from the tears in the poor girl's eyes that it was most assuredly *something.* She wanted to ease her pain but wasn't quite sure how to go about it. She never had a thin skin. With Francis Harrow as a father, she couldn't afford to bruise so easily. As she let her eye linger over Madeline's features, her protective instincts flared. This delicate little flower had no one to protect her.

"Can I ask you something, Lady Madeline?"

Madeline nodded.

"I don't want to overstep but . . . do you want to marry the duke?"

Madeline paused, letting her hand slip away from Rosalie's arm. "Is it not what any girl should want? To be married to one of the most illustrious men of the land? But he'll never have me now," she murmured. "Oh, I should have just played the game!"

Rosalie pulled her to a stop. "Listen to me. You are the only lady of quality in that nest of hornets. His Grace would be lucky to be your husband. In fact, I think it quite possible he would never come to deserve you."

"Why are you being so kind to me?"

"Because I like good people," Rosalie replied. She dropped her hand away and kept walking down the shaded path. "I like to think good people can prosper in this world . . . we can be assured the bad ones will."

"You can't really think that, Miss Harrow."

"Of course, I do. You cannot convince me this world doesn't reward avarice and vice, especially in those who can easily afford both."

"You speak your opinions so freely," said Madeline, her tone equal parts awestruck and anxious.

"I speak as I find," Rosalie replied. "I'd like to say I've learned to temper my strong opinions with time out in society, but it's only getting worse. If I'm not careful, I shall talk myself into serious trouble someday."

This earned her a smile from Madeline. "I believe it."

"I'll *really* know I'm in trouble when I can't talk myself back out of it," she added with a laugh.

Madeline's smile grew.

"I shall speak another observation aloud . . . if you'll let me."

"Go on, then."

Rosalie paused her steps again, meeting Madeline's soft gaze. "You'd do wrong to think your only option is marriage to this duke."

"Father wants the matter of my position settled—"

Rosalie scoffed. "You're what? All of sixteen? Seventeen?"

"I turned seventeen in May."

"And just out in society?"

Madeline nodded.

Rosalie took a deep breath. She owed it to sweet Madeline to be a lone voice of reason. "If marriage is in your future . . . and I'm not saying you have to resign yourself to that fate . . . dare to cast yourself a wider net than the man currently being thrust before you."

"You don't like the duke?"

Rosalie shrugged. "The truth is I don't know the man. Not well, at any rate. But what I've seen gives me pause . . ."

She could tell Madeline was listening intently. "Why do you pause?"

Rosalie put voice to the observations she'd been making over the last two days. "George Corbin seems to be a useless sort of person, prone to moods and fits of boredom that are too easily explained by his utter lack of enterprising spirit. In fact, I have the sneaking suspicion that he leaves the managing of his estate entirely in the hands of his brother."

"You judge him harshly."

"I speak as I find," Rosalie repeated. "His Grace is not the only eligible man here at Alcott . . . perhaps he is not even the *most* eligible man. While not equal to the duke in title or wealth, the others each seem to have merits His Grace utterly lacks . . ."

"Such as?"

Rosalie considered. "Well . . . modesty, for one. I very much doubt Lord James would ever juggle candlesticks."

Madeline giggled into her lace-gloved hand.

"Integrity, for another," she added. "The lieutenant seems to be an upright and honorable man. He'd never embarrass you before the others like His Grace did back there. He'd never seek to do a lady harm."

Madeline considered this. "But . . . is it really my place to have an opinion on how His Grace treats me? I'm not his equal—"

"Says who?" Rosalie snapped. "You may not be his equal in title, but you are flesh and blood, same as him. You don't have to settle for a man who would mock you to your face and laugh at your expense before others. That is not a good man, Madeline. Find yourself a modest man, a gentleman who *earns* the name—"

Madeline paused in her steps, wary as a rabbit. "Do you hear that?" she murmured, turning around to peer behind them down the path.

Rosalie stilled too, her own senses sharpening to amplify the sounds of the forest. Over the birdsong and coursing stream, she heard voices. A laugh. A few shouts. "Perhaps the group is catching up with us . . ."

"No, it's not coming from behind us. It's up ahead," she said, pointing towards the bend in the stream.

The girls hurried their steps, following the little path until the sound of voices grew louder—deep laughter, a man's keen call. They turned the bend and Madeline shrieked in panic, her gloved hand flying up to cover her open mouth.

Rosalie's eyes locked on Lord James. He stood not ten feet

away, ankle deep in the water . . . completely naked. Before she could help herself, her eye was traveling down the sharp planes of his chest, following a trail of dark curling hair down his muscled stomach to—

Heavens, Rosalie!

She looked pointedly away. Just behind Lord James stood Burke, waist-deep in the water, also naked. His dark hair dripped water down his face. And those broad shoulders . . . Rosalie couldn't decide whether she liked the view of them better with or without his coat. The muscles of his chest tensed as he felt her gaze and his eyes narrowed, his smile widening to meet hers.

Without. Definitely without.

Lord James recovered his senses with a few audible curses and quickly slapped his hands over his exposed manhood, which, Rosalie noted with a grin, did little to conceal himself from the ladies' eyes.

Next to her, Madeline lost herself in a fit of giggles.

"Heavens, let us avert our gaze." Rosalie snatched Madeline's parasol and flipped it in front of their faces to block both gentlemen from view.

From center stream, Burke roared with laughter as Lord James retreated into the deeper water with a splash.

Madeline still giggled, her cheeks a deep crimson. The ugliness of the picnic was now utterly forgotten. "Yes, I see what you mean," she said through her laughter. "Quite the gentlemanly display of modesty."

23

James

JAMES WANTED TO die. He was quite sure if he sank under the water and waited long enough, he could accomplish the task. Two ladies . . . two *guests* in his house, just saw him naked. Damn Burke and his stupid bloody ideas!

The girls stood together behind a parasol, their faces hidden from view. Little Lady Madeline twittered as Miss Harrow shushed her.

"Good afternoon, ladies," Burke called, his voice full of mirth. "How goes your strawberry picking?"

"Yes," came Miss Harrow's strangled reply. "Quite diverting! I believe we shall go back now, sirs. Please enjoy the day!"

James couldn't help but smile as they made a show of turning their backs, keeping the parasol between them like a shield.

"I can't speak for Lord James," Burke called. "But when you next see me, I promise to be more formally attired!"

James lunged for his friend to the sound of both girls breaking into peals of laughter as they hurried away down the path. Burke let himself get caught and James shoved him under the water. "You arse!"

Burke resurfaced with ease, still laughing.

"What the hell am I going to do now?" James said, trying desperately to hold on to his anger, even as he began to laugh. "How will I face them again?"

"Very easily," Burke said, swimming safely out of reach. "Why should you be ashamed? It's not as if you're missing any parts."

James groaned, standing waist-deep against the gentle pull of the current.

"You're a rich and handsome lord," Burke added with a roll of his eyes. "I'm sure the ladies considered it quite the treat. If they don't both blush furiously the next time you see them, I'll give you ten pounds."

"Ten pounds of my own money?" James scoffed. "How generous of you."

"Fine, what do you want?"

James considered. What he wanted was Miss Harrow to look at him again. He wanted her in his arms, to watch those cheeks blush pink as she took his cock in her hand and—

Where the hell did that come from?

He shook his head, trying to clear it of the unbidden visions. Rosalie Harrow was completely off limits. She was penniless and all but alone in the world, with only a widowed aunt to her credit. She had no social capital, no title, no breeding or education. James shouldn't give her a second thought. So why couldn't he get her out of his mind?

Goddamn it, he had better control than this. He wasn't going to give little Miss Nobody from Nowhere another minute of his time. He couldn't afford it. Let Burke be impetuous. James would be rational and steadfast. He was married to his work.

"You're plotting something," Burke mused. "Care to share?"

"Not plotting," James said quickly, still trying to push away that image of Miss Harrow and her wandering eye. "More like . . . musing."

"On?"

James scowled. "Do I need you to know my every thought?"

Burke ran his hands through his slicked-back hair and laughed again. "Only the indecent ones. I care nothing for your thoughts on land conveyances or farming innovations . . . much as you've tried to reform me."

James laughed too. "You're not half as useless as you like to pretend."

"Lies," Burke replied, daring to look affronted.

James' smile fell as he studied his dearest friend. "Why do you try so hard to be idle? What does it gain you?"

Burke just shrugged and began making his way out of the stream.

"You know, if I was the duke in fact, I would make you my steward in the next breath," he called to Burke's retreating form.

Burke paused, glancing over his shoulder. "And I would graciously decline. I already bring enough shame being your wastrel bastard of a friend," he added under his breath. "Imagine if I actually put in effort. How they would all laugh and sneer then." He snatched up his breeches and put them on.

James sank into the water, considering Burke's words. "Is that it, then? Is that why you won't try to be more? Why you give up every position I've ever offered you after a six-month?"

Burke sighed, tucking his shirt into his breeches. "It's selfish enough of me to stay at Alcott knowing I draw whispers and derision. If I were a better man, I'd leave. I'd save your family the disgrace of my connections—"

"Stop," James called, his ire rising as he waded out of the stream. "I've told you once, and I'll tell you again: I don't care who your mother is. Damn the world and everyone in it for making it your cross to bear. But you have a chance here to use me to your advantage, so *do* it." He placed a hand on Burke's shoulder. "My family name is more than powerful enough to protect us both. You're my dearest friend, Burke. I want to see you get everything you want in life, and I *know* this isn't it." He gestured to the quiet countryside all around. "Wasting away here at Alcott, helping me manage George's moods, catering to my mother's demands—you can do and be *more*. Take a position. Use my name if you want, Lord knows you've earned it after all your years of loyalty."

Burke raised a dark brow. "Use your name?"

James shrugged. He'd thought of this solution often enough, but never actually voiced it aloud. "If the Burke name holds you back, then let's change it. Become a Corbin, and every door in society will open to you. I will finance entry into whatever profession you want. You could set up in Carrington or Town—"

"Are you trying to get rid of me?" Burke said with a laugh, but James heard how hollow it was, how false.

"Never," James replied. "But I'm done sitting by and watching you waste away as if you have nothing to offer the world."

Burke shrugged out from under James' hand and reached for his waistcoat. "And what if what I want isn't suitable in the eyes of your high society? What if the things I want bring even more shame to the Corbin name?"

James lowered his brows as he reached for his own breeches. "You're not . . . you don't want to marry a goose or something, do you?"

"No," Burke said with a laugh.

James smiled, happy to see he was easing his friend's mind. "You'll not take to the continent and become a nudist standing for paintings all day?"

Burke raised a brow at this suggestion. "I won't say it doesn't appeal, especially as an escape from the harsh English winter . . . and I do dearly love Florence."

James just laughed as he worked himself back into his clothes. Burke finished first and went to unhobble the horses. As James leaned against the tree, shoving his foot inside his leather riding boot, Burke approached, reins in hand.

"And I know what you were thinking about," Burke said. "You could never hide anything from me."

James glanced up with a grunt as he gave the sides of his boot an almighty tug. Damn, this was always easier with a valet's help. "What?" he huffed, snatching his other boot out of the grass.

"Earlier," Burke said. "When you were *musing*."

James slipped his other foot into the top of the second boot. "Oh, yes? And what was that?" He gave the second boot a Herculean tug.

"Miss Harrow."

"*Christ*—" James lost his balance and nearly toppled over, shoving out his elbow to brace against the tree. He glanced up sharply, as if it were Burke's fault he couldn't put on his own damn boot. "What the hell are you talking about?"

Burke gave his horse's neck a pat. "You were musing on the fine eyes and handsome figure of Miss Rosalie Harrow."

James swallowed, still holding on to the sides of his boot. He tried to give nothing away in his face. "And why would I waste a moment thinking about her?"

Burke's answering smile turned positively devilish. "Because your mother told you not to."

24
Rosalie

IF ROSALIE THOUGHT Lord James might be embarrassed to meet with her again, dinner quickly put him to the test, for they were seated next to each other. Not only that, but Burke was seated on her other side.

"Good evening, my lord," she murmured as Lord James drew out her chair. "I trust you had a productive day in the village?"

"Aye, it was," he replied. "Thank you, Miss Harrow." He sat quickly next to her and took a sip of his wine the moment the footman filled his glass.

She fought to control her smile and realized with a jolt that Burke was busy doing the same.

"Come now, man," Burke muttered, leaning in so close she could smell the fresh soap of his hair. "Don't make this awkward for the lady. So, she saw you naked. Let's acknowledge it and move on—"

"Burke—" Lord James hid his mouth behind his napkin. "Take your own damn advice, for it is *you* who are discomfiting her."

Rosalie just smiled. She wanted to join in their teasing.

Would they let her? Only one way to find out. "Don't take this the wrong way, sirs, but I'm afraid you'll have to do much more than appear naked to discomfit me."

"Saints alive," Burke breathed. "What else must we do?"

She met his gaze, noting the way it narrowed on her. To be an object of his interest felt somehow even more thrilling than braving a storm. He leaned in until his shoulder brushed hers, the corner of his mouth tipped into a grin. She wanted to trace it with her finger . . .

She blinked, taking control of herself again. Heavens, but attention from this man was heady. How did all the other women dare show him such disdain? "That's hardly appropriate dinner conversation, Mr. Burke," she said, recovering her wits. "Please restrict your interests to my accomplishments and my opinions on Fordyce's Sermons."

Burke choked on a laugh as he set down his glass of wine. He leaned in again, voice low. "The day I waste a moment of your time asking your opinion on Fordyce's Sermons is the day I'll eat James' pocket watch."

From her other side, she felt rather than saw Lord James smile. Burke had spoken loud enough for him to hear their exchange. But the lord's attention was quickly snagged by the countess, who sat to his opposite side. She dragged him into a conversation on new farming equipment that Rosalie only heard in bits and pieces.

They settled into their first course of veal collops with white sauce. Rosalie noted the mixed seating arrangement down the table. Each night the duke found himself winged by eligible ladies. Tonight, Lady Olivia finally had her turn, while Elizabeth sat to his other side. Next to Elizabeth sat Lieutenant Renley, and on his other side was young Mariah.

He looked miserable as Mariah tried to enchant him with her silly stories. And he kept casting a wary eye across the table, as if trying to catch the attention of Burke or Lord James.

"Your friend looks ill, sir," she murmured to Burke.

Burke glanced down the table with a frown. She noted the way the two men seemed to have a silent conversation with just their eyes. Something was wrong. She could tell by the way Burke's shoulders tensed, by the way Lieutenant Renley's eyes narrowed and his jaw clenched.

"He's fine." Burke tore his eyes away. "No doubt the fatigue of the day."

Rosalie nodded, even though she was sure that didn't explain the lieutenant's attitude. Something was most certainly wrong.

Burke's eye kept darting down the table. She leaned in, watching him watch his friend. "Can I ask you a question, Mr. Burke?"

Her voice pulled his attention fully back to her. "I thought we were dispensing with formalities?" he said.

"Perhaps I'm not yet used to it after such a short acquaintance," she replied. "Most men must earn the comfort of familiar names with a lady."

He smiled at her subtle jab. "Ask your question . . . should I brace for impact?"

Now that she had this chance with him, she couldn't waste it. Especially not while the lieutenant was so clearly agitated. "Why are you so determined to make the lieutenant a match from among these ladies when you and I both know his heart already belongs to another?"

Burke's smile fell and he slowly lowered his knife and fork. "Christ, but you're observant," he murmured.

"Hmm, and cautious too," she added. She leaned closer, careful that only he should hear her. "I don't like being set out on a fool's errand. Why would I help you secure a lady's affections for the lieutenant when his own affections are firmly engaged elsewhere?"

"You *are* observant," he repeated, "but you don't have all the facts . . . and we shouldn't speak about this here." He gave a pointed look to his left.

She glanced over his shoulder to see his other seat mate was Sir Andrew, and beyond him sat the marchioness. "Then when and where?" she pressed. "For until I have all the information, I'll not be helping you snare one of these ladies."

He frowned, glancing down the table again at the lieutenant. "Let me speak with Tom after dinner. If he's agreeable to it, we'll tell you everything tomorrow."

She raised a brow. "And if he is not agreeable?"

He smiled. "Well, then I'll just have to risk Poseidon's wrath and tell you anyway."

25
Tom

TOM WAS IN agony the entire dinner. He answered the Swindon sisters' questions about life in the navy, trying to control the roll of his eyes as Mariah accused her sister of getting seasick, to which Elizabeth retorted with an animated story of her sister's notable history of being terrified of thunderstorms. Elizabeth found no less than three occasions to drop her napkin, leaving Tom duty bound to retrieve it for her.

As soon as the ladies left the dining room, Tom swept out of his chair and came around the table, dropping into Miss Harrow's empty chair between Burke and James. "I need to speak with you both," he muttered.

Burke was ready for him, for they'd been sharing covert looks all evening. But James blinked, leaning back in his chair as he drew his eye away from the conversation George had struck with Sir Andrew.

"Now," Tom added. "In private."

James tossed his napkin on the table. "Let's go to the morning room."

The men stood and made their excuses to the others. Tom walked between his friends as they crossed down the grand gallery. A footman led with a candelabra, and the three of them sat on the pair of sofas in the middle of the morning room as the footman lit some additional candles.

As soon as the footman was gone, Burke leaned forward. "Well?"

Tom sighed. There was no point in delay. "Colin had word this week from Yew Warren, from Sir John himself . . . Marianne's husband is dead."

"Christ," Burke sighed, at the same time James asked, "How?"

Tom shrugged. "Colin didn't say, but Young is definitely dead. Marianne is a widow."

Burke launched from the sofa and paced the carpet. After a moment, he turned, eyes narrowed. "You mean Marianne is *available*. Now that she's a widow, you're thinking about throwing yourself at her feet again. Christ, Tom, I thought we got you past all this!"

"You're biased," Tom challenged. "You always wanted to see the worst in her, to convince yourself she was not worthy of me—"

"Who are you trying to convince now, Tom: me or yourself?" Burke replied.

Tom scowled. Was Burke right? Was his whole design in telling them just to have Burke talk him down?

Apparently, Burke was more than willing to play his part. "She strung you along for years, Tom. She spun every line about waiting and loving and dying of want. She gave you everything . . . *except* her hand in marriage. When the choice was set before her, she jilted you for that toadying fool Thackeray Young. A man so useless as to be no fit companion for fencing, riding, shooting, or Christ, even ambling through the park. But he *did* have seven thousand a year," he finished with a scoff.

Tom let his friend's words sink in. "Yes, she had a choice between love and comfort, and she chose comfort," he reasoned. It was a line he'd said a thousand times before.

"If you care nothing of this news," said James, "why were you practically laying an egg at dinner? Either you're over her . . . or you see this news as the chance to try again—"

"Goddamn it, James, don't give him any ideas," Burke barked.

"He's already had the idea, else he wouldn't be so distressed," James countered.

It was true. How many times had he considered riding to London and hunting down that idiot Young? How many dreams did he have of running the gentleman through with a sabre and taking Marianne right there on the floor of his foe's drawing room?

James leaned forward. "What do you want from us, Renley? Do you want us to convince you to let her go? We'll play our parts. Burke is clearly willing," he said with a slight frown at his friend. "Or do you want us to advise you to offer yourself to her again?"

"I won't do it," Burke replied sharply. "James will have to be the one to say those lines. I'll not sit idly by and watch as that woman twists you up again, Tom."

Tom dropped his head in his hands. "Christ, I hate her. *That's* my truth. I hate her down to the bones of me . . . but I love her too. She has me bewitched . . . I can't explain it. I want this feeling gone from me, but she haunts me like a ghost."

James sighed. "While I don't share Burke's outright contempt for the lady, I will admit that I always thought you built her pedestal rather too high. I think her glorified status comes from you not finding any others to compare with her."

"Too true," Burke echoed.

James shot him another glare but continued. "If you had spent more time moving in society, perhaps you would have met other ladies that rivaled Marianne in beauty, wit . . . and most assuredly devotion." He shrugged, stating the obvious. "But you went to sea. So, none could ever supplant Marianne in your mind as a paragon of perfection."

Tom sighed and sat back, arms crossed over his chest. He glanced from Burke to James. "What would you do?"

James considered for a moment. "I believe, if it were me, I would go to London. I would want to face the ghost that haunted me and determine for myself whether I could ever put her to rest. It's been eight years, Tom. Perhaps you will meet with Marianne again and not like who you see . . . perhaps you'll realize she was never meant to sit so high on her pedestal."

Tom's frown deepened. "Burke?"

"I would have let her go eight years ago," Burke replied without hesitation. "I don't want anyone in my life who doesn't want me."

Tom had to appreciate Burke's feelings. The man was loyal to a fault. If you loved him, he returned your love with a ferocity unmatched. Surely that's what came of living in high society as the bastard son of a whore. Tom felt a kind of twinge in his chest to realize he'd somehow been deemed worthy of such devotion.

Burke sighed, his face softening. "But . . . seeing as you have most decidedly *not* moved on, my method will not work. James urges you to meet the lady again and gauge your feelings as well as her own. I recommend caution. I admit it is possible that Marianne loved you . . . in her way," he begrudgingly admitted.

Tom was surprised. Across from him, James smiled. "Who is this new rational creature, and what have you done with my Burke?"

Burke went on. "I put to you a challenge: Keep waiting. If her husband is dead, and she is now his sole inheritor, she is rich and can make her own decisions. If she loved you, and fortune was the only impediment, she is now in a position to compensate for you."

Tom saw the wisdom of this approach. After all, it was quite possible that Marianne jilted him and never gave him a second thought.

James cleared his throat. "I can't believe I'm saying this, but I agree with Burke. Caution ought to win the day. Besides, we don't want you looking too desperate—"

"Though we three know the truth," Burke added with a laugh.

Tom dared to let himself laugh too. He felt calmer now that he had a plan of action. He would wait and see if Marianne wrote to him. If she ever cared for him, let *her* be the first to reach out.

"Speaking of truths . . ." Burke's face suddenly looked decidedly guilty. "We may need to tell Miss Harrow about this new development."

James' smile fell. "Why would we do that?"

Burke's guilty look landed on Tom. "I may have . . . enlisted her help."

Tom's glower was matched by James' in ferocity. "Help with what?"

"Courting the ladies," Burke admitted. "Making them jealous by flirting with you—"

"Christ, Burke," James snapped. "I ought to thrash you!"

Tom leaned back against the sofa. It hadn't escaped his

notice that Miss Harrow's attentions had been pleasing. He noted the way she smiled, the way she leaned in and tried to make him laugh. Here was the truth: She was on orders from Burke. None of it was real.

James groaned. "Christ, Burke, what could have possessed you?"

"Come on, she's perfect," Burke replied. "She's gorgeous and clever and . . . off limits," he added quickly. "That's what I meant by perfection. James will eat his own hat before he lets himself be bothered with such a thing as romantic connection—"

"Hey!" James had the audacity to look affronted.

"And you know you don't want her," he shot at Tom. "She knows it too. So, she can flirt with you with no fear of consequence, and it draws the other ladies in. And the ruse *was* working . . . even if you could be putting in more effort."

"So why do we need to bring her in to our confidence?" James pressed.

"Because, as I say, she's clever," Burke replied. "She sensed something wrong with Tom and threatened to break our deal if I didn't explain why she should help him court these ladies when he's so clearly still lost to Marianne."

Tom fought a growl. "She knows about Marianne?"

At the same time, James asked, "Deal? What deal?"

"She heard us talking of her the other night, remember? She put the pieces together," Burke explained. "Like I said, clever girl."

"What deal, Burke?" James said again.

Burke cast Tom a look. "It's nothing—"

"That's what you were doing in the library the other day," James realized. "What the hell happened that she would feel forced to make a deal with you?"

Tom couldn't help but laugh again. "Christ, just tell him."

James looked ready to burst. "One of you better start talking right fucking now, or—"

Burke laughed too. "Keep your wig on, James. It was a silly prank. Remember Lady Olivia and the salty tea?"

James blinked. "What . . . yes . . ."

"Well, it wasn't the footman. It was Miss Harrow," Burke replied.

Tom's grin spread, remembering the moment she came to them.

James blinked again. "Miss Harrow salted Lady Olivia's tea? Why?"

"Because she was rude to Tom," Burke explained. "Well, rude to everyone. She salted the tea and then Lady Gorgon blamed the footman, so Rosalie came to me to beg clemency for the footman. I think she was too afraid to approach you directly—"

"Why should she be afraid of me?"

Burke laughed. "Because you're usually so aloof you may as well be made of stone. Or if not aloof, you're brooding behind us all like a wolf with a toothache."

Tom still wanted to punch him. "Christ, Burke, I *told* you to leave me to my own devices—"

"Well, that was never going to happen," Burke muttered.

"I'm telling you to stay out of it. I will manage my own affairs—"

"Whoa, wait. There will be no affairs with Rosalie Harrow," James barked.

"That's *not* what I meant," Tom replied, growing increasingly exasperated.

"But it was sort of implied," Burke jabbed.

"Shut it!"

"Make me, sailor—"

"Enough!" James was standing now. He pointed a direct finger in Burke's face. "Burke, leave Miss Harrow alone. Compromise the lady's honor while she's in this house, and I will flog you in the yard. Do not test me."

Tom smiled as his friend was chastised, until James rounded on him.

"And *you*, man up and handle your goddamn business. You want Marianne, go get her. You want to get married to one of the ladies here and snag her fortune, get married. You want to wallow in self-pity like a brokenhearted poet for the rest of your goddamn days, be my guest, but do it elsewhere."

He took an angry breath and charged ahead. "If you're going to stay under my roof, you must find the strength you need to stop being such a goddamn bore. I'm sick of you moping about like a whipped dog. Burke is too. I want fun Renley back. I want the Renley who entered any ring with both fists raised, ready to take on the world. Find him or find your way back to your brother's house with your tail between your legs."

Tom blinked, winded by the ferocity of James' speech. He felt something shift inside him, as if he'd been encased in a shell of hard stone. Tom felt a crack in that shell, and he took an unrestricted breath. One breath turned into two, and before he realized what was happening, he was gasping, clutching at his cravat, trying to loosen it. The breaths couldn't come fast enough. He wanted to fill his lungs until they burst.

"Renley?"

"Christ—*Tom*—"

Both men were on their feet. James dropped to his knees

and took over for Tom, untying his cravat and unwinding the black cloth, tossing it aside.

"Breathe, Tom," Burke said, placing a hand on his shoulder.

Tom took a few more gasping breaths, raising his own hand and wrapping it around Burke's wrist. "I'm fine," he panted after a moment.

"What happened?" James muttered.

Tom sagged back on the couch, letting his head fall against the cushion as he slowly began to laugh.

James cast a wild look at Burke. "What the hell just happened?"

Burke grinned. "I think you broke the evil spell."

"The . . . *what?*"

"He's fine," Burke laughed, holding out a hand to help Tom to his feet. "Or he will be. Right, Tom?"

Tom took another steadying breath. He felt lighter than he had in years. "Yeah . . . yeah, I'm fine."

26

Rosalie

AT HALF PAST nine the next morning, Rosalie found her way to the duchess' parlor for tea. She was ready for it this time when the footman barked out her name as she passed through the open door.

"Ah, Miss Rose . . . may I call you Miss Rose?" said the duchess from her usual place in the center of the window-facing sofa.

"Of course, Your Grace," Rosalie replied.

"Well then, sit yourself down here and we'll get straight to business," she said, gesturing to the closest chair. "I'm quite pressed for time this morning."

Rosalie could well believe it. The duchess seemed to be situated between a mess of paperwork—sample menus and seating charts for the ball, dance cards, stacks of unopened correspondence, folded newspapers. The woman never seemed to cease working.

A footman served Rosalie tea, which she accepted gratefully, taking deep whiffs of the floral oolong.

"Well, Miss Rose?" the duchess said, not looking up from her reading.

"Your Grace?" Rosalie replied, lowering her cup back to the saucer.

"Report," the duchess replied with a huff. "Is that not why I sent you out these last three days?"

Rosalie nodded, setting her tea aside. "Yes, well . . . the ladies you assembled are all of fine breeding, well-mannered and accomplished. They seem to come from good families—"

"Stop right there," the duchess snapped, tossing her reading aside and slipping the glasses off the tip of her nose. "If I wanted an accounting of their pedigrees, I would read their entries in the latest edition of *Debrett's Peerage and Baronetage*. I'm asking you, Miss Harrow, what is your opinion of them. You are my impartial observer, for you do not know these ladies from Eve. I'm relying on you to tell me what you think."

Rosalie blinked, too surprised for words. Was it possible that her opinion was actually going to hold any weight with a duchess? Her mind wandered back to the stack of bills hidden in her trunk and she took a deep breath. The duchess really wanted her opinion? Rosalie would oblige.

"The Swindon sisters are perhaps a bit vain, and Mariah in particular is very silly," she began. "But she is young, Your Grace. She could learn, especially given the right guiding influence . . . *your* influence."

The duchess nodded. "Go on, Miss Rose."

"Lady Olivia is haughty in the extreme," she went on. "She sees herself as better than everyone. She talks down to everyone—servants, the other guests. She was even rude to your son. Lord James was quite fair about it when I would have shown my teeth."

"I heard about the incident," the duchess replied. "Olivia comes by it naturally enough. Her mother is a cold-hearted bitch. I hate her . . . and I respect her. She's a hell of a businesswoman."

Rosalie nodded. In a strange way, she could see how the attributes of Lady Olivia might actually be good for an estate like Alcott, even if she shivered at the prospect of her being paired with George Corbin. It would be only the second worst pairing of the bunch. Rosalie lifted her eyes to the duchess. Those sapphire-blue eyes watched her, waiting.

"Lady Madeline is not a good fit for the duke," Rosalie said on a whisper. "They would be miserable together, and she would be miserable in her role here. The coronet would always wear her, never the other way around."

The duchess frowned. "And Blanche Oswald?"

"She is ridiculous," Rosalie replied. "She would drive you quite mad here, always under foot, always talking in your ear day and night. I fear you might snap and shove her out an open window . . . if Lord James doesn't beat you to it. Mr. Burke would help in either case."

The duchess contained her amusement, though Rosalie saw a flash of it in her eyes. "And you consider yourself a good judge of character? You think these opinions hold weight?"

"I speak for myself alone," Rosalie replied. "But . . . yes, Your Grace. Like you, I see myself as a good judge of character. And I have no reason to lie to you. These are my honest opinions."

"If only every conversation I had with all my acquaintances could be so to the point. It is our Richmond blood, I think," she mused. "We Richmond women don't suffer fools, nor waste our time with frivolous words."

Rosalie blushed under the duchess' muted praise.

"I think it's time we talk about my primary design in

bringing you to Alcott," the duchess went on, shuffling around some of the paperwork in her lap.

Rosalie held her breath. She'd been hoping for this, as much as she was dreading it. She never liked feeling like she was being kept in the dark. "I will hear anything Your Grace wishes to tell me," she murmured, reaching for her tea to give her hands some distraction.

"I'll not deny it, Miss Rose, you've impressed me. I've watched you, and you are everything I hoped for . . . and everything I dreaded."

Rosalie shifted uncomfortably, taking a sip of her overly floral tea. "I'm not sure if you mean to compliment me, Your Grace," she admitted.

"You are clever, Miss Rose," the duchess went on. "I'm pleased to see you have more than two thoughts in your head. You seem curious about the world, and you make easy conversation with people of high and low rank alike. Even my servants seem to enjoy you. You've earned a glowing recommendation from your maid."

Rosalie *had* been getting on well with Sarah. The girl was a veritable font of gossip. It was through her she learned Mr. Burke had an older half-brother who was a curate in Devonshire. And that Sir Andrew was having an affair with his wife's maid.

"I don't know about your accomplishments," the duchess added. "But you'll soon have opportunities to exhibit them. No, on the whole, you were just what I hoped to find in Elinor's daughter."

Rosalie smiled faintly. "And . . . what do you dread, Your Grace?"

The duchess frowned. "You are too beautiful by half and

your charm is infectious. You have an air of mystery about you that lures men in. Without lifting a finger, you've already managed to turn the head of every man in this house. You have the damnable ability to make a man question everything he owes to family and duty. It's infuriating . . . and dangerous, and I won't tolerate it. Not when you are a nobody with nothing to offer."

Rosalie felt her pulse quicken. "Your Grace, I would *never*—"

"Oh, I know you wouldn't wield your wiles on purpose. But that's what makes you all the more alluring," the duchess replied.

"I told you, I am not considering marriage."

"Well then," the duchess said with a haughty sniff, her brow arched in that imperious way she now attributed to all three Corbins. "If you are sincere, then I believe we may be able to make an arrangement."

"Arrangement?"

The duchess smiled. "You seek to pay off your debts to me. You seek a position that does not involve marriage, and I have one to offer."

What turn of events was this? Rosalie didn't dare breathe. "A position, Your Grace?"

"I want you to come and stay here at Alcott Hall," the duchess declared. "Stay as my ward. You'll have room and board, pin money, new dresses. Let the next few weeks be a trial, if you wish."

Rosalie's heart was in her throat. "And . . . why would you want me here?"

The duchess set her empty cup and saucer on the table. "Because it seems quite certain that my son George will make an inappropriate match, if he makes one at all, and this estate needs management. It needs a *proper* duchess. By your own estimation, if he were to choose Madeline or Blanche, I'd sit back and watch as they ran this estate into the ground."

Rosalie's mind spun. "You want me to . . . to be a duchess? But you just said—"

"No, dear," the duchess said with a soft laugh. "As we've already decided, you are quite out of the question as a prospective bride. But I will not trust the running of Alcott to whichever new duchess dares take my place on George's arm. She's certain to be a useless creature, and I will not allow the Corbin name or this great estate to suffer her ill attentions."

Rosalie saw sense in this solution, even if it was a bit unconventional.

"I want you to be my ward," the duchess continued. "You'll learn at my side how to run an estate such as this, at least the feminine side. My son James handles the rest. You'll plan menus and events at the house, handle charity and patronage for the tenants. In a word, you will be me: a guardian and manager of both Alcott and the Corbin family. You will work discreetly, allowing George and his new bride to live their lives as unencumbered by responsibility as possible. Trust me when I say, this arrangement will be better for everyone."

"But . . . Mrs. Davies," Rosalie pressed. "Surely a trained housekeeper already fills these roles—"

"A housekeeper lives in the shadows," the duchess explained. "The mark of a good one is that a guest might never see her in the whole course of a visit. No, I need someone who can balance *between* the worlds, the shadows and the sunlight. A manager who can plan events, but also a lady who can assist in the hosting of it. If I take you on now, and train you at my side, it will be no discomfort to those within the duke's circle to see you at balls and assemblies, comings out and christenings and church bazaars."

"I don't understand why you would possibly want *me* to fill this role," Rosalie admitted, still trying to wrap her mind around it all.

"Are you Elinor Greene's daughter or not?" the duchess snapped. "My Elinor was a force of nature—creative and clever, loyal to her friends. She was reliable and resourceful. Do you possess none of the traits that made her such a worthwhile companion?"

"I think . . . I am very much like her," Rosalie murmured, trying to keep any emotions she felt about her mother safely in their box.

"Good, excellent. Because I want someone with a clear head on her shoulders," the duchess replied. "Someone clever and resourceful and unafraid of hard work." She sat forward. "More importantly, I *need* someone who will not have their pretty little head turned by the empty promises of lovers or social climbers. This is a dangerous world for a woman, and predators are everywhere. I am trusting that your status as a wholly worthless marital prize will protect you from unwanted suitors." She paused, once again raising her arched brow. "To swim in these exalted waters is to know sharks abound, Miss Rose. So, tell me, are you a good swimmer?"

Rosalie fled the duchess' study with promises to consider her proposal. She retrieved her bonnet and found the first exit that led out a side door, taking off for the comfort of the trees. Her breath came out in sharp pants as she clutched her hands into fists at her sides. She didn't slow her pace as she slipped under the trees and followed a shaded path directly away from the house.

What a turn of events! It was beyond anything Rosalie had ever dreamed possible. It was not enough that the duchess was canceling all Rosalie's debts. Now she was offering a chance for Rosalie to make something of her life beyond settling into an unwanted marriage or selling herself in servitude as a governess. The duchess wanted to give Rosalie a position. Rosalie could make Alcott her home and live in the shadow of a duchess, learning how to run a grand house for one of the most illustrious families in the realm.

How could she refuse? How could anyone in her position refuse?

And what did the duchess expect in return? That Rosalie commit herself to her tasks and work hard? Easy enough, for Rosalie hated being idle and longed for a new challenge. Show resolute loyalty to the Corbins and the estate? The duchess was now Rosalie's redeemer. And Lord James was a good man, determined to do right by his family and the people here. She would gladly show them loyalty. As to the estate, it was beautiful beyond words. To think of it as her home gave her no small amount of pleasure.

And then there was the last request of the duchess: that Rosalie marry herself to her work and not let her head be turned by men. The duchess said herself that Rosalie's position as a penniless, low-born woman of no social consequence would surely protect her from anyone who navigated in high-society circles. This gave her pause . . . not the part about marriage. Rosalie was happy to sign an oath here and now declaring her intention never to marry. But the duchess' words unsettled her. She said Rosalie turned men's heads. Was Rosalie turning heads here?

She'd be a fool to say the tension with Burke wasn't heavy

with mutual attraction. The man was handsome beyond words, clever and curious. He was just what a good man ought to be. But the duchess had been explicit: Burke was not for consumption. Neither was Lord James. Could Rosalie stand to live in a house with these men and watch as they tried to dash themselves upon her rocks? Was this not a recipe for disaster?

But then another thought crept in with the stealth of a morning shadow: Could she stand to live without them?

"Miss Harrow?"

A deep voice behind her made her gasp. She turned, taking an involuntary step back to see the lieutenant standing before her.

27

Tom

"ARE YOU WELL?" Tom stepped forward.

Miss Harrow wiped at her eyes and tried to laugh it off. "Yes, quite."

"You're crying . . ."

"Happy tears," she replied with a weak smile. "The duchess did me a good turn and I was overcome for a moment."

He glanced around, taking in their isolation as they stood together in the middle of the forested path. "Were you seeking solitude? I can return the way I came . . ."

"I was, sir," she admitted. "But your intrusion is not unwelcome."

He gave a curt nod. A dapple of sunlight filtered down through the trees, landing on her face and illuminating her soft features—dark eyes and porcelain skin. Damn, she was gorgeous. Why did it strike him like this every time? "Shall we continue on this way together?" he offered.

She nodded, turning slightly to make space for him on the path at her side. For a moment they were quiet, Tom listening to the tranquil sounds of the forest.

"Where is Mr. Burke this morning?"

"He went with James into Finchley," he replied. "And apparently there's to be music tonight, so all the young ladies are determined to practice . . . I found I needed a moment of peace," he added with a grin. "The trees called to me, and I answered."

She smiled. "And does the sea call to you as well? Do you miss your ship, sir?"

"Aye, it can be a hard life to balance between ship and shore," he replied. "The rules are so different, the daily living . . . I find myself restless when I'm in the country. To go from such a confined space to such a state of unconfinement is . . . well, jarring."

"Is that why you are so prone to walking? Because you feel you must navigate the space around you while you have space in which to move?"

He mused on that with a slow smile. "Perhaps there is something in that, Miss Harrow . . . like a caged animal set to roam. I fear the day I come to prefer the cage."

"Speaking as a creature well familiar with life in a cage, I fully comprehend your feelings, sir."

He paused. "You see yourself as caged?"

She shrugged, letting her bonnet hide her face from him. Damn, he hated when women did that. Men had no such effective shield as part of their attire.

"All women live their lives in a cage, sir. It is our blessing and our curse. A blessing when men fill the cage with comforts and sweets and place the cage with a goodly view of the outside world . . . a curse when we are left beating our wings against the bars, isolated and alone . . . with no way out."

"Christ," he murmured. "I never thought of it that way. You must despise me for comparing my life at sea to being in a cage."

"Of course not," she said with a laugh. "As I said, the situations are indeed similar. I don't envy you your feelings. Rather, I appreciate that you can understand mine. It is a gift to be understood, is it not?"

"Indeed," he replied.

They walked in silence for a few minutes, taking a turn in the path that allowed them to spot glimpses of the house and grounds through the trees.

"How goes your wife search?" she said, the hint of a smile in her tone.

Christ, when she said it like that. "You make it sound so despicable."

She laughed. "That was not my intent, sir. I understand the rules of our society. You are simply making your way in the world. As we all must. Playing the game . . ."

"I've never been much of a game player," he said, lost in renewed thoughts of Marianne. Could he really sit and wait for her to want him again? How pathetic did that make him on a scale from hopeless to downright pitiable?

"Nor I. Which perhaps accounts for why we are both still unmarried . . . though your friends seem determined to help you change your status."

"Yes," he said with a groan. "Perhaps *too* determined." He paused, meeting her gaze. "Listen, Burke told me what he asked of you. I'm sorry for it. He never should have done it."

He'd spent the night and half the morning pretending that it didn't matter that she had no interest in flirting with him outside her agreement with Burke. But he was just vain enough to admit that it *did* bother him. Increasingly, he found he wanted to see her smile and know he was the cause. He glanced over at her. "Miss Harrow?"

She blushed and turned away. "Would it be terribly wrong of me to admit that I was enjoying it?"

"Enjoying what?"

There was a long silence, filled with the sound of leaves rustling on a wind.

"Flirting with you."

It was the last possible thing he expected her to say. His body responded with a warm feeling that spread from his chest down to his fingertips. He gripped tighter to the top of his walking stick. "I enjoyed it too," he admitted.

Her smile widened and she glanced his way. He took in the soft blue of her dress, the curve of her neck, half covered by a dark curl of hair come loose from under her bonnet. He wanted to tuck it behind her ear, wanted to run his fingers down the length of her neck, feel the tips brush over her collarbone as she took a gasping breath, his lips on hers . . .

Fuck. She was talking again. *Focus, you arse.*

"There is something so freeing about flirting with someone and knowing it will come to nothing," she said, clearly oblivious to the scenes now flashing through his mind. "How comforting for both of us that we may flirt without fear of unwanted consequence."

"My thoughts exactly," he replied.

That was a lie. Those were not his exact thoughts. In fact, his thoughts were the reverse. In this moment, all he seemed to want to do was press her against the nearest obliging tree and imprint her taste on his lips, drinking of her until he was drunk.

The others in this house party may ignore her and dismiss her as that little bird in a cage, but Tom *saw* Rosalie Harrow. He felt the fire burning inside her and wanted to dance with it. She wasn't a little starling on a branch. She was a phoenix.

He wanted to feel her heartbeat and taste her fire, smell the sweet violets on her skin. Just thinking about holding her made his cock twitch.

"Well, who shall the lucky lady be?" she said brightly. "Have you decided?"

"I suppose I haven't made a decision," he replied, still doing everything in his power to cool the fire she'd so suddenly stoked in him. He led the way farther down the forested path. "There are many factors to consider . . ."

Horse shit, crying babies, George's stupid face. Calm down, Tom.

She hummed a noncommittal response.

He glanced her way again, noting how a soft wind fluttered that loose curl on her shoulder. "Which would you choose, Miss Harrow?"

She gave him a surprised, affronted look. "Sir, I would never dream of commenting. It is not my place to have an opinion on such matters." A tip of her lip told him there was some secret joke to her comment and he was desperate to be in her confidence.

He gave her a nudge with his shoulder. "And yet, why do I presume myself correct that you are never without a ready opinion?"

"I'm sure I don't know what you mean."

He followed the arch of her neck with his eyes, settling on her lips, memorizing the way her upper lip bowed. He took a step closer until he could smell that intoxicating scent of sweet violets and rosemary. He let his breath fan across her neck, noting with pleasure the way she jolted. "I mean to say that the length and breadth of your ready opinions must surely rival the Old Testament."

They both laughed. It felt strange to be so comfortable

in a lady's presence. The other ladies bored him to death, but laughing with Rosalie felt right. Tom couldn't remember a time when he felt so at ease. He noticed her shoulders stiffen. "What is it, Miss Harrow? Don't go silent on me now."

She glanced up at him through dark lashes. "Sir, may I . . . may you permit me one of my ready opinions?"

"In this moment, Miss Harrow, I'd enjoy nothing better, and please stop calling me 'sir.' I know Burke asked you to be more informal with him. I should appreciate the same."

"I must admit that your purpose has not gone unnoticed," she began.

"And?"

"Well, it's only that . . . well I can't help but feel that your heart isn't really in it."

He glanced her way, his brow raised slightly, waiting for her to keep going.

"To be perfectly frank, you've been flirting with the other ladies with the warmth of feeling of a cold ham."

The analogy was so ridiculous, so accurate, Tom could do nothing but burst into laughter. Without meaning to, his free hand reached out and gripped her arm at the elbow, giving it a squeeze as he kept laughing. "Perhaps I seek to find that perfect maiden who will indulge my love of *jambon à la moutarde*."

God, he loved teasing this woman, seeing her cheeks blush as beautifully pink as the rose in her name. He could make a hobby of finding all the ways to bring that color to her cheeks.

But she didn't rise to his teasing. Instead, she came to a halt and turned to face him, not caring that his hand was still inexplicably wrapped around her elbow. "You will not turn a lady's head unless she believes you *want* it turned," she said, her tone suddenly serious. "If you want their heads turned, you'll need to put in more effort. But if there is . . . some reason why you would *not* want them turned . . . I think it would be best to admit that as well."

He knew exactly what she was implying. She knew about Marianne. Perhaps not about her recent change in circumstance, but enough to know that Tom was still tied to her. Marianne was the albatross he couldn't escape . . . yet. But perhaps if he was forced to choose between a dead albatross and a caged phoenix yearning to be free . . . *fuck*, this woman did things to his mind he couldn't understand. He needed space, needed to breathe.

"That's all I had to say," she murmured. "And now I've said it, and we shall drop the matter. Because, as I said, it is not for me to have an opinion."

"I have heard your remarks and accept them gladly," he replied, dropping his hold on her elbow. "I vow to you that I won't court any woman here in bad faith. 'Tis true, there is a prior claim on my affections. I know you heard mention of Marianne. The lady was my first love and when she—" He frowned, unsure whether he wanted to reveal the whole truth.

Now it was her turn to reach out and stroke his arm. "She died?"

He blinked, too focused on the feel of her hand on him. "What? No . . . no, she's alive."

"Ahh . . . she jilted you. Which for a man, of course, is worse than if she *had* died."

He met her gaze. "What makes you say that?"

She lowered her hand away. "Because if she died, you'd have a clean break. The heart can heal and move on. When one is jilted, it becomes a wound that festers. I see the sickness in you now," she whispered, those dark eyes narrowed on him.

Her gaze made him uneasy. Where moments before he felt her lust, now he saw only pity, and he hated it.

"I didn't understand your melancholy before, but I see it now. She's your sickness."

It was as if he watched her seal away her emotions behind a mask. Christ, but that was a useful skill to have. The phoenix was carefully back in her cage.

"I will wish you well, sir." She turned to walk back down the lane in the direction of the house, but paused, glancing over her shoulder. "And if you dare tell anyone I've been so forward with my opinions, I shall deny it to St. Peter himself. This never happened," she added, gesturing between them with a pointed finger.

He smiled. *Oh yes it did.* She admitted so much in such a little exchange. She admitted with words how she was watching him with the other ladies. She admitted in looks how she wanted him, how her fires burned. She admitted with those steps inching closer to him how easy it might be for him to lure her back out of her cage.

But she also admitted a truth that had him ready to punch the closest tree: She had no interest in continuing to flirt with a man who was lovesick for another woman. As long as Marianne Young was in his life, Rosalie wasn't going to give him another minute of her time.

28

Rosalie

ROSALIE WASN'T SURE what to expect when she arrived in the duchess' study to begin her informal training. The housekeeper, Mrs. Davies, was waiting as well. She was an austere older woman with absolutely no smile lines. She wore her grey hair in rigid curls that peeked out around her face under a frilled mop cap.

"Right then," the duchess said, getting to her feet as soon as Rosalie entered. "Let's begin."

The morning passed in a blur as Rosalie was shown every nook and cranny of the house. Mrs. Davies prattled off a host of maintenance and cleaning concerns, which the duchess took very seriously. They examined the lower floors—the large and small library, the music room, ball room, large and small drawing room, the grand gallery. And they went even further, marching through the new wing to examine the billiards room, a card room, an unused parlor, and three storage rooms.

"When you have a moment, return to my study and fetch the catalogs," the duchess directed, snapping closed the door to the red storage room.

"Catalogs, Your Grace?" she said, trotting to keep up.

"You're an artiste, are you not?" the duchess replied. "There are three leather-bound volumes in my study that catalog all the paintings in Alcott Hall—dates of purchase, artists' names, reason for commission, and any other notes a former duke or duchess wished to preserve. I want you to examine the lists and tell me if there is anything that ought to be on our walls that we are wasting in storage."

Rosalie fought the urge to blush. It was a great honor to be asked to curate the art of a house such as Alcott. If Mrs. Davies thought the request was odd, she pointedly said nothing. Instead, she showed them into a new wing of the house Rosalie had yet to enter.

"This is the servant's wing, miss," Mrs. Davies said over her shoulder.

Rosalie let herself be led through a string of interconnected rooms—a gun room, boot room, sewing room, three kitchen larders, a drying room. Servants scurried about, ducking out of the way of the duchess as she swept through.

The last stop on the tour was the grand Alcott kitchen. Rosalie blinked wide to see how large the space was, how busily all the staff worked within. Cooking three meals a day for a party as large as this one must surely be an all-day affair. She took in the massive open hearth, framed on either side by ovens built into the brick. A haunch of pork turned on a spit over the hearth fire, sizzling as drops of fat dripped onto the flames. It was enough to make Rosalie's stomach groan with hunger.

A set of two prep tables took up space in the middle of the flagstone floor, piled high with all manner of produce and meats in various stages of readiness. A trio of maids chopped and diced as they chatted. Activity ceased as the room took note of the new visitors. All eyes turned to the duchess and bowed with murmurs of "Your Grace" and "M'lady." Rosalie realized there was already someone else in the room who didn't quite belong.

Lord James stood at the end of the prep table, a beam of sunlight shining through the open window onto his almond locks. For the first time, she noticed a bit of an auburn glint in the tips of his curls. He took her in with a frown, glancing from her to his mother.

"Ah, James, dearest. Right on time," the duchess said, sweeping forward.

They looked so out of place in this space—he in his fine blue morning coat and yellow waistcoat with a crisply tied white cravat. The duchess wore a fuchsia gown patterned with bright blue flowers, her golden curls piled fashionably on the head. All around them, the staff waited, swaying on their feet, one eye on their unfinished work, as the duchess made her inspection.

"Please don't stop on my account," the duchess called with a wave of her hand.

The servants slowly resumed work, keeping one eye on their mistress.

"What is she doing here?" James growled, both eyes still locked on Rosalie.

The duchess sighed, accepting his perfunctory kiss on her cheek. "Heavens, James, is that any way to greet Miss Harrow? I know I raised you with better manners."

His jaw clenched tight as his eyes flashed. Two young kitchen maids tensed with nerves at being so intimately close to this conversation. He made a shallow exhale. "Fine. Good morning, Miss Harrow. What are you doing here?"

Rosalie tried to smile. "Good morning, my lord. Your mother was taking me on a tour of the house."

"Miss Harrow is an artist, James. I was showing her our collection. She's agreed to peruse the art in storage to see if we need to make any rotations," the duchess explained.

"I didn't know we kept art in the kitchen," he said drolly.

The duchess ignored him, turning her attention instead to an imposing man with a thick black mustache and icy blue eyes. "Ah, Monsieur Dubois, our man of the hour. Please tell me you have everything under control."

Rosalie listened quietly for the better part of half an hour as the head cook walked them all through food preparations for the ball. She had no idea how much had to go into planning for such an event. Three additional cooks and two pastry chefs were already en route from London, and they had commandeered the use of additional kitchen space from the inn in Finchley. She didn't envy Monsieur Dubois his busy schedule.

"Well, we shall not keep you, Monsieur," said the duchess, accepting his offer to sample the pistachio prawlongs. "As the date gets closer, you know you have my permission to make all executive decisions. We shall settle accounts after."

A muscle ticked in Lord James' jaw, but he said nothing. The duchess had hinted multiple times how fastidious the lord was with accounting. Rosalie could only imagine the monthly bills for running such a grand estate. She wasn't surprised to learn from the duchess that he struggled with sleep. Such responsibility would make Rosalie lose sleep too.

She followed them out of the kitchen back into the sunny hall.

"You have a meeting with Wiggins now, right dearest?" the duchess said, looking at her son.

"Yes, I'm late for it, actually," he replied, checking the time on his pocket watch.

"Why don't you take Miss Harrow?"

Rosalie stilled as the lord glared at her again.

"Is Miss Harrow a groundskeeper now as well as an art curator?" he said with a raised brow.

"Really, James, this rudeness is growing tiresome," the duchess replied. "You will take her because I asked. You could use a lady's opinion and she could do with stretching her legs."

"I really don't want to intrude—" Rosalie began, her eyes darting between mother and son.

"Nonsense, it will do you good. Be my eyes and ears. I can never trust James to give me a full accounting of his meetings. You'll be invaluable, dear," the duchess said with a pat to her hand. "Mrs. Davies, come. You and I still have much to discuss."

The women swept away, already talking low.

Rosalie stood alone with Lord James.

He gave her a level look before shaking his head and stuffing his timepiece back in the pocket of his waistcoat. "Fine. Let's go, Miss Harrow. I'm already running late, so I intend to stride out. Do keep up."

He pushed his way through a side door into the back garden, and it was all she could do to match his longer stride as he took off in the direction of the pond.

"So, are you both still resolute in obfuscating the purpose of your visit here?" he said.

"My lord?"

"You're meeting in her study for long hours, now you're touring the house and discussing menus, curating our art, monitoring me while I discuss a delivery of ornamental trees with our groundskeeper. Should Mrs. Davies soon expect her notice?"

"Of course not," Rosalie cried, now practically trotting

behind him. "Mrs. Davies is indispensable. Her Grace absolutely relies on her—"

Lord James slid to a halt, eyes flashing in annoyance. "Then what the *hell* is going on? Why is my mother so interested in you?"

Rosalie took a breath, fighting the urge to shrink back under his angry glare. There were many possible answers to this question. Some Rosalie understood better than others. Some she was not yet at liberty to discuss. But she had to give him something. "Do you want my honest opinion?"

"Of course," he huffed.

"To own the truth . . . I believe I discomfit her more than I bring her any pleasure."

He blinked, his mask of righteous anger faltering. "Why would you discomfit her?"

"Because I look remarkably like my mother," she replied with a shrug. "I think when she sees me, she sees Elinor again. She wants me close at hand because it feels like she's holding on to my mother's memory."

The lord resumed walking toward the lake. He slowed his steps, letting her walk at his side. "And you don't mind being treated like her pet ghost?" he said after a moment.

"Grief is different for everyone," she replied. "My method has been harsh denial. I put everything about my mother in a fine box in my mind, trimmed with lovely blue velvet . . . then I shut the lid." They walked on, following the curve of the lake as it angled towards the trees. "For your mother, I think my face keeps Elinor alive . . . until she looks in my eyes."

At this, Lord James couldn't help turning. She felt his gaze and smiled weakly, letting him see her eyes too.

"My mother's eyes were blue," she explained. "Each time

Her Grace meets my eye, I see the flicker of recognition, the resignation. Elinor dies all over again."

"That is . . . morbid," the lord muttered.

"Perhaps a bit," she replied. "But I don't mind. I know you see our time together as me conniving to some nefarious end. You assume I mean you and your family harm."

"I don't—"

"Oh yes you do," she said with a smile. "And I can play the villain if you'd like. Shall I pretend to twirl my mustache? Perhaps I can stuff my pelisse to give myself an unsightly hunchback. Will that better complete your image of me in your mind?"

"No," he said, letting loose a tight laugh.

Her smile widened for a moment . . . then fell. "The truth is, we are just two souls adrift in a sea of memory and loss. For whatever reason, we found each other. I'm not sorry about it. I like your mother. I like how she includes me in her grand life here. It's no secret the other guests dislike me . . . as you clearly do too."

He groaned. "Miss Harrow, if I've given that impression . . ."

She laughed. "Come now, my lord. Let us not go changing our natures. I respect the man you are. You're protective of your family and your home, as you should be. All I can do is prove to you that I am not a threat. But I think that will take some time, as your friendship is not a prize easily won . . . is it?"

They were quiet for a minute, walking along the lake's edge. He paused, glancing down at her. She tried to read the complex web of emotions swirling in those forest-green eyes. "I don't want to dislike you," he admitted quietly.

She smiled. "I am glad. Perhaps this can be the start of our friendship."

He smiled too. But before he could reply, a rustling in the bushes had them both turning. A swan pushed its way out of the shrubbery, waddling on its way towards the lake.

"Bloody hell," Lord James murmured. "Don't move." His shoulders went rigid as he slowly raised one arm before her.

"It's just a swan," she whispered.

"No, it's a devil," he replied, his body tense. "Be quiet."

The swan honked as it took them both in, ruffling its feathers. Its beady black eyes watched them, and Rosalie felt a sudden sense of foreboding. James' arm pressed against her chest as he slowly took a step back, drawing her with him. The swan screeched, flapping its wings as it approached. Rosalie cried out, stumbling back as James shouted, waving his arms.

The angry swan honked again, leaping off the ground in a flurry of wings.

"Fucking dead piece of shit!" James raged, kicking at the bird.

Rosalie stepped back a few more paces, watching with wide eyes as the lord battled the swan, landing one more kick before it fluttered away and splashed into the lake.

James stood at the water's edge, chest heaving. He spun around. "I fucking hate swans!" He stormed back over to her, snatching her hand. His was cut and bleeding.

She practically had to run to keep up as he led her back towards the house, one eye constantly looking over his shoulder to make sure it wasn't following. "Where are we going?" she asked, letting herself be dragged along.

"I'm through! Mother insisted on having swans on the property, but they're a goddamn nightmare. Territorial and aggressive. That cob is a devil. He's attacked me twice."

Rosalie fought the urge to laugh. Apparently, Lord James

was fending off constant threat from all corners—man and beast. No wonder he struggled to sleep at night.

He held tight to her hand as he charged into the kitchen. "Burrow! Bring me a shotgun!"

Rosalie was giggling now, one hand over her mouth to stifle the sound. She prayed he wouldn't turn around and see her laughing, not when they'd made a little progress at last.

"What happened, m'lord?" one of the maids cried.

"Dubois," James barked, taking the shotgun the hall boy offered him. "Change of plans. The second course for tonight's dinner is going to be swan."

29

Rosalie

AFTER THE EVENTS with Lord James and the swan, Rosalie was too excited to return to the house and sit quietly with embroidery or a book. She was relieved when Blanche and Mariah decided to walk into Finchley and invited her to join. Her smile turned into a stifled groan when Lady Olivia determined to join too.

They were an odd quartet, Blanche and Mariah in the lead, walking arm in arm in their brightly patterned frocks, bonnets pressed together, as they giggled. Rosalie walked behind, Lady Olivia strutting at her side. This country lane was a far cry from Hyde Park, but the lady still wore a fashionable silvery promenade dress with a lemon-yellow spencer and matching gloves. A crisp, frilled ruff peeked out around her throat, with matching frills at her wrists.

Rosalie felt quite drab striding next to her in a simple blue frock with a plain brown spencer and gloves. All her clothes were a few seasons old and looking decidedly worn. She hadn't had a moment to think about ordering a new frock since before her mother's sickness took its final turn. As if the lady noticed how plainly Rosalie was dressed, Olivia gave a pointed frown and rolled her eyes.

Rosalie typically wasn't one for feeling envy, not towards someone so far above her socially as the daughter of a marquess. Why should the rabbit envy the owl? But sometimes, she could admit to wanting more from her life, to feeling jealousy . . . feeling shame. Perhaps if her father had been a better caretaker, like Lord James. Perhaps if he had put the needs of his family first. What might Rosalie's life look like if Francis Harrow had been a good provider? Might Rosalie be wearing a pretty pair of lemon-yellow gloves? Would someone like Lady Olivia Rutledge deign to speak to her with a look less pained?

She took a deep breath, swallowing down all the pain and resentment she tried not to feel. Francis Harrow was dead. Each moment she spent thinking of him was a moment he did not deserve. His debts were paid. She was free. If she accepted the duchess' offer, she might soon find herself walking into Finchley ready to spend pin money on new bonnet ribbons, art supplies, or even a book of her very own.

Finchley was pretty as a picture. It had a narrow main street that boasted a smithy, a pub, an inn, a small assembly room, a post office, and a few other shopfronts. The muddy street bustled with activity—shoppers hurrying to and fro carrying parcels, children running and laughing. Crates of squawking birds sat stacked next to a pen of pigs in front of the butcher's shop. A boy stood with a tray by the bakery door, calling out sales on sweet rolls. The *clang, clang, clang* of a blacksmith's hammer echoed all around.

Rosalie was nearly pushed aside as a man hurried past with a muttered "'scuse me, misses" as he herded a gaggle of geese. She fought a smile, thinking of poor James and his aversion to waterfowl.

"Oh, just look at those pretty laces," Mariah cried, peering into the display window of the haberdashery with hungry eyes.

"And those buttons," cooed Blanche. "The military style is quite fashionable now. Epaulettes and double-breasted jackets. Have you seen some of the designs in Town?"

"Miss Harrow, do you prefer the blue or the green?" said Mariah.

"Don't be silly, Mariah. You know she must say green," Blanche replied, fluttering her lashes.

"And why must I say green?" said Rosalie.

"Because that green ribbon there is the exact shade of Lord James' eyes . . . and we all know how smitten you are," Blanche replied as both girls twittered into their gloved hands.

"I certainly know nothing of the sort," Rosalie replied, fighting a blush.

"Oh please, we all saw you from the window this morning," Mariah jabbed. "He held your hand so tightly as he led you into the shade of the house. Tell me, Miss Harrow, are his lips as soft as they look?"

In any other circumstance, Rosalie might have laughed. "Believe me when I say you did not see what you think you saw. Lord James and I were accosted by a vicious swan. He held my hand merely to lead me away from danger. He dropped it quite forcefully as soon as the threat of danger had passed," she admitted.

"And why were you in a position of being alone with him in the first place?" asked Lady Olivia, an imperious brow raised in excellent imitation of the duchess.

Rosalie sighed. She didn't deserve to be interrogated. "I was asked by the duchess to inspect some ornamental trees," she explained. "Lord James was showing me the way. You can all rest assured that nothing occurred. In fact, he as much as admitted that he dislikes me."

Olivia snorted. "Because he has taste."

The younger girls glanced from Rosalie to Olivia, curious to see if Rosalie meant to reply. But she knew better than to start a row on the Finchley high street. It would do her no favors to be accused of tossing the daughter of a marquess into a pigpen.

"Come, girls," she said, holding out her hand to Blanche and Mariah. "Give me the letters you have, and I'll post them. You can go shop for your ribbons and baubles."

The girls reached into their pockets, eagerly placing letters into her open hand, jostling each other to be the first through the door of the haberdashery.

With a haughty sniff, Lady Olivia reached into her own pocket and produced a letter. "I want this posted express," she said, placing it in Rosalie's hand.

Before Rosalie could move away, Olivia closed her yellow-gloved hand around her wrist, holding her still. She was taller than Rosalie by a few inches, which meant she could quite literally look down her nose at her. "Who are you?"

"Excuse me?"

Olivia sneered. "I asked who exactly you think you are."

Rosalie sighed. Perhaps this lady was going to see the view from inside a pigpen before the day was done. "I am plain Rosalie Harrow. I have neither fortune nor title."

"That's right," Olivia hissed. "You are nobody. Like an irksome flea, you've been buzzing about our party, trying to catch the attention of the men. Do you really think they could ever care for you? That the attention they show you is anything more than wanton lust? They see you quite the same as any slattern in a London alley." She stepped closer, lowering her voice. "They will use you and discard you faster than a pair of worn-out stockings."

Rage and shame warred within Rosalie.

"You may look and talk like a lady, even if these clothes are cheap," Olivia scoffed, gesturing to Rosalie's worn spencer with its fraying cloth buttons. "You may reel them in, but you will never deserve them . . . and they will *never* be yours."

The wretched woman still held tight to her wrist. A muscle ticked in Rosalie's jaw as she fought the urge to slap her hand away. Her palm itched with it. But Rosalie knew how to handle a bully. She put on her best forced smile. "What a relief it is to be understood," she said. "You have me painted exact, Lady Olivia."

Olivia's eyes flashed as her hand on Rosalie's wrist tightened. Before she could respond, a deep voice called from just behind them.

"Good afternoon, ladies."

Rosalie turned, heart pounding, to see Lieutenant Renley standing mere feet away. His deep blue eyes were thunderous. She had no idea how much he'd heard of their exchange, but he'd heard enough. Olivia dropped her hand away.

Lieutenant Renley stepped to Rosalie's side, looking as imposing as ever with those broad shoulders framed by his burgundy coat. "Lady Olivia, I believe a widow and her young children are selling flowers over by the smithy. Why don't you do us all a favor and go spit on them? Best leave no one in doubt of your ugliness."

Rosalie blinked in surprise as the lady gasped.

"You dare speak to me that way—"

"You broke the rules of civility first," he replied, leveling a leather-gloved finger in her face. "I will speak to you in whatever manner I see fit."

"I shall tell the duke—"

He scoffed. "You do that. Spare me the trouble of telling him myself how you so roundly abused his guest. Say what you will about George Corbin, but he doesn't take kindly to anyone who punches down."

Olivia's cheeks flamed crimson. "You cannot—I won't—you're a *beast*!"

"Aye, and so are you. Don't think I didn't hear you just now." He stepped closer, lowering his face to hers. "Mark me, my *lady*." The word dripped with disdain. "Sharpen your claws on Miss Harrow again, and you will see the beast *I* can be. Dare to insult her, and you will feel my bite."

Olivia blinked twice, then snatched the letters out of Rosalie's hand. "Give me those," she shrieked. "They need to be posted at once!" Not waiting another second, she stormed off, letters clutched in her fist.

Rosalie watched her leave, chest heaving as she took a few deep breaths. "I wish you hadn't done that," she murmured.

"She deserved it." His voice simmered with anger, but he softened as he glanced down at her. "You would have done the same."

She turned, letting herself look at him. He was so beautiful. She wanted to sketch the fall of his curls over his forehead, his prominent cheekbones, the line of his jaw. He noticed her staring with a raised brow and she blinked.

"Are we even now?" she said with a smile. "I stood up for your honor, now you have championed mine?"

"Don't think of it as a solitary trade," he replied. "I meant what I said. If she bothers you again, you come to me, understood? I will put that gorgon in her place. No one deserves to be spoken to as she just spoke to you. If James knew of it, he'd probably send her packing."

"Oh, please don't tell him. I don't want any trouble on my account."

He held her gaze for a moment before nodding. Then he glanced around. "Did anyone else accompany you?"

"Blanche and Mariah," she replied.

"Christ, well hurry then and take my arm," he said, holding it out for her. "I'll not get caught walking them home for anything. Let's cut round behind the inn and cross over the field back to the lane."

She took his arm, letting him lead her behind the inn. A little field sat beyond, just large enough for a few piebald sheep to graze. They both laughed as they stomped their way through the tall grass, cutting through a thin stand of trees that led back to the lane.

"What brought you into the village?" she asked.

"My evening coat is too tight in the shoulders," he replied. "I'm having them let out the seams."

She smiled, thinking how well he looked in that blue and white coat. Blanche was right: The military style was quite fashionable.

"Why do you smile?" he said, looking down at her.

She cast around for something to say that wouldn't give away her true thoughts. "I must admit, you're not quite what I expected from a naval officer."

"Oh, yes? And what did you expect?"

"Well . . . most of the officers I've met all had rather high opinions of themselves. Hard-jawed, no-nonsense types who would care little for interfering in the petty squabbles of ladies."

He laughed. "Aye, we can be an insufferable breed."

"I sense an air of duty about you," she added. "But there is a playfulness too. I've seen it . . . when you're alone with Mr. Burke." She raised a brow, seeking confirmation, and he smiled. "I imagine your men must adore you."

His smile fell. "I do my best to do right by them," he admitted. "Everything feels so much easier on a ship. Every man has a place. No one man is more important than the others. Sure, the heart has a greater function than the hands for keeping the body alive, but when it comes time to load the cannons, or mend what is broken, I'm mighty grateful for strong, hardworking hands."

"Those are very fine words, sir," she replied. "And I can tell you mean them."

"Aye, I do. But when I'm back in society . . ." He groaned, rubbing a hand over the back of his neck. "I'm all twisted like a sheet in the wind. A lady like Olivia Rutledge has never had to learn the importance of being part of a greater whole. She has no respect for the servants who trim her flowers or the maid who ties her laces. I can't tolerate such people."

Rosalie mused on his words, taking in the view of Alcott, framed in on both sides by trees as they ventured up the lane, still arm in arm. "I take it you won't be asking Lady Olivia for her hand, then?"

His arm tensed as he glanced her way. "Do I seem like the type that would choose a life of misery just for the chance to claim a title?"

She considered her next words carefully. "But to gain your captaincy, will you not be setting all thoughts of love aside to marry a lady of wealth . . . and all to claim a title? True, it is not an aristocratic title . . . but 'captain' is a title all the same."

He blinked, his steps pausing. "Christ," he muttered, lowering his arm away from hers. "You must think me the worst kind of hypocrite."

"No," she said quickly. "You are a second son making his way in the world. It is too easy to think we can all marry happily and stay happy. Marriage is so tricky," she replied. "So hard to get right . . . so disastrous when it goes wrong. And the suffering a bad marriage creates . . ." She sniffed, trying to control the memories that sought to invade her mind. "I think it's fair that you set conditions for yourself. You seek a business partner, not a wife. Surely you will make a more sensible choice."

He stopped there in the lane, using his body to block the sun as he looked down at her. Slowly, he lifted a hand and gently touched her cheek.

She stilled, torn between fleeing, and leaning in.

"I would gladly kill the man who hurt you," he said, his voice somehow soft, even as he threatened violence.

She swallowed, heart racing as those deep blue eyes looked into her soul and saw her for the frail, wounded thing she was. But his heart still belonged to another. It was his goodness, his need to protect others, that made him speak these words now.

"I believe you," she whispered, raising her hand to wrap around his. She gave it a gentle squeeze before she pulled it away from her face. "But I am not yours to protect."

He blinked, dropping his hand away. "Miss Harrow—"

"We will be friends, Lieutenant," she pressed, her eyes

pleading. "I know we both like to flirt, and there is no harm in it," she added. "And I sincerely hope you don't stop. But we will be friends . . . or we will be nothing. Push me on this, and you will push me away."

His eyes flashed and a long moment passed between them, but at last he nodded. "Friends it is, then."

30

Rosalie

THE NEXT DAY passed in a blur as Rosalie once again trailed behind the duchess through a series of meetings. First with the butler, then the head florist, then the orchestra leader, who arrived express from Town. Rosalie helped the duchess organize her correspondence and the duchess gave her free rein to explore the art catalogs. She was shocked to learn the house boasted not one, but *three* Rubens. She was scandalized to find there was a recently acquired piece from Marguerite Gérard still wrapped in paper. If Rosalie truly had a say in Alcott's curation, that would be the first piece taken out of storage.

Dinner was a long affair, seated as she was between Sir Andrew and the marchioness. She would have loved nothing more than to retire to her room with a book, but the young ladies had other plans. Any moment not spent showcasing their talents was a moment wasted, so after dinner, Rosalie found herself seated in the far corner of the music room, watching as Elizabeth played a piece from "The Marriage of Figaro" on the piano. Next to the instrument, young Mariah sang in a pretty soprano.

As soon as the piece ended, the room clapped appreciatively.

The girls made their bows and flitted aside to make way for the next exhibitor. Conversation hummed as a few people rose to refill their drinks. Before Rosalie could protest, Burke dropped into the chair next to her. "You've been busy this week, Miss Harrow."

"As have you, sir," she replied, hating the way her body leaned towards him. "How goes your sporting?"

"The birds are proving difficult to bag," he said with a smirk.

"Perhaps they are wise to your strategy, sir. More caution is sometimes required."

"Hmm, so is persistence," he replied. "And a novel approach."

Something in his tone had her turning her head sharply to take him in. He looked as handsome as ever . . . so handsome she wanted to curse the heavens. He was in a teasing mood again. She saw the grey storms roiling in his eyes.

"Do you play?" he said, gesturing to the piano.

"Only when forced . . . and nothing quite so grand as Beethoven or Boyce."

His voice suddenly rose louder. "Well, of course, you must play, Miss Harrow."

Half a dozen sets of eyes looked their way.

"Did you wish to exhibit, Miss Harrow?" called the countess.

"She's just been telling me her skill is not quite so proficient as the Swindon songbirds, but we don't stand on ceremony here," Burke replied for her.

Rosalie sat frozen, too stunned to speak. She was going to kill him. The fire irons were near at hand. Those would surely do the job.

"Well, you must play, Miss Harrow," came Blanche's coo of encouragement.

"Yes," Burke said, still smiling like an imp. "You surely must."

Rosalie caught the eye of Renley, who was sitting by Lord James on the far sofa. He had a curious brow raised, eyes darting between her and Burke. It gave her an idea. She stood, brushing down the folds of her dress. "I would be more than happy to take my turn. And I have a treat for you, ladies. I too will be performing a duet . . . with Mr. Burke."

His smile fell ever so slightly as all the young ladies cooed and clapped.

"Nothing better than a male accompaniment," called the viscountess.

"I quite agree. We ladies cannot have all the fun," Rosalie said over the sound of Mariah and Blanche twittering their excitement. "Come now, Mr. Burke, let's put all your boasting to the test and showcase your musical talents."

The storms in his eyes raged. But he stood and put a wide smile back on his face. "Your wish is my command, Miss Harrow."

She led the way over to the piano, slipping her long white gloves off as she walked. "Well, Mr. Burke?" She lowered her voice. "You got us into this mess, do you have the talent to get us out of it again?"

"I can carry a tune," he replied.

She considered the list of piano pieces she could play tolerably well. It was a frightfully short list. "Do you know O Waly, Waly?" He nodded and she breathed a sigh of relief. "Fine. I shall sing the first verse and you the second. I the third, and we will dare to harmonize in the fourth. Agreed?"

The storms in his eyes were still swirling. In the flickering of the candlelight, she could almost imagine they sparked with lightning. He was hatching another plan. "Lead on, Miss Harrow."

She dropped onto the bench and took a deep breath,

trying to control the shaking in her hands. Burke took up his position at her shoulder. From this angle, no one could tell how close he was, but Rosalie knew. She could feel him with every fibre of her being. She played the first few chords of the tune and licked her lips, readying herself to sing. Taking a breath, she sang out in a clear alto voice:

The water is wide, I cannot get o'er
And neither have I wings to fly
Give me a boat that will carry two
And both shall row, my love and I

The open top of the piano all but blocked her from view, which she appreciated. What she did *not* appreciate was the sudden feel of fingers brushing up her back, pausing at her neckline. Giving nothing away of his movements, Burke dared to let his fingertips trail up the line of her spine, sending heat shooting through her body. She barely kept her fingers on the keys as that warm hand found a perch on her shoulder, his thumb touching her bare skin. She bit her bottom lip to contain a moan as she played the few notes signaling the transition to the next verse.

Burke stepped closer until he was flush with her back, his hand still on her shoulder, that devilish thumb stroking small circles into her skin. She would die if anyone noticed. This was agony. Damn this man, for playing every game better than her. Pausing the movement of his thumb, Burke sang out in a deep voice:

O'down the meadows the other day
A-gath'ring flowers both fine and gay
A-gath'ring flowers both red and blue
I little thought what love can do

It was all Rosalie could do to keep playing as she was

transported by the beauty of his voice. It was rich and melodic. As he finished, he gave her shoulder a gentle squeeze. She nearly missed her own entrance as she dared to look up at him, anchored by his warm hand on her shoulder. The heat in his gaze sent desire pooling to her core. She wanted him . . . and he knew it. There was no denying this tension or that it was a mutual burning. She let her mask fall away, lowering her lashes and giving him a single look of longing.

His hand clenched on her shoulder as his body went still as stone. He might hold power over her, but she had power over him too. She turned away, a smile of satisfaction on her lips, as she sang out the next verse:

I leaned my back up against an oak
Thinking that he was a trusty tree
But first he bent in and then he broke
And so did my false love to thee

Heavens, what could have possessed her to pick this song? She swallowed her nerves as she met Burke's gaze again, ready to try and sing the next verse with him. He gave her a reassuring nod and they did their best to blend their voices into a passable melody:

A ship there is, and she sails the seas
She's laden deep, as deep can be
But no so deep, as the love I'm in
I know not if I sink or swim

As the last notes of the song faded away, Rosalie took her hands from the keys and peered around the piano. The room was utterly silent. All eyes were on them, and more than one lady was crying.

"That was Elinor's favorite," the duchess murmured. "Will you please finish it?"

Rosalie glanced up at Burke. He nodded, stepping back. His hand slipped from her shoulder, and the loss of his warmth raised gooseflesh down her arms. Taking a breath, she stroked the keys back to life and sang the last verse alone:

O, love is handsome and love is fine
And love's a jewel o while it is new
But when it is old, it groweth cold
And fades away, like a morning dew

A deep, aching heaviness settled in her heart as she finished. How true it was. Every word. She glanced up to see the crowd still watched her. Slowly, she stood. Burke stood next to her and offered out his hand. She took it, feeling his fingers close possessively around hers. He led her around the front of the piano and the pair bowed as the room broke into applause.

"Well done," called the duke.

"That was beautiful," Mariah cried.

"You have the voice of an angel, Mr. Burke," said Blanche.

Even Lady Olivia begrudgingly clapped.

Burke led her back to her seat. She sat heavily, her soul still full of the lyrics to the old folk song. Her mother used to sing it while they sewed, while she brushed Rosalie's hair. It was her anthem, full of the life lessons she wanted Rosalie to learn: Love is fleeting, love is false, love is full of trials and suffering, it is confusing . . . and ultimately fades away.

"Did I pass your test, Miss Harrow?" Burke murmured once he was seated next to her.

She glanced up, noting the way the storms in his eyes seemed to have eased. *Because of me*, she mused. All ships need a port in the storm . . . but what about the storm itself? Who will comfort it? Who will protect it? Like Tempestas, goddess of storms, Rosalie need only extend her hand and she could calm him . . . or bring him to a rage . . . drop him to his knees.

But this will fade. It must fade. It always fades.

"Rosalie? Are you all right?"

Another jolt of want hit her core as he said the three syllables of her name. It was a song on his lips, an incantation . . . a summoning.

If I reach out my hand, he will take it.

She said the only honest thing that came to her mind. "I know not if I sink or swim."

31
Rosalie

ROSALIE WOKE EARLY, even before sunrise. Her dreams were filled with Burke and their piano duet. Thinking of him gave her an idea. Slipping into her blue dress, she tied her unbound hair back with a ribbon and snatched up her sketchbook. She'd had precious little time to draw since arriving at Alcott. Burke mentioned last week how he loved best the view from the roof, and she'd learned from the maid Sarah which set of stairs would take her up. If she hurried, she could catch the sun just before it broke above the trees.

She slipped out her door, walking on soft feet down the darkened hallway towards the east wing. From the duchess' endless tours, Rosalie knew this was where the family lived, or at least Lord James and His Grace had rooms at this end of the third floor. She stopped before what Sarah called "the portrait of the ugly man with an uglier horse." Rosalie had to stifle a snort, for Sarah was right. This was quite possibly the most tragic artistic representation of a horse she'd ever seen. The features of its face made it look demonic . . . and why was the neck twisted that way? She dropped her shoulder and tilted her head, trying to see if that helped the proportions seem more correct, but it was no use.

Thump. From somewhere nearby she heard a giggle . . . perhaps a maid up early? A man's voice barked a laugh. She glanced around the dark hallway, trying to trace the source of the noises.

Bidding farewell to the ugly knight and his uglier horse, she pushed her way through the narrow door directly to the left of the painting. A tight, spiraling stair led up and down—a servant's stair. She imagined the house was full of them. She slipped inside and shut the door, reaching for the rail with her right hand as she began spiraling up.

"Oh god—oh, don't stop—" a woman moaned.

"*Fuck*—"

"Yes—"

Rosalie froze as the source of the laughter came into sharp focus. There, on the small landing immediately above her, stood the duke, pants around his ankles, rutting into a maid. She faced the wall, breasts bouncing free, as she braced against the stone with both hands.

"Oh, Your Grace, spear me with your mighty cock!"

"Shut up, I'm close," he grunted, gripping tight to her hips as he made deep thrusts.

Rosalie tried to slip away without being seen, but she miscalculated how the stair narrowed and nearly fell. She gasped, dropping her sketchbook and clutching the rail, rolling her ankle painfully in the process.

The pair paused, their eyes landing on her.

"Who's this, then?" the maid panted.

"Ah, the little Cabbage Rose," the duke said, still sheathed. "You're up early."

She looked pointedly away as she tried to regain her feet. "I—I—"

The duke chuckled. "Either join in or get out. I plan to finish before my balls turn blue."

Fighting her furious blush, Rosalie fled down the stairs to the sound of the maid's laughter, the duke's groans, and a symphony of slapping skin.

Rosalie stumbled back into the hallway and shut the door with a snap. Even through the door, she could still hear the moaning of the duke and his maid. Wincing on her tender ankle, she took off back down the hall. She rounded the corner to make for the stairs and nearly tumbled again as she ran straight into another soul in the dark.

A pair of strong arms steadied her. "Miss Harrow?"

She looked up to see Lord James. His face was unreadable. His eyes darted over her shoulder. "Lord James, I—"

"Where were you just now, Miss Harrow?" His voice simmered with anger. She could feel it in the way he held her, his grip a little too tight. She fought the urge to whimper.

"I was going to the roof," she whispered.

"You didn't come from my brother's rooms?" His grip tightened, those green eyes molten with unspoken demand.

"No—*never*—he—" Her mind was a jumble as she tried to push the images from the stairwell away. "That's not what happened."

One hand moved from her shoulder to cup her face. His fingers brushed her loose hair back behind her ear. It sent a chill down her spine to receive such an intimate touch from a man who was so clearly ready to burst into flames. "What happened?"

"Servant stairwell," she murmured.

He looked down the hallway. A low growl rumbled in his throat that made her stomach flip. What did this man look like when he lost control? He dropped his hands away from her. "Stay here, Miss Harrow."

His order rattled her bones as he took off. He flung open the far door and disappeared.

Recovering her senses, Rosalie moved down the hallway, stopping halfway when she heard the unmistakable sounds of shouting—Lord James' gruff voice, then the duke. A scuffle, cursing, stomping . . .

Lord James emerged a few moments later, his cravat looking decidedly ruffled, his cheeks a little flushed. His almond-colored hair bounced across his brow as he stormed back to her side. "Miss Harrow, a thousand apologies aren't enough, but let me start with one: I'm terribly sorry for what you endured just now. It's unpardonable. When His Grace is more presentable, he will make his own apology."

"It's nothing," she replied, trying to keep her blush under control.

He narrowed his eyes at her. "We both know that's not true."

"I shouldn't have been in there."

"Neither should he," Lord James countered.

He let his eyes drop down her form to take in the odd combination of her loose hair and her morning clothes. She shifted uncomfortably. She hadn't bothered to button her pelisse, and her hair was a tumble of dark curls around her face and down her back. As his heated gaze settled on her face, she blinked slowly, raising a self-conscious hand to flip her hair off her shoulder. The movement made a muscle twitch in his jaw, and she paused, slowly lowering her hand. Why was he looking at her like that?

"What were you doing in this part of the house?"

His gruff voice had her flinching away. Had she done wrong? His emotions were so hard to read. "I . . . um . . ."

"I'm not angry," he added more gently. "Just curious."

"I was hoping to sketch the sunrise from the roof. My maid told me where to find the stairs," she quickly explained. "I'm sorry if I've done wrong—*oh*—my sketchbook!"

"What?"

"I dropped it in the . . . it's in the stairwell."

Lord James frowned. "If it's all the same to you, Miss Harrow, I think we should retrieve it later."

She smiled. "Yes, my lord."

"James," he murmured.

"What?"

"I prefer you call me James."

She swallowed, fighting the urge to step back . . . or closer. "James," she repeated.

Before she could decide what to do, he was the one closing the space between them. He cupped her face again. Her heart thrummed at his closeness. Surely, he could hear it beating too, like the wings of a bird. This was dangerous. She risked her position if she let him take this any further. She was about to say as much when he lowered his face inches from hers. He surrounded her—his warmth, his control, the clean wool smell of his morning coat.

"Miss Harrow . . ."

She could feel his warm breath fanning across her lips. The tension between them simmered. Oh heavens, why were her hands on his waistcoat—

The servant stairwell door snapped open, and James and Rosalie jolted apart, hands dropping to their sides.

The duke emerged fully clothed. "If I can't get fucked this morning, neither can you!" he called down the hall, slamming his door hard enough to rattle the paintings.

"I'm sorry," James said as soon as the echo of the door slam dissipated.

"It's fine—"

"No, I'm sorry. That was—I shouldn't have done that."

He looked desperately miserable. Rosalie wanted to offer him comfort, but she didn't trust herself. Thank heavens the duke emerged when he did. This was Lord James Corbin, Viscount Finchley. He was the definition of unavailable. If his mother found out about this, she'd be putting Rosalie on the next coach back to London. It wasn't worth the risk. She took a firm step backwards. His eyes narrowed at the act. They stood there like that, an arm's breadth apart, chests rising and falling in sync. Rosalie began to turn away.

"Do you ride?"

She paused, glancing over her shoulder. He watched her with that intense gaze, his eyes the color of a forest glen in summer—deep green with little flecks of gold. "I . . . yes."

"I needed to ride into Finchley. You can join me, if you'd like."

Riding was done outside . . . on separate horses . . . in full view of anyone who happened to pass by. Riding involved sweat and horse dung and many layers of clothes. Yes, riding was a good idea. "I'd love to," she replied.

He sighed with clear relief. "Perfect. Get changed and meet me at the stables in fifteen minutes."

32

James

CHRIST, I ALMOST *kissed her.*

James ran a hand through his hair, sweeping it back as he donned his top hat. What the hell just happened? He knew Burke was besotted. That exhibit at the piano was enough to have James ready to throw a bucket of water on them both. Even Renley was on the edge of falling and he'd been resolutely wound around Marianne Edgecombe's little finger for the better part of a decade. What magic did this woman wield?

Nothing good would come of this. The last thing he wanted was either of his friends pursuing an inappropriate match that would do nothing to further their prospects . . . and he definitely didn't want them fighting over the *same* unsuitable girl. She bothered him to the point of distraction. Her every soft-spoken word, every lingering glance, the rapier cut of her wit, the music in her laugh.

Damn . . . I might be falling for her too.

If Rosalie wasn't more careful, she'd soon have three fools chasing after her like eager dogs on the hunt.

No, this wasn't happening. She was fine as a dinnertime distraction. He'd let himself appreciate her smiles and her laughs.

But he absolutely must draw the line at emotional connection. And there would be no more physical touch. The blessing was that they only had to endure her for two more weeks. After that, she'd be on her way back to London, and he'd never see her again.

James didn't wait long at the stables before Miss Harrow came walking down the path from the great house. She wore a simple riding habit of rust-brown with a crisp white cravat and a small ladies' style top hat. She smiled, but it was a bit forced, not quite meeting her eyes.

"Miss Harrow," he said with a nod.

"Lord James," she replied. "Sorry to keep you waiting."

"Not at all."

"It's a beautiful morning for a ride," she added.

"Indeed."

Her mouth quirked into a grin.

"Miss Harrow?"

"I'm sorry," she snickered. "I'm afraid . . . I don't think I know how to so quickly go from seeing His Grace without his pants to calmly discussing the weather."

"Oh, thank Christ. Me either," he laughed. "You have now seen both the Corbin men in an ungentlemanly state of undress. Let's drop the formalities and just be two people joined in mutual mortification. Agreed?"

She smiled. "Agreed."

The groom brought forward two horses. James took the reins of the smaller horse, a snow-white gelding outfitted with a lady's side saddle. "This little fellow is Magellan."

"Oh, hello," she cooed. She showed no fear as she patted his neck and fished an apple from her pocket. "He's such a little dear."

Magellan happily munched the offered apple, crunching it and sending a mess of apple bits falling to the cobblestones.

"He's well used to a lady's touch," James explained.

She laughed as Magellan snatched the rest of the apple.

"If you'll permit me?" he said, gesturing to the saddle.

She smiled and took the reins, looping them over the pony's head. Then she took up her position at the saddle. James stepped close, his chest brushing against her shoulder as he reached down with both hands to cup her booted foot. He gave her a boost and she swung up, settling herself with a few tugs of her thick skirt.

James moved around to the other mount and swung into the saddle. "Ready?" he said, glancing down at Rosalie.

Her face was all smiles. "Ready."

They rode in companionable silence as James led the way down the lane. They broke into a canter, letting the horses stretch their legs as they put some distance between themselves and the house. He had business in Finchley, but nothing was set to a given time, so he could afford to amble . . . anything to keep Rosalie to himself a little while longer.

He groaned. Apparently, he now had to actively stop himself from thinking about her. Perhaps on his way through Finchley he'd stop at Doctor Rivers' and have himself checked for tumors or head injury.

The manicured gardens gave way to rolling hills and a verdant stretch of forest awash in all its autumnal glory—bright reds and golds, muted browns, dark greens. In the near distance curled the bend of the river, while bare barley fields stretched beyond. James never tired of this view. He was made for country life.

"I should leave Town more often," she said on a sigh. "What is your favorite part about running Alcott?"

He considered the question. "I suppose I enjoy the variety. In one day, I might do the work of a magistrate, a farmer, an accountant, a steward. I like to apply my talents to many subjects, otherwise I get bored."

"I can see how that would be diverting. To never know what one day might bring, and yet be ready to adapt and solve problems as they arise."

"But I am not the duke," he added perfunctorily.

"Of course," she murmured. "And what is his favorite part of running the estate?"

James frowned. Would his honest answer shock her? "That it runs best without his influence or attention."

She was quiet for a moment. "He does seem to have little interest in his position," she conceded.

James just scoffed. "My brother George is the unluckiest of men. He was born with the soul of a medieval poet in the body of a modern duke."

She frowned. "I think you mean for me to laugh, but I see nothing funny. His reticence to fill his role pains you."

He shrugged, disliking the way she read him so easily. "His life is his own. I cannot make him be who I want or need him to be . . . much as I've tried."

"So, you compensate by being everything he's not and more," she replied. "You are the strong fortress, the shelter in the storm, the center of justice and commerce, the arbiter of change. You are the silent, stalwart Duke of Norland."

He glanced her way, noting how she looked at him with an odd mix of pride and pity. The pride he was pleased to accept, but the pity raised his ire. He disliked pity at the best of times, but he most certainly disliked it coming from her. "You make my position sound so grand, but do not envy me, Miss Harrow."

"How can I not?" she replied, those dark eyes turning suddenly sad. "I'm lucky if I can boast of mattering to exactly one person on this earth. While you are everything to everyone. Without you, their worlds would fall apart—His Grace, Her Grace, the staff, the tenants, your friends, and business partners."

"You have an observant eye," he conceded. "Few so quickly see through our ruse."

"People see what they want to see," she replied. "It is the great failing of man that so few look beyond the superficial to see what lies within."

Had he not been playing on this weakness for four years? "So, you haven't been taken in by the charms of His Graceless? Do you see through him too with your sibylline gaze?"

She considered for a moment. "Your brother enters a room, and people unwittingly think it must turn about him, for he wears the title. They can't see that their world is already turning . . . and *you* are the axis point." She gave him a look that he felt deep in his chest. He'd meant it as a joke, but Christ, maybe she *was* a witch. Her smile softened as she said, "Are you not tired, brave Atlas, from holding up all the world on your shoulders?"

Before he could respond, shouts had them both turning in their saddles. James reined his horse to a halt, as did Rosalie. Their mounts pranced as a groom's horse came racing towards them.

"What is it, Jack?" he called to the groom.

"Mr. Reed bids you return to the house, m'lord."

"Why?"

"His Grace ordered the carriage brought 'round," Jack replied. "Says he's goin' to Town, m'lord."

Damn George straight to hell!

At least James knew where the loyalties of the staff lie. He told them to report immediately should George try to leave. "Ride back now and tell Charles and Wallace that if they so much as strap a harness to horse, I'll withhold their wages for a month. *Go.*"

"Yes, m'lord!" Jack was already wheeling his horse around.

James glanced apologetically over at Rosalie. "I'm sorry about this, but we'll have to cut our ride short."

She gave him a weak smile. "No rest for weary Atlas."

He gathered his reins with a grimace, ready to let his horse run.

"Would you mind terribly if I continued on for a bit?" she said, those dark brows raised in question. "It's such a beautiful day . . ."

James' immediate thought was to say no, but she didn't require a chaperone, and she clearly had an excellent seat. "Just . . . stay in view of the house," he said, wheeling his mount around.

"Please go easy on His Grace," she called. "I don't think he could ever admit it, but he admires you. No man in his position would ever let a younger brother usurp him as you do if he didn't understand, in his heart, that you are the better man. He may be a duke, but I doubt very much whether for one moment he's ever actually felt like one."

James didn't know what to say in response to such a soulful

insight, so he merely nodded and urged his mount on, determined to reach George before he could follow through with his threats.

A few footmen bustled in the hall outside George's rooms. Several trunks stood open around the room in various states of packing. George stood in the middle, still wearing only his dressing shirt and a billowing banyan, directing his valet and a pair of maids.

"No, I want the blue coat and the burgundy. No black. I'm not in mourning."

A maid hustled to do his bidding.

James wanted to handle his brother in his usual way, which would be to storm in and have a full row, likely ending with punches thrown as the brothers wrestled on the floor. His way shattered valuable keepsakes and made for blood on the carpets. He wondered if perhaps Miss Harrow's approach might not be worth a try.

"George . . . what are you doing?"

"I'm leaving!"

James sighed. Whenever they were in the country, his brother threatened to leave at least once a month. "Leaving to go where?"

"London first," George replied. "Then the continent. I'm thinking Spain."

James set his hat on the side table and leaned against the wall. "Why are you leaving?"

"Because I'm sick to death of country life! I need a break from this house, from these people, from *you*. You always suffocate me."

"You seem to be breathing just fine."

George turned sharply around and chucked a book.

James ducked as the book slapped against the wall before it flopped to the floor. It was all he could do not to rise to that challenge. He took a steadying breath. "Michaelmas is in less than two weeks, and you must be here to host it. Mother expects—"

"I don't give a fig what she wants," George snapped. "I am my own man, and I will do as I wish, and I wish not to marry. She cannot make me."

"She can—"

"She can't! I'll not say the words!"

"Then she'll just bribe Selby," James replied. "It will be expensive to pay him off, but she's always had extravagant tastes . . . and she always gets what she wants, George."

"Why are you so intent on helping her?"

James sighed. "You can fight it all you like, but you are a duke, and a duke has obligations. You must stay here and see to your guests. You must pick a wife. You must announce your engagement—"

"Must, must, *MUST!*" George bellowed. "I'm sick of the word. May it be banned from this house, never to be uttered again!"

"Use whatever words you like; only do as we ask. As soon as you've announced your bride, you can celebrate with a trip to Town. I'll even go with you."

"I'd rather dance with Reed naked under a full moon," George replied.

Standing watch from the corner like a solemn crow, Reed tactfully made no response to this invitation.

"You could end this misery now," James reasoned. "All Mother wants is a name. Give her one, and she'll let you go."

"You think it's so easy? I'd like to see *you* handle this,"

George snapped. "My little brother, always so eager to be considered Duke of Norland. But you have none of the responsibility! You're not married either. Hell, I don't even know if your cock can get hard. If you've ever used it for anything other than taking a piss, I'll eat Reed's waistcoat."

"We're not here to talk about my marital status," James replied. "As long as I'm the second son, what I do with my cock is of concern to absolutely no one but me."

George snorted. "Yes, and I'm sure you make no exaggeration. Have you ever let someone other than yourself pet your little worm, James? A maid, perhaps? Or Burke? Christ." He barked a laugh. "No, if anyone will be petting cocks in that situation, it would be you petting his—"

"I'll thank you to stop picturing me and Burke and our cocks in any capacity whatsoever, before I turn unfriendly and set fire to these trunks."

"You wouldn't dare," George hissed.

"Give me a name and I'll leave you to your packing. One name of one unmarried maiden that I can bring to Mother, and you will be free as a bird, George."

"*Ugh*, I don't care! I swear to Christ and Jupiter and bloody Osiris that I don't care. God, it bores me to tears. *They* bore me to tears!"

"So, just pick one," James replied. "Put their names into my hat here and draw one out. If you really care so little, let fate be your guide."

George's eyes lit with interest. "I like fate . . ." He dropped the handful of books in his arms and moved over to his desk. Snatching up a quill, he scratched out what James could only imagine were the names of the eligible ladies.

"Bring us the hat, then," George called.

This was stupid, but James would use any method to distract him. He crossed the room, weaving between the open trunks, and thrust his hat at his brother.

George tore the paper into strips, folding each, and dropped the names inside. "Are you watching, Reed? I want a second witness in case Mama asks."

James sighed. "Just pick a name, George."

George shoved his hand into the hat with a flourish and pulled out one of the little papers. He unfolded it and groaned. "Well . . . there we have it, I guess. Fate has spoken."

James snatched the paper and read the words scratched on it with a deepening frown:

Cabbage Rose

33
Rosalie

MAGELLAN TURNED OUT to be the perfect companion. He was a happy fellow who put one foot in front of the other, marching along with the occasional snort. As promised, Rosalie kept the house in her sights as she made a circuit of the park, following random lanes.

Her morning might have started in an unexpected way, but nothing at Alcott had so far met her expectations. In most cases, all her expectations were exceeded—the comfort of her room, the hospitality of the Corbins, the entertainment, the food. She had an offer of employment to ponder . . . and a mystery yet to solve.

The more Rosalie sat with the duchess' words, the more they unsettled her. What could possibly be motivating her to show such kindness? Rosalie had told no lie: Her mother *never* mentioned her dear childhood friend the Duchess of Norland. It left Rosalie feeling unsettled. She wanted to understand more about what happened between them. Her Grace said they merely drifted apart. Surely there had to be more to the story. If Rosalie knew the whole truth of their parting, would she still be willing to accept the duchess' offer? Perhaps James might know something—

Magellan jerked to a halt, ears alert, head raised high. Before Rosalie could register what was happening, a small herd of deer leapt from the trees right in front of them, bouncing through the grass with tails raised in alarm.

Rosalie jerked back on the reins as little Magellan spun around and darted into the trees. She pulled with all her might, but he just grabbed the bit in his teeth, jerked his head down, and ran. It was all she could do to protect her face from the branches as the spooked animal darted through the trees.

In a single moment—slowed until she could feel each pulsing beat of her heart—Rosalie saw the oncoming low-hanging branch. She braced for pain, the smashing of teeth, the cracking of bone. Then her eyes spotted a wide patch of green to the left. She unhooked her leg from the saddle, dropped her stirrup, and leapt.

The world flipped and she had the odd sensation of flying and falling. Her head and shoulder slammed into roots barely concealed by a thin layer of forest moss. With the wind thoroughly knocked out of her, she wheezed, rolling over on shaky arms, fingers clutching the ground. Little Magellan crashed away through the trees with a whinny.

Everything went hazy as Rosalie stumbled to her feet. She placed one hand on her aching head and the other gripped the closest tree. Her ears rang and the whole forest seemed to spin . . . or perhaps *she* was the one spinning. Flashes of sunlight danced through the trees, casting long shadows that made her dizzy. She wanted to retch. Her heartbeat echoed in her ears, pulsing like the waves of a great ocean.

"Magellan!" she called, taking a couple unsteady steps forward.

Neither leg broken. Both arms in their sockets. She was lucky. Now she just had to find Magellan. She couldn't leave him out here. He could snag his reins on a branch or put his leg through them and stumble. How could she face James or the duchess again if he got hurt?

"Magellan!" Blinking back tears of pain, she took another stumbling step forward, following the sound of scared whinnies. "Magellan, please come back!"

34

Burke

LUNCH WASN'T DUE to be served for another thirty minutes, but Burke had no interest in spending any more time outside. He escaped to the dining room and propped his legs up on a chair, newspaper unfolded in his lap . . . but he hadn't read a word. He was far too distracted.

Renley begged off early to go visit his brother, and Burke was annoyed to find that Rosalie skipped breakfast too. When he found out from a footman that she'd slipped out with the sunrise to go riding with James, it was all he could do to keep calm and not demand another horse be saddled. There had to be a good reason why they were riding together, why neither made mention of their plans last night—

The dining room door slammed open and in swept George, followed closely by James.

"George, you cannot be serious!" James barked.

George snatched up a glass, filling it with wine and draining it. "Of course, I am. Fate has spoken. I am but her humble servant—"

"You've never been humble a day in your goddamn life!"

Burke swung his leg off the chair. "What's happening?"

"George says he's going to propose to Miss Harrow," James snapped.

Some monstrous beast uncoiled deep in the pit of Burke's stomach as he suddenly fought the urge to leap across the table and strangle George. No one was going to touch Rosalie but him, especially not George fucking Corbin. "What?!"

"It's not like I *want* to marry her," George groaned. "But it was your idea for me to pick a name out of a hat." He turned to Burke. "I did what he asked, and now he's mad!"

"Walk me through it," Burke said, moving around the table to stand next to James.

"George was being a petulant child again," said James. "He was packing to leave *again*, and I told him the only way he was leaving was if he picked a bride first."

"So, James bid me put all the ladies' names into his hat," George added. "And I'm sorry if you don't like the result, but it's out of my hands at this point. Fate has spoken."

Burke glanced at his friend. "Oh James, you didn't . . ." Why on God's green earth would James play into George's superstitions? It was—

"It was a mistake," James muttered to Burke. "And I never for one moment expected you to take this so seriously," he threw at George. "Miss Harrow's name wasn't supposed to be an option!"

The monster inside Burke purred with delight at this. James hadn't forgotten his ironclad principles after all. Burke turned to George, determined to help James put him back in his box. "She'll never agree to marry you," he said at George.

George just scoffed. "Of course, she will. Any of the ladies would fall over themselves to become duchess. Why do you think I detest this all so much? Why would any man want to go pheasant hunting if all the birds throw themselves at you and beg to climb in your sack? If my torture ends with her, so be it."

"I'm telling you, she'll not agree," Burke repeated.

"Why not?" George said with a scowl.

"Because she's far too principled. She's like James here," he said, jabbing a thumb at his friend. Linking her in any way to James was a surefire way to make George retreat.

But his response wasn't quite what Burke expected. George narrowed his eyes between Burke and James, landing on his brother with a glower. "Really, James? Your own sex life is so boring you have to go and talk to Burke about mine?"

Burke blinked. "What?"

"I'm flesh and blood, James. I have needs! I'll not be ashamed just because *you* live like a monk—"

"I don't care if you fuck every maid in this house. I clearly can't stop you," James countered. "But there's a time and a place!"

"What happened?" Burke repeated, eyes darting between the brothers.

George raised a surprised brow. "*Ahh*, so you didn't tell him. That's interesting."

Burke could feel himself getting angry again. "Tell me what?"

James groaned, glancing at Burke. "Miss Harrow caught George in the stairwell this morning . . . with a maid."

He left the rest unsaid, but Burke could well imagine what Rosalie saw. What George probably said and did. Burke wanted to lunge forward and punch George in the face, but that was a line he couldn't cross. As much as Burke might want to on occasion, only James could get physical with George with impunity.

"And Burke's right," James added. "Now that she's taken the measure of you, she won't say yes."

"Well, what do you expect me to do now?" George said, sinking into his chair. "Pick a different name from the hat?"

"*Yes*," Burke and James replied together.

"But . . . that feels like cheating," George said with a pout.

"Give me that fucking hat." Burke snatched the hat from James' hand. He dug his hand inside and scooped out all the little papers, tossing them on the table and opening them as he read each. "George . . . what is this?"

George didn't look up as he refilled his glass with wine. "What is what?"

Burke read the papers aloud. "Mousey, Ice Queen, Red One, Red Two—what the hell is this?"

George shrugged. "What? I can't be expected to learn all their names. There's too many—"

"Jesus *fucking* Christ, there's only five, George," James groaned, rubbing his temple with a tired hand.

"Six if you count the lovely little Cabbage Rose."

Burke clenched his jaw. "What?"

"His name for Rosalie is Cabbage Rose," James murmured, holding out the crumpled strip of paper in his hand.

Burke snatched it and read the moniker scrawled in slanted black ink.

"Come on," George snickered. "It's funny. She's poor, so she's like a little cabbage rose. I mean, I know *you* don't find it funny," he shot at James. "But you want to fuck her so—"

"George, enough," James barked.

The beast inside Burke was ready to breathe fire. "What the hell is he talking about?"

"Ignore him." James rounded on his brother. "You can't

pick your duchess by drawing a name from a hat. The woman you pick will stay in this house. Her portrait will go on the wall, her children will be born upstairs."

"Yes . . . I suppose you're right." George let out a deeply agitated sigh. "Frankly, I think I dodged a bullet, because that Miss Harlow seems like a nightmare."

"Harrow," Burke corrected.

"Whatever."

James chanced a hesitant step forward. "So . . . will you stay?"

George frowned, glancing from James to Burke. Suddenly, his eyes flashed with mischief. He leaned forward, elbows on the table. "If you really want me to stay . . . the two of you have to kiss. Right here, right now."

Burke choked on a laugh as James' face went from pink to red with swallowed fury.

"Get fucked, George," Burke replied for the both of them.

"Oh, I plan to," George replied. "Perhaps later again this afternoon. Meanwhile, the two of you will be stuck holding your own cocks as you cry into your pillows tonight about the Cabbage Rose and how she'll never have any of us. Those principled types die old maids." He stood, pushing his chair back from the table. "Tell Reed I'll take a tray for lunch in my room. James, you can handle the guests until dinner."

As he turned to leave, a cacophony of shrieks and screams had all three men running to the window.

"What the hell?"

"I can't see anything—"

More screams. Clattering. Smashing.

"Get it open—"

"Bloody—*fuck*—"

All three men fought with the latch of the window until it

gave, and Burke shoved the glass panel open. It was the work of moments to swing one leg over and climb out. James was out just behind him and George last. Just as they were rounding the corner, George grabbed hold of Burke by the coat and jerked him backwards.

"Look out!"

"Christ—" Burke gasped as a white horse went streaking past. "What the—"

George let go of Burke's coat. "How did a horse get loose?"

"It wasn't loose. It had a saddle," Burke replied, eyes narrowed as he searched for the fallen rider. He charged around the corner to see that the ladies were in hysterics.

"Oh, Mr. Burke, that animal was wild," shrieked Elizabeth, her red hair fluttering around her face.

"It came charging through our game like a hurricane," her sister added.

Burke's eyes darted around the group looking for Rosalie.

"Burke!" James called.

"Your Grace, thank heavens," another cried.

George stood dumfounded, surveying the tipped tables and ladies in various states of swoon.

"Burke!" James called again.

"We were nearly trampled," shrieked the marchioness, fanning her daughter's face. "That animal should be shot!"

Burke didn't care about any of this. Where the hell was Rosalie?

"Christ, man, *come on!*" James was suddenly at his side, one hand snatching at his lapel and jerking him around.

"Where is she?" Burke said. "Where's Rosalie?"

James' face was stricken. "That was her horse."

"What? I thought she rode in with you—"

James took off at a run towards the stables. "George, come on," he called to his brother.

Burke easily caught up. "James, tell me what happened! You just left her out there?"

"She's got a good seat and she was just walking the park. Something must've happened. *Damn it*."

"What's going on?" George called, running after them.

"Saddle horses!" James shouted as they neared the stables. It was already in pandemonium as the grooms did their best to catch poor little Magellan, who was trotting in circles in the courtyard.

"We need horses," James ordered. "Jack, Wallace, take to foot. Find Miss Harrow. Last I knew she was heading towards Finchley Hill, but that was an hour ago."

Rage flooded Burke. "An *hour*? She could be anywhere by now—"

"You don't think I know that?" James spun around. "Look, I'll let you thrash me later. Right now, she's the only priority. Shut up, mount up, and help me find her."

Burke fumed. If anything happened to her, he'd be taking James up on that offer. He'd beat James bloody. But Rosalie was missing, possibly injured. She was his only concern. He snatched the reins of his horse and swung into the saddle. Wheeling it around, he took off towards Finchley Hill.

35

Rosalie

ROSALIE STUMBLED TO the edge of the tree line, tugging on her heavy riding skirt as it caught on another branch. What a sight she made—broken hat in hand, riding habit torn, hair a tangled mess, skirt six inches deep in mud . . . and with no sign of Magellan. It was time to trudge back to the house and admit to James that she lost the horse.

She broke through the trees at the edge of a grassy field and paused, one hand clutching her side as she winced in pain. Her head, shoulder, and side all ached, and her vision still felt fuzzy in the bright light. She raised a hand to shield her eyes. From this angle, the great house sat perched like a bird of stone on a hill of grass. The gardens were just visible, peeking out like a colorful nest. How had she stumbled so far away? Fisting her skirts in both hands, she took a deep breath and began walking.

What had she done in a past life to deserve such terrible luck? To walk every moment through trial after trial, her life becoming just one long lesson in pain and self-denial. A cruel, wastrel of a father, dead too soon. Debts that ate at her mother's soul until they killed her . . . far too soon. An aunt of no means who couldn't afford to care for her.

Now, for the first time in her life, Rosalie had a chance. She could have a position, respectability, the protection of one of the most illustrious families in the land. But each time she thought of accepting the duchess' offer, she thought of Burke's hand on her at the piano. She thought of Renley's laughing, bright eyes as he discussed his travels. She remembered the feel of James' breath fanning over her lips. Was she really going to risk it all by doing the one thing the duchess warned her against and form an attachment with one of these men?

No, Rosalie couldn't allow it. She had to be strong. She had to—

"Rosalie!"

She turned, trying to track the direction of the caller. Hoofbeats pounded the ground. She could feel them pulsing in her bones. He was coming for her.

"Rosalie!"

She spun the other way, facing into the sun as the imposing figure approached. A dark-haired man on a powerful black horse.

Burke.

Her shoulders sagged with relief. She was so used to fighting her own battles. She was utterly, wretchedly alone. She'd learned to live with it. Heavens, she *embraced* it. No one wanted or needed her, so she had to learn to want the same. And she did, with every fibre of her being. It was safer this way. She didn't get hurt this way . . .

Burke reined his horse to a halt and swung out of the saddle, the tails of his coat fluttering behind him. He had eyes only for her. That look sang through her, coiling around her bones, burying itself in her lungs as she took a gasping breath. The storms in his eyes were as violent as she'd ever seen them.

225

He crossed to her side, head and shoulders towering over her as he blocked out the sun. His hands cupped her face, firm but gentle, as his fingers slid into her hair, pushing back the mess of her loosened dark curls.

He pulled her closer, taking a deep breath, filling his lungs with her scent as she dared to do the same. His usual mulled sweetness was gone. Now he was all sweat and salt and sun. Her soul calmed at his touch, even as a fire raced in her blood.

Safe alone. Always alone, the voice inside cautioned. It was a habit formed over a lifetime, and so difficult to break. No, Burke was different. He came for her, seeking her out, missing her, wanting her. *I'm not alone when I'm with him.*

She raised her hands, clutching the lapels of his coat. His relief sang out as he lowered his face to hers. Those beautiful eyes locked on her, asking a silent question, begging to be let in. His forehead pressed ever so gently against hers as they shared one fleeting moment of perfect understanding.

Come in, her soul whispered.

His lips pressed to hers, warm and eager and determined. She lost herself in the feel of him, in the way his body pressed against hers. His hands dug into her hair as he tipped her face up, opening her to his kiss. She drank of him, tasting the salt on his lips, feeling the heat of his mouth ready to consume her.

She was shaking, core molten as she pressed closer. She moaned softly into the kiss as his tongue flicked against her bottom lip. The sound had him tensing as one hand dropped away from her face, banding around her shoulders. As he pulled her closer, she winced. Burke heard and felt her pained reaction. He let her go with such speed it left her spinning. They stood together, her hands still clenching his coat.

His stormy eyes narrowed on her. "Christ, love, are you hurt?"

The use of an endearment made her stomach flip. She wanted to hear him say it again. She felt certain she could hear it a thousand times and still find joy in it . . . even as she knew her impulse should be to tell him to stop.

He tipped her chin left then right, gently stroking the tender spot on her temple. She winced and he dropped his hand away. She could only wonder what she looked like. His fingers brushed the large tear at her shoulder. "Are you hurt?" he repeated, his voice a command.

"I'm fine," she replied. "My shoulder took the worst of it," she said, gesturing at the frayed sleeve. "And I bumped my head. It aches, but I'm fine. Nothing bruised but my pride."

"Thank God," he said, placing a soft kiss at her temple. "What the hell happened?"

"A herd of deer," she said. "They came out of nowhere, and my mount bolted into the trees. I let myself fall as we approached a low-hanging limb."

"Christ, it could have been so much worse." He kissed her forehead again. "The horse found his way back already. He appeared without you and the whole house was in uproar."

Relief flooded her. "Oh, Burke, is he all right? I've been looking for him for ages. I couldn't just go back empty handed. I couldn't leave him out here to get hurt—"

Burke put a comforting hand on her cheek, and she leaned into it. "He's fine, love. Safe and home . . . where you should be." He said this last as he lowered his face to hers again, his voice soft in her ear. It sent another jolt of heat straight to her core. As if he sensed the change in her, his shoulders tensed. Heavens, they were almost *too* in tune.

"Can you bear to ride again? It will be faster than walking, and we need to call off the search," he said.

"What search?"

"James and George and the others," he replied, stepping away to go retrieve his horse. "It was quite the event when Magellan came tearing through the ladies' lawn games." He laughed as he snagged his stallion's reins.

Her mind filled with the image of little Magellan crashing into the middle of a garden party and she smiled, cheeks burning with mirth until a laugh bubbled out of her. She glanced up to see Burke watching her, his eyes hooded.

"I feel your every laugh in the center of me. Right here," he murmured, pressing his fist against the middle of his chest. He looked almost surprised that he was admitting so much. He tugged on his mount's reins, leading it over.

She let her eye drop down his handsome form as he walked, taking in those broad shoulders, the narrow cut of his hips, his long legs. Those breeches where a gift from Aphrodite herself. Rosalie's mouth tipped into a grin as she noted the strength of his thighs through the tight fabric.

He crossed the distance between them and stepped in close, tipping her face up to meet his eyes. His lips were slightly parted as he leaned in, his voice heavy with want. "Look at me like that again, and I'll gladly take you into those trees and kiss you until you come apart." He dared to trace his thumb over her mouth. "Before I'm done, my name will be a prayer on these perfect lips."

With a shuddering gasp, her resolve shattered into a thousand tiny pieces. She kissed him again. This time she took charge, raising her hand to grip the back of his neck and pull him down to her. He kept one hand on the reins, but the other dropped around her waist. His touch was overly gentle as he tried to be cautious of her injuries. But she didn't care about the pain. She wanted him on fire, burning as she was from the inside out. With a whimper, she opened her mouth to him. A shiver of desire had her trembling as his tongue eagerly pressed in. She wanted more, *more*.

He pulled away first. "Christ, Rosalie," he cursed, taking a step back. "We can't do this here," he said, eyes darting around the clearing.

Riding the high of his kiss was everything, but his words sent her plummeting to earth like a heavy stone. "You're right," she murmured, feeling her emotions closing in on her, readying themselves to be forced back in their cage. "We can't do this."

36

Burke

ROSALIE'S WORDS HIT Burke like a shot. What he'd meant to imply was that they couldn't keep kissing *here*, exposed as they were in the middle of the field. He'd be damned if that was the first and last time he kissed Rosalie Harrow. She was sweet as honey and so responsive to his touch. Her every whimper and sigh was an aria sung just for him.

He raised a hand to his mouth. She kissed like a goddess too. Damn, he already wanted more. He had to step back or be consumed. He felt himself the luckiest of men that she would trust him with that first kiss. She'd trembled in his arms. He was a man bewitched when she dared to claim the second.

But now she was looking at him with regret in her eyes and he wanted to die.

"That's not what I meant," he said gruffly, pulling her closer.

"But it's what we both know to be true," she replied, eyes downcast. She was sealing herself away.

"Don't," he said, jaw clenched tight, desperate to stop her emotional retreat. How could she be in his arms, yet so far away? "Rosalie—"

"*You* don't." Her cheeks bloomed pink, even while her eyes

were still glassy with desire. "Don't call me that, and don't push me on this. We both know our respective situations. This can go no further. It was a beautiful moment, and I thank you for it—"

"You thank me," he scoffed, bitterness lacing his words as he dropped his hands away. He didn't care if he was being selfish. In the span of one achingly perfect moment, he tasted ambrosia on her lips. Now this goddess was sentencing him to Tartarus, where he'd live trapped in this memory forever, knowing it would never be repeated.

"I do thank you, Burke. But we *can't*—"

He heard the quiet sob in her voice. His every instinct begged him to touch her, comfort her, kiss away her tears. But he knew if he touched her now, he risked breaking the trust he still had. If he wanted any hope of a repeat of those kisses, if he wanted to remain in her confidence, he'd have to play this game by her rules.

Good thing he liked games . . . and he was playing this one to win.

He raised a hand in mock surrender. She loved the devil in him, and he was determined to see her duel with it before he tasted her again. He narrowed his eyes in challenge. "Your wish is my command, Miss Harrow. I won't kiss you again . . . until you ask me nicely."

37

Tom

"YOU SEEM DISTRACTED today, Tom. Trouble at the great house?"

Tom glanced over at his brother as they slowed their mounts to a walk. He'd arrived that morning at Colin's request. Since their father's death, Colin had proven to be more open-handed when it came to collecting rents. This meant he was more well-liked than the late Mr. Renley of Foxhill House, but it also meant his tenants tried to cheat him left and right. Tom didn't mind lending his weight as another Renley to bolster the effectiveness of Colin's visits. It did good to remind some of their wilier tenants that the rents must be paid.

Colin watched him with a raised brow. "You've been so far away. Is it just this marriage business? Do none of the ladies at Alcott suit? Perhaps you'd do better going to Town."

Tom sighed. He *was* distracted. He couldn't get the image of Burke and Miss Harrow out of his head. Christ, what had the man been thinking, touching her like that? The angle of the open piano lid had been such that only Tom and James saw their little exhibit, but still . . .

"I heard Miss Blanche is staying at the house. Sir Andrew is set to own half of Carrington soon. She'd surely come with a pretty dowry," Colin teased with a smile.

"I'd sooner marry Blossom," Tom said with a nod to his mount.

Colin snorted. "Then who *are* you pondering over? With such a hive of bees buzzing between your ears, it must be a lady."

Tom shrugged. He'd never had a very open relationship with his brother. They were friendly, but not quite friends. His truest friends were Burke and James. He could tell them anything . . . usually. But damn if Burke wasn't a devil last night. He had his hands all over Miss Harrow. Tom's jealousy warred with his arousal as he watched her cheeks blush pink. She liked it. Hell, she *craved* it. She had been practically leaning into Burke's touch. It left Tom with a painful ache. Sure, in his cock . . . and he had very few options as to how to scratch that particular itch while he was stuck in the countryside.

But the ache went deeper. In truth, it went soul deep. Tom was lonely. Rosalie's words had stayed with him. He didn't want to marry some high-society lady for her money, counting his new guineas as he cashed in her bride-price for a set of braided shoulder lapels. He wanted what Burke had last night. He wanted a beautiful woman looking at him with a passion that burned white hot.

Tom lost himself in the memory of her looks, her blushes, her soft, panting breaths. He couldn't remember the last time he was so turned on. That little phoenix was ready to set fire in her cage. How Tom longed to be the one to let her out.

Christ, he wanted Rosalie for himself. He almost laughed aloud at the realization. What was worse, he desperately wanted her to want him too. He wanted passion and love. He wanted hunger that verged on obsession. Instead, he was empty . . . empty . . . empty.

He thought he had that once . . . with Marianne. Had she taken the best of him? Perhaps he wouldn't be able to turn Rosalie's head. After all, she thought he still harbored feelings for Marianne. Did he? He hardly knew. His love for Marianne was so wrapped up in his resentment, like some great Gordian knot.

But he remembered that look Rosalie gave him in the forest, and again walking in the lane. It stung with the pain of dismissal. She would never settle on being anyone's second choice. His respect for her grew, even as he felt an uncomfortable jealousy churn in his stomach at the thought that Burke might be the one to win her instead.

Nothing about this was simple. Tom's career, Rosalie's position, Burke's competing interest. Was Tom willing to risk their friendship by courting her in earnest?

Be my friend, she said. She didn't want his sincere attention even if he offered. That was the truth. She wanted a friend and nothing more. Could he stand to be only her friend if Burke got to become more?

"You'll go cross-eyed thinking that hard," Colin said with another laugh.

Tom blinked, pulling himself from his thoughts long enough to notice they were almost home. A few of the children called out their welcomes as they saw Colin and Tom approach. Tom glanced at his brother, snagged by a sudden thought. "Colin . . . why did you marry Agatha?"

Colin barked another laugh. "What kind of question is that?"

"I know we don't typically talk about matters of the heart—"

"No, we most certainly do not."

It seemed somehow important that Tom know this truth. "Colin, be serious. Did you marry her for her fortune? It was not a great sum, I know."

Colin mused for a moment longer. "I believe any gentleman ought to say you marry for duty's sake first. Then perhaps comes love. Least of all, but still quite important, comes that whole 'avoiding carnal lusts and appetites' angle that curates love to preach about."

"Bloody hell, Colin, I'm not asking some country gentleman in a crowded men's club. I'm asking my brother. Did you love Agatha?"

Colin narrowed his eyes at Tom. Eventually he sighed, giving his horse's neck a pat. "Tom, I love her to distraction. If you hadn't noticed, we have six children. Five of them in a row came out boys. We could have stopped with an heir. We could have stopped with the spare. But here we are, six children later, and the sun still rises and sets on that woman's smile. Gods alive, man, I'm mad for it."

Tom felt a lightness in his chest as his brother admitted to his happiness. He wanted that joy for himself. No woman since Marianne made him think it was even possible . . . until Rosalie Harrow.

They rode into the stable yard and dismounted, leaving the horses with a groom.

"Staying for supper?" Colin asked, leading the way towards the house.

"Of course, he is," came Agatha's voice. She stood in the doorway, one hand on her hip. "Just try and weasel out of it, Tom, and I'll have Mark and Thomas tie you to a chair."

"I'll get the rope!" cried Young Tom, bounding off around the side of the house.

Mark took off like a shot, eager to chase his little brother down. "Thomas, come back! She was *joking*!"

Colin and Tom laughed. Tom's smile fell as he considered her offer. Perhaps he needed a night of distance. He needed to get his head on straight. "Fine, I'll stay," he said, placing a kiss on Agatha's cheek. "Just the one night, mind."

"We'll see." She smiled, victorious, and turned to go back in the house. "Oh, Tom, wait." She pulled a letter from her apron pocket. "This came for you shortly after you'd both gone."

Tom took the letter and felt a fist clench tight around his heart. He knew that handwriting like it was his own.

"Tom?" Agatha put a hand on his arm. "Are you all right? You've gone pale."

"I . . ."

"Heavens, what is it?" Agatha's tone sang out her concern.

"It's nothing," Tom muttered. "I'll just . . . go change for dinner."

"But we've not had luncheon yet—"

He pushed into the house, angling for the back stair. As soon as he was safely to his room, he locked the door and tossed his hat and gloves on the bed. The sounds of the full house faded away as Tom picked up a paper knife and sliced open the green wax seal. He unfolded the letter and read:

Dearest Tom,

I can only imagine your surprise at hearing from me again. It was remiss of me not to write to you sooner, but I must confess, I was afraid you would not wish to hear from me. And then I was afraid I wouldn't know where to write to have a letter be received by you. One hears such horror stories of letters to naval men going astray. Why, a friend once said her letter went all the way to India before it found its way to her brother stationed in Lisbon.

You can imagine how relieved I was when I heard from Lady Braddock that First Lieutenant Tom Renley of Foxhill House was not only back in the country, but back in the very county of our youth. I can only imagine the fun you must be having in this golden autumn. How is dear James? I hope your brother fares well, and Agatha and all the children.

I have news of my own that might cause you some distress. Again, I confess I am not certain whether this news will be received with any interest, but I shall tell you all the same. In June, a cruel twist of fate took my husband. It was a carriage accident. (How many times did we take reckless drives in the phaeton? You always drove too fast for me, Tom.)

The service was a pretty one, and Thackeray is buried in his family estate near Cornwall. I am still in mourning, but when the time for sadness is done, I look forward to renewing our friendship. If you ever tire of country life, please know you always have a friend in Town who would await a visit from you with eagerness.

Give all my love to Agatha and the children. I will be praying for your health and happiness. I always have, Tom. I always will.

Yours,
Marianne Young

38

Rosalie

THE RIDE BACK to the house was torturous, worse than their first ride together. Rosalie sat sideways, pressed against Burke. She tucked her head under his chin, trying not to wince as the horse cantered down the lane. Burke kept an arm around her middle, holding her against him, while the other held the reins.

They cantered over the crest of the hill, and his arm shifted slightly lower on her hip. With the angle of her body, the press of her legs together, the movement of the horse—his arms around her, his breath in her ear, the ghost of his kisses on her lips—she couldn't help the soft moan that escaped her.

"Damn it," he growled. "Keep making those noises, and I'll change my mind."

She smiled. It was almost too easy. Not that she wanted to torture the man. If she had her way, she'd have let him drag her into the woods. She was hungry for it, hungry for *him*. And she already knew what waited for her under this coat. She saw him at the stream—his broad shoulders, that muscled abdomen, the dusting of black hair across his chest leading down, down, to what the water kept concealed. She swallowed another moan.

"Rosalie, *fuck*, play fair." His voice was low in her ear.

"I'm not doing it on purpose," she replied. "I know you feel this too. When we touch," she whispered. "Heavens, even when you just look at me, I want . . ." She left the rest unsaid. "But neither of us are in a position . . . we owe the Corbins more. You know they wouldn't approve. I'm sure Lord James has already said as much to you."

"They don't own me, Rosalie," he muttered. "James is my friend."

"Nor do they own me," she replied. "But we are guests in this house, and there are rules of conduct. I know it would trouble the duchess to think of the two of us . . . entangled."

He lowered his face to nuzzle against her ear. "Christ, you can't use words like 'entangled' when you're pressed against my cock."

"Control yourself, sir, or I will walk the rest of the way," she challenged.

"You're the one saying you want me, moaning like I'm already inside you. Who needs lessons in control?"

Heat flooded her core, even as she bristled in annoyance. He was too good at playing these games. "Careful, Burke. The more you vex me, the longer you'll have to wait to kiss me again."

"I've waited twenty-seven years to find one single person who could hold my attention the way you do, love," he replied. "I'm a patient man. It will make it all the sweeter when you set aside this ludicrous notion of restraint. We are inevitable."

Those words sent a chill through her, cooling the fire in her blood. What was he hoping might come of all this? She had dared to assume that, given his position, he might not be interested in forcing their relationship to fit convention. Was Burke looking for a wife? If he was, she'd have to stop this before it went any further. Otherwise, the only inevitable outcome would be his pain, her tears, and two irrevocably broken hearts.

They arrived back at the house, and Burke handed her down into Lord James' waiting arms. He took his leave with a softly spoken, "Miss Harrow." Wheeling his horse around, he trotted out of the yard, leaving Rosalie and James standing together, watching him ride away with surprised looks on their faces.

"Do I want to know?" James muttered, one arm still wrapped around her.

"Know what, my lord?" she whispered, still watching Burke ride away.

"Never mind. Come along," he said, guiding her gently back towards the house.

James called Doctor Rivers to examine her, and the duchess placed a moratorium on any other young lady riding out without an escort. In the end, Rosalie begrudgingly agreed to follow the doctor's orders and submit to two days of bed rest.

She passed the first evening sitting quietly by herself, with nothing to entertain her but Renley's book on astral navigation. She was grateful in the morning when Madeline came to visit. They sat together, sketching the large vase of flowers on her bedside table. Rosalie had to borrow paper from Madeline, as her sketchbook was still in the servant's stairwell.

"They're exquisite," Madeline murmured after a while.

Rosalie smiled. They *were* exquisite. Spikes of blue delphiniums, little bunches of pink rambling roses, larkspur and hydrangea blooms. "They were an apology gift from Lord James," she replied. "He still blames himself for my fall. Which is ridiculous," she added. "It was no one's fault."

"Of course," Madeline echoed, her fair brows lowered in frustrated indecision.

Rosalie set her cup of tea aside. "What's troubling you?"

Madeline sighed, not looking up from her sketching. "It's only . . . there are whispers . . ."

Rosalie's smile fell. "Whispers?"

"Whispers of Lord James . . . and you," she added. "Apparently you were seen together yesterday morning."

Rosalie fought hard not to scowl. "There was nothing improper in our riding into the village. I needed to post a letter to my aunt."

"That's not where you were seen," Madeline replied, still not looking up.

"Where, then?"

"Outside his room . . ."

Rosalie took a shaky breath. Of course, they were seen. By whom? A maid? Nosy Mariah and Blanche? "My presence in that hallway yesterday morning was completely innocent," she declared. "I'm sure Lord James would be more than happy to put any officious lies to rest. I'll do the same just as soon as I'm able."

Madeline shrugged. "It's not my business, but I'd not mention the flowers outside this room. It would only fuel the fire . . ."

"Am I to assume the other ladies are preparing my pyre as we speak?" she said. "Shall I be burned at the stake for accepting his innocent attentions when no other lady seems inclined to do so?"

Madeline dared to glance up, those large, doe eyes looking at Rosalie with quiet confidence. "Just because the other ladies don't approach him, doesn't mean they don't want to. And they don't take kindly to encroachment from . . ."

Rosalie raised a brow. "From?"

Madeline settled back into herself, lowering her eyes away.

"From a penniless, grasping social climber who ought to know her place?"

Madeline smiled. "Maybe not those words exactly."

Rosalie pursed her lips, fighting a smile. No, she couldn't imagine any combination of those words escaping Madeline's gentle lips. "Why are you telling me this?"

"Because I like to think that good people can prosper," Madeline replied with a blush, echoing Rosalie's words from the other day. "You need to know what weapons they will use if you're to fight them."

Now Rosalie smiled. "Are we going into battle, then?"

"I've been taking fencing lessons since I was six," Madeline replied with a shrug. "I can protect you if it comes to it."

The images conjured in Rosalie's mind were so absurd, so delightful, she burst into peals of laughter that made her tender side hurt. Before long, Madeline joined in, and the ladies passed the rest of the morning with Rosalie asking Madeline how she might win in a duel against each person in the house.

"Mr. Burke is strong, but I'm fast," Madeline argued. "I would sting him like a bee."

Rosalie laughed again, determined to do everything in her power to keep this delightful creature out of the hands of George Corbin. He could never deserve her.

Renley was the next to visit after lunch, his golden curls unruly as ever, with a nosegay of yellow roses clutched in his hand. "How's the invalid?" he said as he entered.

"Perfectly well, as you can see," Rosalie replied from her perch on the bed. Sarah rose and made a great show of fluffing her pillows so she could sit up more comfortably.

"I only just heard about your accident," he said, brows

lowered in concern as he surveyed her for injury. "From the way they talked downstairs, I half expected you to be partially decapitated . . . and for that horse to be Lucifer's own steed."

She laughed. "No such luck, I'm afraid. Nothing more than a tender shoulder and a bruised ego. And Magellan has been most egregiously maligned."

He came around the side of the bed and offered out his flowers. "I thought you might like a little nature to admire . . . but I see you have a far superior arrangement here."

The bouquet from James sat in a beam of sunshine.

"These are most welcome," she said, reaching for the nosegay. "A lady can never have too many beautiful things." She let her eyes settle on him, feeling a flutter inside as she realized she wasn't only talking about flowers.

Sarah bustled over with a little vase in hand. She inched in front of him, breaking their eye contact, and took the flowers. She set them on the opposite bedside table.

Renley cleared his throat as Sarah reclaimed her seat. "Don't get too excited about those," he said. "I stole them from a vase downstairs."

They both laughed.

"Your secret is safe with me," Rosalie replied. "I believe I appreciate them even more knowing they were pilfered. Nothing so delicious as a stolen sweet." She blushed anew, but this time it had nothing to do with the man standing before her. It was all for memories of a tall, dark, handsome man with firm hands and the softest lips . . .

She didn't know how to rationalize the way her heart so quickly fluttered at the thought of each of these men. All she knew was that attraction to one in no way affected attraction to the others. Here she was, sitting before the most beautiful man she'd ever met. He was kind and attentive. Her heart softened for him each time their acquaintance grew . . . even as she accepted that she could never be what he needed.

Burke. Renley.

Both.

All to say nothing of the enigma that was James Corbin . . .

"How I'd love to be inside your mind right now," Renley mused, dropping into the chair next to the bed.

She swallowed. That would be dangerous in the extreme. "Only thinking of how the ladies must have reacted to a horse joining their game of lawn bowls."

"Yes, I heard it was pandemonium," he chuckled. But she could see in his eyes he was thinking of something else too. Something that required his eyes to fall to her lips. She needed to change the subject.

"Have you been riding the park in this heat?"

"I just arrived back from my brother's house," he replied. "I stayed there last night. My sister-in-law only just let me get away." He glanced to the bed, where her series of flower sketches sat scattered. He picked up the top one. "These are very pretty."

She reached for the sketch by her knee. "Yes, Madeline and I—*ahh*—" For a moment, she'd quite forgotten her pains and reached with her injured shoulder.

Renley was forward in a flash, one hand on her elbow and the other lightly touching her shoulder as he helped her sit back. The sketch he'd been admiring fluttered to the floor.

"Thank you," she murmured, her skin heating at the points he touched her. His thumb made one gentle stroke along the soft inner bend of her elbow, and her breath caught. He was close enough for her to smell that intoxicating scent of salt and leather.

He held on for a moment longer, their eyes meeting, until he abruptly let go and sat back. She was grateful for the space, even as she wished he would still touch her.

"Does it ache?"

Her eyes still held his, dark brown meeting deepest blue. What was his question? Did it ache? "Terribly," she murmured, not knowing what particular ache she implied.

"This tea's gone cold, miss," came Sarah's voice from across the room.

Rosalie jolted. Heavens, Sarah was still here. "Oh . . . yes. I haven't offered you any refreshment," she said, looking back at Renley. "Would you like some tea?" Not waiting for the answer, she turned. "Sarah, would you mind?"

"Not at all, miss," Sarah replied. She was already gathering the old tea things on a tray. She flashed Rosalie an excited smile as Renley's back was turned, her intention clear. She was leaving Rosalie alone with the handsome lieutenant.

39

Rosalie

"I'll be back in a moment, miss," Sarah said as she left, tray rattling in her hands.

Renley sat with one leg crossed over the other, hat perched on his knee. By all accounts, it should be a relaxed position, but Rosalie felt the tension coiling in him. He wasn't looking at her—rather, he seemed to be studying the pattern of the wallpaper.

"You seem far away," she said.

Flipping his hat over, he tossed his gloves inside and set it next to the flowers. "Miss Harrow, I wonder if I might . . . you said we could be friends."

She blinked. "Yes, I would be happy to call you my friend."

He leaned back again. "You know about Marianne. Or at least, you know some of it."

"I know only what you've told me."

"Would it be terribly forward of me if I sought your advice? I don't know the rules here," he added with a shrug. "I've never considered a lady a friend before. But you make me feel so at ease, and I really fear I might be going mad."

This had her leaning forward. He felt it too . . . whatever

it was between them that felt so natural. He wanted her in his confidence, and she wanted to be there. "You may tell me anything. I will listen as a friend and do my best to offer advice."

"I . . . I don't want to offend you."

She smiled, even as something inside her clenched tight. Heavens, what was he about to tell her? "I think you'll find I'm made of stern stuff, Tom. Best to haul anchor and sail full speed ahead."

They both grinned at her nautical reference, and his eye flashed at her use of his name.

"Marianne was my first . . . everything," he began. "We were young and in love. The height of our passion lasted about a year. I asked her to marry me. She asked time to consider. Within a fortnight, she was engaged to another man. They married in the spring, and I set sail for my first tour of the West Indies. That was eight years ago."

It was a common enough tale: the young lady torn between two suitors. She felt for him his pain at not being chosen, but it was hardly surprising given the circumstances. "Has something happened, then? Why does the lady still haunt you so?"

"I've had a letter from her. I had the news already from my brother, but her letter confirms: Her husband is dead, and she now finds herself a wealthy widow."

"And . . . was her letter cordial?"

He pulled it slowly from the inside pocket of his coat and held it out, the dark green wax seal broken. "Would you like to read it?"

Her hand reached out, ready to accept the letter, but she paused. "I don't think—I shouldn't read it, no." She dropped her hand away. "If this were *my* letter to you, I don't believe I would want it shared with another lady . . . even only a friend."

With a curt nod, he tucked it away. "She is cordial," he said. "She makes it quite clear that she would like to renew our friendship."

Her heart sank. It was she who forced the idea of friendship and nothing more . . . and she meant it. She had to be a friend now and counsel him, even if it meant she pushed him into the arms of another woman. "Well then, perhaps this is your second chance. If you loved her and she loved you, perhaps this time there will be no obstacle."

Renley scoffed. "No obstacle except the past eight years. I loved her, Rose. She told me every day she loved me. But when her love was put to the test, she walked away. Without a second look or a second thought. She had the audacity to invite me to the bloody wedding!"

He stood and stalked away, only turning when he'd reached the open windows. "In the end, my love wasn't enough. Why should it suddenly be enough now? If I value my pride, how can I accept her renewed attentions?"

Rosalie worried her bottom lip. "The gentleman she chose . . . was he as handsome as you? As lively and engaging?"

Renley scoffed again. "Thackeray Young was a man nearing thirty with little wit and dull manners. She settled herself on him for his seven thousand a year."

"I believe you might be giving the lady too much credit to assume she really had a simple choice between you and the other gentleman. In fact, I imagine if you ask her, she'd say she made an impossible choice. In the end, it was no choice at all."

His eyes narrowed. "No choice? We *always* have a choice. She had me on my knees, heart in hand, offering her the world. All Young had was a London townhouse and deep pockets. She didn't even know the man! She chose her own comfort over a love match. Is she now to be rewarded with me falling to my knees yet again?"

How was it possible that even the cleverest of men could be so blinded? She sighed, shoulders sagging slightly from the weight of having to explain womanhood. "Tom, do you have any idea what it means to be a woman in this society?"

He blinked at her, confused.

"Do you have the slightest notion of our constant, debilitating fear? Knowing that at every moment, our fortunes depend upon staying in the good graces of the men in our lives? That we are all, at every moment of the day, one step away from ruination, whether we are a lowly gentleman's daughter or even a queen."

He had the good sense to look ashamed. Crossing over to the bed, he sat down, taking her hand. "I hadn't considered it from that angle."

"Your Marianne chose safety and security, yes. She chose fortune over risking it all on a throw of the dice with you. What were you then, all of seventeen, eighteen? You're a second son with no guarantee of position or fortune. You think your love was not enough for her, but that is a childish notion. Only men can afford to hold to such romantic ideas."

"You surprise me, Rose," he said. "You don't think love ought to matter between two people? That it should not be the foundation of a marriage?"

"Love rarely has any role in the marriage calculation. Not for a woman who prizes her life and the living of it. It was never about whether she loved you, Tom. She simply chose a fate that would move her further from the brink of ruination."

He looked down at where their hands were joined, and his thumb moved softly back and forth. She tried to control her breathing. Each time he touched her, she felt warm and jittery. Now was no different.

"You must think me heartless for hating her all these years," he muttered.

"You've been uncompromising with the lady," she admitted. "Unjust and unfair . . . and frankly a bit naïve."

He blinked twice before barking out a laugh. "Oh, is that all, Miss Harrow?"

She blushed, worried she might have made him angry. "Yes, that is all."

"Christ, you give your opinions so freely," he said. "I've never spoken like this with a woman. I feel like it was *I* who was just thrown from a horse."

She couldn't hide her smile. "That is your fault too."

"*Ahh*, is it? Add it to the list, then," he said with a dramatic wave of his hand.

"You told me to treat you like a friend," she reminded him.

He sighed in annoyance, even as his mouth tipped into a smile. "I suppose I did."

"And do you now regret your decision? Should we go back to behaving as mere acquaintances? Shall I call you 'Lieutenant Renley' again?"

He leaned in, their faces inches apart as he muttered, "Don't you dare."

They held each other's gaze, her hand still held in his. "I don't know to what end you seek my advice. But if your plan is to go to her and renew your courtship, I'll have to say . . . you seem quite miserable about it."

He laughed again, but it was hollow. "I wear my heart on my sleeve," he admitted. "More often than not, it feels like a runaway kite, string pulled taut as the winds batter it to pieces."

She mused on this with a soft smile. Not like a kite . . . like a ship adrift at sea. Yes, Burke was the rogue knight, James the lonely fortress, and Renley was a powerful ship, battered by the sea, desperately in search of a calm port in the storm. She fought the urge to raise her free hand and brush those hopeless curls off his forehead.

Thinking of the men together made her mindful. "Can I ask . . . what does Lord James think about it all?"

Renley sighed heavily, his thumb still making absentminded strokes on the back of her hand. "James thinks I should go to London. He thinks I will never lay her ghost to rest until I have seen her and spoken to her. He says I must face my past."

She couldn't help but smile. She expected nothing less from the lord. "That sounds quite sensible. And Burke?"

"Burke thinks I'm well shot of her. But he never liked her, so . . ."

This gave Rosalie pause and—dare she say it—hope? Was it possible that the woman truly right for Tom Renley could ever be disliked by one of his dearest friends? What kind of person must she be that Burke would disapprove? "Can I ask the reason for his dislike?"

Renley shrugged. "They never got on."

"Surely it must be more than that . . ."

"He always said she smiled too much and that it never met her eyes . . . though what that means, I have no idea," Renley replied.

Rosalie puzzled over this. Was Marianne an actress, then? Did Burke see through her artifice? He certainly had the ability to read people. Perhaps Renley, young and innocent as he was, read more into Marianne's love than was ever there . . .

"Your friends have given you their advice, and now I shall give you mine."

He scooted closer. "I'm all ears, Rose."

"Do not love her again if it's not in your heart to do so . . . but forgive her," she said. "For your sake and hers, forgive her everything. Tell her you have done so, and let her move on. Or take the gift fate has bestowed on you and go to her now that you can. And choose to be happy."

"You really think it's that easy?"

"No, of course not," she replied. "But life is about our choices, as you said. If we make enough of the right kind of choices, we might find happiness. Even if ultimately our choice is to soldier on alone. There can be happiness in that too."

He held her gaze for a moment. A thousand thoughts flashed through those blue eyes. Had she said too much?

"You are wise, Miss Harrow," he murmured.

She was Miss Harrow again. Not a good sign.

"I speak as I find," she replied, regretting her loose tongue.

"Yes . . . you do."

"Have I offended you?" she dared to ask.

Before he could respond, Sarah came bustling back in with a heavily laden tea tray. "So sorry about my delay, Miss Rosalie."

Renley bolted off the side of the bed, snatching up his hat.

"I'm afraid I've taken up enough of your time, Miss Harrow," he said, clearing his throat. "You need rest and relaxation, and burdening you with my problems affords neither. I'm glad to see you are on the mend."

"Thank you," she replied, feeling increasingly empty. Burke was already avoiding her, now she'd just pushed Renley away.

Renley turned to leave, but paused, suddenly patting the pocket of his coat. "Oh, I did have another gift for you."

"Is this one pilfered too?" she asked, forcing a smile.

"In fact, it is." He pulled out a small book. "I stole this from the library. You cannot possibly be enjoying the last one I gave you," he said with a nod to the book currently sitting at her bedside.

"I confess, astral navigation is not my favorite subject."

"Perhaps this will be more to your liking."

"What is it about?" she asked, examining the cover. She glanced back up to see he was watching her.

"Read it and report back." With that, he turned and left, walking right past a confused Sarah, who was ready at last to pour their tea.

It was a novel. More accurately, it was a romance novel. A dreamy tale of a young princess swept off her feet by a mysterious knight. It was the perfect distraction to avoid thinking about Burke and his teasing dare, Renley and his sudden dismissal, James and his rigid rejection.

She read all through the evening. Madeline peeked her head in to say goodnight. Hours later, the candles in her room burned low. Rosalie lay atop the covers, for it was too warm for a blanket. She curled up on her good side, inching towards the candle's light, her bare legs stretched out behind her. The daring knight was ready to profess his love.

Rosalie was so entranced, she didn't hear the rattle of the door handle. She didn't even hear it squeak open. But she did hear it shut . . . and she most definitely heard the deep sound of a man clearing his voice. With a gasp she rolled over to see Burke leaning against the door, his stormy grey eyes trailing up the line of her bare legs, settling on her surprised face.

"Look who's still awake."

40

Rosalie

"Burke." She sat up with a wince. "You cannot be here. You must leave at once."

Heavens, he looked divine. His black trousers were slung high on his hips, and his shirt was undone at the neck, exposing him down to his sternum. His sleeves were rolled to the elbow. He had the audacity to smirk. "No one saw me," he said, voice low.

She rolled off the bed, letting her shift fall to cover her legs, as she snapped her book shut and tossed it on the bed. "That is *not* the point! You cannot be in here."

"I'm not hearing that you don't want me in here," he said in that teasing tone. "Only that I *ought* not to be . . ."

Heat pooled in her core. Oh, she wanted him here. But he was most definitely not invited. To take such a liberty was an affront she couldn't excuse. She crossed her arms over her chest, for her shift did nothing to conceal the outline of her peaked nipples, the curve of her hips. The idea of him seeing her like this made her tremble, even as she fought her righteous indignation.

"Fine, I don't want you in here. There, does that satisfy?"

A muscle twitched in his jaw as he made no move to leave. Should she throw the book at him? No, it would probably make too much noise . . . but dropping her shift to the floor would make no noise . . .

Rosalie Harrow, don't you dare.

He leaned casually against the door, but his eyes burned through her. "Tom said you were hurting," he murmured. "*Aching*, I believe, was the word he used."

Her pulse raced faster at that possessive look. "Oh, I see," she whispered. "Tom came to see me today, and now you're jealous. Is that it?"

"Don't call him 'Tom.'"

Her anger flared. "I will call him Tom if I wish, and it can be nothing to you. If you want me to call you by *your* Christian name, you'll have to reveal it first." Her chest rose and fell rapidly as silence stretched between them.

"Is Tom right?" he said at last. "Are you aching tonight, love?"

"I'm fine."

"Prove it. Lift your arm."

Her heart fluttered at the command, but her mind rebelled. "You lift *your* arm. Lift it to turn the handle, and leave."

He glared at her as he took a step forward. "Rosalie, lift your fucking arm."

A soft whimper escaped her lips as she dropped her hands to her sides. She lifted her left arm chest high. "See? I'm fine. Doctor Rivers has already seen me—"

"Lift it higher."

She hated the way her body felt so ready to follow his commands. She raised it another inch. "There. Happy?"

"Higher," he growled, taking yet another step closer. "Above the shoulder."

With a huff, she jerked her arm up. "God, you're impossible—*ahh*—" She winced and dropped it to her side.

His eyes flashed in triumph. "See? You're hurt."

"Doctor Rivers said it would heal in a few days," she replied, rubbing the curve where her shoulder met her neck. If she moved it wrong, it felt like being stabbed.

"Rivers is fine when it comes to fevers and birthing babies," Burke scoffed. "But he's hopeless at tending this kind of injury. Let me help you."

She blinked, mouth opening slightly. She snapped it shut before narrowing her eyes. "You're not a doctor, Burke."

"No," he replied. "But I've sustained a lifetime's worth of similar injuries and fully recovered. You jarred your shoulder in your fall. I know how to ease the pain."

She ought to show him the door. There was too much left unspoken between them. She didn't want to hurt him or lead him on . . . any more than she already had. "Burke, we can't . . ." She blushed, falling into silence as she fought to control her trembling. She was a coward. *But if you tell him the truth, he might leave . . .*

"I can't sleep knowing you're hurting," he admitted, voice low. "If you're in pain, I can help. Just say yes, love."

Yes.

"What will you do?"

He slipped a hand into his pocket and pulled out a corked vial. "Hot oil massage."

Yes, yes, yes. She was screaming inside.

"You'll have to permit me to touch you," he added, the corner of his mouth tipping into a smile.

The words went straight to her core. "Burke, I don't think—"

"Neither do I," he said, stepping closer. "Not when it comes to you. I just . . . do. You're in pain and I want to help you. Please let me."

His words hung in the air between them.

Finally, Rosalie took a deep breath. She was surely going to hell. "Fine."

Burke raised a surprised brow. "Yes?"

"Yes," she said on exhale. "What should I do?"

He glanced around the room. "Get the candle," he whispered. "Set it on the table next to that chair." He pointed to one of the striped chairs near the empty hearth. He moved past her to the dressing table in the corner and grabbed the cushioned stool.

Rosalie picked up the candle, praying her hand wouldn't shake. Two more still burned on the mantel. Shadows played in the corners as she moved across the room.

Burke was waiting. "Sit here," he said. "Face away from me."

Taking a few shallow breaths, she sat on the stool, back straight, hands folded in her lap. Burke filled the space behind her, his long legs stretching to either side of her as he grabbed the stool and slid her a few inches closer.

"This will only take a moment."

She glanced over her shoulder to see he was holding the glass vial over the flickering candle, warming the contents. "What is it?" she whispered, terrified he might be able to hear the pounding of her heart.

"Just a simple oil infused with comfrey and frankincense . . . and a bit of lavender," he replied. "Untie your shift and expose your left shoulder."

She froze. "Burke—"

"Relax," he murmured. "I made you a vow yesterday and

I'll not break it. If you expect me to kiss you tonight, you're going to have to ask me nicely first. Agreed?"

She turned away with a nod. Nothing was going to happen without her permission. She could trust him. She could wait to tell him she would never marry him. Two people could enjoy each other's touch without it leading to the altar.

You're cruel and deluded, Rosalie Harrow.

Raising a shaking hand, she tugged at the tie between her breasts until it gave. Loosening the collar of her shift, she exposed more of her injured shoulder.

He scooted closer. "If this hurts too much, tell me and I'll stop."

She gave another nod.

He uncorked the little vial. "Move your hair to your other shoulder."

She swept her dark curls over to her right shoulder, leaving her left shoulder bare. An intoxicating smell filled her nose as he rubbed his hands together: spicy and warm, with soft notes of lavender. The sound of the slick oil in his palms made her stomach flip. He was so close she could feel his breath fanning over her neck. She couldn't contain her shiver. It raised gooseflesh down her arms, and she bit her lip to keep from letting out a moan.

He started with one hand. The warmth of the oil felt amazing, and the smell was heavenly. A soft sigh escaped her as his other hand joined in, both working to define the shape of her shoulder and the curve of her neck.

"Hold still," he murmured.

She groaned as his touch turned from gentle strokes with soft fingers to an iron grip. He kneaded the stiff muscles, holding her tight with both hands. Her body turned to jelly as he worked the aches away. It hurt, to be sure, but it was a hurt she didn't ever want to end. He paused twice to add a bit more oil to his hands.

"I'm going to start moving the joint a bit," he cautioned. "This may hurt."

She readied herself for the pain.

He scooted all the way to the edge of his chair. With one hand tight on her shoulder, he used his other to move the arm.

A groan turned into a gasp, which she quickly had to stifle as a cry. "*Ouch—*"

"Sorry," he soothed in her ear, his hands going soft as velvet as they stroked over her shoulder, up her neck, down her arm. "Once more. Be strong. I'm rotating it back a bit."

It was painful as he kneaded the muscles, all while rotating the shoulder. She sighed, doing her best to stay quiet. Before he was done, he had her raising her arm at the shoulder until she felt more of a dull ache than the sharp, piercing pain of a knife stabbing her.

"How's that?" His hands were smooth as silk again.

"Better," she whispered, lips barely moving. "So much better . . . thank you, Burke."

He dropped both his hands away, leaving her swaying on the stool, desperate for his anchoring touch. She awkwardly tugged on her shift, trying to cover her naked shoulder.

Burke corked the little vial and wiped his hands with a handkerchief. "If it still pains you tomorrow, we can do this again," he offered.

She made no response. Her senses were swimming. Then her breath caught as his fingers trailed softly down her neck. He started just behind her ear, setting a fire in her skin as the tips of his fingers brushed their way down her back to the point where her shift sat askew.

"Rosalie," he whispered, the warmth of his voice making her burn. He pressed his forehead lightly against her shoulder. "I'll say goodnight."

He was leaving, and she wanted to scream. Not yet. It was too much . . . and not nearly enough. It was right that he should go. He shouldn't even be here.

He shifted away from her and stood. "Try to get some sleep," he murmured.

Her hand shot out as he passed, and she held on to his wrist. "Wait," she heard herself say. "Not yet. I—"

Burke's arm tensed under her grip. "Miss Harrow . . . did you want something else?"

She gasped as he turned, using her grip on his wrist to pull her up off the stool. He spun her around and tucked her tight against him. Then he dropped his hands to her hips and lowered his head to run the tip of his nose along her bare shoulder and up the curve of her neck. She couldn't contain the moan that escaped her lips.

"What do you want, love?" he whispered against her ear. "Say it."

She wanted to feel his hands on her. Just a few more seconds of stolen ecstasy. But Burke liked to tease, liked to circle his opponent, liked to *win*. She knew he wanted to kiss her. Not for what it would feel like, but for what it would represent: him claiming her resolve. She moaned, pressing her hips against him, feeling the way he eagerly pressed back.

He dug his fingers in her hair, pulling her head back to look in her eyes. "Those sounds are driving me mad. Please—*god*—"

She grinned. "Should it not be me begging for your kiss? Am I not to ask nicely?"

"Yes, *beg*," he rasped, his hot breath sending shivers through her body. His hands roved, sliding over her bare shoulders and under the edge of her shift to stroke the swell of her breasts. "Tell me what you need, you temptress . . . you fucking siren."

She *was* a siren, for she had lured him in without knowing what he wanted, what he expected from her in return. It was too cruel. Rosalie couldn't do it. She stiffened in his arms. "Burke—"

He stilled too, his fingertips grazing the swell of her breasts. "Tell me to stop," he whispered, his voice pained. "If you need this to stop—"

"No." She turned in his arms, sliding her hands up his chest to his shoulders. She loved the feel of him in just his shirt. No coat, no waistcoat. She wanted to press her face into his chest and breathe him in. "I want you so badly . . . but I'm not . . . I don't—"

He tipped her chin up with a finger. "Don't be afraid of me. Speak plainly."

"Whatever happens tonight, I will not consider myself ruined in the morning . . . and if you try to propose to protect my honor, I will say no."

He chuckled. "Are you trying to tell me you're not pure as the driven snow? Did you really expect the bastard son of a whore to be fastidious about that?" He tucked a few loose strands of her hair behind her ear.

"Don't call yourself that," she whispered, leaning into his touch.

"Why not? It's the truth."

She closed her hand over his wrist, meeting his gaze again.

"You are so much more than that. I don't . . . labels cage us in, they trap us. Could you ever accept me without one?"

"I do accept you."

"Please don't try to cage me," she whispered, pressing her face against his chest. "I couldn't bear it."

"Hey," he pushed gently on her shoulders, willing her to look at him again. "I would never hurt you." He lowered his forehead to hers and sighed. "Let me make you feel good."

She felt his hardness at the small of her back as he turned her around with firm hands. He groaned deep in his throat, both hands plunging inside the top of her shift to cup her breasts. She gasped, the sound turning into a whine as he caressed them. She squirmed, wrapped in his arms, her head lolling back against his chest.

"Tell me what you want, little siren. What will ease the ache?" The gravel in his voice made her shake as she pressed wantonly against him with her hips. "Do you want me to kiss you?"

There was her teasing Burke, still trying to get her to break. Her smile grew with her resolve. Whatever game they were playing, she was winning this round. "No kiss," she replied, " . . . but don't stop."

"Fuck," he growled. His hands seemed ready to ravage her. One slid back inside her shift to cup her breast, while the other pulled down on her sleeve to expose her shoulder. She moved her hips against him and let out another soft moan, loving his immediate response. He tweaked her nipple and she hissed.

"*Christ*—say it," he growled in her ear. "Put me out of my misery."

She sighed out another breathy, "No."

His hands dropped to her hips, grazing downward as his fingers reached for the edge of her shift. She was practically writhing as he slowly dragged it up her thighs, not stopping until it was bunched around her hips and her sex was exposed to the room. She gasped as she felt him caress her naked skin, his thumbs gently circling the bones of her hips.

"And now?" he whispered. "Tell me what you want now."

She tipped her head to the side, exposing more of her neck, desperate to feel him everywhere. "Touch me, Burke. Please—"

His right hand cupped her sex, and she felt sure she would die. "Are you wet for me?" he whispered. "Are you aching with it?" His fingers pressed against her as he slid them up and down, opening her. At the first proof of her desire he groaned, burying his face against the curve of her neck. "You're so wet. My sweet siren is aching."

"I am," she whined. "For you, only for you." She was going to break. She was going to kiss him, and then it would all be over.

"That's it, love," he whispered, his fingers moving in slow circles over her wet sex. "Do you want more?"

"God, Burke—*yes*—don't stop—"

He groaned. "Yes to kissing you . . . or yes to my fingers in your cunt?"

She trembled all over. He wasn't playing fair. "No kissing. More—*ahh*—"

He gripped her hip with his left hand, holding her tight against his hardness. His right hand slipped through the curls of her sex until he pressed a finger inside her. He moved the finger slowly in and out.

"Please, please," she whimpered, her own arms wrapping backwards to brace against his hips.

"You're so responsive," he groaned. "So sweet, so beautiful, so fucking perfect. I've never wanted anyone the way I want you." The words spilled out of him as he held her tight. He dragged his finger in and out until she was ready to collapse with need. Then he pressed a second finger inside her.

"Oh *god*—"

She was losing control. Was this still a game? Did she even care? She raised her good arm, snaking it around his neck as she rose on her toes, pressing herself closer to him. His fingers began pumping in earnest.

"Don't stop—*don't*—" she whined, chasing her release.

His left hand dropped lower until both were working her inside and out. "You're close, little siren," he whispered in her ear. "Your cunt is so tight. Come for me. Just do it quietly, or you'll wake the marchioness."

She swallowed her gasp, legs shaking as she shattered. Her greedy core clenched around his fingers, as she felt a wave of pleasure roll through her entire body.

"That's it," he murmured, his left hand moving back around her waist to help keep her standing. When her core stopped fluttering around his fingers, he pulled them out. They were both panting. "So wet," he murmured. "Such a goddess . . . just one taste."

She watched as he lifted his shiny fingers to his lips and sucked them clean. It was the most sensual thing she'd ever seen. If Rosalie was a goddess, Burke was surely a god—he stood there, dark hair sweeping over his brow, those haunting grey eyes locked on her. Now he had her taste on his tongue.

This man couldn't play a game fair if he tried. He was born to break the rules, to live outside them. Rules and conventions and social niceties were for mere mortals. Burke was something . . . *else*. They both were, she realized with a smile.

He pushed her gently back, willing her to look at him.

When she did, he stroked her cheek with an impossibly gentle hand. "Tell me this is real."

She knew he referred to the magic between them. The force that sent sparks flying like they were a pair of firecrackers. She stroked his face in return. He closed his eyes, leaning into her touch. His need was so genuine, so raw—to be accepted by her, to be wanted.

"Burke . . . look at me," she whispered.

He sighed against her hand, not opening his eyes.

"Look at me," she repeated.

His eyes opened: so vulnerable, so beautiful.

"This is real," she admitted. "Nothing has ever felt more real."

He dropped his head back to her uninjured shoulder, nuzzling his face against her hair as he took a deep breath. "I want you," he whispered. "Don't ask me to stay away."

She wrapped her arms around him, her petite frame dwarfed by his broad shoulders. She didn't know what this would mean for their futures, but heaven help her, in this moment she could only give him the truth. "I want you too."

He pulled her tighter against him. "Christ, love. Will you let me kiss you *now*?"

She smiled. "No . . . but that was a very valiant effort. I *shall* kiss you again, but not tonight."

He pulled back. "Why not?"

His look was so petulant, so pouting and pathetic, that she couldn't help but laugh. "Because you broke into my room quite uninvited and risked scandal and the ire of the Corbins, and we cannot reward such reckless behavior . . . as much as I might want to," she added with a smile, pressing her hip ever so gently against the proof of his own desire.

He groaned. "I miraculously healed your shoulder," he challenged.

"Hmm, I'm pretty sure Doctor Rivers did most of the work," she teased. "Now I think it best we say good night before we're caught."

He sighed and tipped her head back, about to give her a parting kiss. Realizing his intent, he pulled away with a scowl. "Fucking temptress," he muttered under his breath.

She understood his frustration. Kissing him felt like it ought to be the most natural act in the world. There was breathing, tying a bonnet ribbon, and now kissing Burke. She couldn't wait to do it again. But now that she'd drawn her line in the sand, she felt it only right she stick to it . . . at least for tonight.

Perhaps tomorrow. Yes, she felt quite sure that, after another night of restless sleep, another night of waiting and wanting and aching for his touch, all bets would be off.

41

Burke

BURKE WAS GOING to hell. That's what happened to men who stole things, right? Men who broke faith with their friends. Men who lied and cheated and manipulated others into getting what they wanted. Men who abused generosity and would happily see debts go unpaid. It was bad enough he could admit to having *one* of those vices. Surely, owning all of them together would earn him a place in the fiery pit.

But if Rosalie Harrow was his consolation prize here on earth, then Burke felt certain that burning in hell would be a perfectly lovely way to spend his eternity.

He shifted on the stiff bench, wedged as he was between James and the duchess in the duke's pew box. He gazed across the church to the other set of boxes, where the young ladies all sat listening to the Sunday sermon. Directly across from him sat the woman who had slowly begun to occupy his every thought.

Hello, sweet siren.

Rosalie wore her hair down, dark curls tumbling around her shoulders. A bonnet framed her face, tied with green ribbons. Her soft cheeks bloomed pink as she felt his gaze on her. She glanced up, and a jolt passed through him as their eyes met. Her blush deepened, and she was the first to look away, her gaze settling pointedly on old Mr. Selby as he continued to prattle on from his pulpit.

Burke cracked his knuckles in annoyance. He couldn't go to her last night, for the men kept him occupied too late with billiards and drinking. He could think of no excuse to leave when they needed a fourth for their game. By the time he managed to slip away, it was so late that all her lights were out. Had she waited for him?

"Stop fidgeting," James muttered.

He took a deep breath. If he looked overlong at Rosalie, his cock would get hard. He really didn't feel like having to explain a cockstand to the duchess.

God, but Selby knew how to prattle. Burke had no patience for the church. He only went out of obligation to the duchess. He didn't need Selby's sidelong eyes whenever he mentioned man's carnal lusts and appetites. Burke smirked. His appetites *did* tend towards carnality. Not that he made a habit of indulging. That was the thing about being the bastard son of a whore: He knew the very real ramifications of losing himself too deep to those lusts and appetites. He'd only let a rare one woman in fifty ever get close enough to indulge.

His mother may have been a whore, but Burke was not.

Which was why a very small part of him was glad he hadn't been able to go to Rosalie last night. She was his weakness. For her, he seemed ready to break all rules. The heat of her kisses, the feel of her wet sex. Did she ever pleasure herself? Would she let him watch? She admitted she wasn't a total novice, but she was still nervous, shaking and trembling in that sweet way that made his cock ache to be inside her, eager to teach her everything he knew.

He wanted her like he'd never wanted anything in his life. It was so much more than her beauty, her responsiveness, her exquisite taste—

Fuck, do not get a cockstand next to the duchess.

He took another breath, ignoring the raised brow James shot his way. No, Rosalie was . . . *more.* She was clever and caring. He loved the way she teased and liked being teased. Most of all, he loved the way she looked at him. Rosalie *saw* him. Not Burke the cocky bastard, Burke the Corbins' charity case, nor even Burke the sometimes-gentleman who could play at respectability. She saw through all those masks. When Rosalie looked at him, their eyes connected, and he felt seen.

It was heady. It was intoxicating. And he wanted more.

He sighed, looking over at Rosalie again. Her face was in profile. He followed the line of her gaze, and that monster that lay curled in the pit of his stomach rose its ugly head.

Fucking Renley.

When Renley admitted to being alone in her room, Burke had wanted to flatten him. Renley assured him nothing happened, but he knew exactly what kind of pull Rosalie had. If he had to watch her walk into Renley's waiting arms, he might die.

I want you too, she'd whispered. *This is real.*

"Burke," James muttered, jabbing him in the ribs.

He blinked, pulled from his thoughts to realize the sermon was over and everyone was getting to their feet.

"Burke, Christ, get up."

"Sorry," he muttered.

"What's wrong with you this morning?" James tucked his hair behind his ears as he adjusted his hat. "You're all in a daze."

The duchess cast him a side glance as she raised a hand and he quickly took it, ready to escort her out.

"Are you ill?" the duchess murmured.

"Not at all," he replied. "Fit as a fiddle."

"And did you enjoy the sermon?"

"*Mmm*, quite inspiring."

"He was speaking of tithing, Burke. It was duller than watching grass grow."

The carriage waited just outside the doors, and George stood beside it with the marchioness, ready to allow the duchess to be seated first.

"Do I want to know what distracted you so?" she said as he helped her within.

"I very much doubt it," he replied.

"Hmm." She arched one of her perfect brows. "And do I *need* to know?"

"I am confident James has me well trained by now."

Her other brow matched the height of the first before she lowered both, blue eyes narrowed. "All the same . . . I think I shall remind him to give your lead a tug."

"I look forward to the course correction," he said with a tight smile.

She pursed her lips and waved him away.

Two more carriages were lined up behind the first. Lady Gorgon and the Oswalds were settled in the middle carriage. The last carriage was saved for the Swindons, Lady Madeline, and Rosalie.

His eyes narrowed as he saw Rosalie standing off to the side of the carriage, hand draped casually on Renley's arm. They spoke quietly together, her face concealed by her bonnet. Damn, but he hated that about bonnets. Was she blushing again? He could see Renley's face clear enough. He had his brows knit together, his face all seriousness. *Fuck*, why did he look even more handsome when he was serious? It wasn't fair. Damn Burke's rotten luck that he had to compete with a bloody Adonis.

Burke was already moving, his feet crunching on the fine gravel, determined to step between them and know what new secrets they shared.

I want you too, she had whispered with love in her eyes. *Nothing has ever felt more real.*

By the time he wove through the crowd, Renley was helping Rosalie inside the carriage. He stepped back with a nod to the other ladies as the footman shut the door and flipped up the step. Burke stopped at Renley's side, noting the way Rosalie's eyes went wide at seeing them standing together. The carriage rattled into motion and her bonnet quickly blocked her face from view. He watched for a moment, waiting, but she didn't turn around.

"What was that about?" he muttered.

"Hmm?" Renley put on his dashing naval officer's hat.

"With Miss Harrow," he said, trying his best not to sound petulant.

He failed.

Renley's frown deepened. "I need to go to Town. I had planned to take luncheon at my brother's and leave from there. Will you tell James for me?"

Burke blinked, still distracted. "Town? That's rather sudden."

"I have some business to attend to," Renley replied. "I'll check in with the officer's club and have dinner with my captain."

Burke raised a dark brow. "But you'll be back in time for the ball?"

"Undoubtedly," Tom replied.

The truth hit Burke like a punch to the gut. Tom's agitation since returning from his brother's house, his serious looks, his quiet moods. "Oh, fuck's sake, Tom. She wrote to you, didn't she?"

Renley sighed. "Burke—"

"Christ, man, why didn't you say anything? When did she write? What did she say?"

Renley's jaw clenched. "She requested a renewal of our friendship. She asked to see me. I feel . . . I feel I should go."

Burke was suddenly at war with himself. Should he protect his friend, or sabotage him? Provide measured counsel that may lead Renley to stay and continue to pursue Rosalie, or gleefully throw him to the wolves?

Well, *a* wolf. A cunning actress of a she-wolf named Marianne Young.

"What will you tell her?" Burke asked.

"I hadn't . . . I'm not sure I've quite formed the words. I think I need to see her before I know for certain. But Rosalie said I ought to forgive her—"

"*Rosalie* said?" Burke's monster snarled. First, he hated hearing her name on Renley's lips almost as much as he hated hearing Renley's name on hers. Second, what did Rosalie say? His mind was spinning even as the monster began to purr. Rosalie wanted Renley to forgive Marianne. Would she dare do such a thing if she had designs on Renley for herself?

Yes. For she was the soul of heroism—salting the tea of gorgons, befriending frightened maidens, saving runaway horses, and seeing people for who they were instead of what society wanted them to be. She would shove Renley right into the arms of another woman if she thought it was what he wanted.

"Tom . . . have you brought Miss Harrow into your confidence about all this?"

Renley nodded. "Aye, she had many useful things to say on the matter." He chuckled dryly. "But damn if her tongue doesn't smart like the crack of a whip."

Burke *really* hated Renley making any mention of Rosalie's tongue. Christ, he wanted to taste it again, wanted it tracing along his collarbone, wrapped around his cock. *Fuck.*

"I think I may have been an arse all these years," Renley admitted. "She said something that's had me mindful the last two days. I can't let it go . . ."

Burke readied himself for the worst. "And what did she say?"

Renley met his eye. "It was about choices. About choosing to be happy."

"And . . . are you ready to choose to be happy?"

Renley gave him a half smile. "Not yet . . . but god, I hope soon." He clapped Burke on the shoulder. "You'll tell James I'm away?"

Burke nodded. "When shall you return?"

"A few days at the most. I'll see you when I see you." He gave Burke's shoulder a squeeze.

"Sure," Burke muttered. "See you when I see you."

He watched Renley walk off towards the far side of the church yard where Colin waited. Renley was leaving, and Rosalie had known before Burke. She *encouraged* him to go. What had they said to each other? What was Renley planning to do? Would he return from London heart-healed with Marianne Young on his arm . . . or perhaps heartsick for someone new? Perhaps a young lady with dark lashes, the softest curls, and the sweetest rosy blush . . .

42

Rosalie

ON HER RETURN from church, Rosalie went straight upstairs to deposit her bonnet and pelisse. She opened the door to her room and paused, hand still on the knob. "Sarah . . . what?"

"I don't know," the maid cried. "T'was all here when I came up to change the linens."

Rosalie took in the three large, rectangular dress boxes stacked on her bed. A blue hatbox sat next to them, and another small, yellow parcel sat atop the hatbox. The duchess hinted that Rosalie would have an allowance for dresses should she choose to stay, but she'd yet to give the duchess her answer.

"But . . . where did it all come from? I ordered nothing."

Sarah hurried forward. "The modiste in Carrington. There was a note on top, miss."

Rosalie took the envelope and slipped out the card within. It contained two short lines written in a slanting hand:

Consider this repayment for any damages.
Yours respectfully,
J.C.

EMILY RATH

Her heart fluttered. James Corbin. She slipped the card back inside the envelope and tucked it safely in her pocket.

"Who's it from?" Sarah pressed.

"Lord James," she replied, setting her bonnet on the chair as she stepped forward. She eyed the top box. It was the largest of the three. Swallowing her nerves, she lifted the lid and folded back the stiff paper.

"Oh, heavenly," Sarah whispered. "Did you ever see such a pretty blue?"

Rosalie couldn't contain her smile as she lifted out the dress, letting it fall in heavy folds to the floor. Not a dress . . . a new riding habit, with fashionable sleeves, a high collar, and beautiful, double-breasted silver buttons. It was the loveliest shade of robin's egg blue.

"This must have cost a pretty penny." Sarah touched the fabric with awe. "He must like you very much, miss."

Rosalie cleared her throat. "No, he's just being gallant because he blames himself for my fall," she replied. "I tore the sleeve of my habit, remember?"

Sarah blinked. "But . . . I've already mended that for you."

Rosalie fought her smile. "Help me with these other boxes."

In moments, Rosalie's eyes were misting as she took in all the pieces of a full riding ensemble. Not only had James replaced her torn habit with a far more extravagant one, he included a fashionable riding hat in a darker shade of navy, with a pretty net veil that swept across the face. There was also a new walking dress of softest butter yellow with ivory lace trim. The bottom box contained a new petticoat and stockings. In the smallest parcel was a pair of kidskin riding gloves, also dyed a fashionable dark blue.

No one had ever given her such an extravagant gift. Why

276

would he go to such trouble and expense? Her heart sank as she admitted the truth: She couldn't possibly accept it. Might it not send the wrong impression?

"Do you want to put on the new dress, miss?"

"No," Rosalie said too quickly. "No, I . . . I shall speak to Lord James first. I need to . . . I don't know that I can accept this . . ."

"Oh, but you *must*. He'll not be pleased if you decline."

Everyone in the house would surely take note of new clothes. Madeline already warned her that the other ladies were ready to sharpen their knives at the mere idea of Rosalie *talking* to Lord James. What might they think if she paraded about the house in all these fine things?

"Put it away for now, Sarah. Back in the boxes, if you please. I must . . . I'm going to speak to Lord James."

Sarah looked wary as she folded the dress. "I hope you know what you're doing, Miss. Lord James is not a person easily gainsaid."

Rosalie set her shoulders. "Unhappily for him, neither am I."

The door to the duke's study was ajar. Rosalie rapped twice and waited.

"Enter," a deep voice called.

She swung the door open, saying, "Lord James, please forgive the intrusion, but I—" She paused, blinking as she found the duke leaning back in his chair, feet propped up on the desk, a book open in his hands. "I—I'm sorry, Your Grace." She dipped into a curtsy. "I did not think to find you here. I was looking for Lord James . . ."

The duke scowled at her over the top of his book, snapping it shut with a huff. "Well, it is *my* study. I am the Duke of Norland, am I not?"

"Of course, Your Grace. I . . . I'll just go then." She took a few steps back.

"Not so fast," he said, swinging his legs off the desk. "Now that you've caught me alone, we may as well have it out. Sit down."

She stilled, eyes darting from the duke to the empty chair. "Have it out, Your Grace?"

"You clearly angled to find me alone," he said. "You must mean to have harsh words with me over my conduct the other day."

She swallowed her nerves. James said his brother would apologize for the scene in the servant's stairwell, but she never actually expected it of him. "Your Grace, I did not—this is not—I'd never dream of monopolizing a moment of your time."

He chuckled. "Relax, I had no idea of you actually looking for me. But take a seat all the same, for I am weary of work and need the distraction."

Work weary? It was a Sunday afternoon before luncheon. She glanced down at the book he'd set on the desk and saw from the cover it was a historical reference on battles from ancient Mesopotamia. Taking a breath, she stepped forward and sat in the chair he offered.

"Remind me of your name," he said, propping his elbows on the desk and crossing his fingers until he rested his chin atop them.

"Harrow, Your Grace," she said. "Rosalie Harrow."

"Yes, of course," he said with a grin. "The famous Cabbage Rose. Mama's little pet project. Has she offered to take you in yet? God, she collects strays like I don't know what."

She blinked, unsure how to respond. The duchess hadn't

yet given her permission to make their plans public knowledge. Perhaps her sons already knew?

"No need to answer if you fear you're in her confidence. But I had a feeling she might make you such an overture. How I'd *love* to know what secrets she holds that make her so interested in you. I've tried winkling them out of her, but the woman is a veritable vault of unknowable mysteries."

Rosalie stilled. Clearly, she was not the only one curious to know why the duchess was bothering to show her attention.

"You don't like me, Miss Rose. I can tell."

She tried to read his mood. "Your Grace, if I gave the impression—"

"No, it's fine," he said with a wave of his hand. "I have a nose for this sort of thing. I can sniff out disappointment better than my best pointer. Burke's right; you're the principled type, aren't you? You have to be principled, for you've got nothing else going for you."

She tried not to cringe. Burke was talking about her with the duke?

"You've no money, no status, no prospects of any kind from what I can see beyond that face and those tits," he said, gesturing with another wave.

As his eyes flicked down to her breasts, she fought the urge to slap her arms across her chest. Heat flooded her cheeks.

"I find people like you to be insufferable," he went on. "You see yourself as always in the right. My dear brother is just the same. It doesn't matter that he usually *is* right . . . that just makes him even more intolerable. Thank God he talked me out of marrying you the other day."

Rosalie felt like she'd just been thrown from a horse all over again. "You . . . what?"

The duke raised a brow. "James didn't tell you? Yes, we were picking names from a hat to choose my duchess, and your name was first out. But, in the end, he and Burke talked me out of it. Thank God too, for we would have driven each other quite mad, I've no doubt."

She felt faint. Lord James and Burke stood around with the duke drawing names from a hat? That's how they planned to choose the next duchess? She was sure if the duchess knew, she'd have the men horse whipped.

"As of now, the only thing you *do* have to your credit is the attention of my mother," he went on. "It's a curiosity, you see? It vexes me. What is your allure for her, Miss Rose?" He narrowed his eyes. "Your mother was friends with mine, yes?"

"I believe so," she replied.

He leaned back in his chair. "So, we must speculate wildly. An affair of the heart, perhaps? Love gone wrong? My money is on betrayal, for very little motivates my dear mother to act outside her own material benefit. Guilt is one of her few weaknesses."

Rosalie considered his words, letting her own imagination spin.

But he was watching her with a curious look on his face. "If I were a lesser man, I would use you to my own ends. Don't think I haven't considered it. With the way James and Burke are panting after you, it would be all too fun. It would drive them all quite mad to think I've formed a sincere attachment on you."

Rosalie couldn't help but flinch, leaning back slightly in her chair.

The duke scowled. "Oh relax, Miss Harrow. God almighty, there's those iron-clad principles again. Your perfect match is James, but he's too proud and stupid to see it."

Rosalie's heart fluttered at the words, even as she wanted to take the horse whip to herself. Siren indeed, luring not one but *three* men to dash themselves against her worthless rocks.

"Hmm, you know . . . if I *was* that better man, I might connive to bring you both together." He paused, his deep blue eyes, so like his mother's, inspecting her.

She shifted under his gaze. It didn't feel anything like when the others looked at her. She desperately wanted him to look away.

He huffed. "But James is an insufferable, self-righteous prig who can fight his own battles. I sincerely hope his cock rots off with longing for you."

Rosalie didn't know how to possibly respond to this, so said nothing.

The gong rang for lunch, and he stood, stretching his arms out to his sides. "If you get a chance to corner my mother, do see if you can't winkle out the reason why our mothers fell out. I'm betting ten guineas on a sordid betrayal. If I'm right, and you bring me proof, I shall happily pay you. If the betrayal leans in the direction of a secret love child, I'll double it."

Rosalie fought to contain her gasp, and the duke laughed.

He leaned down as he passed her chair. "Just imagine the cabbages you could buy with twenty guineas, eh Miss Rose?" Then he swept past her with a chuckle, making no attempt to escort her to the dining room.

She rose to her feet, her mind in a daze. She'd come to thank James for her new riding habit . . . or chastise him . . . now she couldn't quite remember which. Her head felt thickly fogged. Was the duchess a villain who'd used her mother abominably and now owed Rosalie a debt? The duke almost proposed? Burke and James knew and said nothing . . . James, who longed for her . . .

She didn't know how long she stood in the empty study, staring down at the book on ancient Mesopotamian battles, before a new, slightly surprised voice spoke behind her.

"Miss Harrow? What are you doing in here?"

She spun around to see James standing in the doorway. A surge of resentment shivered through her. "I was looking for you, my lord. I came to thank you for your kind gesture . . . but I'm afraid it will be impossible for me to accept. I'll make sure Sarah has the items returned to the modiste at once."

A muscle ticked in his jaw. "The purchases have already been made. I'll not have a debt between us."

"There is no debt," she replied. "But for me to accept such a needlessly extravagant gift would create one. Not to mention it would raise the ire of the other house guests. I'll ask you to please understand and take no offense."

His green eyes narrowed as he stepped fully into the room. "What happened?"

She smiled, knowing it didn't meet her eyes. "Nothing at all, my lord. I am merely ensuring that we avoid any awkward situations. We can't leave anything to *chance*, don't you agree?"

Before he could make a response, she curtsied and scurried away in search of the safety of the crowded dining room.

43
Rosalie

ROSALIE SLIPPED INTO the dining room on the heels of the Swindon sisters. She glanced quickly around to see Burke was already seated. He caught her eye and smiled. The seat next to him was open. She clenched her hands at her sides as she followed the Swindons to an empty chair at the opposite end of the table.

The group was lively as the ladies discussed the ball that was now only a week away, while the men discussed some case of political intrigue noted in the Sunday papers. Rosalie sat between Madeline and Mariah, who quickly swept her up into a loud conversation about ball gowns. She shifted uncomfortably in her chair, feeling the eyes of Burke and James flickering down the table at her. They'd been whispering, both wearing frowns, and now they wouldn't stop looking at her.

"Everything all right?" Madeline murmured.

"Perfectly fine," Rosalie replied, taking a bite of her food and not tasting it.

Burke and James are panting after you.

The duke knew. She wanted to die of mortification to think of him playing matchmaker. Who else knew? Heavens, was the whole table aware of the way the men kept looking her way?

"I realized earlier that we've been remiss, Lady Madeline," Burke called down the table.

Some of the chatter stalled as eyes glanced from Burke to Madeline.

"We promised you a sketching adventure and have yet to deliver. I've just been speaking with James, and we think tomorrow might be the perfect day—"

"Tomorrow the ladies go into Carrington for their final dress fittings," said the duchess from her seat at the end of the table.

"Tuesday, then," Burke replied with a smile. "Any of the young ladies are welcome to join," he added.

"What a capital idea," said the duke. "Where did you have in mind?"

Now all the young ladies were interested, twittering out ideas.

"By the lake would be lovely," called Blanche.

"Or the top of Finchley Hill," said Mariah.

"It could be an expedition," her sister added. "Painting and sketching for those so inclined, and perhaps a search for walnuts for us adventurers."

"But I didn't bring any of my watercolors," Mariah cried.

"Oh, I'm sure we can find suitable supplies," the duke replied. "I myself have been known to dabble in watercolors. In fact, I think I shall join the party."

There was much exclaiming at this, and Rosalie smiled as she saw how it annoyed Burke and James to have the duke insert himself into their plans.

The young ladies went on discussing possible sites and

Rosalie found she just couldn't help herself. What were the duke's words? *If I were a better man* . . .

"With so many wonderful options, I doubt we can go wrong," she said, immediately drawing all the eyes at the table. She leveled her gaze at Burke and James and smiled. "Perhaps we can leave it to fate and simply draw from a hat."

Both men went still as stone.

"Oh yes, what fun," said Mariah, clapping her hands.

"Where shall we get a hat to draw?" Blanche asked, looking around as if she meant to do it right there at the table.

"I believe Lord James has one you can borrow," Rosalie replied.

James' eyes blazed with violence as he shot his brother a feral look. The duke raised a glass in mock salute before flashing Rosalie a playful wink.

It was all Rosalie could do to avoid the looks of the gentlemen as she waited for lunch to end. As soon as the duchess excused herself, Rosalie slipped out of her chair too, desperate to escape. She took off down the hallway. Her feet gravitated towards the safety and comfort of the library.

"Miss Harrow—"

She kept walking, the tail of her sprigged muslin dress trailing the carpet.

Burke kept pace just behind her. "Rosalie—"

"Please don't," she panted, pushing her way through the doors into the sunny library. Her eyes darted around the room, desperate to determine if they were alone. She longed for it, even as she prayed there might be someone lurking along the shelves.

He shut the door behind them. "Rosalie, talk to me. Let me explain—"

"You don't need to explain, sir," she said, turning on her heel only when she managed to get a sofa between them. "His Grace explained everything."

Burke's countenance was stormy. He leaned over, his hands gripping the back of the sofa as if it were the only thing keeping him from launching over it and snagging her in his arms. "What the hell did George say?"

Her tongue flicked out to wet her lips and she nearly whimpered at his reaction—his eyes narrowed as his hands gripped tighter to the sofa. "That you are to blame for why I shall not be receiving an offer of marriage from His Grace."

His jaw tightened. "Tell me precisely. What did George say?"

She crossed her arms, eyes darting towards the door. "He told me about your decision to pick his new duchess by drawing names from a hat. My name was drawn first, and he resolved to marry me. That's when you lost your nerve."

"Fuck." He pushed off from the sofa. "Rosalie, that is *not* what happened."

Her eyes flashed with fire. "So, our names were *not* put into a hat with the indifference of choosing a raffle pie at a county fair?"

"Yes, but—"

"My name was *not* the first drawn from the hat?"

He pressed the palms of his hands against his eyes with another pained groan. "It was, but—"

"And was it not the point of the horrid game that the first name drawn would be the new duchess?"

He swept around the sofa towards her. "Goddamn it, Rosalie. *Listen*—"

Her back stiffened at his approach. "So, it would appear your meddling just cost me a duchess' coronet."

He stopped right before her. His grey eyes were thunderous. "You would marry George Corbin?"

She tilted her chin up in defiance, holding his gaze. "You would let me?"

"Never," he growled, leaning into her space, claiming her air. "I'd kill him first."

His hands shot out, fingers tangling in her hair as he pulled her close. She moaned, her own hands snatching his lapels. His lips descended, and he was just about to break his promise and kiss her when the door snapped open. Rosalie and Burke shot apart. She was trembling as she turned away, too embarrassed to see who caught them.

"What's going on in here?"

Her stomach flipped. This was too much. Alone with Burke and James in the same room? Let someone enter and save her. She hadn't the strength—

"Burke, what the hell is going on?" James' deep voice sounded murderous.

Rosalie spun around, her anger still boiling. "I was just thanking Mr. Burke for his interference that led me to be denied your brother's hand in marriage. Whose scheme was it?"

"I had nothing to do with this." Burke pointed a finger at his friend. "This was all James."

James went rigid, his eyes locking on Burke. "Shall I order the carriage brought 'round? Then perhaps you'll be so good as to *shove* me in front of it." He slammed Burke in the chest with both hands, sending him stumbling backward.

Burke recovered, shoulders squared as if he meant to take a swing at him.

"Enough," Rosalie cried, stepping forward with her hands raised. Her heart raced as both sets of eyes locked on her. "Just tell me what happened."

James looked away from Burke. "It was nothing. A harmless distraction for George. I was trying to keep him from running off. If he slips off the estate, I'll not catch him again for months. Hell, he may even follow through with his threats and immigrate to Australia at last."

"So . . . you never intended to pick a duchess by—"

"No," James said. "It was a game taken too far. It can be difficult to rein my brother in. Burke did nothing to encourage him. This was all me."

Rosalie let herself take a shallow breath. "So . . . you didn't want me to accept him?"

Both men were carefully quiet, casting a glance at each other she couldn't catch before Burke asked, "Would you have said yes?"

"No," she whispered. "Whatever my fate may be, I know it will not involve wearing a duchess' coronet. His Grace is quite safe from me." She could feel the sigh of relief neither man would let escape him. She fought her tremble as she let her eyes dart from one to the other. "I think you should both know something . . ."

"Know what?" James pressed.

"You should know that the duchess has made me an offer. She wants me to stay here . . . beyond the end of the season. She wants me to move into the house and serve as her ward."

Burke's eyes flashed with hunger, while James' belied a sentiment she could only describe as horror.

"Why would she do that?" James said with a glower.

"She, um . . . well, it's to do with His Grace, really. She doesn't believe he will secure a duchess interested in . . . being duchess. And Alcott must be managed."

"So, she's enlisting your help?" Burke glanced at his friend. "Imagine that, James. Your mother has found her own replacement and has seen fit to insert her right under your nose. What a happy little family we'll be: His Graceless and his idiot duchess, the dowager, the beleaguered shadow duke, the shadow duchess, and the bachelor bastard."

James shot him a look meant to quiet him.

Burke ignored him, his eyes back on Rosalie. "What conditions did she make?"

"She offered me room and board, an allowance for dresses—"

"Her conditions," Burke repeated. "The duchess never does anything without claiming some measure of control. How does she seek to control you, Rosalie?"

She fell quiet, her heart thudding dully in her chest.

"Just say it."

"I am to draw no attention to myself . . . of any kind," she added softly.

It was James who spoke this time. "Meaning what?"

She cleared her throat. "Meaning that I made it clear to the duchess I had no intention of ever marrying. She approves of my decision. It is that condition on which her offer hinges."

"Fucking hell." Burke stepped away.

James stood perfectly still, that muscle twitching in his jaw.

Rosalie chanced a look at him, for she didn't dare say the next words and look at Burke. "So, you see, Lord James, I must ask you not to include me in any more marriage schemes. If I am to stay here at Alcott, I cannot entertain them."

That muscle ticked again.

"But more to the point," she whispered. "I do not *want* such attention . . . from anyone."

Without waiting for either man to make a response, she slipped between them and made for the door. Neither tried to stop her as she fled.

44
Rosalie

"PAY ATTENTION, MISS Rose. You're all in a daze today." The duchess sat across from her, the plans for the ball spread out across the tea table between them.

"I'm sorry, Your Grace," Rosalie murmured, setting aside her teacup.

"I was saying I think I ought to move the Fords to table ten. Then I can move the Oswalds to table four, and that will open space for the Chamberlains at my table. Make note of it."

Rosalie scratched out the note. They'd been at this for two hours, making minute changes to set lists for the dances and moving couples to preserve the order of rank. All the while, Rosalie was distracted.

What is your allure for her, Miss Rose? We must speculate wildly . . .

"Tomorrow, I'll do a final check with the cooks, the florist, and Mrs. Davies," the duchess continued.

An affair of the heart, perhaps?

Rosalie pushed his words away. "Shall I attend you, Your Grace?"

"Of course not," the duchess replied. "You'll need to be in town with the others to get your dress sized."

Rosalie nodded, but she hardly heard the words. The duchess was showering Rosalie with blessings—debts and medical expenses paid, new dresses, a position in this house. What Rosalie didn't understand was *why*. There had to be a reason beyond citing an old childhood friendship. She didn't even notice she was standing when she spoke with a voice not quite her own. "Why are you doing this?"

The duchess frowned, peering over the top of her list. "I told you, Miss Rose, you can't stand at my side dressed in whatever bit of old lace you brought with you—"

"I'm not talking about the dress," Rosalie snapped. Her heart thundered in her ears. "Why do you want me here?"

The duchess lowered the papers with a huff. "We've been through this already—"

"No, not why you *want* me here," she said. "Why do you want *me* here? Me, Rosalie Harrow. What am I to you?"

The duchess' nostrils flared at being cut off. "Sit down, Miss Harrow, before your remarkable rudeness begins to offend."

Rosalie sank back onto the sofa. "Your Grace, please don't leave me in the dark. I *must* know. Why did you fall out with my mother? What did you do?"

The duchess' face was set in a determined scowl. "You dare presume *I* am at fault?"

She couldn't back down now. "Yes, Your Grace . . . and I am not the only one with questions—"

"You've been speaking to my sons," the duchess huffed again. "I thought you had the good sense to keep our conversations private, Miss Harrow. I don't recollect giving you permission to speak freely as it concerns me."

"His Grace approached me," she protested. "And the others in this house hate me. They despise the attention you give me. If I am to weather it, I must know why."

"Of course, George would rile you up. He's been nagging me for weeks. James asked at first, but I cowed him with threats of exorbitant spending. He was always easier to manage." She glanced up, eyes narrowed on Rosalie. "Let me put it to you like this. If I won't tell my own sons my motives, what makes you think I would ever disclose them to you?"

Rosalie took a steadying breath. "Because I believe you when you say you loved my mother. And I believe the reason you fell out is because she wanted nothing more to do with you . . . and my mother was not the type to form resentments easily."

The duchess watched her with pursed lips.

Rosalie leaned forward. "So, I believe you must have done something you regret that resulted in *her* walking away from *you*, denying herself the help and comfort of having a duchess for a friend, even when it could have prolonged her life."

A flicker of emotion passed over the duchess' face. The duke said guilt was her motivator. Rosalie had to use it. "It was brutal, Your Grace," she said on a whisper. "Elinor suffered to the very end. The coughs, the fevers, the slow dying of it all. At any moment she could have reached out to you, written to you, begged your help . . . but she didn't."

A single tear slipped down the duchess' cheek.

"Whatever you did was unforgivable," Rosalie went on. "Beyond any pains suffered at the hands of my father—and believe me, there were many—*your* sin was sealed inside her heart. So, I find myself in the awkward position of either respecting my mother's wishes and having nothing to do with you . . . or accepting your generosity. To make this decision, you must tell me: What did you do?"

The duchess wiped a finger under her eye. "I was married to the duke for thirty-two years. In all those years I never loved him . . . and he never loved me. I had his children, I supported this estate, I catered to his politics . . . I ignored his string of whores." She paused. "The gambling, the debts, the poor investments . . . I kept this estate together and I *never* made a complaint. I made sure the names 'Corbin' and 'Norland' shined like silver."

"I'm sure you've been essential—"

"And I never complained, because I made my choices, Miss Harrow. I chose advancement over love."

Rosalie waited, sure the point must be coming soon.

The duchess narrowed her eyes at Rosalie. "I will tell you what you want to know, but it will go no further than the two of us. And once I've told you, you will never mention it again. If you ever dare speak it aloud, I will deny the truth of it as I see you to the door."

Heart fluttering, Rosalie gave a slow nod of agreement.

The duchess sighed. "I never loved the duke, and he never loved me. He was in love with another . . . with my dearest friend."

Rosalie's heart skipped a beat as her eyes went wide.

The duchess knew she was understood. "Yes, the fifth duke was in love with Elinor Greene. They met in London at some society event. Elinor wrote to me and told me of their passion." She paused. "I arrived in London. I saw their attachment and tried to win him away, but he was besotted."

Rosalie felt an ominous air fill the room as the duchess went on.

"There was a society ball, and he became deep in his

cups. I saw my chance, and I took it." She cleared her throat. "When we learned of my pregnancy, he proposed. George was born eight months later."

Rosalie leaned back with an ache in her chest. "And my mother?"

The duchess shifted uncomfortably. "Naturally, it broke her heart. Not only the betrayal of her lover, but the betrayal of her friend. Later I heard reports . . . from your Aunt Thorpe . . . she had a stillborn daughter one week after the birth of my George. You see, she was too late to tell the duke she was pregnant . . . and then too proud to ask him to break his promise to me. After all this time, that is the shame that has burrowed deepest in my heart. She didn't fight. The duke wasn't worth it . . . and neither was I."

A tear slipped down Rosalie's cheek. "You were both so young."

"I knew better."

"It was a mistake—"

"I knew better," she snapped. "And my jealousy cost me everything. Cost *us* everything. I was trapped in a loveless marriage, and she trapped herself too." She reached distractedly for her cup of tea.

Silence stretched between them.

"So, Miss Harrow, you have a choice to make. Walk away now, and hate me as you should, as your mother did until she died. Or accept my apology and let me care for you in the way I could never care for her. I denied her a chance at this life. I can rectify it with you. I'd like the chance to try."

Rosalie's mind raced. The duchess trapped her duke in marriage, breaking Elinor's heart and resigning her to a life with a husband she hated. Elinor died wretched and alone with nothing but bad debts and broken dreams. Meanwhile, the duchess lived like a queen, surrounded by comforts. But Rosalie saw the truth: The duchess had lived unhappily too. She mentioned infidelity, debts, loneliness. Despite all odds, Rosalie found herself feeling sorry for a duchess. She glanced up, tears in her eyes. "Do you regret what you did?"

"Every day," the duchess replied.

They were both quiet for another moment.

"Do you think it would have worked between them," Rosalie whispered at last. "Was their love enough?"

"The fifth duke was entirely his own creature, with his own habits and failings. But they were young and in love . . . so perhaps."

"I have no need for pretty words, Your Grace. Please, just tell me."

The duchess pursed her lips. "No, Miss Rose. Knowing them both as I do . . . as I *did* . . . I doubt very much she would have been happy had they ever married . . . but she would have been rich," she added with a sad smile. "And that is its own kind of happiness, I suppose." She cleared her throat. "But enough of all that. You know my side now, and you must do as you see fit."

Rosalie's heart was tight in her chest. "I think I need some time, Your Grace. I need . . . this is a heavy truth to ponder."

The duchess narrowed her eyes but gave a curt nod. "Fine. Now, let us discuss George. Is he ready to make a sensible decision?"

Rosalie stilled. This felt like a new kind of trap. Gossiping about the other ladies was one thing, but she couldn't possibly be expected to speak openly about the duke in front of his mother.

As if the duchess saw her thoughts, she huffed. "Come,

come, surely the two of us have crossed the ocean of rank in the last ten minutes. Tell me your thoughts, for we cannot afford for this to go wrong. Which lady should my son pick? You've spent more time with them, and I need your opinion."

Rosalie took another breath. "His Grace is a charismatic person. He is an entertainer . . . and he likes to be entertained. He likes spectacle . . ."

The duchess narrowed her eyes. "What are you implying?"

"None of the girls interest him," she replied. "They are wholly unspectacular in his eyes." She looked back on her own encounters with the lord and stifled a smile. "In fact, I think it possible he has not even bothered to learn our names."

The duchess scowled. "You think he means to choose none of them."

"I think if he does choose one, it will be under duress, yes. Perhaps if there was a lady with a little more . . . excitement. It may mean that Your Grace will have to do away with a few qualifications on your list . . . perhaps less fortune, or a name that is not quite so polished. But if she had an air about her of mystery or excitability or—"

"*Shh*, enough." She stood, the sample menus tipping onto the carpet and scattering. "Oh, you are brilliant. I believe there is still time. I shall send out the invitation at once." She rushed over to her desk and began scribbling a note. "Fawcett!"

The door opened and a footman entered. "Your Grace?"

"Tell Reed I have an urgent letter to post. It needs to get to London straightaway."

"Very good, Your Grace." He bowed his way out, and the duchess stayed at the desk, finishing her note.

"Shall I go, Your Grace?"

Silence as the duchess continued to scribble. Rosalie

watched as she finished with a flourish and set the ink, already preparing wax to seal it.

"Your Grace?" Rosalie tried again.

"*Hmm?* Yes, off you go," she said with a wave of her hand. "You've been most helpful. This idea is possibly one of my best."

Rosalie turned towards the door.

"Oh, and Miss Rose . . ." The duchess' voice was hard again. "Remember, breathe a word of this to anyone, and I will hound you to the ends of the Earth." She stood with her head held high, surrounded by all the finery of the estate she connived to earn for herself. She was not a woman to be crossed. Ever.

Rosalie swallowed and nodded, seeing herself out.

45

James

THIS WAS A bloody disaster. How did everything go so wrong? James stormed down the gallery. There were only a few places Burke would hide, and James knew them all. He'd already checked the small library.

James had thought his suffering would be over at the end of this week. He was letting himself pine until after the ball. Then Miss Harrow would go, and his life could return to normal. He was hoping for it, waiting for it, needing it like he needed air. She would go, and all would be as it was before. She would *fucking* go.

But no, Rosalie had just smashed that dream with a hammer, and now he was living inside a nightmare. Of course, his mother wanted her to stay. Someone had to learn to be the duchess, and George was certainly incapable of attracting the right sort for himself. So, his mother managed everything. Rosalie would move into his home. She would greet him every morning and discuss menus and plan village bazaars. She would walk his park and use his baths and be always underfoot until he gave in to his desires and claimed her body and soul—

No. There will be no claiming of any kind.

She was only here under the express condition that she make no attempts to woo or be wooed. Trust his mother to set impossible standards for everyone. But this was so much worse. It wasn't enough that Rosalie couldn't accept his sincere attention. She had looked him square in the face and admitted she didn't *want* to accept. She fled the library, and James didn't dare follow. Burke left soon after.

Bloody hell, James should have stepped in sooner. Burke didn't give his heart away easily. Ever. Burke *never* gave his heart away. If this little vixen thought she was going to be the one to take it and shred it in her hands . . .

He took a deep breath. He needed to find Burke.

As children, they liked to play in the storage rooms—games of hide and seek, burrowing under old tables and behind frameless art. Over time, James arranged himself a reading nook in the corner. It was just a faded chaise wedged behind a folding screen, but it was angled just right to catch the light. Once Burke found it, James was resigned to fighting him for the spot. It had been their favorite hideaway ever since, far from the bustle and noise of the main house.

James entered the red room and sighed. Burke's riding boot was sticking out from behind the screen. He wove his way across the room, stepping over a rolled carpet and around a dented suit of armor. "Sulking, are we?"

"Get lost," Burke muttered. "I was here first." He was stretched out on the chaise, his coat flung over the back, cravat untied. He had one arm raised up over his face, blocking his eyes from the harsh sunlight. In his other hand, he held a glass of brandy.

James sighed, leaning against the wall. "It's a bit early for brandy, don't you think?"

"If we set our conduct by George's standards, I'm merely catching up." Burke sat up and drained the glass, setting it down with a clatter. "I can't take a sanctimonious speech right now. Try again after I've had a few more of these."

As Burke reached for the decanter, James leaned over top of him and snatched away the glass. Burke righted himself, reaching for the glass, and glowered.

"I have no speeches to give," James said, rolling the glass gently between his hands.

"Yeah, right," Burke scoffed.

Burke showed his hand in the library. It was only right James do the same. This was new territory for them. They'd never lusted after the same woman before. But Burke meant more to him than any passing infatuation. He sighed, setting the glass down. "I am not such a hypocrite to think you warrant a speech and I do not."

Burke stilled, lifting his head off his hands. His expression shifted from wary jealousy to surprise. "Christ," he sighed with a shake of his head. "She got to you too."

"Not quite in the same way I believe she may have gotten to *you* . . ."

Burke made no response. Apparently, he wasn't in a sharing mood. But James had to know. "How far has it gone? Should I be—"

"We kissed," Burke admitted. "I kissed her . . . she . . . we kissed."

"When?"

"When I found her at the edge of the wood," Burke muttered. "She stumbled out looking like some kind of forest nymph. Her petticoats deep in mud, eyes wild. She was so . . . *alive*. I couldn't stop myself. It was like she was the shore and

I the tide." He glanced up, grey eyes hardened. "I'm not sorry it happened."

"What do you intend to do now?"

Burke shrugged. "Leave for the continent, I suppose. Join the military? Tom has been on me enough about the opportunities naval life can afford. Or perhaps I'll join George when he makes his trek to Australia."

"Burke, don't be rash—"

Burke dragged his hands through his hair. James had never seen him this way about a woman. "If she's moving into this house, and pushes me away, I can't stay," Burke muttered. "She thinks it can just be about sex, that I'll pine after her body and not want to claim her soul. She's mad. She doesn't understand the power she holds over me. I can't be here watching her, feeling her presence in every room. I can't see her face everywhere, hear her voice, and not be with her. It would haunt me, James. I can't—"

"That bad?"

"Worse," Burke croaked, his face a mask of misery.

"Let's just . . . get through this week. If Miss Harrow is staying, we'll have time to sort things out. For now, we need a plan for Tuesday."

Burke flopped back on the chaise. "What about it?"

James kicked the heel of his booted foot. "Your brilliant idea for a sketching party. Where do you want to take them?"

"I don't bloody care—"

"I am not doing this by myself. Get your head out of your arse and stop moping. You are not falling apart over a girl you've known for two goddamn weeks. You wanted to take the ladies sketching, now tell me where. Finchley Hill? The west lawn?"

Burke just scowled.

"Fine. You're bloody useless." He turned away.

Burke's voice called through the screen. "The waterfall . . . in the woods, by the—"

"The old mill," James finished. It wasn't a waterfall, more of a slight declination that made for some rapidly flowing water. But it was still a lovely spot, full of fond memories. As boys, they played knights and kings in the abandoned mill, using it as their keep.

"Make it a picnic," Burke muttered. "Blankets on the grass by the stream's edge."

"It's a fine idea," he replied. "I'll arrange everything." Then he paused, not quite believing what he was about to say. He was glad Burke was hidden behind the screen. "She never said she wasn't interested in you; she's just not interested in getting married. Perhaps she has a good reason. Perhaps that reason can change . . . given the right incentive."

He could feel Burke's stillness. "You would approve?" Burke muttered through the screen. "You would let me have her?"

James forced a laugh. "I doubt very much there would be any 'letting' you do anything when it comes to Miss Harrow. And don't forget Renley's interest. He might come back from London a changed man . . ."

Burke scrambled off the chaise. "Rosalie told him to forgive her. He's going to throw himself at Marianne again. If anything, he'll probably come back engaged. And she doesn't want him like that. He said she was adamant they be nothing but friends."

James met his gaze. "Right . . . like the two of you are just friends . . ."

Burke's eyes roiled with storms. Yes, Renley was most

assuredly in this contest too. These idiots were fighting for the hand of a woman who didn't want to be won, a woman who was just as much a fool for not realizing she'd already won. Both men could be hers for the taking. Christ, what a joke.

James was so busy for the rest of the day, he hardly had a moment to turn his attention to the problem of the unsuitable Miss Harrow. The afternoon ran so long, he missed dinner. By the time he returned home, he headed straight for his chambers, where he had his valet prepare a steaming hot bath. It was only when he was settled in the bath, steam spiraling off the water's surface, that he let himself think about her.

For all he knew, Burke had approached her today. Did they kiss again? Did she whisper sweet nothings in his ear, promises to love him forever, like Marianne had to poor Tom? Would she do the same to Tom when he returned from Town?

That didn't seem like her style. To own the truth, she'd impressed him in their time together. There was an honesty to her that he could appreciate, for it mirrored his own. She said what was on her mind, and she didn't hold back . . . but she also didn't seek to harm. That was rare in a person in general, and virtually unheard of in a woman. For what lady did not secretly live to tear others down?

But this was an infatuation and nothing more. Burke may be ready to make a fool of himself, but James had a family, a title, a reputation. He couldn't go ruining himself over a passing fancy. And that's all Rosalie Harrow was. Then he would let nature take its course. For when had he not eventually found fault with every girl he'd ever fancied?

A sudden thought had him sitting up in the tub, sloshing water over the side. He was taking Rosalie sketching . . . but she wasn't in possession of her sketchbook. He very much doubted she retrieved it herself, likely too traumatized by seeing George's hairy arse. And servants never had occasion to go up to the roof . . . unless George was in the mood for a shag with a view. No, the sketchbook was probably still there in the dark of the stairs.

He finished his bath and snatched up a candle. This late at night, there would be no one walking the halls, so he didn't care he was barefoot with his shirt undone. He pulled on his favorite green silk banyan and stalked out of his room. He moved down the dark hall, passing George's suite. He paused for a moment, listening for sounds within. There came the un-mistakable sounds of giggling—masculine and feminine.

Fucking George.

James stalked down the hallway, his candle flickering as he paused before his least favorite painting in the house. What the hell was wrong with that horse? If James ever became duke, one of his first acts would be to see it taken down and burned in the yard.

He pushed through the servant's door and took the few steps spiraling up to the next landing. The stone was cold against his bare feet. He paused. There on the steps was Rosalie's abandoned sketchbook, spine bent, pages abused. He picked it up and flipped it over. His eye flickered over the page and his heart stilled.

It was *him*. She hadn't drawn anything above his nose, but he knew his own face well enough to recognize the shape of his jaw, his lips. She'd clearly put time and effort into shaping them just right. Had she been watching him? Or was it done from memory? Either way, it made his cock twitch.

He knew it was wrong. This was a lady's private sketchbook. He may as well be reading her diary. But he found himself dropping down to the stone stair. He set his candle a few steps above him and leaned back, holding the sketchbook in both hands as he flipped through the pages. Most were done with ink or charcoal, but some were colorful pastels—flowers in a vase, the Swindon sisters, a handsome sketch of a horse in profile. And then his chest tightened. Renley smiling, his mouth quirked at the corner, his handsome officer's hat pulled low over his brow.

He flipped the page and felt his chest grow tighter. Burke in profile. Burke's stormy eyes. Burke's hands. How did James know the man so well he could identify him by his hands alone? How did Rosalie know his hands so well she could draw them from memory?

He flipped the page. Another sketch of James. The general shape of his face was there, with some hatching filling in his jaw. The only defined feature was his lips. Two sketches. A study of James Corbin's mouth. Bloody fucking hell. All she had to do was ask, and he would show her what his mouth could do. What sketches might she draw, then?

A rattling below made him jump, and he snapped the sketchbook shut. Who the hell would be moving around at this hour? He snatched up his candle and stood, tucking the sketchbook under his arm as he spiraled down the stair. His brows lowered as he readied to catch a pair of servants in a midnight tryst.

"Who's there," he barked.

He swung around the corner to see Rosalie yip and step back, nearly tumbling down the stairs. Her candle tipped off its stand as she smacked it against the wall. He shot an arm out and caught her, closing the space between them, turning her towards the wall. He dropped her sketchbook and caged her in with his arms. It all happened in a blink.

"Heavens," she panted.

He took in her flushed face, her dark hair tumbling around her shoulders. She wore a nightshift with only a blue velvet robe to cover her nakedness.

"Why is there always a Corbin in this stairwell?" she hissed, slipping out from under the cage of his arms.

He couldn't help but grin. "Well . . . it *is* our house."

Her eyes dropped to take in his open shirt and bare feet. Flustered, she sank to her knees, reaching for her candle in the dark.

"What are you doing up here?" he said, voice low. His eyes caught on the little yellow ribbon in her hair. He fought the urge to reach down and tug loose the bow. He wanted her hair completely down, framing that heart-shaped face.

"I came for my sketchbook," she replied. She righted herself and met his gaze, always so defiant. "I could ask you the same."

His grin widened as he visualized her drawing his lips with such care. "*I* came for your sketchbook."

She gasped a little breath. It sounded so good, he wanted to find a way to make her do it again. He prayed she wouldn't see the way his cock was half hard for her. When was the last time he was alone with a woman? He couldn't think. She smelled heavenly. Something floral and spiced. It filled his senses, tugging at some memory he couldn't place. Was it frankincense?

"Where is it, then?"

He watched her mouth make words. If he had any talent, he might return the favor and make a study of sketching *her* lips. Wait, she was speaking. What did she say? God, he was an idiot. How could a woman make him feel so out of control? Why was she still looking at him like that? Oh right, they were speaking. He took a breath. "What?"

"My sketchbook," she said on a huff, hands on her hips. "You said you had it."

He glanced around. "I dropped it. I was rather distracted by the damsel threatening to tumble down my stairs."

She glanced around, spotting it with a little gasp. She bent down and snatched it up, tucking it under her arm. Her cheeks were still deeply flushed as she held out her snubbed candle. "Would you give me a light, sir?"

He dropped down a step and held out his candle. The new flame flickered into life, expanding the circle of light around them. He watched the twin flames dance in her dark eyes. They stood there in the quiet, chests rising and falling as they breathed. Christ, she was so beautiful. He wanted to touch her face—those dark brows, her full lips, her blushing cheeks. Would she let him? Would she ever crave his touch like she did Burke's?

Damn it . . . Burke.

Burke was in love with her, mad for her . . . and here was James, coveting her for himself, daring to jeopardize his friend's happiness. Burke called her the shore pulling in tides, but James knew better, for was he not feeling the same inescapable pull? James had been suffering under the delusion that when Rosalie left, the urge to be near her would ease. Out of sight, out of mind.

But Rosalie Harrow was not the shore. She was the moon. There would be no escaping her pull for either of them . . . *any* of them. The moon is everywhere—always coaxing, always claiming. Even when she cannot be seen, she is felt. And James felt her everywhere.

Damn it all to hell.

Those beautiful dark eyes were trying to read him. Impossible.

He had to shut these thoughts down. He refused to get involved. More importantly, he refused to hurt Burke.

Walls, James. Retreat.

He shut down his emotions, finding the strength to detach. He saw recognition flicker in her eyes as if she knew exactly what he was doing.

Her countenance fell. "I'll just . . . I'll go then . . ."

"Yes. Good night, Miss Harrow."

He frowned. Why wasn't she moving? She was just standing there, holding tight to her candle like it was a shield and he a dragon. Was she afraid of him? He lowered himself down a half step, and she pressed herself back against the wall, giving him more space to pass by.

"After you," he muttered, gesturing down the stairs.

She turned and their shoulders brushed in the narrow space. He was fighting the urge to reach out again—

SLAM.

"What was that?" she whispered, nearly stumbling back against his chest.

James' every sense was on high alert. One hand braced her hip to steady her.

"Frigid *whore!*"

46

Rosalie

JAMES LED THE way down the stairs, flinging the door open. Rosalie slipped out behind him and gasped as she took in the scene. The doors to the duke's room were flung wide, light pooling into the hallway. Lady Olivia sat on her knees in nothing but her chemise, a few mussed curls framing her face. She sobbed into her hands as the duke tossed her clothes into the hall. First a shoe, then her beaded silk dress, her stays.

"Just get out—waste of time—"

James blew out his candle, dropped it to the floor, and charged towards his brother before Rosalie could reach out a hand to stop him.

The duke saw his approach with wide eyes. He lifted his hands in defense. "Not the face—*not* the face," he squawked as James lunged for him.

The Corbins crashed into the duke's rooms as James punched every piece of his brother he could reach.

Rosalie dashed forward.

"Get her out of here," James barked through the doorway, his arms around his brother's neck on the floor of the plush blue carpet. The duke tried to squirm free.

"Where?" Rosalie rasped. She didn't know this part of the house well enough.

"Water closet—" James grunted. "Three doors down—"

Rosalie put a hand on Olivia's shoulders, still holding her candle. "Come on, we have to move. They'll wake the whole house with that racket."

Olivia just kept sobbing.

Rosalie dropped to her knees and snatched up Olivia's dress and stays one-handed, trying to hold her candle still with the other. "You have to get up. *Now.* Come with me, or the house will find you here and you'll be ruined."

Olivia gave a weak nod, and Rosalie flung her hand with the candle around her shoulders, pulling her to her feet. They shuffled down the hallway. Rosalie opened the door to the water closet and pushed Olivia inside, shutting the door and locking it. Olivia sank back to her knees. Rosalie dropped the clothes to the floor and set the candle on the washstand, leaning against the door as she fought to control her breathing. She could still hear the men arguing through the door.

"Unacceptable—"

"Her idea—came on to me—"

"Fucking *kill* you—"

She let Olivia cry for a few minutes as a door slammed. Then another. James had enough control of the situation to get the duke back behind closed doors. She heard the unmistakable sound of feet trotting down the hallway. More than one pair. Probably footmen.

Muffled voices.

Knocks on the far door.

All the while, Olivia continued to cry.

Rosalie shrugged out of her robe and dropped to her knees,

Olivia scoffed. "I never even met him. I had a miniature portrait of him that hung on a green ribbon, and two letters." She shrugged. "But he died, and that was that. It took almost two years before I secured another offer—the second son of the new Marquess of Bath. Johnny was a lovely lad, and I fancied myself lucky to get him. He was so handsome . . . *is* so handsome . . ." Her voice trailed away as her gaze fell to the floor.

"What happened?" Rosalie whispered.

Olivia gave a bitter laugh. "Why should he settle for a marquess' daughter when he could marry the daughter of a duke? He jilted me for Maude Manners, eldest daughter of the Duke of Rutland. They just had their second child." Her voice turned quiet. "I was invited to the christening . . . Mama and I came to Alcott instead . . ."

Rosalie's heart ached for her. Wealth and status were certainly no guarantee of happiness in this life. "What happened tonight?" Rosalie murmured. "Did His Grace—"

"No," Olivia rasped. "It was me. I can't—I couldn't—I needed this to go well. I couldn't face returning to Town without . . . God, I'm so embarrassed."

Rosalie tried to put the pieces together. The duke throwing her out, his calloused words. "You couldn't go through with it," she whispered.

"I thought I could," Olivia replied, cheeks red. "We've been dancing around each other for days. Flirting and a few stolen kisses. Tonight, I let myself into his room and I . . . I tried. I just . . . couldn't—"

Rosalie sighed with relief to know that—whatever else he might have done—the duke didn't force her.

"I don't think I'll survive another year on the circuit," Olivia muttered. "What man will tip his cap at a twenty-seven-year-old maid?" Her voice broke. "I—I've ruined everything. I should never have—oh *god*!"

Rosalie flipped forward onto her knees and pulled the woman into her arms. Olivia slumped against her shoulder, sobbing. "*Shh*," she murmured. "You did nothing of which you should be ashamed."

Olivia jerked away. "What do you know about any of it?" she spat. "How could you possibly understand?"

Rosalie sighed. There was the delightful gorgon. She gave the lady a stern look. "Believe it or not, I know the way the world works too. I know the pressure you're under, even if I do not feel the same pressure in quite the same way."

Olivia had the good sense to look slightly less haughty. "I'm sorry," she muttered. "God, I'm such a bitch. I hate who I am—who I've become. You know, I used to be a good person. I used to be more like those idiot Swindons."

Rosalie couldn't help but smile, seeing how Olivia couched her compliment in an insult. "We survive the best we can. That's all you're doing," she added. "You're surviving, and I'm surviving, and there's nothing wrong with that."

Olivia took a steadying breath. "I hate him," she whispered. "He's a disgusting pig and I *hate* him. I'll die before I marry him."

Rosalie tucked a curl behind Olivia's ear. "He doesn't deserve you." A sudden thought occurred to her. She felt instinctively this was the right course of action. Olivia needed this affirmation. "Do you know what they call you?" she whispered.

Olivia blinked. "Who?"

"The men in this house," Rosalie replied. "They call you Lady Gorgon. They see you as some mythical monster. You are fierce and untamable. Men don't like a woman who defies expectations, a woman that unabashedly shows her strength. It angers them. I think they would like to be Perseus and slay you."

Olivia's eyes were wide as she listened.

"I think you should *use* it," Rosalie whispered. "Be yourself. Be fierce and don't apologize for it. You are Lady Olivia Rutledge, daughter of the Marquess of Deal. You are one of the most illustrious women in the land. Do not waste your time with the likes of George Corbin or any other man who cannot contend with your strength."

A spark of hope flickered in her eyes. Olivia wanted to believe. "But . . . I must marry . . ."

Rosalie laughed. "You are the daughter of a marquess. Your brother will be a marquess. You don't *have* to do anything. You could remain unmarried and never want for a thing. Better to be unmarried and free, then marry George Corbin and be trapped."

Olivia's eyes narrowed. "Is that why you are unmarried? Your fear of being trapped? You have all the beauty, charm, and wit a man might desire. I see the way the men here watch you. You could have any of them kneeling at your feet."

Rosalie shrugged. "I know what marriage is . . . or perhaps I should say I know what *bad* marriage is. Until I can be convinced that not all marriages turn sour, I shall never allow myself to walk into such a trap."

Before Olivia could reply, there was a soft knock on the door. "It's me," came James' voice. "The coast is clear."

They scrambled to their feet, and Rosalie helped Olivia dress. Olivia put the stays on without tying them, slipping her gown up over her shoulders. Rosalie fastened her in, while

Olivia smoothed down the front. Rosalie moved to the door and unlocked it, swinging it open to reveal James.

He stood in the dark hallway, no candle lit. "Lady Olivia, words cannot express—"

"Please," she whispered. "I think it's best we all say nothing."

He nodded and held out her satin slippers.

Olivia took them with a steady hand. She passed through the door, pausing to look back at Rosalie. She gave a curt nod and disappeared into the darkness.

Rosalie looked through the doorway at James. Some unspeakable tension settled between them.

"Is she all right?" he whispered.

"I think she will be," Rosalie replied.

"George didn't—"

"No. Olivia stopped it before . . ." She fell silent and he nodded.

"And you, Miss Harrow? Are you all right?"

What could she say? Was she all right? Did she even know? For a moment on the stairs, she thought he might kiss her. He was leaning in, those green eyes blown black with desire. Did poor Atlas ever let himself feel an emotion as useless as lust? He was so focused on caring for everyone else, being everyone's strength, a veritable fortress of calm and control. How she longed to muss his hair just to feel like one thing was out of place.

Every soul in this house—in the whole county—was cared for in one way or another by Lord James Corbin, Viscount Finchley. Perhaps he needed a solitary friend who would care for *him*. She found herself aching to fill the role.

He raised a brow, still waiting for her response.

"Yes, my lord," she whispered. "I'm perfectly well."

He shifted awkwardly, focusing his attention at a point over her shoulder. "Miss Harrow . . ."

What was wrong now? Her nerves were already frayed. "What?"

He cleared his throat. "You were wearing a robe before . . ."

She gasped, looking down to see she was only in her chemise. The material was thin, and it hung off one shoulder. Heaven only knew how much of her he could see. Surely, he'd noticed the naked curve of her collarbone, the swell of her breast. She ducked down behind the door and snatched up her robe, shrugging it on. "I used it to block the light," she whispered hurriedly, tying it closed. "I didn't want a footman to see us."

"That was quick thinking," he replied, slightly less uncomfortable now that her breasts were off display.

"I'll, umm . . . bid you good night, then," she whispered.

His jaw tightened as he stepped back with a nod. Ever the gentleman, he seemed determined to prove he was in control. There would be no late-night kisses in the hall, not after the duke's disgusting display.

She took a few steps, pausing to glance over her shoulder. He stood there in the dark, watching her with that miserable, strained expression on his face. "You're not like him," she whispered. "Just in case you were worried . . . you are nothing like your brother. In fact, I have it on good authority that you are one of the best men breathing."

She heard his sharp inhale. "And whose authority do you accept so willingly?"

Her mouth tipped into a smile. "Burke's."

Silence yawned between them before he muttered, "You should speak to him. He's hurting."

"Nothing I say can change that," she replied.

He stepped closer. "Is his love doomed to be unrequited?"

The words floated in the air between them, and Rosalie wondered if, in some small part of his mind, James was not merely inquiring about the fate of his friend. Her heart thrummed. "No," she whispered. "But I refuse to ruin him. And a love requited by the likes of me can only end in ruination . . . for both of us."

He took a step closer until she could feel his warmth at her back. "Miss Harrow—"

"Good night," she whispered, not waiting another second before she stepped into the darkness.

47

Rosalie

ROSALIE HARDLY SLEPT. Her dreams were full of whispered words, soft caresses, and warm green eyes. When she woke to Sarah pulling open her curtains, she groaned. Her legs were tangled in the sheets, and she was sweating.

"Morning, miss," Sarah called brightly.

"Morning," she replied, rubbing her hands over her face.

"The carriages will be around at eight to take any ladies into Carrington who require a dress fitting," Sarah went on. "Lady Oswald has arranged for you to take lunch at Oswald House. Which dress did you want for this morning, miss? The sprigged muslin again? Or perhaps the new yellow . . ."

Rosalie couldn't help the way her heart fluttered. She wanted to think of James Corbin as a friend. Accepting his gift was a small step, but a step nonetheless. "The yellow, I think," she replied. "With the—"

"The green spencer?" Sarah replied with an excited smile. "Yes, I think that will look lovely."

In no time, Rosalie was dressed, her hair fashionably arranged. Most of the guests were already in the breakfast room, with the young ladies twittering about the day's plans. The duke shuffled in just after Rosalie, and everyone stood to attention. He waved them back into their chairs. Rosalie was pleased to see he was not sporting any black eyes. She chanced a look at Olivia, who didn't lift her eyes away from buttering her toast.

Rosalie sat down, eager to clear her mind with a cup of tea. As she reached for the sugar, a high, musical voice called out from the doorway.

"Well, aren't we a dreary lot!"

There were a few gasps and clattering of dishes. Rosalie looked up and had to struggle to keep her mouth from falling open. Standing in the doorway were two women she'd never seen before. They were beautiful beyond words, with honey-yellow curls and dark hazelnut eyes. They wore matching grins, wide as anything. They wore matching dresses too—pretty things of peony pink. In fact, everything about them was matching down to the last detail, for they were twins. Identical twins.

A few voices exclaimed and the men at the table stood to admit them.

"Miss Prudence Nash," called Reed from the doorway. "And Miss Piety Nash."

"Saints alive, what a treat," said the duke, slapping his napkin down on the table. "The Nash sisters in my breakfast room." He snapped his fingers. "Collins, bring extra place settings."

A footman shuffled forward to comply.

Rosalie sank back in her chair. These ladies needed no introduction. They were famous across London. They were new money, not usually the type to orbit in the same circle as a duke. But as their father's star rose, so too did their popularity. And being identical twins made them a spectacle wherever they went. The papers said they were beautiful, but Rosalie had no idea. These things are so easily embellished.

"What brings you here, Misses Nash?" the countess said, her voice thickly sweet, even as she ravaged her stewed tomato with sharp strokes of her knife.

"Oh, well that was ever such a good surprise," said the one on the left, fluttering onto a chair. "We were just returning from dinner with the Talbots when we received a letter posted express. Was it not so, sister?"

"Indeed, sister. Such a good surprise." The other rapped a spoon on the edge of her teacup with three sharp taps.

Sir Andrew looked cross-eyed at them. He pointed a finger at one, then the other. "Which of you . . . is which?"

The sisters laughed, as did His Grace. "I'm Prudence," said the one on the right.

"And I'm Piety," said the left. "I'm taller by half an inch," she added.

"And I have a beauty mark . . . though I shan't tell you where," Prudence said with a flirtatious smile.

Sir Andrew leaned away with a grimace of confusion as, beside him, Lady Oswald pursed her lips.

"You were telling us why you're here," said the stony-faced marchioness.

"Oh yes," said Piety. "Well, the duchess wrote to apologize for the delayed invitation to the Michaelmas Ball. She was so out of sorts by the oversight, she asked if we might not come down a little early and join in the fun. Of course, we couldn't pack our cases fast enough, could we, sister?"

"No, indeed," twittered Prudence.

The duke was on the edge of his seat, enraptured by watching them play off each other.

"Daddy has always wanted to see Alcott, Your Grace," Piety added with a charming smile to the duke.

"He'll join us on Friday," cooed Prudence.

Rosalie jolted in her chair as the truth hit her. Heavens, this was *her* doing. This was the great idea her words inspired in the duchess. *Twins.* The duke wanted spectacle, and the duchess delivered with a set of social climbing, identical twin sisters. Rosalie couldn't decide if she wanted to laugh or scream. Why didn't she ever learn to keep her mouth shut?

She glanced around the table, seeing at once how each person slowly realized the truth: The game was up. For who could compete for the heart of George Corbin against fun, flirtatious, wholly unsuitable twin sisters? Sir Andrew disappeared behind his paper. The Swindon sisters pouted, casting anxious looks at their mother. Blanche looked like she was ready to cry into her eggs.

"James, look here," the duke called with a wide smile. "Look who decided to grace my table."

Rosalie glanced up sharply to see James and Burke standing in the open doorway.

The Nash sisters turned as one to take in James and Burke, their matching smiles and fluttering lashes practiced to an art. "Good morning, my lord," they chimed.

"It's the Nash sisters," the duke added, positively gleeful.

"So I see," James muttered. "Ladies, welcome."

Next to him, Burke stood still, stormy grey eyes taking them in. Neither of them seemed to be in ignorance. Had the duchess told James to expect these new arrivals?

"And this must be the delightful Mr. Burke we've heard so much about," Prudence said, lifting a dainty hand towards him.

Burke took it, bowing slightly over it. "As I've heard about you, Miss Nash."

Rosalie's stomach clenched into knots. She wanted to slap their hands apart. The feeling was so intense she had to turn away, lest she bolt from her chair and actually do the deed. She drowned out the sounds of the rest of their conversation, resolutely committed to adding a dash of milk to her tea.

She almost didn't notice when the men moved towards her end of the table. James passed by her first, helping himself to the buffet. Burke paused behind her chair. She felt his presence so close, pulling the air from her lungs. She raised her cup to her lips, hoping it might keep her from letting out a sigh of longing.

"I believe this is yours, Miss Harrow," he murmured, slipping his arm between her and Madeline to slide her sketchbook onto the table. "You might need it for tomorrow."

"Thank you," she replied, placing her hand protectively over it.

Without another word, he moved off around the table and joined James at the buffet. When James turned, he paused. She lifted her gaze to meet his, offering a smile. He was taking in the cut of her yellow dress. His gift. A muscle twitched in his jaw as he nodded once. He moved to his seat, busying himself with his breakfast. Burke joined him, and Rosalie waited only a few moments before she excused herself from the table.

It was only when she was alone in the hallway that she dared to flip through the pages of her sketchbook. Her breath caught as she looked down, one finger running over the torn edges of a page. Her sketches of Burke were missing.

Everything was in chaos as the ladies prepared to leave

for town. The Nash sisters already had ball gowns, but they were determined to "join in the fun," which required calling another carriage. Blanche and Mariah were still close to tears, while Elizabeth seemed poised to take over Olivia's title as resident gorgon.

It was a restless ride, with Rosalie wedged between Madeline and Mariah. Elizabeth and Blanche sat across from them, and the whole ride was taken up with the other ladies complaining loudly about every feature, word, and deed of "those horrible Nashes." While she certainly disliked the way Prudence so confidently took Burke's hand at breakfast, she wasn't about to admit it aloud. After all, it was *her* fault the Nash sisters were here.

The ladies made their way into the modiste with much twittering and sighs of delight. Rosalie tried to blend in with the fabrics as the others jockeyed for position to be the first to try on their dresses. She was accosted by both Nash sisters almost at once. They had the consideration to at least wear different colored spencers over their matching dresses.

"And who are you?" said Piety in lemon yellow.

"Oh sister, isn't she beautiful? Those eyes, that little chin," cooed Prudence in lavender.

Rosalie stilled as Prudence tipped her chin up with a finger. "I'm Rosalie Harrow," she replied, shifting away from the overly familiar touch.

"Harrow . . . Harrow," Piety mused. "*Oh*, are you with the Harrows of Harley House?"

"I don't believe so," Rosalie replied.

"The Harrows of Harrow and Wright Manufacturers?"

Rosalie shook her head. "I doubt very much you've heard of my set," she replied. "My father is dead, and his only brother immigrated to the East Indies. No one has heard from him in nigh on thirty years. I'm the only Harrow left."

"Heavens," Piety murmured. "So . . . are you of any fortune?"

"None whatsoever," Rosalie replied.

"Then . . . whatever brings you to Alcott?" Prudence asked. "We heard it was a race down the aisle. Surely, you're not our competition," she said with a laugh, flicking one of her tightly coiled blonde curls over her shoulder.

"I have no designs on His Grace," Rosalie replied.

Prudence narrowed her dark eyes over those perfectly pink cheeks. "But you have designs on *someone*. Who is it, so we shall know if we will be friends or rivals?"

Rosalie was saved from replying by the seamstress calling her name. In no time, she was standing before a trifold set of mirrors, eyes wide as she gazed at her reflection. Several of the other young ladies stood huddled, staring daggers at her as she turned slightly left, then right. All except Madeline.

"Oh, Rosalie," Madeline murmured. "It's beautiful."

The gown was the most gorgeous shade of cornflower blue. It had little capped sleeves, and the bodice was framed with a brocade ribbon in jade and gold. The waist was pleated across the front and fell in folds to her feet. She'd never worn such a bright color to a ball. All her gowns were secondhand debutant dresses in ivory or blush. It made her self-conscious to think of wearing something so fine, so bold.

"We'll take it in here and here," said the seamstress, giving the bodice little tugs as she pinned it. "Do you like the longer train, miss?"

Rosalie glanced down, noting the length trailing behind her. "Umm . . . no," she murmured. "I want to dance."

"Not to worry." The seamstress dropped to her knees to pin up some of the train.

Madeline stepped closer. "He won't be able to look away," she whispered.

Rosalie watched the blush grow in her reflection's cheeks. "Who?"

Madeline boldly met her gaze in the mirror. "You tell me."

For the rest of the day, Rosalie could only watch in awe as the Nash sisters swanned their way through every conversation. Their every look, touch, and laugh was easy and artful. By dinner, poor Mariah finally broke. The Nash sisters asked for dancing in the music room after dinner to practice their steps for the ball. The duke announced with a flourish that they should lead the first dance on his arm. That was around the moment when Mariah burst into tears. The Nashes giggled and pretended to fret about how they could both dance with the duke at the same time, so he begrudgingly offered Burke as his second.

As the ladies left the table, the duchess looped her arm into Rosalie's with a smug smile on her face, leading the way to the music room. "Well, Miss Rose? What say you now? Is it enough spectacle for my George?"

Rosalie put a smile on her face. "An inspired idea, Your Grace. They are charm itself."

"They are vile," the duchess replied. "Grasping, devious little social climbers. Of course, George is enthralled." She lowered her voice. "And I tell you now, if Prudence doesn't keep her hands off Burke, I will have them removed with the third duke's broadsword. I might be willing to accept one Nash into the family, but I absolutely draw the line at two."

Now Rosalie's smile was genuine. She mirrored the

duchess' thoughts exactly. "The third duke carried a broad-sword, Your Grace? That's rather eccentric," she mused, enjoying their moment of intimacy.

"Heavens, no," the duchess laughed. "He was a frail little thing by all accounts, but he was a great collector of art and artifact. His Viking collection is on display in the bachelor's corridor. I'll have Reed take down the sword and Fawcett can wield it. It takes a strong arm to heft a broadsword, Miss Rose."

Rosalie couldn't quite believe she was laughing on the arm of a duchess about removing the hands of one of her guests. "But . . . you would be happy? If His Grace chooses one of the Nash sisters as his bride?"

The duchess frowned again. "They are not as rich as I would like, nor is the Nash name nearly polished enough . . . but they are on the rise. No scandals that cannot be weathered. What matters most to me is that George is settled, and an heir is on the way. If spectacle is what he needs to settle . . ."

At that moment, Prudence took to the piano. A merry jig filled the air as the rest of the group filtered into the room. The footmen had already pushed back most of the furniture, leaving enough space for dancing.

"Snag Burke before those Nashes descend," the duchess directed, giving Rosalie a little shove.

Heart in her throat, Rosalie let her feet guide her across the room. Burke turned, his eyes locking on her with that steely gaze.

"The duchess demands we practice our steps before Friday," she said in a voice that didn't sound quite like her own.

Burke glanced over her shoulder to where the duchess was now sitting. His Grace was already in the middle of the room with Piety on his arm. James was letting himself be led forward by Elizabeth, while Mariah took the hand of the be-grudging Sir Andrew.

"I should be very happy, Miss Harrow," Burke replied at last.

He held out a hand and she took it, feeling the way their skin jolted at the contact.

"You feel it too," he muttered, placing his hand on the small of her back.

She shivered at the touch. "Of course, I do. I didn't lie to you, Burke."

He turned her slightly and dropped his hands away, taking his place across from her. Her body longed to be touched by him again. She was aching with it. Prudence broke into the reel, and the group danced and clapped, modifying the moves in the tight space. Rosalie laughed as Burke spun her round. She felt breathless, clutching her chest as the music pounded to an end. The group clapped, urging Prudence to play another.

Burke stepped into Rosalie's space, eyes alight, his hand brushing the soft skin just above her gloved elbow. "You're a beautiful dancer." His deep voice flowed through her like warm honey.

"You're not so bad yourself, sir," she replied.

"I stole the sketches," he murmured, speaking against her temple as he feigned trading places with her for the next set.

Her heart raced to feel him so close. "I know."

"You can have them back," he whispered. "If you ask me nicely . . ."

Her core went molten. He still wanted her. He was sore at her for keeping secrets, and he needed answers, but the magic between them still thrummed like the strings of a beautiful harp. She wanted to kiss him again here and now. Her eyes gave her away as she met his gaze. There was no Prudence Nash with her overly familiar touch. No Lord James with his disapproving looks. No duchess pulling their strings. There was only Rosalie and Burke.

And Renley . . .

Rosalie gasped, eyes wide as she glanced over Burke's shoulder. There, standing in the doorway to the music room, stood Renley, handsome as ever in his officer's uniform . . . and he was looking right at her, wide smile on his face.

48

Tom

CHRIST, ROSALIE WAS just as beautiful as he remembered. Her eyes went wide as she found him in the doorway. They practically glowed in the candlelight, her cheeks flushed from dancing. He longed to go to her immediately, but jealousy coiled in his gut. He saw the way she was looking at Burke. The lust in her eyes, that open longing. Were they even trying to hide it anymore? What else had changed in the two days he was away?

Burke followed her gaze, spinning on his heel.

"Renley! Good god, man, come in," James called, stepping forward to shake his hand. "Have you eaten?"

"Aye, I stopped at my brother's on the way in and begged some scraps. I didn't want to interrupt your dinner."

"Rest easy, ladies," George called to the room. "Your handsome sea captain has returned from journeys afar, ready to whisk you all onto the dance floor. Who's first, then? How about you, Red?" he laughed, flashing a smile at Elizabeth.

Burke stepped forward, offering his hand and a smile. "Back so soon? You must be dead on your feet."

"Not at all," he replied. "The journey was most invigorating."

"Not too tired to dance, I hope," James muttered. "I don't know that you'll escape before you've danced at least a few sets. The ladies are ravenous tonight."

Tom couldn't help the eye that slipped over to where Rosalie stood. "Well, we must sate their hunger."

George laughed. "Take a swig of something fortifying and get back to your stations, gentlemen. I can't balance all these birds in one hand . . . much as I might wish to," he added.

As George moved away, Tom tried to grab the elbows of Burke and James. "We need to talk," he muttered.

James patted his shoulder. "Let's just get through this and we can talk later."

Burke was still being stoic, which was unlike him. Christ, what happened?

"Right then, gentlemen, line up if you please. Ladies, be ready to fight for a partner. Ground rules first: no eye-gouging, or left hooks—"

"George," James growled in warning.

Tom couldn't help but laugh. George at least was in excellent spirits tonight. It was then that he noticed the presence of a new lady among the group. Bloody hell, two of the *same* lady. Was he drunk? He'd only had a glass of claret with dinner.

James caught his confused gaze. "Ah, Renley, you haven't met the Nash sisters. This is . . . Pruu—"

"Piety, my lord," the closer twin said with peals of laughter. "My sister Prudence is at the piano."

"Miss Nash, this is First Lieutenant Tom Renley," James added.

Miss Nash sized Tom up in a way that made him feel quite exposed. "Well then, Lieutenant. Do you have a pair of wobbly sea legs, or can you spin a lady about the room?"

"I can dance, Miss Nash."

"Excellent," she cooed, curling her arm around his. "You shall be my partner for the next two dances. Prudence, play the Virginia Reel!"

Tom was dragged into place at the top of the set next to George and Blanche. Down the set, he saw Burke paired with Madeline, while James stood across from Olivia. Rosalie stood at the end of the set, partnered with Sir Andrew. He lost himself in the music, letting himself spin his new partner 'round. It was a proper reel where every man danced with every lady. He waited until it was time to pull Rosalie into his arms.

"You're back," she called over the clapping, wide smile on her face.

"I told you I'd come back," he replied, loving the feel of her in his arms.

The moment was over too soon, and he was back leading Miss Nash down the line of dancers. It took a few more turns before it was Rosalie dancing down the middle with Sir Andrew. The poor man was a sport, but dancing was not his forte. His brow was already glazed with sweat. Rosalie spun 'round him and reached for Tom with both hands.

"You had a pleasant trip, I hope?" she said, still all smiles.

"I accomplished my goal—"

Those were all the words they could exchange before she was twirling away again.

When the reel finally ended, he clapped with the others and readied to lead his partner off the floor.

"You promised me a second dance, sir," Miss Nash said, fluttering those lashes at him. "Or if not me, allow me to take my sister's place at the piano."

He had no reason to refuse so found himself nodding,

even as his eyes trailed to where Rosalie now stood in the corner, patting the shoulder of the wheezing Sir Andrew.

The other Nash sister swept forward, putting herself between Tom and his view of Rosalie. "Well, Lieutenant Renley, if you are not the handsomest man I've ever seen—"

"That's quite enough of that talk," George barked, pushing his way in. "Renley may be a handsome devil, but I'm a filthy rich one," he said in the lady's ear.

She giggled and batted his arm playfully away. "Your Grace should know better than to try to woo a lady with riches. We are far too principled to have our heads turned by such banality. Give me good humor and a lively conversationalist . . . and make him a divine dancer if possible. This I pray, dear Lord." She mocked crossing herself and folded her hands in prayer with a wink.

Christ Almighty, these Nashes were born to flirt. Tom felt like he was being swept away on a strong current, utterly powerless to stop or change course.

"I'm taking this one, Renley," George said, a fire in his eyes. "Find another partner."

She squealed as George took hold of her by both hands and spun her into the middle of the room, nearly knocking over the Swindons. Tom made his escape, moving across the room to try to catch Rosalie alone. The timing was perfect, as Sir Andrew had found himself a chair and was still fanning his sweaty face. Tom crossed behind the pushed-back sofa only to find his way blocked by Burke.

"You came back sooner than we expected," he said.

Tom tried to gauge his mood. "And that displeases you?"

"Not at all," Burke replied. "You noticed the new additions?"

"Did I ever," Tom said with a forced laugh, glancing over

his shoulder to make sure they were both safely distracted—one behind the piano, one in George's overly familiar embrace. "I've seen tempests act with more subtlety."

Burke smirked. "It's caused a bit of an uproar. None of us quite understood why the duchess invited them . . . or we didn't until now. They work fast, don't they? George always did love novelty."

"How ever will he pick just one?"

"You seem . . . better," Burke hedged, those grey eyes studying him. "London went well for you? You're happy?"

Tom sighed. "Are we not friends? Ask me plainly what you want to know."

Burke's jaw clenched tight. "Did you propose to her?"

Before Tom could respond, the Miss Nash at the piano plinked out several loud chords. "Places everyone, next up is the cotillion! Four sets of partners at the ready!"

Burke groaned. Tom knew well how much Burke disliked dancing, but there were far too few men to sit out even one set.

"Later," Tom said, turning away to find three pairs of eyes watching him expectantly. "Miss Mariah, will you do me the honor?"

The girl nearly burst with excitement and almost tripped over her skirts in her rush to step up and take his hand. Burke followed behind him with the elder Swindon on his arm. James was the last to join the set with Blanche.

He glanced over his shoulder to see Rosalie sitting between the duchess and Madeline on the sofa. It was impossible to miss the feel of Rosalie's eyes on him each time his back was turned. But why would she not meet his gaze?

The dance was lively, and Tom only missed the steps twice. It had been a while since he danced a cotillion. As the group broke apart, he made a second attempt to go to Rosalie. This time, his way was blocked by James handing him a glass of port.

"So, how's the family?"

Tom sighed with frustration, taking the glass. "My brother is fine. He complains of a rheumatism. Agatha is expecting again, had I told you?"

"No . . . Christ, that's how many now?" James said, brow furrowed.

"This will be number seven," Tom replied.

"Seven children. Poor Agatha," James muttered.

"Perhaps she'd not have quite so many if she wasn't so much a fan of the method," Tom said into his glass.

James barked a laugh. "I guess not."

Tom set his glass aside, done with this charade. "James, why are the two of you determined to see me cut off from Rosalie? What happened that I cannot go speak to her?"

Unlike Burke, who may have attempted another round of denial, James had the good sense to say, "We should talk first . . . before you go saying anything you'll regret."

Tom frowned, glancing over to where Burke watched them from across the room. He was only pretending to be in conversation with Sir Andrew. The happiness and confidence Tom built on his journey back from Town was slowly ebbing away like sand through his open fingers. "What the hell happened while I was gone?"

49

Rosalie

"Heavenly," Rosalie sighed, taking a deep breath of sweet autumn air. The heat was finally abating, a sure sign that summer was indeed over. She stood at the water's edge, watching it ripple down over the rocks. Behind her sat an old mill, with crumbling stone walls and a roof with holes in the thatch. Ivy crept up the sides, and thick sprays of wildflowers grew right against the stone like something out of a fairy tale. It was nearly a mile walk to get to the spot, but it was well worth the exercise.

"We used to play here as boys," James explained to the group. "If anyone wishes to forage, we have some baskets here. There are usually beds of chanterelles up that way and berries in the hedge."

"What do you think?" came Burke's voice from behind her.

"It's a beautiful spot," she murmured.

"I'm glad you like it," he said, his breath warm on her neck.

A chill shot down her arms as she spun around to face him. This tension between them couldn't last much longer. She needed to get him alone. Needed to explain herself . . . needed to feel his lips. Most of all, she needed him to stop looking at her like that! She frowned. "You still have my sketches. I want them back."

"And I'd like you to ask nicely," he said with that teasing grin.

"It was beastly of you to take pages out of my sketchbook. You have no right to them."

Damn that smirk. Did he practice it in a mirror? "No right to my own likeness? One might argue I have the only right—"

"Come on then, Miss Harrow, get yourself to an easel," called the duke. "I'll be giving a gold sovereign to whichever lady paints the best portrait of me." He stomped through the grass over to a large rock at the water's edge. As a few of the other ladies giggled, he climbed atop it and struck a stately pose.

Rosalie couldn't help but laugh too. For all his crude manners and lack of interest in performing the role he was born into, she could admit that she sometimes found George Corbin good company. Well . . . perhaps not *good* company, but he was entertaining.

The day passed pleasantly. James and Burke took turns with Renley and the duke to lead the young ladies into the trees to forage or explore the mill. By midmorning, the clouds began to roll in, deepening the shadows on the forest floor. By lunchtime, the first roll of distant thunder rumbled. A September storm was on the way.

"We may have to cut this outing short," Madeline said, glancing up at the sky.

"Oh, but His Grace was going to show us the best spot to search for truffles," said Elizabeth.

Burke snorted into his cucumber sandwich. "If His Grace can correctly identify a truffle from a toadstool, I'll marry Magellan."

A few of the ladies giggled.

Rosalie met his eye, controlling her own smile.

"Burke, why must you always ruin my fun?" the duke pouted.

"Don't worry, Your Grace," said Prudence, giving his arm a coquettish pat, even while she narrowed her eyes at Burke. "There are more important distinctions than truffles and toadstools, like discerning good society from bad."

The barb was so pointedly a rejection of Burke that Rosalie found herself swallowing a gasp of indignation. She sat forward.

Surprisingly, it was Lady Olivia who spoke. "And which sort of society are you, Miss Nash? For while that bonnet and those clothes are the mark of good society, your manners belong in a Cheapside alley."

Prudence's cheeks flamed pink. She huffed and got to her feet. "Well, I never—what a disagreeable—I'm going in search of my sister. Would you care to join me, Your Grace?"

The duke stared daggers at Olivia, who was resolutely ignoring him as she busied herself with her scone. "Happy to," he said, looping Prudence's arm in with his. They stalked off, leaving the group in awkward silence.

"You didn't have to do that," Burke murmured.

Olivia gave an airy laugh. "What, put that mortal in her place? Of course, I did, Mr. Burke. Tell me, what happened when Icarus flew too close to the sun?"

He smirked. "The wax of his wings melted, and he fell from the sky."

"Quite right."

He mused for a moment, casting Rosalie a look that had her smiling too. "So . . . in that analogy, is Miss Prudence young Icarus and His Grace the sun?"

Olivia huffed, adding a dollop of orange marmalade to

her scone. "Who said anything about him? *I* am the sun, Mr. Burke. You see how effectively I manage the sky around me. Take note."

Burke's grin spread. "Oh, it's noted."

By the time James and Renley returned with Mariah between them, the mood at the picnic had improved drastically. Elizabeth and Blanche were taking it in turns to recite verses of a Byron poem, while the others relaxed. Prudence and the duke were still missing.

"We should start heading back," James called. "It's going to rain."

The ladies sighed their discontent.

"I've told the lads to start packing up," he added.

The servants bustled through the woods behind him carrying two large trunks.

Burke was on his feet as James crossed the clearing to his side.

James looked around. "Where's George and Miss Nash?"

"They went off in search of the other Miss Nash a while ago," Burke replied. "Did you not cross paths with them?"

"Miss Piety said she was coming to join the lunch," Renley said, lowering a laden basket to the grass.

Rosalie sat up, fighting to control her frown. The duke was alone in the woods with the Nash sisters?

James spoke quietly to Burke and Renley. "See that the ladies start on their way back before the heavens crash down on us. I'll go find George."

Burke grabbed his arm. "Let me go."

"Why you?"

"Because I can promise not to break his legs," Burke replied. "He needs them for dancing. Can you promise the same?"

James tugged the brim of his hat lower. "Fine. Renley, help me with the other ladies. Burke—"

"I'll handle it," Burke replied, stepping off into the woods without a backward glance.

Rosalie didn't bother to pretend she wasn't listening. When James turned and caught her eye, she gave him a sympathetic look.

He just clenched his jaw and turned away. Poor Atlas, always beset by worries and strife. "Come then, ladies. We must start back," he called to the group.

Before they could get even a step out of the clearing, the heavens opened, and rain started to fall. The echoing of distant thunder promised a deluge to come. The ladies squealed, holding their shawls up over their heads as they ran for the trees.

"Careful," James called, snatching up a parasol and running after them. "Let me lead the way!"

Madeline and Rosalie held back, laughing as they tried to protect the art. Madeline flipped over the canvas of her watercolor. Rosalie reached for hers, knowing it was too late. The rain was washing away all her hard work.

"Best leave it, ladies," came Renley's voice. He was busy helping the lads toss sodden pillows and dishes into carrying cases.

With a giggle, Madeline dropped her canvas to the grass, abandoning it to its fate. "Come on, Rosalie."

"Oh, but we can't just leave this mess behind," she cried. She tossed her ruined painting to the grass, snatching up the other canvases and adding them to the pile.

"Madeline! Miss Harrow!" Olivia shouted from the safety of the trees. She was one of the only ladies armed with a parasol. "Come away!"

"Go," Rosalie said. "You are far more valuable than I am."

"Rosalie—"

"I'll be right behind you," Rosalie added with a laugh, reaching for one of the easels.

"Madeline, come!" cried Olivia.

Madeline turned on her heel and took off across the wet grass. She joined Olivia under the parasol, and they turned away together down the path.

Rosalie put herself to work, snapping the easels shut and stacking them next to the ruined paintings. Then she collected all the brushes and supplies and tipped them into a basket.

"Rose," Renley called. "What the hell are you doing? Go back!"

"And leave these poor lads to clean up our mess?"

He crossed to her side. "We'll take care of this. Just go."

The rain fell harder around them.

"Go with her, m'lord," one of the lads called. "We got this here!"

"Get them ladies back safe," shouted another.

Renley twined his fingers with hers. "Come on, before we have to start swimming." He pulled her towards the trees. As they passed under them, the rain eased a bit, protected as they were by a canopy of leaves. Renley led the way, weaving down the path.

"You know where you're going, right?" she called over his shoulder.

"Do you doubt my skills in navigation?"

"Well, I know you can chart stars, but it is day, sir. A rather stormy day," she added. "Even the sun can be no guide in a thunderstorm."

He slowed to a halt, nearly making her tumble into him.

He caught her with both hands on her shoulders. Rain softly fell all around them. "I know these paths like the back of my hand. I will not see you lost."

The depth of the blue in his eyes was like pools she wanted to sink into, but she couldn't allow that to cloud her judgment. For all she knew, he was engaged. She swore she'd wait until he volunteered whatever truth he wanted to give . . . but she still found herself whispering, "What happened in London?"

His gaze softened. "I took your advice," he replied. "I forgave her everything."

Rosalie nodded, looking down at her feet to hide the burning sensation in the corners of her eyes. Heavens, this was ridiculous. Why should she feel loss that he took her advice and sought out his true love? Was this not all she hoped when she saw him again? If his heart was safely in another's hands, it would not be hers to take and break.

"Rose—"

"I'm happy for you, Tom," she said, forcing a smile. "I'm sure you must feel better. To offer forgiveness is always such a relief. And she sounds—your Marianne sounds lovely," she added. Not giving him a chance to respond, she ducked around him and squelched her way down the muddy path.

"Rose," he called again, easily catching up on his longer legs.

"It's nearly a mile back—"

"Rose, *look* at me." He spun her around. "I am not engaged to Marianne. I said I took your advice. I forgave her, I wished her well, and I went on my way. I came back to Alcott. I came back to—" He swallowed the rest of his words with a groan.

Oh God, was he about to say *to you?* Tears threatened to mix with the rain on her cheeks. They were not tears of joy. "Tom, *please*—"

He cupped her cheek. His skin was so warm, the pads of his palm calloused from a life at sea. "Rosalie, look at me."

She met his eyes again. "I can't—I don't want to hurt you—"

"You won't," he whispered. "I know where you stand. I know you don't want to get married right now, that you intend to move here and work for the duchess. It's admirable, truly."

Right now, he said, as if he fully expected her to change her mind. Was that not always the way whenever a lady said something as brash as not wanting a husband? Surely, Rosalie *must* change her mind. When the right man came along, she'd gladly enter the matrimonial cage. It was the natural situation for a woman to want one man to own her until she married another, and with any luck she would birth a third to take his place. Father, husband, son. Always holding the keys. Always in control.

Her anger rose as she took in his full meaning. Why would he be here talking to her about marriage? She scowled at him. "So, is it safe to assume that's where you disappeared to last night? You and James and Burke slipped away to gossip about me? You're worse than old maids at their knitting!"

She spun away as Renley let out a laugh. He caught up again quickly. "Rose, stop. Rose, I'm sorry! *Yes*, we talked about you. Can you blame me?"

"I blame all three of you," she huffed, picking her way down the muddy path. "Rotten gossips—"

"I had to know where I stood," he explained. "I saw the way you looked at Burke last night. God, I'd give anything to have you look at me like that—"

She paused in her steps, and he nearly bowled her over. He wanted her to want him? What happened to Marianne? Heavens, what was happening to *her*? In the span of a fortnight, she went from being resolutely independent to *this*—waiting and hoping that Renley might come back and say these beautiful words, even though she had no intention to marry him. She was a monster. She didn't deserve his smiles or his goodness.

"Tom, I refuse to string you along, giving you hope where there is none. You want to marry. You *need* to marry. You have a career and a life. And you love Marianne. Surely whatever is between you is not insurmountable. I want you to be happy—"

He cupped her cheek, and her breath hitched. He searched her face, holding her captive with the earnest look in his eyes. "Why are you trying to push me away? Why can only Burke and James be close to you?"

She jerked away from his touch. "Why are you bringing them into this?"

"Because they *are* in this." He stepped closer, reaching for her again. "Tell me I'm wrong—"

"You're *wrong*," she hissed. "James Corbin doesn't want anything to do with me." She spun around and kept walking down the path, hands clenched at her sides.

"Fine, maybe James is still being a stick in the mud," he called after her. "But that doesn't mean he doesn't want you. Trust me, Rose. I've known him all my life—"

"Are you trying to make him interested in me? Please do us both a favor and stop!"

"No, of course not—"

She was already back on the path, marching away.

"Look, I'm out of my depth here. All I know is how I feel—*Christ*, will you stop walking!"

He grabbed her arms again. She didn't turn around as the rain continued to fall, pattering the leaves overhead. In the distance, thunder rumbled. Renley stepped closer until he was nearly pressed against her back. His touch gentled, his hands sliding down the wet fabric of her spencer from her shoulders to her elbows.

"This is not a proposal," he murmured, his breath warm against her ear and making her shiver. "I know you don't want that. Hell, I'm not even sure *I* want that anymore. I was lost for so long, Rose. Lost to my heartache, my resentment. I was drowning in memories of Marianne. Your words humbled me and made me see how foolish I'd been. I don't want to live with another moment of anger or regret."

"Then what do you want?" she whispered, feeling the way her body longed to lean against him. She turned slowly to face him, needing to read his expressions.

"I want . . ." He shrugged, looking desperately around, as if the answer might be tacked to a nearby tree. "I don't understand this," he said, gesturing between them. "I've never counted a woman as a friend before. I've never wanted . . . I feel as if part of me has always known you. It's so easy with you. So . . . right." He groaned, eyes settling on her. "Tell me you feel it too."

Slowly, she lifted her chin, peering into the depths of his blue eyes. "I do."

He leaned closer. "You said we could be friends. What does that mean to you? What does that allow me?"

"What do you want?" She prayed his answer wouldn't send her running. *No commitment, please no commitment. No promises of love and ownership.*

"I just want to be close to you," he replied, clearly trying to find the right words. "I want you in my life, in my confidence. I won't ask you for anything you don't want to give. Can you let me be close and not create ties that bind us?"

She raised a hand and touched his face, a fingertip tracing

along his strong jaw. "Yes, that is just what I want. I want to be close to you," she replied using his word. "I am not . . . I've lived my life very differently than the ladies here," she explained, still trying to follow his lead and speak in thinly veiled metaphors. "Part of it was my upbringing, but there has been choice involved too. I like men. I like feeling . . . all the things that come with love. I'm . . . I think I might be broken. But if you will let me be close to you—"

"Enough," he whispered, stroking his thumb over her lips. "We understand each other. We're friends. *Close* friends," he added with a knowing smile.

She felt something inside her settle into place. "When I look at you, I don't see an angry man full of resentment and regret," she whispered.

His hands settled on her hips. "What do you see?"

"I see a good man," she replied. "Steadfast as a sunrise." She smiled. "It is a rare man who dares to love after all hope of its return is gone. I pray someday you meet a lady deserving of such devotion."

The weight of his hands on her hips drew her closer. "And what do you feel here in my arms?"

What *did* she feel? She hardly knew. Being near Burke was all fire and passion and longing. It was intoxicating, even if it sometimes scared her. Renley made everything feel so simple, so easy. Her breath caught before she whispered the only words that made sense. "I feel . . . home."

She didn't know who moved first, but it didn't matter. His face lowered as she tipped up on her toes. Their lips met and she sighed into his kiss. His arms wrapped around her. It felt strange to kiss him in the rain. His lips were already wet. She relaxed into him, loving the feel of his muscled arms around her.

As their faces turned, their hat brims brushed, sending water dripping onto Rosalie's cheeks. With a smile, Renley used a finger to flick her bonnet back, then his lips were on hers again. His tongue teased softly against her bottom lip, opening her mouth. She ran her hands down his lapels, gripping them with both hands as he deepened their kiss. His teeth grazed her lip and she sighed.

Time stood still until the only things that existed were the soft pattering of the rain all around them and the feel of his mouth, so warm and inviting against hers.

Home. Friendship. Peace. A place for her heart to rest.

"Christ, Rose," he murmured, breaking their kiss.

Her eyes fluttered open, and she gasped, immediately going stiff in his arms.

Renley pulled back, searching her face. "What is it? I'm sorry—"

"Burke." Rosalie gasped his name as the man himself charged towards them, his eyes murderous.

50

Rosalie

"BURKE," ROSALIE SAID again, her heart hammering in her chest.

Renley turned to face him as he approached. He put up a hand, as if readying to block a hit. "Burke—*wait*—"

Burke growled deep in his throat, eyes only for Rosalie. The heat of his gaze stole her breath away. His eyes were obsidian. No grey. No storms. *He* was the storm. He pushed past Renley, his hands cupping her face as he backed her against the closest tree.

"Say it," he said, voice deep with longing.

Renley put his hand on Burke's shoulder, ready to pull him off. "Burke, don't—"

Burke tensed, eyes still locked on Rosalie. "Christ, Rosalie, *say* it."

She knew what he wanted. She wanted the same thing. She'd been aching for it since that first kiss. Could she dare say the words in front of Renley? He was standing right there, ready to step in, ready to protect her. His kiss was still fresh on her lips. Oh god, he would see . . . but some dark part of her wanted him to see, wanted them both to understand how she felt.

She lifted her chin, looking into Burke's eyes, and whispered the words that would send her straight to hell. "Burke, will you please kiss me—"

The words were hardly spoken, and he descended. It wasn't the sweet, rainswept kiss she'd shared with Renley. She burned molten as Burke claimed her, holding tight to her face with both hands as his tongue forced its way deep into her mouth. Her core clenched and she went boneless in his arms, clinging to him.

"*Fuck*," she heard someone groan. It had to be Renley, for Burke's mouth was occupied with stealing all her air.

As soon as it had begun, Burke pulled away, both of them panting. She sank against the tree, too embarrassed to look over Burke's shoulder and see Renley's hurt face.

Burke leaned against the tree, caging her in with his arm. "Look at me," he murmured.

It was then Rosalie realized she had lowered her face, using her bonnet as a shield. Slowly, she lifted her face, knowing her cheeks must be blazing with desire . . . and shame. She looked first at Burke, whose eyes were still obsidian. Then she let her gaze drift to Renley. He was standing there, soaking wet, his shoulders rising and falling as he stared at her.

Burke cupped her face. "You want me."

Trust the rain to wash away all artifice. "Yes," she whispered, putting everything she felt into the word.

"This is real." His fingers trailed down her jaw.

She shivered at the touch. "Yes," she repeated. Of course, it was real. Burke was the fire in her blood. He was her twin soul longing to fly free. She wanted him like she wanted air. She thought he might kiss her again, but instead he put a hand on Renley's shoulder. Renley stiffened, but he didn't jerk away.

"You want him too . . . don't you?"

She saw the confusion in Renley's eyes, the curiosity, the stifled hope. He'd been burned once before. The scars of that love were still so raw. She couldn't bear to hurt him. "Yes," she whispered. "To earn his friendship would mean everything to me."

"Show him."

She glanced from one man to the other.

Renley looked just as confused. "Burke, what are you—"

"Show him the kind of friend you want him to be," Burke pressed. "Here in these woods, with no one else to see, show us how we make you feel."

She gasped. Apparently, Burke was happy to burn in hell with her. Would Renley join them? Only one way to find out. Burke stepped back as she moved into Renley's arms. She lifted both hands, running them up his lapels. She rose on her toes, pressing closer. Renley's eyes were wide, his perfect lips parted in surprise.

"Stay in this dream with me," she whispered, touching her lips to his with a featherlight kiss.

He was still for another half a second, his entire body coiled with tension, until he murmured the words that made her moan. "Never to wake." He claimed her mouth in another heated kiss. His arms wrapped around her, holding her tight as he left all hesitation behind.

Rosalie couldn't quite believe her luck. She knew logically that not all men must be good kissers. Sir Andrew, for example, with his bushy mustache and thick lips, must surely kiss like a horse. How spoiled she was that both Burke and Renley were divine. Burke's kisses felt like fire, a molten heat that burned across every inch of her skin. Renley's kisses went deeper. Like a dam bursting, she felt a flood of desire cascading through her.

Renley's mouth slanted over hers and she sighed against him.

"*Fuck*," came Burke's curse.

He was watching everything, close enough to touch. Her core clenched as she remembered the feel of his fingers so deep inside her, claiming her release. But then Renley bit down on her lip, sucking it into his mouth, and she whimpered, all thoughts back on him. She stepped backwards, seeking the bracing comfort of the tree, but Burke was there instead, his hands on her hips.

Renley pulled away with a groan. "Bloody hell, you kiss like a goddess," he panted. "How will I ever stop?" he added, almost to himself.

"She's a siren," Burke murmured, stroking her neck with his fingertips, his breath hot against her skin. "She's perfect."

Rosalie beamed with feminine pride. It was one thing to know Burke and Renley were masterful kissers. It was quite another to hear praise that she too was accomplished. She barely had a moment to catch her breath before Burke was turning her, his hands tight on her hips. She gasped as his mouth caught hers, his tongue warm and seeking. She trembled, clinging to his coat, even as her back pressed against Renley.

Renley's hands slid up her sides as he pulled her body flush against his. She felt the tightness of his muscled chest, the rise and fall of his every breath. He lowered his head until his breath was warm on her neck, even while Burke feverishly claimed her mouth.

Oh god, they were *both* going to kiss her. She wanted their lips on her, claiming her, setting her on fire. She leaned into Burke's kiss as she twisted slightly, bringing one hand around to tug Renley's coat, desperate to feel him closer. Renley latched on to her neck, the heat of his mouth sending a jolt straight to her core. She moaned into Burke's mouth. When Renley's teeth scraped her skin, she cried out, breaking Burke's kiss.

Renley pulled away too, and she stood there, shaking like a leaf between them, her hands clutching tight to each of their coats. Burke lowered his forehead to her shoulder, panting with need. Renley seemed dazed, his eyes unfocused as he looked at her. The rain continued to patter down all around them.

"Rosalie," Burke began after a moment, his voice gruff. "I have to know . . . what do you want? You don't want marriage. I'm clearly not enough."

The pain in his voice had her turning, both hands raising to cup his beautiful face. "It's not like that. Not for me. There is no enough. I feel what my heart tells me to feel."

His large hands wrapped around her wrists as she stroked his face with her fingers.

"I want you so badly," she whispered. "I want you." She kissed him again, her lips barely touching his. "I want you." She felt him sigh with relief against her lips.

She turned slightly to look at Renley. "Everything with you has been so confusing because of Marianne. Your love for her seems so genuine, so all-consuming. I'm afraid to trust you. Afraid you could never care for me like you do her—"

"Don't." He pulled her closer, resting his forehead against hers. "Don't compare yourself to her. Don't think of her at all." He lifted his head to meet her eyes. "You called this a dream, and maybe it is. Never in my life did I think I'd be standing in the rain with Burke kissing the same girl," he said with a laugh. "But I'm here. I'm not asking for anything. If my friendship is all you seek, then you have it. Every kiss you give me is a gift I don't deserve."

"You do," she tried to say, but he silenced her with his lips. When he pulled away, she was breathless. She could so easily get drunk off these men and their kisses.

"This is your dream, Rose," he said, a smile tipping his lips. "What do you want?"

Her heart pounded in her chest as thunder rumbled overhead. What she wanted was indecent. It was sinful and . . . everything. "I want—"

CRACK.

A bolt of lightning flashed less than a hundred yards off, snapping into a tree and making all three of them jump. Rosalie clung to both their arms as the men laughed.

"Come on," Burke said, taking her hand. "Let's go back before God gets creative and smites us." He tugged Rosalie forward, laughing as Renley followed.

Burke led the way across the soggy back gardens as the storm raged overhead. He pulled open the door to the new wing, letting her and Renley pass through. She nearly slipped on the polished parquet floor. Renley caught her with a hand to her elbow.

Burke shut the door with a snap, calling the footman over. The poor lad looked at them with wide eyes. "Bates, be a good lad and run and fetch us some towels. The duchess won't be pleased if we ruin her fine carpets."

The footman nodded and ran off down the hall.

"Heavens, what must I look like," Rosalie sighed, feeling

every inch of her dress slicked to her body. Water dripped from her nape down her neck.

Burke towered beside her. "Listen, I bought us maybe three minutes."

She blinked, confused, as she tried to make sense of his tone, the look in his eye. "Burke, what—"

"You have two choices, little siren." He took a step closer, his heated gaze making her molten. He pointed down the hallway. "Walk that way, and Bates will meet you with a towel."

She glanced quickly over at Renley, who was watching her with the interest of a hungry fox. She looked back at Burke. "Or?"

Burke smirked. "Or come with me." He held out his hand, an open invitation in his eyes. She swallowed her whimper, desperate to say yes. Then he slayed her when he glanced at Renley and added, "Just know he's coming too."

51

Rosalie

ROSALIE COULD SCARCELY breathe as she raised her hand and placed it in Burke's. This was madness. This was quite possibly the worst decision she'd ever made . . . and nothing was going to stop her now. Burke turned, pulling her behind him as he led them through the second door on the left. Renley followed close behind.

Her eyes had to adjust to the half-light of the storage room. The shutters on all the windows were closed, save the one in the corner, which was only partially open. Lazy motes of dust swirled in the slanting sunlight. A maze of furniture and abandoned art dotted the room—towers of musty leather-bound books on an old writing desk, rolled carpets, a dented suit of armor missing an arm.

The lock on the door clicked into place and the sound rattled her very bones.

"Away from the door," Burke muttered. "Give poor Bates a minute to realize we took off without our towels."

She couldn't conceal her smile as they inched their way around teetering stacks of ballroom chairs. There was a handsome painted screen set up just in front of the window. It was responsible for blocking most of the room's light.

Renley looked around. "You still use this place?"

"Aye," Burke replied. "It's our favorite reading spot," he added for Rosalie. "James and I have been fighting over it since we were kids."

She peered around the screen to see a cozy setup—a comfortable chaise covered in a sheet, a side table stacked with all manner of books, evidence of empty drink decanters. It was a perfect hideaway. Rosalie was about to say as much when a voice echoed from the hall.

"Mr. Burke?" Poor Bates was back with their towels. "Lieutenant . . . Miss?"

She covered her mouth with her hand as her shoulders shuddered. Burke and Renley stood to either side of her, Burke's hand slipping around her waist until his thumb brushed her hip. Her laughter died as her body began to tingle. There was really nothing funny about this.

"Give him a minute to bugger off," Burke said, leaning against the wall.

Feeling supremely uncomfortable in her sodden clothes, Rosalie did the bare minimum to relieve herself. She pulled out the pin holding her bonnet and took it off, breathing a sigh of relief.

Renley stroked her cheek with the back of his hand. The gentleness of his touch raised gooseflesh down her arms. "You are so beautiful, Rose."

She didn't typically like when people shortened her name, but on Renley's lips it sounded like the sweetest endearment.

Burke's hand was still around her waist. He gave her a

little tug, breaking Renley's contact. "In the woods you were about to tell us what you wanted," he said, voice low.

She shivered, fighting the urge to close her eyes. There was no way this was real, but she didn't want the dream to end yet. "Have either of you ever done this before?"

The men exchanged a look over her head. With two of them, she couldn't read both their faces at once. "Yes," Renley replied.

Her jealousy warred with her excitement to imagine these beautiful men together. "Wait, you've shared a woman . . . or you shared one together?"

Burke took the bonnet from her hands and set it aside. "If our pasts matter that much to you, I'll tell you I have never been with Renley in any situation like this. As to the rest, a gentleman doesn't kiss and tell . . . just as we'll not ask you for details of your past."

She nodded. She was jealous by nature, so knowing too many details was going to hurt more than it helped. Her body gave another shiver at the chill of her wet clothes, and she wrapped her arms around herself. Both men noticed, their eyes narrowing.

"Let us take care of you, little siren. Tell us your limits and we'll go from there."

Limits? Did she have any? Surely, she must. "I can't . . . um . . ." Why was it so hard to say the words? She blushed furiously as she squeaked out, "I can't get with child."

Burke chuckled, kissing her again. "Wouldn't dream of it. I don't have a French letter to hand, but we'll make do . . . unless Tom wants to surprise us?"

Tom laughed. "Don't look at me. I may be a sailor, but I

don't carry French letters in my pockets to go truffle hunting with George Corbin."

"We'll take care of you, love. Now, come here and let us help you out of these wet clothes." Burke led her behind the painted screen.

Renley followed, dropping his coat to the floor with a sodden flop.

Burke let go of her hand and did the same, tossing his coat and waistcoat aside.

Her core fluttered as she watched them strip out of their wet upper layers until they were both only in their shirts.

"Face Tom," Burke directed.

Rosalie turned slowly as Renley tugged off his shirt. He dropped it to the floor and Rosalie stifled a gasp. Like Burke, he was well muscled. But what most drew her eye were the dozen or so tattoos peppering his chest, shoulders, and arms. A large anchor over his heart, a ship in sail at his shoulder, some words she couldn't make out along his ribs and down his forearm, a mermaid down his other arm, a cross in the middle of his chest.

"I thought our little artist might like those," Burke teased. He settled his hands on her hips, giving her a push towards Renley.

She raised a hand, a question in her eye, and Renley nodded. She stroked the anchor, just over his heart. "I've never seen a tattoo before," she admitted.

"No, well you wouldn't," Burke said with a laugh. "They're not exactly accepted in polite society."

"They're beautiful," she murmured. "Did they hurt terribly?"

"Terribly," Renley replied. He cupped her face as he pulled her close and kissed her.

She sighed into his mouth, her hands stroking the hard planes of his chest. She thrilled at feeling his skin. He broke the kiss and dropped his hands to her chest to start fumbling with the buttons of her spencer. He peeled it down her arms, tossing it aside.

Behind her, Burke stepped closer, his hands at the back of her dress. "Stop us at any time." He placed a kiss on the nape of her neck that made her shiver again.

"Eyes on me, Rose." Renley's devastating blue eyes held her captive. His thumb brushed over her lips before he was pressing it into her mouth. She opened to him, feeling his thumb slide against her tongue. She moaned as she sucked on it gently. "Fuck," he growled, pulling away.

Burke slipped her dress off her shoulders and dropped it to the floor. Renley's fingers were already working the laces of her stays. He tugged at them, moving expertly hand over hand until he flicked it off her shoulders too. She took an unrestrained breath, her ribs expanding fully for the first time in hours.

Now she stood before them in nothing but her stockings and chemise. It clung to her, showing off all her curves. No doubt Renley could see her nipples through the wet material.

Burke snatched the sheet off the chaise. "Take that off and wrap up warm before your teeth start chattering."

She nodded, heart in her throat as she shimmied out of the chemise. Renley's eyes went wide as he eagerly took in her nakedness. Before she could feel too embarrassed, Burke was behind her, wrapping her in the folded sheet. It was blessedly warm and dry. Burke used his large hands to rub her arms vigorously, warming her up. Renley just watched, a smile playing at his lips.

Burke pulled her a few steps backwards. "The boots are coming off too," he said, peppering kisses down her jaw.

She let him steer her to the chaise. He undid the laces of each muddy boot, tugging it off and tossing it aside. The last piece of clothing that stood between her and total nakedness was her sad excuse for stockings. Burke reached under the folded sheet, his hands sliding up the length of her calves until he found the garters tying them in place. He tugged the string of each garter, then slid the wet stockings down her legs.

She sat there, heart pounding, looking up at her two shirtless men. Burke was perched on one knee, his gorgeous, muscled chest on display, the swirl of black hair across his chest trailing down his stomach and disappearing into his trousers. Renley stood just behind, tattooed and beautiful, his eyes fixed on her. They waited, holding their breath.

Slowly, Rosalie got to her feet. Burke did too. She looked from one man to the other. "We stay in this dream a while longer," she whispered. "But when we wake . . ."

Renley and Burke exchanged a glance. "We both know what this is," said Renley.

She nodded, but the words needed to be spoken. "No one must know," she whispered. "I'll be ruined. Please, I'll—"

"No one will ever know what happens here," Renley replied, voice firm. "This dream belongs to the three of us alone."

With more confidence than she felt, she opened the sheet and dropped it back down to the chaise. Both men groaned as they took in her nakedness—the swell of her breasts, the peak of her nipples, her soft curves. "Well . . . are you just going to stand there?"

"Fuck," Renley muttered again, stepping past Burke to wrap her in his arms, his mouth claiming hers in another heady kiss. His hands roved from her shoulders down her back, all the way to cup her bottom. He lifted her slightly, pulling her hips flush with the hardness of his erection. It pleased her to know how strongly she affected him.

Then Burke was behind her, his hands sliding over her ribs. He gave a little tug to break her contact with Renley. She moaned, desperate to feel herself pressed against Renley's warmth, but the moan turned into a sigh when Burke cupped her breasts, using thumb and forefinger to tweak both her nipples.

"Oh god," she cried, leaning into Burke.

Renley held her by the hips as he dropped kisses down her neck. Burke moved his hand away so Renley's mouth could close over her nipple. He licked and kissed and teased until she was shaking. Before she could recover, Burke came around the other side of her and dropped his head too, taking her other breast in his mouth. They kissed her in tandem, Burke sucking while Renley flicked with his tongue.

Burke dropped his hand to brush lightly over the curls of her sex. "Is this perfect cunt ready for us?" He raised his head to kiss her neck and she leaned into his touch. "Do you want to let Tom taste it?"

"Yes," she panted. "Yes, more—"

"You heard her, Tom," Burke said, tucking her in front of him. He palmed both her breasts with measured strokes.

She wiggled her hips against him, seeking the hardness of his cock.

He growled in her ear, biting the lobe until she hissed. "Play fair. I'm trying to share, which doesn't come naturally to me. If cocks come out, I might go feral and rip off his fucking head." Renley just gave a dark chuckle. "Now, let Tom please you."

She whimpered again as Renley's hand slid down to her

sex. He used one finger to gently open her, testing to see if she was ready. Silly sailor, she'd been soaking since they were in the woods.

Renley groaned. "She's so wet."

"I told you," Burke said, kissing her neck. "She's perfect. Wait till you taste."

Rosalie was utterly at their mercy. She let herself be held upright by Burke as Renley slid his fingers up and down against her sex, swirling with each stroke at the top of her legs. She wasn't going to last long. She chased his fingers with her hips, trying to get them to stay at the spot where she wanted them.

"Don't get greedy," Renley warned, his breath hot in her ear. "Good girls who stand still get to come more than once."

She sagged against Burke, trying to stay focused on her pleasure. Then Renley slid two fingers into her. "Oh—god—" she cried out, her core already clenching around him.

Both men groaned.

Renley pumped his fingers in and out, teasing her with his slow pace.

"Please, please," she whispered.

"She's insatiable," Burke said with a chuckle, tweaking both her nipples in time with how Renley stroked her.

In moments she was doubling over as she came. It was quick and brutal, burning through her.

"There it is," Burke murmured, kissing her shoulder. "That's one, love."

Renley panted, pulling out of her. "We're nowhere near done with you." He gripped her face with his soaking fingers and kissed her deep, opening her mouth with his eager tongue.

Burke broke their kiss, dragging her back. "All right, enough. That sweet cunt is mine now. Rosalie, sit."

She flinched at the command in his voice, but her legs were already taking her to the chaise. She sat down, eyes wide as Burke dropped to his knees in front of her.

"Lean back," he said, pressing gently on her abdomen. "Your next release is mine."

She leaned back on the chaise. It was an odd angle, but she didn't care. All she cared about was that Burke's fingers were on her sex. It was almost obscene how wet she felt. She could hear it as he moved his fingers with lazy strokes.

"God, I need to taste you," he groaned. "I'm dying from wanting you." He leaned into her spread legs, kissing and licking up her thigh. Then his mouth was on her, and she thought she might die. No man had ever done this to her before. He lapped with gentle strokes, his tongue like warm velvet. When he sucked, she dropped her head back, melting into the chaise.

She moaned, raising both hands to grip the back of the chaise as her hips began to move on their own, pressing into Burke as his tongue teased, working with his fingers to send her over the edge again. As she sighed out her pleasure, Renley was there to swallow the sound, his tongue licking inside her mouth.

"I want more—*ah*—" Her legs trembled as Burke pressed his tongue in as deep as it would go, rubbing her with his fingers on that sweet spot. She broke the kiss with Renley, panting for air. "Oh—Burke—yes, *ahh*—"

Burke switched his order, shoving two fingers deep inside her as he dropped his mouth to the top of her sex, sucking on her bud until she shattered. Her core clenched over and over, as her whole body shook.

"Good girl," Renley murmured. "So beautiful. Fuck, you're so responsive. You're like poetry, Rose." He dropped his head to her shoulder, nuzzling her neck, one hand cupping her breast.

Burke placed lazy kisses down her leg as he slowly pulled his fingers out of her quivering core.

She sighed with contentment, eyes closed, one hand stroking Renley's golden curls as she reached blindly for Burke with the other.

Burke rose off his knees and sat on her other side. "Do you want to taste?"

She opened her eyes to see his soaking wet fingers. Her heart skipped a beat. Was she allowed to want this? Too blissed to care, she parted her lips and nodded.

"Oh, fuck yes. God, Rose, taste yourself," Renley groaned, lifting his head off her shoulder to watch as she opened her mouth and let Burke slide his wet fingers inside.

She moaned softly at the intrusion, trying to control how deep he pressed with her tongue. The taste on his fingers was sweet, a little salty.

"I want you so badly." Renley kissed her shoulder as one hand dropped to cup his erection.

"This time is only about her," Burke replied, his tone firm. "If she lets us have a next time, we'll make this a mutual claiming."

She blinked, looking from one to the other. "But I want to make you feel good—"

"This *does* feel good, love. This is amazing. *You're* amazing. You're taking a leap of trust by letting us both touch you like this. Next time, you can show us what that talented tongue of yours can do."

"Do you want to come again?" Renley asked as his fingers traced down her sternum.

She moaned, hips squirming. Was she pulling away or pushing closer? She could hardly tell. Both men took their time kissing her face, her lips, her shoulders, her breasts. They touched her all over, sliding their rough fingers over her smooth skin. She secretly thrilled at the coarseness of their hands. Renley's were rougher, the pads of his fingers driving her wild with new sensation as he traced along the line of her collarbone.

Burke slipped a hand under her leg and pulled it wide as Renley dropped off the couch and settled on his knees in front of her. She whimpered, not ready for another round, and aching for it at the same time. These men were going to ruin her. There would be no other men after this. No other kisses. No other caresses. The adoration they showed her was so tender. She felt precious, promised . . . sacred.

Burke wrapped her in his embrace, holding her open. "Come one more time for us, love."

"So perfect," Renley whispered, kissing and licking her sex, stroking his hands over her hips, making her twitch in Burke's grip. Renley's tongue lapped at her with slow, even strokes and she began to shake.

Burke tightened his hold. "Good girl," he whispered in her ear, his thumb stroking the underside of her thigh while his other hand cupped her breast, kneading it softly. "Feel how he touches you, how he worships you. Do you like it?"

"Yes," she moaned.

Renley pressed his fingers deep inside her and held them still, filling her up, as he continued his slow, steady strokes with his tongue. She wiggled her hips, trying to get his fingers to drag along her inner walls. "Hold still," he growled, nipping the inside of her thigh.

She squeaked and sank back, body going limp as he kept his fingers inside. The tension made her pant.

"What do you want, siren?" Burke whispered. "Where does it ache?"

"There," she moaned. "Everywhere."

"What do you want?"

Renley hummed against her sex as he started to move his fingers at last. He twisted them as he dragged them in and out, and she wanted to die. With his free hand, he pushed on her other thigh, opening her even wider. He pulled his mouth away, glancing up at Burke. "She's close. If we're doing this—"

"Are you?"

"I'm willing if you are."

She tried to listen as they had one of their special conversations where less than half the words were spoken aloud.

"What do you want, siren?" Burke pressed again. "Do you want to come? You have to say it. We don't finish unless you say it."

She moaned. She'd give anything to chase the high of being theirs a little longer. When this ended, they'd all go back to being . . . whatever this was. Friends? Housemates? Acquaintances with a primal urge to possess?

"I want to come," she whispered. "Please, god—"

Burke kissed her neck as he slid away from her.

Still on his knees, Renley shifted over. Burke dropped next to him. Her perfect, shirtless men rubbed shoulders as they each took hold of one of her legs. What were they doing? What was happening?

"Oh god, I can't—it's too much—"

"Want us to stop?" Renley asked, hearing her incoherent protests.

"Don't you dare—*ah*—"

Burke descended, his tongue making her quiver. After a moment, he pulled back, twisting his torso and putting an arm around Renley, pulling him forward to take his place. Renley sucked and flicked at her with his velvet tongue as Burke watched, one hand still on his shoulder.

She was writhing under them, her hips desperate for more friction, more everything.

They switched places.

"Hold still, and we'll tongue fuck you together until you come apart," Burke growled, keeping his face low to her sex.

She whined, taking short, labored breaths. Just when she thought she couldn't take any more, they muttered a few low words to each other, their breath hot against her thighs. Then they attacked. Both tongues worked her over at once. Her head fell back, eyes shut tight.

In the end, she was too cowardly to look. She couldn't bear to see the way their hot mouths came together, tongues stroking each other as they consumed her. She didn't even know whose fingers plunged inside her, but as soon as they did, she came harder than either of the first two times. It rocked through her, sending her body curling forward with wave after wave of euphoria.

Once the cresting ceased, she felt weak and boneless, utterly spent. Her naked body wanted to curl up on the sofa as she fought sleep . . . and the urge to cry. The dream was over. They were done . . . and this might never happen again.

Renley sat next to her and pulled her into his lap, hugging her to him as he slowly stroked her naked back. "You did so well," he murmured. "You were so perfect. You're amazing, Rose. So beautiful." He dragged the sheet out from under them and wrapped her in it, all while kissing her wet hair and whispering more soft words.

She soaked up his praise, pressing her cheek over his steady heartbeat. It calmed her to feel him so calm, so perfectly comfortable with what just happened between them. She smiled against his warmth, knowing her cheek was pressed against his anchor tattoo. How fitting. Without realizing the how or when of it, he was becoming *her* anchor.

Burke gathered all her clothes and brought them over. "I'm sorry, love, but if we don't get you back in these wet things and upstairs, you'll miss the dinner gong, and they'll likely send out a search party."

"Can you stand yet?" Renley asked, stroking her loose hair behind her ear.

She shook her head, not yet capable of speech either. She was right to worry. These men ruined her. The violence of their passion, their dedication to her pleasure . . . and they were holding back. What might it be like when they were fully unleashed? When they let her give them pleasure in return? The very idea made her tremble all over again.

52

Rosalie

THE NEXT TWO days passed in a whirlwind. Rosalie hardly had a moment to herself as the duchess kept her busy preparing for the ball. It was exciting work, and Rosalie found a kind of pleasure in feeling at home enough to speak a command and have it followed. She finalized menus, prepared dance cards, and toured the greenhouses to inspect the flower shipments with the duchess. They opened the ballroom to have all the sconces and chandeliers prepared with eight-hour waxes.

On Wednesday, the musicians arrived, and Rosalie got to oversee their rehearsal. A few of the other girls slipped in, and before long, they were taking turns reeling around the wide-open space. There were no gentleman for dancing because the last of the shooting had all the men in the heather, bagging as many birds as they could before the season closed.

Even with all the distractions, Renley and Burke were as attentive as they could be . . . without drawing unwanted attention. On the first night, Renley escorted Rosalie into the dining room, leaning in as they passed through the door to whisper, "You look beautiful tonight." As he lowered her to her chair, he gave her hand a squeeze and winked.

She stilled, her gloved hand closing around a hidden slip of folded paper. She dropped her hand to her lap, fist clenched tight, watching as he walked away. She opened the piece of paper under the table and read:

I still taste you on my tongue

Heat flooded her core as she glanced up, trying to meet his eye. But Renley was turned away, dutifully pretending to listen as Elizabeth told an animated story that involved many a flutter of her lashes. It gave Rosalie no small thrill to think that she held sway over this man, that he could speak to Elizabeth and yet be thinking of her.

From across the table, Burke met her gaze and smiled. She took a deep breath, trying to control the fluttering of her heart. She needed to feel their kisses again . . . and soon.

But it was impossible to even contemplate getting them alone, for the house was bursting with people. From morning to night, additional staff hurried everywhere—footmen carrying trays, maids dusting everything, laborers moving furniture and rolling up rugs, men from town with endless deliveries. It was usually all Rosalie could do to stay out of their way.

Not to mention the new wave of guests arriving each day who were privileged enough to stay in the house the night before and after the ball. On Wednesday morning, the stately Duchess of Somerset arrived with her comely spinster sister. Shortly before dinner, Madeline's father arrived, the large and imposing Viscount Raleigh. He shared a carriage down from Town with the Earl of Waverley. By luncheon Thursday, another viscount and his countess joined the party, along with a few other aristocrats and friends. By Thursday dinner, the house party had grown from sixteen to thirty-six.

Rosalie actually enjoyed herself at dinner, seated as she

was between Madeline and a friendly young man named Charles Bray. He was the nephew of Mr. Selby. Apparently, the Corbins were supporting his education at Cambridge.

"So, you will graduate in the spring, and what comes next for you, sir?" she asked, taking another sip of her white soup.

"I hope to be assigned a position," he replied. "I've never been much for city life. A little parish in the country would suit me quite well."

"And how shall you like making sermons?"

He smiled, tasting his wine. "Oh, this is very good," he murmured, enjoying another sip. "A man in my position can't really afford not to have a position, Miss Harrow. Second son and all that," he said with a wave of his hand.

She stifled a smile. She was well aware of the responsibilities of second sons. She glanced across the table, feeling Burke's eyes on her. She gave him a little smile that he did not return. His jaw was tight, his mouth a thin line. He was seated next to Olivia, so Rosalie could only imagine the gorgon was making him miserable. She gave him a sympathetic look before turning her attention back to Mr. Bray.

"But what about you, Miss Harrow? How are you connected to the Corbins?"

"My mother was friends with the duchess," she replied. "They grew up together in Richmond."

"Well, you're a long way from home."

"Oh no, I live in Town now," she explained. "My aunt keeps a flat in Cheapside."

"Cheapside, eh? You must be quite a fish out of water in this set," he said, his eye trailing around the gaudy opulence of the room.

"Well, I . . ."

"I mean no offense," he added, leaning in. "I'm miserably awkward at these events. Poor Uncle Selby always invites me, and I always leave feeling as though I've been beaten about the head with a stick. It's a relief to talk to someone who actually looks me in the eye and doesn't judge me for my sec-ondhand dinner clothes."

She smiled. "I fully understand you, sir. Most of these ladies wear their diamonds to breakfast."

They both laughed.

By the time the dinner ended, Rosalie was contentedly chatting between Madeline and Mr. Bray. Even Madeline seemed taken in by his easy charm. It warmed Rosalie to watch her smile and laugh with confidence, asking him ques-tions and following his stories.

The duchess led the way to the drawing room. As the ladies crossed the hall, Rosalie grabbed Madeline's hand. "Make my excuses, and I'll go slip into the library and fetch that book you mentioned to Mr. Bray," she said in a whisper.

Madeline's eyes went wide. "Oh, Rosalie, don't—"

"You can give it to him when the gentlemen come to the drawing room."

"I couldn't possibly," she replied on a blush.

"Oh, yes you can," Rosalie said, giving her hand a squeeze. "I think he's lovely, and you get on so well. It doesn't have to come to anything," she added when she sensed Madeline's hesitation. "Just have a little fun. I'm not taking no for an answer."

Madeline frowned. "I'm not sure if you're proving to be a good friend or a bad one."

Rosalie laughed. "Stick with me, and you'll learn that sometimes it's good to be bad," she said with a sly wink.

Madeline groaned and let her go.

Rosalie retrieved a candle from a footman and slipped into the dark library, making her way over to the section reserved for novels. She held out the candle, reading the spines of each book as her finger brushed over the cool leather. She smiled as she pulled free *The Mysteries of Udolpho*, the tale of a young maiden sent to live in a dark, mysterious castle. She was surprised by Mr. Bray's interest in Gothic romance. She was equally surprised to learn Madeline was a voracious reader of the genre too.

"Looking for something, little siren?"

She turned with a smile to see Burke standing in the corner near the door. The man had a talent for entering a room unnoticed. With his dark hair and black evening clothes, the only thing she could see clearly was the white of his shirt and his crisply tied cravat. "What are you doing in here?" she whispered.

"I could ask you the same thing."

His tone set her on edge. Heavens, but Olivia must have put him in a sour mood. "Did anyone see you?"

"Do you take me for an amateur?" He took a few steps closer. He wasn't so much crossing the room towards her as he was stalking. She swallowed, unsure whether she was meant to feel frightened or excited by this feral display . . . perhaps both. "Why are you in here?" he repeated.

"We discussed a book at dinner with Mr. Bray." She held up the leather-bound novel. "I just wanted to retrieve it before the gentlemen came through. Am I too late? You can't possibly be done with your brandy yet."

He closed the space until he was standing right before her. His pull was magnetic. The others may have upset him, but she knew she could bring a smile back to those beautiful lips. She set her candle and book aside and reached out to him with both hands. "What happened?"

He stepped back with a scowl, staying just out of reach. "Is Bray next, then?" he growled.

She dropped her hands, feeling the sharp sting of his rejection. "Burke, tell me—"

"I said is Bray next?"

She blinked. "What are you—"

"I'm just trying to determine how many of us you will try to juggle," he said, his voice dripping with disdain. "Surely there must be a limit. Even George can't manage more than four candlesticks at once."

His full meaning hit her like a slap to the face. Her breath escaped in a gasp. "Oh . . . you *devil*." She squared her shoulders at him, which still made her little more than a lamb before a lion. "Speak plainly, Burke. What is it you accuse me of?"

"I saw you at dinner," he snarled. "I saw your simpers and your smiles, the way you leaned into his every laugh. Do you now intend to throw yourself at Charles Bray?"

"No, what you *saw* was me performing my duty by being perfectly cordial to a guest of the Corbins," she countered, hands on her hips. "I spoke to him because it is the *polite* thing to do. I smiled because Mr. Bray is friendly. I laughed because he is funny. That doesn't mean I plan to 'juggle' him, as you so condescendingly put it."

He scoffed. "Can you blame my confusion? You've made it clear you have no interest in us beyond the pleasure we give you. Am I wrong to think you would gladly add another man to your harem? Would you add this idiot Bray before you even consider James—"

"Stop," she hissed. "I will not let you bully me. If Renley were here and heard you being so cruel, I'd like to think he would thrash you for it."

A muscle twitched in his jaw, but he said nothing.

"But I'm used to fighting my own battles," she said. "I could never best you physically, so let me use words as my weapon. Burke, you do not own me. You will *never* own me. If you think to keep me in a cage, I will have to tell you I will *die* first."

"Rosalie—"

"No, I am speaking," she said, cutting him off with a heated look. "You insulted me. Once, I would have let you, and maybe even thanked you for it. Once, I let men hurt me. I accepted every cruel word, every vicious, cutting look. I handled tempers and rages. I took beatings in silence, and—"

Burke's countenance changed so fast it made her head spin. He stepped into her with a different kind of fire burning through him as he gripped her shoulders with both hands. "What the hell are you talking about?"

She shrugged away from him and raised her chin in steely defiance. "My life is no fairy tale. My father was a monster. He blamed my mother for every setback, and he hated me. He liked to see me cry. You think you can tear me down with your petulant remarks? Throw my love back in my face the second you begin to doubt it? Well, you can go to hell. Anything you can think to try, Francis Harrow has already done. He broke me in every way you can imagine. I rebuilt myself stronger. So, go ahead and do your worst."

"You can't say these things to me," he said, voice tight.

She crossed her arms over her chest. "And why not?"

"Because it makes me want to *kill* whoever hurt you," he replied, leaning into her space, trying to claim her air. "Give me their names, and I'll bring you their heads."

Her stomach flipped, but she was too angry to give in. Had Renley not threatened to do the same? She was luring them too close. This was impossible. She had to put a stop to it. She snatched up the book and candle. "Don't trouble yourself. You cannot kill a dead man, and I'm clearly not worth the effort."

"Rosalie—"

"Not that it's any of your business," she added, stepping past him, "but I was retrieving this book so *Madeline* could give it to Mr. Bray. It was she who recommended it at dinner. I think he might be perfect for her, so I am meddling, as any good friend would. Not for one second did I think of him for myself, because I imagined myself falling for *you*. But no man who calls me whore gets to call me his."

"Rosalie, wait." He caught up to her, reaching for her arm. "Please—"

"Don't," she hissed. "I am the jezebel who simpers at all men, remember? Surely you can have nothing left to say to me."

"Rosalie—" He reached for her again, but she pulled away. "I was mad with jealousy. I was resentful and—*fuck*—I just want you so goddamn much. I feel like I can't breathe—"

"None of that is my problem," she said, sealing her heart behind a wall of stone. "Sort yourself out, Burke. I intend to accept the duchess' offer whether you want me here or not."

"I do—"

"And I intend to live my life exactly how *I* choose, without consideration from anyone else, least of all a man who uses the same pair of perfect lips to kiss me and curse me."

"Rosalie . . ."

"Good night, Mr. Burke." Without looking back, Rosalie left him standing in the dark. She just barely made it out the door before tears started falling down her face.

53

James

THE MORNING OF the ball arrived at last. James couldn't wait to put this whole day behind him. He was sick to death of having the house bursting with people. He stormed down the grand gallery, weaving between a trio of men toting away a rug and a harried florist carrying an arrangement so large he couldn't see around it.

"Christ's sake," James growled as the florist nearly crashed into him. "Bates, help this man get where he's going!" he called over to the footman. "And someone tell me where the *hell* is Burke!"

Something was wrong. He noticed last night but couldn't get Burke alone to ask. Then the man disappeared like a puff of smoke. Burke had agreed to lead some of the guests down to the lake this morning, but he never showed. He skipped breakfast too. James would have asked Renley about it, but he left after dinner too. He wouldn't be back until tonight, with his brother and sister-in-law in tow.

He took a sharp right out of the grand gallery towards the new wing, determined to hunt Burke down in the storage room. Before he could get that far, the man in question came through the door at the end of the hall.

"Where the hell have you been?" he called.

Burke looked miserable. His black hair was untidy, his eyes hooded with lack of sleep. He wasn't dressed properly either. He wore only half an ensemble—his riding boots and high slung tan trousers were to be expected, but he wore no waist-coat or cravat, not even a coat. No hat, no gloves, no walking stick.

"Where have you been?" James repeated.

"Walking," Burke grunted, stepping past James.

James struggled to control his frustration. "Where have you been walking looking like that?"

Burke swung left, making his way for the back staircase. "Fuck off, James. I'm in no mood."

"I know where you *weren't* walking," he called after Burke's retreating form. "We agreed you would take a group down to the lake at half eight, did we not? It is now half nine."

"Are you a talking pocket watch now?"

James growled, following quickly after his friend. "Tell me what happened."

"Just leave me alone."

"Damn it, don't walk away from me!"

"You're my friend, not my master," Burke barked over his shoulder. "I don't follow orders."

James felt the tenuous hold on his patience snap. Burke wasn't going to get away with pouting and being petulant for the next week as he mulled whatever grievance plagued him. James had entirely too much on his plate to manage without Burke's help. He thought fast. Nothing had ever been as effective at rousing Burke from one of his moods quite like physical exercise. This was going to be fun.

As Burke reached the bottom of the stairs, James took a few running steps and launched himself on Burke's back. He twisted both his arms under Burke's, wrapping them around his shoulders and linking them behind Burke's neck, effectively locking Burke's arms in place.

Burke stumbled forward. "James—*fuck*—"

James kicked out Burke's leg, dropping him down to one knee.

Burke growled like a bear, twisting and grunting as he tried to break James' hold on his shoulders. "Ouch—*get off*!"

"Say it," James laughed, holding on for dear life as Burke tried to wrestle free.

"Say what—"

"Call me *master*," James hissed in his ear.

Burke exploded. He heaved with all his might, slinging James free. James rolled to his feet, nearly knocking a vase of flowers off a table. He turned, fists raised. Burke scrambled to his feet too, chest heaving, eyes manic.

"Come on, then," James said with a playful beckon of his hand. "You may be an Oxford-trained boxer, but I'm a fucking Corbin. My ancestors grappled in the mud at Agincourt. Knights' blood flows in my veins. Take me down if you can, you little ponce."

Burke's eyes flashed obsidian as he lunged. James braced for impact as both men went sprawling to the floor. James hit the table with his shoulder, sending the vase and the spray of flowers crashing down. The vase shattered, pooling water over the parquet floor.

James grunted as Burke landed two good punches to his side. "Fucking hell—" He twisted his legs with Burke's, snaking his arms around until he could get Burke in a headlock. "Say it, and I'll let you go," he taunted, tightening his hold on Burke's neck.

"No—"

"Call me 'master' and I'll stop."

"Fuck you—"

James tightened his hold and Burke groaned, panting out what little breath he could catch in his lungs.

"Christ, man, say it before you pass out," James urged.

"God—*damn it*—"

"Excuse me," came a soft voice.

Both men looked up to see Madeline floating down the stairs. She slipped past them both sprawled on the floor. James loosened his hold and Burke took a gasping breath.

"Lady Madeline," James murmured with a nod.

"Good morning, Lord James," she replied, making no comment about their ridiculous display. She navigated the shards of broken vase and went on her way.

Burke used the distraction to scramble out of James' grasp, flopping on his back and leaning against the bottom stair. "What the hell was that?" he said as soon as she was safely around the corner.

James dabbed at his lip and blinked to see a stain of blood on the back of his hand. "Christ, did you split my lip?"

Burke just laughed.

He fished in his pocket for a handkerchief and leaned against the wall, his legs stretched out across the carpet. "So . . . what happened?"

Burke shrugged. "Nothing you couldn't have predicted."

A thousand thoughts flashed through his mind as he paused with the handkerchief halfway to his lip. His cheeks suddenly blazed at Burke's guilty look. "Did you—"

"Not exactly," Burke replied. "But I ruined everything. I pushed her too far."

A feral anger simmered in his chest. "What does that mean?"

"I may have said something stupid. I saw her with Bray last night and I just—I lost control. I had to know—"

"Whoa, stop." James held up a hand. "What do you mean you *saw* her with Bray?"

"It was nothing. She was just talking to him at dinner . . . but I snapped. I want her so goddamn much," he said, dragging his hands through his hair. "I don't think I've ever—I *know* I've never—but I can't stand feeling like she's going to walk away. That I'm not enough. And there's Renley and you, and I just couldn't handle the idea of Bray too. Sharing her is already hard enough."

"What the hell does that mean?"

Burke blinked. "What?"

"Sharing her is hard enough? What do you mean?"

There was that guilty look again. James wanted to punch it off his face.

"I . . . found her kissing Renley in the woods after the picnic. And I may have . . . joined in. I really don't mind Renley. He's a friend and . . . damn if it didn't turn me on," he added under his breath. "I mean, I could more easily share with you . . . but I draw the line at Charles fucking Bray."

This was a lot of information for James to process. Rosalie Harrow was kissing Burke. And now she was kissing Renley . . . and Burke . . . *together*. And if Burke's guilty looks were any indication, it may have gone further than kisses in the woods. The lady ought to show more propriety! It would be enough to ruin her if it were discovered. So why was James' first reaction jealousy? Why did he feel this tightening in his chest and a throbbing at his temple?

Holy hell . . . what else did Burke just say? James could hardly think straight. Burke was willing to share her with him. In what universe could James ever allow that to happen? Would he even want that?

Yes, a dark voice whispered. *Anything for a taste of her.*

He shoved the thought away. He could evaluate the cracks in his morality later. For now, Burke needed him. "What exactly did you say to the lady?"

Burke lifted his face off his hands. "I may have implied she was a jezebel seeking a harem of men." He glanced up. "I was angry and jealous and desperate to know if she really cares for me . . . but I already know how she feels. I feel it every time she moves, every time she looks at me, every time I touch her. Christ, it's electric. She's a goddess—"

"I don't want to hear."

Yes, he did. He wanted to hear everything. Every detail.

"I was a fool," Burke groaned. "She wants me and I'm pushing her away because I don't like her terms."

"And what are her terms?"

"No cages, no labels. She doesn't want marriage. Now I understand why. Her father was a monster, James. He hurt her. I think he might have . . ." He swallowed, his voice hollow. "She has boundaries to protect herself, and I stomped all over them."

"What . . . so she just wants to be free to love you and make love to you, and do the same with Renley, and never consider the idea of marriage to either of you? She expects you both to just live in sin with her?"

Burke just shrugged.

"And . . . what about what *you* want? Do you want to get married? You've never mentioned a word in the affirmative about the institution."

"What could I offer a woman in a marriage?" Burke muttered. "What lady would swoon at inheriting my soiled name and my empty pockets?"

James scowled. "You're being defeatist again, and I'll not stand for it. I told you we have a quick fix for both those challenges."

"James—"

"But you have to *want* to be married. Would you marry Rosalie Harrow if you could?"

"She doesn't want that," Burke muttered.

"I'm saying if she did. If right now she came sweeping down those stairs and said, 'Marry me, Burke' . . . would you do it?"

Burke let out a long exhale. "I don't want to leave you . . ."

James forced a laugh, even as he felt a tightening in his chest. "You've met my mother, right? Does she strike you as a particularly accommodating person? Do you think she'll accept your whirlwind romance and just let Rosalie move into the bachelor's corridor with you?"

"Alcott is my home," Burke replied softly. "As much as I want Rosalie, and as much as I want her to want me . . . I don't want to be forced to choose between her and Alcott . . . between her and you."

James swallowed thickly. This was getting precariously close to the kind of sentimentality that English gentleman were warned against from their earliest breaths. He got to his feet. "You know, I *can* stand on my own two feet. I can manage things here alone while you go find your own life. It won't mean we care for each other any less." He held out a hand, helping Burke to his feet.

"I don't want you to be alone. I want you to be happy," said Burke.

James smiled weakly. "Your happiness is my happiness."

"It's not enough," Burke replied, holding his gaze. "You are the best man I know, James. You deserve to be happy too."

James gave another false laugh. "Well, perhaps you can ask if Miss Harrow has a sister."

Burke's eyes were serious as he put a hand on James' shoulder. "Make jokes all you want, but I know you. I know how you feel about her. I know how you watch her. Don't ask me to make any of this make sense, because I can't . . . but I think she wants you too."

His words sent a stone sinking into the pit of James' stomach. It wasn't possible. What the hell was James supposed to do with this information?

"I know what I must do," Burke went on. "I intend to apologize. If she forgives me, I'm not going anywhere. You of all people know the strength of my constancy. If Rosalie Harrow will have me, I'm hers. She can name whatever bloody terms she wants."

James raised a wary brow. "Why are you . . ."

"Because, you need to know where I stand. If you seek to claim her . . . just know you'll be claiming me too."

54

James

JAMES LEFT BURKE at the stairs, his mind reeling as he went in search of his brother. This day was not going at all according to plan. Hell, this entire month had been a disaster. Rosalie Harrow crept in with the night and disrupted all their lives with the force of a hurricane.

Did his mother have any idea what she was doing when she invited the little vixen to stay? The Dowager Duchess of Norland was as clever as they came. James was sure she had a man investigate the girl. No doubt she already knew all the sordid details of Rosalie's life.

If James were a lesser man, he'd march into his mother's study and rattle all the drawers of her desk until he found the report. He wanted to read it for himself. He needed to know. Who was Rosalie Harrow? Why did his mother want her so badly? And how did James effectively go about disentangling her from their lives?

For that was the only solution, right? He couldn't possibly let her stay knowing she intended to ruin his friends, wrapping them around her jezebel's finger with no intent to marry either of them. That kind of behavior might be acceptable for a common prostitute or an opera singer, but it wasn't going to be the fate of a ward of this house.

Christ's sake, Burke and Renley must have gone mad. James was going to have to put his foot down. He just needed to think of a way to do it without hurting Burke . . . or running him off.

But this was all going to be tomorrow's problem, because tonight James had to survive the Michaelmas ball . . . and to survive in one piece meant guaranteeing his brother did the expected thing for once in his worthless goddamn life and announced his engagement.

"So, who's it going to be?" James said with a raised brow, leaning against the wall just inside George's room. "Mother needs to know now so we have everything arranged for tonight."

"Let me show you what I have planned," George said, smiling. He went over to an armoire in the corner of the room that James knew held all manner of unspeakable items.

James raised a wary brow. "George, if this is a sex thing—"

George tsked. "Do you think I would discuss that with you? I doubt you even know where to put it—"

"George," he warned.

"A joke," George said, both hands raised in mock surrender.

"I just need a name. Mother wants no surprises."

"Yes, look . . . here's the thing," George hedged. "I've delayed in telling you my plans because they're a bit unconventional. But I don't want you to be all up in arms until you've heard me out . . ."

James instantly had to fight the urge to be up in arms. "I'm listening . . ."

"Right, well . . ." George took a deep breath. "I've decided to marry Miss Nash."

"That's wonderful. Which one?"

George gave a sheepish smile. "I'd actually rather determined that I'd like to have the set."

James blinked. "The set?"

"Mother's vision for my life has always been to run the estate, get married, and have children. It's a horribly oppressive way to live, feeling like you have no choice. You can't imagine because you're a second son," George said with a wave of his hand.

James could have punched him. He didn't understand the pressure of being a duke? He lived that pressure every day as his brother ambled about, content to do fuck-all with his life.

"I confess, I've been rather rebellious," George admitted. "But I've seen the light, James. The Nash sisters have been helping me to see the light, and I really feel like a changed man. My new vision for my future is *twins*."

James blinked again. "And by twins, you mean . . ."

"I mean, I shall live here at Alcott with the Nash sisters as my wives. Well, one wife, one mistress, I suppose—though I've never really liked the term mistress," he added under his breath. "It's brilliant, eh?"

James reeled. All the men around him were going mad. "George . . . you *cannot* be serious!"

"Whyever not? Do you really think I'm the first peer to have a wife and a mistress?"

"Most mistresses are not the daughter of a lord," James replied. "They are not related to the duchess!"

George just scoffed again. "I'm sorry, but I believe the Boleyn sisters just popped out of the grave to say, 'I beg your pardon?'"

"Stop trying to make jokes," James snapped. "Christ, you must be sensible. You have to pick one."

"I'll only *marry* one, obviously," George replied, his nose in a drawer.

James crossed the room to his brother's side. "Which one?"

"It doesn't matter to me which one walks down the aisle—*ah*—here it is. This is what I wanted to show you. I plan to give it to . . . one of them." He turned, opening the lid of a box to show James a beautifully cut emerald ring set with diamonds. It once belonged to their grandmother.

"Which one will you give it to, George?" James repeated.

"I just said I don't care. Hmm . . . perhaps I should have two rings. One for each? Fairness and all that," he added. "I know I have something suitable in here." He continued to dig in the top drawer.

"George, you have to choose—"

"No. If I choose, it will seem like I have a favorite, and that's no way to start a marriage. I'll let them choose. They can flip for it."

"Flip for it?"

"Sure," George replied. "You know, flip a coin. Heads a duchess, tails a mistress."

This was how James would die; he was sure of it. He would handle this crisis, then tumble down the stairs to his death. "You are mad," he muttered, sinking onto the bed. "I really think you've all gone mad."

"It does seem to be going around, doesn't it?" George replied. "Here, this ought to do nicely." He turned with a new bauble held flat in his palm. It was a diamond brooch with a pearl drop the size of a quail's egg. He opened his other palm to reveal the emerald ring. "What do you think?"

"I think you are perhaps my least favorite person to ever walk this earth," James replied honestly.

George just laughed again. "Fair enough. But I meant about the baubles."

"I can't be part of this," he muttered. "I can't watch you raise one up while you ruin the other. One gets to be your wife, and the other your mistress? One lauded the realm over as your duchess, the other your whore? It's too cruel for words. They don't deserve you."

George groaned. "Christ, you're such an insufferable prude. Even our dear father kept a mistress at Corbin House. For years, James. And she's a lovely dear, quite fun dinner company," he added. "I had to move her out when he died, of course. Mama wouldn't have it any other way. But we still find time to dine together whenever I'm in Town."

James wasn't a fool. He knew all about his father's French mistress. "You still dine with our dead father's mistress? You're seen together in public?"

"Of course not. I've rented her a nice little flat in Leicester Square."

This had James seeing red. "You still pay for her upkeep?" He took a shaky breath, bracing his clenched fists against his knees. "George . . . I swear to the Almighty, if you are fucking our dead father's mistress—"

"How *dare* you," George said with a glower. "She is like a sister to me. We're *friends*."

James exhaled. This was some relief, at least.

"I couldn't very well put her out on the street. It wouldn't have been the Christian thing. After so many years of loyal service, I figured it was the least she was owed."

James shot off the end of the bed and began pacing. "Does Mother know?"

George gave him an affronted look, one hand on his hip.

"Little brother, it pains me to say it, but sometimes I question how we're even related."

James seethed. "I wish to God every day we weren't related," he snapped. "Burke has been more a brother to me than you have ever been!"

"And Helene is more a sister to me than *you* have ever been," George retorted.

"Who the *fuck* is Helene?"

"Helene!" George cried, hands raised in exasperation. "Father's mistress. Helene! How can you be so unfeeling? You met her multiple times, James."

"Christ, spare me from this madness," James muttered. "Spare me. I can't handle this right now."

"For once, I'm not asking you to do a thing," George said. "I'll get down on one knee and everything. Mama will have absolutely nothing for which to reproach me, I promise."

A bitter laugh escaped him. "Except for the fact that you're proposing to *two* women."

George just shrugged. "Mama is a rationalist. If she expects me to marry, this is the bargain she must accept. The girls are up for it," he added. "I don't know why it should be a spot of bother to anyone else."

Now James quivered. When his voice came out, it was easily half an octave too low. "George . . . tell me you did not already push this idea on the Nash twins. Tell me you have not so disgraced us as to actually pitch this ludicrous idea to them!"

"Of course, I did," George replied. "And they were more than agreeable. They don't care about propriety either. English social mores are far too confining. They understand. All they want is financial security and the protection of my title to live how they see fit."

For a horrifying moment, James felt his life flashing before his eyes. He imagined the Nash twins inserting themselves into every facet of his life—meals together, redecorating rooms, arguing over dress money and imported glass for pineries, catching them in George's arms in all manner of odd places. James would have to move. There'd be nothing else to be done. He'd have to resign the fate of the dukedom to George. Perhaps he'd move into Corbin House permanently, though he hated being in Town. He could go abroad . . . Switzerland or Greece. Anywhere but Alcott Hall, living every day in the shadow of George, his duchess, and his identical mistress.

"What do you expect me to tell our mother?" he asked with a raised brow.

"Tell her whatever you think is best," George said with a shrug. "The twins have impeccable taste. I'm sure they'll put together a lovely wedding by Christmas. I'm thinking Bath in the New Year, and then on to Italy for the spring."

"And you'll . . . just bring them both, I suppose," James said, his tone flat.

"Of course," George replied.

"And the children?"

"What children?"

James scowled. "Children, George. What if you get your mistress pregnant first? The only legitimate heirs will be those from your legal wife."

"Hmm, I hadn't thought of that," George muttered.

James saw a fleeting ray of hope. Could he actually manage to make George abandon this scheme using a reasoned argument?

"I'll acknowledge them either way," George said with a shrug. "I can't imagine the twins would care so long as all their needs are met, but I'll ask. Thank you, James. I'm glad to have you on board with this."

James dragged a very tired hand through his hair. "I really think I hate you."

George gave him a sad sort of smile. "I know. Life has treated us both unkindly. It raised me up, when I am the most unworthy of men, and it keeps you living in my shadow. We both suffer—me from hating my position, and you from hating me. If only the roles were reversed, eh? What an excellent second son I would have made."

James couldn't help the weak smile that quirked his lips.

"What about you, then? Mama will be on you to marry next. Any progress with Miss Harrow?"

James blinked. Why the hell was everyone on him about Miss bloody fucking Harrow? "Miss—what? No, I'm not—she's—"

George's smile spread as his eyes twinkled again. "Very articulate."

James snapped his mouth shut. "It's complicated."

"It's always complicated with you," George replied. "Do you want my advice?"

"No."

"Uncomplicate it," George said anyway. "If you let that one get away, you'll never find another like her."

"Lucky for you, that will not be your lot," James retorted, moving for the door.

George barked a laugh. "Aye, I suppose that's true. If I lose one, I'll have a spare. It's brilliant, no?"

James sighed. "No."

55

Rosalie

ROSALIE FELT AN odd sort of fluttering in her chest as she sat at the mirror. Sarah stood behind her, fixing her hair. It was a far more ornate style than Rosalie was used to. Sarah used powder and pins to make it stay, weaving some decorative pearls into Rosalie's dark strands.

"I'm done, miss."

Rosalie tilted her head, admiring the style. "It's so beautiful," she murmured. "You have a real talent. You could be a proper lady's maid."

Sarah blushed and hurried over to pick up Rosalie's gown. "I've never seen such a pretty blue," she said with a sigh, holding it out.

Sarah helped her shimmy into it, and Rosalie took a deep breath as Sarah latched the hooks and eyes up her back. The dress had cap sleeves and exposed her décolletage in a wide *V*. The jade and gold brocade trim wrapped beneath her breasts, while the soft satin of the skirt fluttered in folds down to the floor.

Before Rosalie could reach for her gloves, there came a knock at the door. Sarah hurried over to open it and exchanged a few words with someone in the hallway. She turned holding a small velvet box in her hands.

"This is for you, miss," she said, a broad smile on her face.

Rosalie knew a jewelry box when she saw one. "Who was that?"

Sarah held out the box. "This is from the duchess."

Rosalie flipped open the lid and gasped. Inside sat a beautiful, three-strand pearl necklace with an intricate diamond clasp. There was a little note folded inside as well. Rosalie took it and read the words twice, tears stinging her eyes.

In another life, this might all have been yours.
Please accept this as a small token of my friendship.
HWC

Sarah took the necklace out of the box and placed it around Rosalie's neck, angling the diamond clasp over her collarbone. The pearls felt cool against her skin. Rosalie turned and faced herself in the mirror, hardly recognizing the woman who looked back. She fingered the lowest strand of pearls. This was a very fine piece of jewelry, finer than anything Rosalie could afford in a lifetime. And the duchess had just . . . parted with it. Knowing what she knew of the duchess, could Rosalie allow her friendship to be bought?

She smiled at her reflection in the mirror as Sarah handed her the white, elbow-length gloves. She slipped on the first glove and touched the pearls again. Perhaps Rosalie couldn't be bought . . . but she certainly didn't object to such a lovely attempt.

The entry hall was full of guests by the time Rosalie floated down the stairs. It was one of her favorite rooms, with the black and white marble floor and walls arching up three stories high, every inch adorned in art. Two dozen people queued before the doors that led to the grand gallery.

Renley was the first friendly face she spied as she neared the bottom of the stairs. He looked dashing as ever in his naval dress uniform. His golden curls seemed less unruly tonight, slicked around the ears and brushed back off his forehead. She had to fight the urge to raise a gloved hand and muss it. She liked it when he looked a little more windswept.

"Good lord, Rose. You're a vision," he said with a wide smile. "Give the other ladies a chance, won't you?"

She smiled in return, feeling a blush in her cheeks as she noted the way his eyes trailed down her body. It had been three days, but she still felt him everywhere. His lips, his tongue, his steady hands. Was he thinking about her in that way?

Friends. You both agreed . . . and when he marries, you must let him go.

He held out an arm to her. "May I escort you in? I'd like you to meet my brother and sister . . . if it's not an imposition . . ."

"Of course," she replied, accepting his arm.

They joined the receiving line, waiting as the duke, duchess, and James greeted each guest. The duchess was resplendent in a mustard-yellow gown with ruby-red accents. A spray of red roses adorned her fashionable powdered wig. Her tiara glittered with a hundred diamonds, while more stones sparkled at her ears, wrists, and throat.

James saw her first, his eye trailing down her face and settling on the pearls at her neck. That muscle in his jaw twitched before he let his eye pass over to Renley. It was only when he looked away from her that she realized she'd been holding her breath.

"Good evening, Renley," said the duke.

"Evening, Your Grace," Renley replied with a bow. "Your Grace," he added a bow for the duchess.

"And who is this delightful—" The duke gasped, wide smile on his face as he jabbed his brother in the ribs. "Why, it's our own little Miss Harrow. James, look. It's Miss Harrow."

"Yes, I see her," James said through a tight smile.

"Your Grace." Rosalie prepared to drop into a curtsy, but the duke stuck out his hand, as if they were old friends. She paused in a sort of half curtsy and slowly reached out her own hand. The duke took it in both of his and bowed slightly, his lips touching her knuckle. Her eye darted over to James, who watched with a veiled expression.

"You shine as brightly as any ornament here," the duke murmured. "I was a fool to ever think you a common Cabbage Rose."

"That's quite enough," came the duchess' stern voice. "George, you're holding up the line. Let Miss Harrow go at once."

The duke gave her a little wink before dropping her hand.

Renley tugged on her arm. "What the hell was that about?"

"I have no idea," she replied honestly.

"Don't worry," he replied. "I'll tell Burke. George can play his little games with the others, but he'll not be playing them with you. If we need to, we'll unleash James on him."

Her stomach did a little flip at the thought of these men protecting her, even from something as harmless as the empty flattery of George Corbin.

Renley led her down the crowded grand gallery towards the ballroom. It felt strange to see the house so full of people. "Colin, you've found the famous Corbin punchbowl already," Renley called.

A handsome man turned, clutching a glass of punch. His

eyes were just the same shade of blue as Renley's. He was narrower in the shoulders. His hair was darker too, and his face was lined with grey at his temples. He had a kindness about him that warmed Rosalie instantly. He glanced from Renley to Rosalie, his quirked smile growing.

"Colin, may I present Miss Rosalie Harrow," said Renley. "Rose, this is my brother, Colin Renley."

"It's very nice to meet you, sir," she said, dipping into a curtsy.

"Gracious, Tom, she's beautiful," a woman cooed at Renley's shoulder. She was terribly short, and with her kinky golden curls and pink cheeks, she looked almost childlike, but there was a strength in the directness of her gaze.

"My wife, Agatha," said Colin.

"Very pleased to meet you, ma'am," said Rosalie. "Renley has told me so much about you both. He's made me quite envious, as I have no siblings. But it would be just my luck that, if I did, they would never be half so kind as you."

Colin and Agatha shared some private look before they both turned to Renley. Colin laughed while Agatha beamed. "What on earth have you told the poor girl?" said his brother.

"Colin, hush." Agatha slapped him lightly with her folded fan. "Miss Harrow, come stand by me, and let me tell you no less than three embarrassing stories about our dear Tom before they start the dancing."

Renley released Rosalie's arm, letting her take a place between his brother and sister-in-law, who immediately launched into a story about a teenaged Renley and Burke, a cricket bat, and a bee's nest.

The ballroom was fit to bursting by the time the musicians played a processional to announce the arrival of the Corbins.

Rosalie was wedged along the wall between Renley and Agatha, a glass of sweet, fruity punch in hand. The master of ceremonies stood at the double doors and announced, "His Grace, the Duke of Norland, Her Grace, the Dowager Duchess of Norland, and The Right Honorable, The Viscount Finchley."

The duke swept in with his mother on his arm, James following behind. He cleared his throat and called out in a clear voice. "My Lords, Ladies, and Gentlemen, on behalf of my dear mama, my brother, and myself, I want to thank you for attending our ball tonight!"

The room clapped appreciatively.

"The annual Michaelmas ball has been a tradition in the Corbin family since the reign of the third duke. It is an event we look forward to every year with great anticipation. This year is no exception." His eye trailed over to the opposite wall, where many of the young ladies stood at attention, including the preening Nash sisters in matching dresses of blush pink, the Swindon sisters with their fiery red hair piled in curls, and Lady Olivia, who seemed to take no enjoyment from the duke's speech and was busy fanning herself.

"The hard work of the harvest is done," the duke continued. "As autumn sets and the long, cold winter begins, let us celebrate with a rousing night of dancing, feasting, and furious frivolity!"

The excitement in the room seemed ready to boil over as the duke swept forward with the stately Duchess of Somerset on his arm. He had to open the dance with the highest-ranking lady in the room. Rosalie watched as James bowed over the hand of Olivia's mother. As a marchioness, she was the next highest in rank. Other couples swirled as the master of ceremonies called out the dance: "Mr. Beveridge's Maggot!"

Renley leaned in, his breath warm against her ear. "Well, Miss Harrow? Is your dance card already full?"

She soaked in his smiles. "It is not, sir."

"Then may I have your first dance?"

She nodded, setting her glass of punch aside. Agatha beamed as Renley took her hand and led her to the floor. They joined the set near the end. In moments, Rosalie lost herself to the dance. It was a complicated reel, and Renley proved himself a little rusty. Rosalie laughed, offering him encouragement as he twice threatened to turn the wrong way.

"I never said I was any good," he muttered as they came together.

"You've had far more important skills worth honing," she replied. "I can't imagine you do much reeling aboard your ship."

"Oh, you might be surprised what sailors get up to when the weather is fine and the grog flows."

"I think I might like to see that," she laughed.

"Give it time, Miss Harrow," he replied. "That Corbin punch is deadly. A few more glasses and I might show the room some talents best reserved for a circus stage."

It was strange to hear him calling her "Miss Harrow" again. She much preferred the easy manner he had when they were alone. She relished the way his hands lingered overlong with hers, only pulling away at the last possible moment. She loved the way he leaned into her, warm smile on his face.

"You dance so beautifully, Miss Harrow," said Agatha as the dance ended.

"Thank you," she replied, glancing down to note the way Renley still held her hand.

Agatha raised a brow. "Well, Tom? Are you going to leave me standing here like a sad little wallflower all night?"

"Of course not," Renley replied, giving Rosalie's hand a squeeze before he dropped it. "Agatha, nothing would give me more pleasure than to claim the next dance with you."

"Hold my fan, dearest."

Colin laughed as Renley led her away to join the next reel. "How about it, Miss Harrow?" Colin said with a smile.

"Sir?"

"Tom may be the more handsome Renley, but I'm lighter of foot. Care to take a spin?"

She laughed and nodded. Colin set down his wife's fan and took her hand, leading her out to the set. They danced a quadrille, and Rosalie was pleased to see Colin had not exaggerated his talent. He was all ease and cordiality, leading her through the steps while tossing teasing remarks to his brother.

She sat out the next set, watching with a smile as Mr. Bray took a turn with Madeline, who looked sweet as ever in a lavender dress. Remembering Burke's cold words, her smile fell, and she glanced away. Colin introduced her to a handsome tradesman who claimed her third dance, and then she danced her fourth with Renley again. He was just leading her off the floor when James materialized from the crowd, his handsome green eyes locked on her.

"Will you dance the next with me, Miss Harrow?"

56

Rosalie

JAMES STOOD BEFORE her, waiting for her answer.

"Yes," she replied on a breath.

Renley frowned but let her go. "Just keep her away from George, eh?"

James offered her his hand. "That's the plan."

Rosalie let herself be led back onto the dance floor. "Why was His Grace's manner so informal?" she dared to ask.

She thought for a moment he wouldn't respond until he said, "To annoy me. Pay him no heed, Miss Harrow," he added quickly. "After tonight, he'll be safely engaged."

She swallowed down her ready retort: Engaged isn't married . . . and even that doesn't stop most men.

The master of ceremonies called out a reel, and Rosalie and James took up their positions. She felt several sets of eyes on her from around the room. Dancing with a Corbin was drawing unwanted attention. Was this a bad idea?

The music began, and James took her through the steps, quiet as the grave. And there was that confounded frown again. Who could glower like that while dancing? Down the set, the other couples smiled and laughed, offering little bits of conversation. She was about to make some polite comment when the reel brought them together. He leaned in and said, "I hear Burke made a fool of himself last night."

She nearly missed her steps as she spun away and wove between the other dancers. She'd been trying very hard to keep all thoughts of Burke carefully sealed inside a box in her mind. If he was sorry for what he said, he would have come to her last night and apologized. Rosalie waited for him. She sat awake on her bed late into the night, candle burning low. She fell asleep atop her covers with her body angled towards the door . . . but he never came.

"You need to forgive him," James said as they took a turn.

She gasped, jerking her hand away as they split. When they came back together, her eyes were blazing. "What did he tell you?"

She watched his jaw clench as he glanced around. The other couples chatted, clapping along to the music. "Everything," he muttered. "You should know Burke tells me everything."

"Oh god—" She hadn't meant for the words to slip out of her lips. Everything? Did James know about Burke coming to her room? Did he know about the woods . . . the storage room? Why would Burke embarrass her by sharing their secrets?

"Talk to him," James said when they came back together.

She bristled. "Surely, he can fight his own battles."

"He is my friend—"

"And what am I to you?" Heavens, she hadn't meant to say that out loud either. What was wrong with her tonight?

His jaw was tight as he glanced around again. "My mother's ward."

Her chest brushed up lightly against his shoulder as they linked arms and spun round. "Why are you trying to mend our fences?"

James lowered his voice. "Because I think I'm partially to blame. He has it in his mind that I have designs on you," he said, voice low. "It's messing with his head."

"And do you, my lord?"

That muscle ticked in his jaw again as his eyes flashed. He glanced over his shoulder. "Brandon," he barked, pulling a man forward by the shoulder. "Take my place."

The gentleman stumbled into James' spot and James broke the set, crossing over to the ladies' side. He gripped Rosalie by the elbow and pulled her backwards. Several couples around them watched with wide eyes and more than a few whispers.

"What are you doing?" Rosalie rasped. This wasn't just highly irregular. It was unthinkable. You didn't break set in the middle of a dance—

"Miss Mariah," James called. "Take Miss Harrow's place. She's feeling faint."

Mariah hurried forward. "Oh, dear, are you unwell?" She cast her eye over Rosalie.

"She's fine," said James. "Just overheated." He tugged on her arm, and they were moving, eyes watching them as he led her out of the ballroom by a side door.

"James, what are you—"

"Not here."

He dragged her through the servant's cupboard, then through another door that led down a narrow back hallway. A few footmen raised their brows in surprise but tactfully focused on their work.

"James—"

"Through here." He pushed another door with his shoulder, and she blinked, wholly disoriented to find herself in the library. The sounds of the ball were quieter here as she stepped into the room, wrapped in the familiar smell of leather and books. The only light came from the full moon outside, flooding the room with a silvery glow.

James shut the door, revealing the other side as a false wall panel she'd never noticed before. "You can't say such things where others might hear," he chastised, one hand still pressed against the door.

"You brought it up," she countered. "And now I must know—"

He spun around. "You don't need to know everything, actually. There are a host of moving pieces on my chessboard, and you, Miss Harrow, are not privy to know my strategy."

"I think I do if *I* am the piece being moved. You're trying to fix things between Burke and me, and I want to know why."

"Because," he growled, stalking off towards the shelves.

She followed. "That is not a proper answer to give a person. Tell me *why*—"

He spun around again. "Because I want him to be happy! Because he is in love with you, but he loves me too, and he's loyal to a bloody goddamn fault." He took a step closer. "Because he's one of the most stubborn men I've ever met, and when he makes up his mind about something, it takes an act of God to change it."

"What does that make me? Am I his act of God? His plague of locusts?"

"You are his redemption," James replied, sucking all the wind out of Rosalie's sails.

She shrank back, tears in her eyes. "By your own admission,

you say Burke loves me. You call me his redemption. Do you want to know what *he* called me?"

"He didn't mean it. He's in agony over it. Give him one minute of your time and you'll see for yourself."

Hope flickered like a candle inside her. Could it be true? She took a hesitant step forward, closing the space between them.

"But you have to reconsider this ludicrous notion that you'll not marry him."

Rosalie paused, heart pounding in her chest. "What did you say?"

James narrowed his eyes at her, trying to read her with a look. "Why won't you marry him? Is it his family history?"

"No, of course not—"

"His lack of position, then? Or perhaps you wish to find someone titled. Someone with a tidy fortune to keep you in the finest fashions?"

"Is this coming from Burke?" she asked, incredulous. "Does *he* ask these questions . . . or do you ask for yourself? I already told you I am not looking for a husband—"

"Which means exactly nothing," he said with a scoff. "A spirited lady like yourself may hold that opinion when she is young and confident and thinks no gentleman will ever love her the way they do in novels—"

"You dare," she hissed.

"But then those spirited ladies become more acquainted with the world, and they learn to manage their expectations. They see what a good man like Burke can be, and they marry him. I'm just trying to save you both whatever misery comes between this trifling argument and your happily ever after. Admit to me now that you want to marry him, and I will settle a sum on him so he can be worthy of you. Go on, Miss Harrow, name your price—"

"You're despicable—"

"I'm pragmatic," he said leaning into her space, claiming her air with his dark energy.

What was wrong with him? This wasn't James. He was honest, but he wasn't cruel. He didn't seek to attack. What was Rosalie missing? Her mind spun as she thought back over all his words since asking her to dance. She took a breath and stepped back. "Where would Burke get such a notion, my lord? For he is neither a foolish man nor prone to reading people wrongly."

James blinked. "What?"

"Burke is the most socially sensitive person I've ever met," she went on. "He reads people like open books. I am sure, given your closeness, he reads you with his eyes closed. If he sees something in you, it must be there. So, tell me, James . . . what am I to you?"

"We're not going to discuss this—"

"What *am* I to you?"

"You are a distraction!" He swept forward, his face inches from hers. "You are a passing infatuation that I cannot afford. You will ruin me, and I have to stop it." His words had her leaning back, eyes wide. "How could you make me a proper wife? I can't even call your connections merely inferior, for you have none! You said yourself you have no family, no money, no title. You are beautiful and good tempered, and that is all."

She gasped, indignation flooding her veins.

"And that is saying nothing about the fact that you've recently had your tongue down the throats of *both* my closest friends. If Burke is to be believed, you even managed them at the same time," he scoffed, his voice dripping with disdain. "If you had any propriety or proper breeding, you'd never dare be so loose—"

Rosalie slapped him as hard as she could. He spun away, one hand raising to touch his jaw. She held her gloved hand suspended in the air between them, chest heaving in her tight stays as she tried to contain her sobs.

"Don't—" she choked out. "Don't you dare judge me. You have no idea what's in my heart. You asked, and I will answer, though you do not deserve my truth. I don't want to get married. Not to Burke, not to Renley, and most certainly *never* to you. For I will not give any man such power over my life. My beast of a father is dead, and I have no brother. I am *free* of the control of men. This bird will know no cages."

He took a step forward. "Miss Harrow—"

"You've said and done quite enough, sir," she said, lowering her shaking hand to her side. "I must beg you to release me now." She spun on her heel heading for the door, desperate to flee before her tears began to fall.

"Wait—" James snatched her elbow and pulled her back, pressing her against the bookcase. "Don't go. I was angry. Not at you." He raked his free hand through his hair, still holding her pinned with the other. "It's George—it's . . . all of it. *Fuck*."

Her breathing was labored as she felt the heat of the hand holding her pinned to the bookcase. He was touching her above the line of her glove. Had he noticed? She swallowed, indignation still pulsing in her veins. He wasn't offering an apology, merely an explanation . . . and a poor one at that.

"James, please . . . just tell me what you want. Do you want me to go? I can turn your mother down. I can leave Alcott. Everything could be as it was before—"

"Nothing will be as it was. Not . . . Burke will never get over you. Even Renley . . ."

Rosalie fought to control the hitch in her breath.

"You certainly work fast," he said with a mirthless laugh. "Was that your design?"

"I did nothing," she hissed. "I came here with only one motive: to accept the condolences of your mother for the loss of mine. All the rest, I neither sought out nor asked for. But you make the rules here, Atlas. You carry the weight of the world. You control all our fates. Tell me what you want me to do, and I'll do it."

She waited, eyes locked on him, trying to read his face. He looked so tired, so full of resentment. "I cannot just say—"

"You are the only one who can say," she cried. "What do you want?"

"I want—*fuck*—" His words faltered as he dropped his hand from her arm.

"For the love of God, just tell me what you want—"

Her words died with a gasp as he pressed her into the bookcase, his hands on her shoulders. She managed one breath before his mouth claimed hers in a bruising kiss. For the briefest of moments, she was ready to shove him off. Without realizing when or how, she pulled him closer instead.

He groaned against her lips as he slanted his mouth over hers. His fingers brushed over the elegant pearls at her throat before he cupped her cheek. She tasted the sweet brandy on his tongue as the intensity of his kiss forced her head back. His fingers slid from her cheek to her hair, weaving into the braids, holding her tight as he begged without words for her to open deeper for him. She clung to him, melting into the heat of his kisses that had her core fluttering.

He grabbed her wrists and jerked both arms up over her head, pressing them to the bookcase as he stepped in. She sighed as she felt his weight press against her, holding her captive. In this moment of vulnerability, Rosalie saw through his angry words. She saw through his thick walls of duty and respectability. Here in his arms, feeling the electric heat of his touch, she knew she was seeing the man who dwelled within that lonely fortress. James Corbin was hungry and desperate, a man too long starved for affection.

Let me in, her heart cried out.

He deserved love. He deserved care and compassion. James needed the warmth of connection, of belonging to another person as more than a friend or a brother or a master. He needed companionship. In this stolen moment, wrapped as they were in the moon's soft light, she would give him what he needed. She pressed her hips eagerly against him and chased each kiss. They fought for control, even as he kept her hands pinned above her head. He was starving, but so was she. Two creatures trapped in cages of their own making, longing to be free.

He pulled away and she gasped as his lips covered the pulse point on her neck. He gave her wrists a press, telling her to stay put, then his hands dropped away, sliding down her arms to cup her breasts. She savored all the ways her body responded to his fevered touch. She arched into him with a soft moan, twisting her wrists until she could grip the shelf.

His fingers brushed back over the pearls at her throat as he claimed her lips again. Something about the way his hand lingered on the necklace pierced her cloud of lust. She let out a soft gasp of panic. She was standing in his brother's house, wearing his mother's pearls, kissing him in the dark. James Corbin was off limits . . . and they both knew it.

He felt her hesitation and groaned, breaking their kiss. They panted for a moment, lips inches apart. Then suddenly, his warmth was gone, sucked away with all her air as he took two steps back. He dragged a shaking hand through his hair and tugged at his waistcoat, quickly rebuilding his stone walls. She sank back against the bookcase. Why did she suddenly feel so bereft?

"I'm sorry," he muttered. "That won't happen again."

Her heart broke for him. Too afraid to want . . . too afraid to be wanted. "James—"

"No," he said, his eyes flashing with determination. "It won't happen again."

A simmering moment stretched between them.

"I need to go," she whispered. They both knew what she really meant.

"Stay."

"But—"

He stepped back into her space, making her head spin. "You will stay at Alcott." His words were spoken almost against her lips. "Don't miss this chance on my account. Stay on your own terms."

"*Hmm-hmm.*"

Rosalie spun with James to face the servant's door. In the time they were kissing, it must have opened, for the butler was now standing with them in the dark.

"Goddamn it, Reed. Announce yourself next time," James barked, using his body like a shield to block Rosalie from view.

"Beg your pardon, my lord," Reed said in that deep voice. "But Her Grace is asking for Miss Harrow."

57
Rosalie

"WHAT DOES SHE want?" James growled.

"Her Grace did not bring me into her confidence, my lord. I know nothing other than that I am to fetch Miss Harrow," Reed replied in that dry tone.

"I'll come," she whispered, putting a hand on James' arm.

James stiffened, his eyes still locked on the butler. "How much did you hear?"

Reed had the good sense to look confused. "I heard and saw nothing, my lord. Ought I to have heard something?"

Rosalie felt the tension flickering between the two men. Was Reed loyal to James . . . or the duchess?

James' shoulders relaxed slightly. "When my mother is finished with Miss Harrow, inform me at once."

"Of course, my lord." Reed moved to open the main door of the library.

She raised a brow in silent question, and James replied with a curt nod. He would find her after and assure all was well. She turned following Reed out the door, leaving James standing alone in the dark library.

Rosalie let herself be led to the drawing room. The duchess

was seated in the center of the room, surrounded by a cortège of high-society ladies in their plumed feathers and diamonds. Rosalie dropped into a curtsy.

"Miss Harrow, there you are," said the duchess. "I heard you were taken ill while dancing. Are you quite recovered?"

"Yes, Your Grace," she murmured, her cheeks warming as she felt all the women's eyes on her, measuring her, judging her.

"Well then, come meet my friends," the duchess directed.

The lady seated next to the duchess pursed her lips and stood, making room for Rosalie. The ladies resumed their gossip, sharing the latest news from Town. Rosalie listened quietly, a forced smile on her lips. All the while, Reed watched quietly from the doorway, one eye on her. She shifted uncomfortably. What might he say as soon as she was gone?

"Are you a distant cousin then, Miss Harrow?" one of the ladies asked. "I know so few Harrows. I'm finding it difficult to place you."

"I am unrelated to Her Grace," Rosalie replied, chancing a look at the duchess. They hadn't made their plans public yet. In fact, Rosalie had yet to formally agree. If Burke and James were going to be this impossible, she may have to decline. Nothing would be worse than living in a house with them if they were determined to bully her.

"Miss Harrow is the daughter of an old friend," the duchess provided. "I've decided to take her on as my ward. She's been indispensable to me as I planned for tonight."

Rosalie stilled.

"What an honor to be so singled out," said the Duchess of Somerset with a smile.

"Yes, Your Grace," Rosalie murmured, feeling a shiver of indignation lick down her spine. The duchess was forcing her hand.

No, she's vouching for you, giving you status, daring the others to question your right to be here.

But still . . . Rosalie had not yet said she wanted the duchess to claim her.

"Harriet, you never said a word about it when you were last in Town," the Duchess of Somerset added.

"Our friendship has only recently blossomed," the duchess replied. "But, given the changes we anticipate in the house, she will be a godsend."

The ladies twittered for a few more minutes, trying to make the duchess reveal her secrets, but she remained tight-lipped. At last, she turned to Rosalie. "If you're fully recovered, you may go. Join the frivolity."

Rosalie bobbed her head and stood, desperate to get away. She chanced a look at Reed as she passed. She prayed he would respect James' wish and stay silent. Otherwise, her dreams of Alcott might be over before they even began.

The grand gallery was crowded with people. Rosalie's eye quickly caught sight of the Renleys. Agatha and Colin chatted with a few acquaintances and Renley stood just beyond, his back turned to her. She breathed a sigh of relief. Of the three gentlemen, perhaps Renley understood her best. He didn't judge her for desiring love without obligation. She needed his comfort now. She moved towards him, already thinking of some excuse to lure him away. She would tell him everything and seek his advice. He would know what to do.

As he turned, her steps faltered. He was already deep in conversation with a beautiful woman with soft brown hair and fair eyes. She wore a fashionable gown and her neck glittered with diamonds. A plume of ostrich feathers added height to her hair. Rosalie watched as Renley leaned in close

413

to say something in the lady's ear. The lady blushed and raised a hand to whisper something back. His smile spread.

Rosalie blinked and turned away, heart racing. Why should she be surprised other women might show an interest in him? He was desperately handsome, with a bright naval career ahead of him. He was a fine prize for any lady. That lady just wasn't going to be her. The afternoon they shared was beyond wonderful, but she knew Renley wanted more. He wanted marriage and commitment and a love of his own. She would never hold him back from that future.

She turned a little half circle, feeling decidedly adrift in this sea of sparkling faces. She moved back towards the ballroom. Maybe Madeline could help restore her serenity. Just as she was about to enter the room, movement caught her eye. A tall, dark, handsome man with broad shoulders stood half in the shadows. Rosalie would know that silhouette anywhere.

Burke.

He is in love with you, came James' voice. *You are his redemption.*

She slipped through the crowd. She had to speak to him. The duchess may have announced it to all her friends already, but Rosalie refused to stay in this house if it would hurt Burke to do so. Was he moving away? Was he arguing with someone?

She stopped in her tracks. Burke wasn't alone either. He stood in his handsome evening clothes, dark hair falling across his forehead, with his hands on the shoulders of a lady. Not just any lady . . .

"Oh god . . ." Rosalie watched in horror as Elizabeth Swindon pressed forward, wrapped her arms around his neck, and kissed Burke square on the lips.

414

58

Rosalie

THE GALLERY SPUN in a clash of laughing faces, flickering candles, and feathered headdresses. Rosalie needed air. She needed to *scream*. Both her men were openly enraptured with the attention of other women, not even caring if she saw. Not thinking of her at all.

Not your men. Never yours.

The cruel voice in her head was Olivia's, taunting her like she did that day in Finchley. Rosalie asked them for no commitment. They were merely holding her to her word. She just had no idea it would hurt quite so much to watch it unfold before her eyes.

She swept down the gallery, looking for some quiet place to collect herself. Her room was two floors and a wing away. *Too far.* She took a sharp left, darting towards the door that led into the ensuite rooms. The duchess wouldn't allow anyone in her private study tonight. The doors would be locked . . . but Rosalie knew where to find the hidden key.

She pushed her way into the dark morning room, shutting the door with a snap. She leaned hard against it. The ball thrummed behind the door. Laughing voices, music, the press of people . . . his hands on her shoulders . . . his lips on her lips . . .

She choked back a frustrated sob. Not Rosalie's shoulders. Not her lips. Burke accused her of throwing herself at Mr. Bray, and then he had to go and do the same. Was this all a game to him? Some kind of cruel retribution? And with Elizabeth of all people! That mewling, desperate, mean-spirited witch with copper curls—Rosalie *hated* her!

He is in love with you.

"No, he's not," she whispered to the empty room.

She panted, trying to regain control. Her stays were too tight. She was gasping for air. What was happening to her? She was behaving like a wronged wife with some higher claim on his affections. The reality was, she had nothing. No right to him, not even the moral high ground, for had he not watched her kiss Renley?

Her pulse quickened as heat flooded her core, leaving her clinging to the door. Oh yes, her body remembered the feel of Burke and Renley standing so close, the three of them sharing breath as the rain battered the trees overhead. She remembered the heat of their lips on her as they worshipped her. Both of them drinking of her mouth, their mingled tastes like ambrosia on her tongue. Nothing had ever felt so natural, so right.

She moaned. No, Burke had no complaints then.

The moan turned into a groan that sounded almost feral as she accepted the truth. She had no claim on him . . . but she *wanted* one. The realization made her shake. Burke was right, she was a temptress. It was cruel to want him to want only her . . . and Rosalie wasn't cruel. She had to stop this. Had to let him go. No . . . *she* had to go. Alcott was his home, not hers. She couldn't stay here and keep hurting him.

She pushed away from the door as she heard voices approach. Crossing the room, she pulled open the door to the music room. Silvery moonlight gave the room a soft glow. Behind her, the morning room door opened, the sounds from the ball echoing around.

"Rosalie—"

She stiffened and turned, dark eyes narrowed on the object of her obsession.

Burke shut the door, muting the sounds from the party. "Why did you run off just now? Don't tell me you're jealous." His gaze feasted on her as he smirked. "Green is a good color on you, love."

"Go away." She spun on her heel and swept into the music room. Light from the moon elongated her shadow.

"Don't walk away from me—"

"Don't follow me!" She stomped over to the side table near the piano and reached for the key resting behind a small angel figurine. The music room door snapped shut and she heard the lock click into place. She jolted upright, key fisted tight in her hand.

"Unlock the door."

He met her eyes with his steely gaze. "No. Not until I've had my say."

That look sent heat racing to her core. She was still mad at him, right? He called her a whore, and then kissed another woman. She was definitely still mad.

He gave a dry laugh, dragging his hand through his hair. "Look, I know you saw me just now with Elizabeth—"

The man *dared* to laugh about it? She slapped the key back down on the table. "I don't want to hear, and a gentleman wouldn't discuss it."

His smile fell. "Well, then it's fortunate that I am no gentleman."

"Truer words were never spoken!"

There was no way he'd let her escape, but at least the piano still stood between them. She had to keep it there, or she risked committing murder tonight. The duchess would never forgive her ruining a perfectly good carpet.

"You didn't see what you think you saw," he declared. "Elizabeth was drunk. She kissed me, and I rebuffed her. Go see her for yourself if you don't believe me. I deposited her in Mariah's arms as I saw you flee."

The words registered, but Rosalie's anger didn't soften. "Why bother chasing after me? You made your position clear last night—"

"I did not make my position clear," he snapped. "Rosalie, I spoke without thinking, and I hurt you. I swore to myself I'd not do it again . . . though I'll admit, I'm enjoying this fit of jealousy immensely," he added, the ghost of a smile on his lips as he inched closer.

She darted around the piano. "I'm not jealous." Her cheeks flamed hot at the lie.

"Right . . . just like *I* wasn't jealous when you had your tongue in Renley's mouth."

She gasped. "You—that's not—same thing—"

"You're right, it's not the same thing," Burke challenged. "You *asked* for Renley's kiss. I didn't ask for Elizabeth's."

Shame filled her. "Burke . . ." Tears stung her eyes as she wrapped her arms tight around herself. She'd never felt such turmoil, such deep and utter confusion. "It feels like I'm being torn to pieces. I don't understand what's happening to me . . . why am I feeling like this? Am I wicked?"

His gaze softened and he took a half step closer. "I said I was jealous," he repeated. "That doesn't mean I didn't like it. What you did with Renley . . . what *we* did . . . it wasn't wrong. And you're not cruel or wicked for wanting us both. I don't blame you or judge. You've been open and honest from the start."

She took a shaky breath. He didn't know all of it. "I want no secrets between us . . ."

He raised a brow in question.

"James kissed me tonight," she whispered, cheeks burning hotter with shame. "In the library."

A shadow flickered in his eyes. "What happened?"

"I don't want to hurt you—"

He shook his head. "The only way I can handle this is if I know everything. Tell me."

"We were dancing and . . . we argued," she began. "I asked him what he wanted, if he wanted me to leave Alcott. He kissed me and . . . Reed found us."

"Shit," he groaned, dragging his hand through his hair. "Well, I can't say I'm surprised. James is going to let his confounded pride stand in the way as long as possible."

"In the way of what?"

He scowled. "Of you, obviously. Of his feelings for you."

"I'm just a passing infatuation," she replied, still hearing James' words echoing in her mind loud as a clanging bell. "He told me he doesn't want me."

"Right," Burke scoffed. "Well, he lied."

"He was quite forceful in his denouncement. He called me worse things than you did."

His eyes heated again. "He's a lord. They always say one thing and think another."

419

She took a hesitant step forward, trying to read him. "You're not . . . angry?"

He sighed, looking down at his feet. "I expected something to happen. Perhaps his timing was poor, but he's had rather a lot on his mind." He glanced up, eyes swirling. "But you should know I have no intention to fight his corner. It's every man for himself."

She couldn't help herself when she replied, "You seemed content to help Renley the other day . . ."

"That was different. I didn't know where we stood. I was afraid the only way to have you was to join in. I'd rather have a piece of you than nothing at all."

"I'm glad you were there," she whispered. "I'm glad it happened . . . are you? I mean, did you . . ."

"Did I like it?" He laughed. "Of course, I fucking liked it. I wouldn't have let Tom touch you if I didn't like watching what he did to you."

Her core fluttered. Burke liked it too. Maybe he'd let it happen again . . .

"Listen," he said, stepping closer. "Whatever tension brews between Tom, James, and me, leave it to us to handle."

"Burke, I'm sorry—"

"Don't." He raised a hand. "Don't apologize. I'm the one who's sorry. You stated your limits and asked me to respect them. I didn't."

Her shoulders sagged. She needed something between them, some barrier she could cling to besides her traitorous arms that longed to hold him.

"I'm covetous by nature," he went on. "And loyal to a fault. But I demand that loyalty be returned. I could never love someone like Marianne Young, who would choose another."

His look of rejection had her stepping forward. "But I *didn't* choose—"

"I know," he said. "At first I didn't understand but . . . maybe your heart works differently. Or maybe it's just the way James and Tom and I are together." He groaned, dragging a hand through his hair. "I thought our tastes in women were different, but perhaps the right one just hadn't come along," he finished with a shrug.

Could she really be hearing him say these words?

"I didn't respect your terms before," he went on. "I want to hear them again, and this time I promise to listen properly. Tell me what you want, Rosalie. Tell me what you're willing to accept from me. Leave no room for misunderstanding."

She took a deep breath. Once spoken, these words couldn't be taken back. "I'm covetous by nature too," she said, her gloved hand dusting the top of the piano. "You want my loyalty. My passion, my obsession. You want me basking in the warmth of your every look and touch," she whispered.

"Yes."

"You call me siren," she said with a soft smile, loving the feel of his eyes on her. "The name is fitting, for if you sail too close, I think I mean to claim you. I will snatch the soul from your chest. It will be mine . . . but I'll not marry you. Any of you. I can't relinquish that power. I want to be free, Burke. Let me be free, and I will freely choose to . . . to love you."

The heat in his eyes flared as she said that four-letter word. She fought her smile. It was working. She was stripping his armor off piece by piece. She wanted to see him undone. She reached out a gloved hand, lightly stroking the lapel of his evening coat.

"I want you, Burke. I want every piece of you—your charm,

your wit. I want your moods and your melancholy, your every infuriating smirk." She glanced up, meeting his eye. "Do you want me?"

He snatched her wrist, holding it tight. "I want you so badly, I can hardly breathe. From the first moment I touched you in that pub, and every moment since." His voice was warm with need. "I never had much need for the church and now I know why." He tilted his head down, resting his forehead against hers. "You are my goddess," he murmured, brushing his lips lightly against her brow. "I worship only you. Claim me, ruin me, own me. I don't fucking care."

She closed her eyes and breathed a deep sigh of relief. Her hands slid over his shoulders. "I know it's not fair, but the siren in me won't let me stay silent," she whispered. "I am too jealous to stand the idea of you with another woman."

He kissed her forehead, her temple. "Your jealousy is a relief, but unnecessary. I only want you."

Those words melted through her core. She took a shaky breath, meeting his gaze. "And . . . what of your jealousy?"

He frowned. "I meant what I said. Sharing doesn't come naturally to me. I won't pretend it will be easy . . . but I'm fine with Tom. And if James ever pulls the stick out of his arse, I'd be fine with him too. But no one else," he added, his voice edged with iron as he cupped her face. "I will not contemplate sharing you outside the three of us. Ask it of me, and the man in question will be a dead man."

She smiled, secretly loving the threat of violence. Feeling daring, she stepped out of his embrace. He raised a brow in curiosity but let her go. She backed away, feeling his stormy eyes follow her as she pressed against the piano. Pulse racing, she raised her hand and slowly pulled off her long, white gloves. First one, then the other. "I'm offering myself to you. Every piece of me. Do you want to claim me, Burke?"

Burke groaned low in his throat. "Yes."

Her lips parted as she dropped the gloves to the floor. "Well then . . . come take what is yours."

He was on her in a second, their bodies pressed chest to chest as his hand wrapped around her nape, his fingers digging into her artful braids threaded with pearls. Their mouths collided in a hungry kiss. Her teeth clicked against his as they both moaned, seeking union with lips and tongues.

He pulled away and buried his face in her neck. His nose was pressed just beneath her ear as his lips brushed her skin. She took a breath too. His spiced currant scent filled her lungs, and she couldn't help the moan that escaped her.

Remembering their fight in the library, she threaded her fingers in his hair and jerked his head back. He grunted as she angled her lips to whisper in his ear. "Hurt me with cruel words again, and I will horse whip you."

"*Ah*—agreed," he growled.

She relaxed her fingers, smoothing them through his hair with a gentle stroke. "Do not doubt my constancy. You are mine, Burke. I am your siren, and you hear only my call."

He grabbed the lobe of her ear with his teeth and bit until she hissed. "Say it again."

She licked his bottom lip before sucking it between her teeth. "You're mine," she repeated, feeling as his cock pulsed against her stomach. "My love . . . *mine*."

His mouth covered hers, his tongue opening her deep. Using both hands, he released the clasps of her dress, letting the cornflower-blue satin flutter to the floor. He didn't bother unlacing her stays, he just jerked the top down, tearing her chemise as her breast spilled into his hand. He ducked his head, taking her in his mouth as she arched into him. He flicked her nipple with his tongue, sending a jolt like a whip of fire straight to her core. She moaned, both hands wrapping around his shoulders. He licked her again and she quivered. When he used his teeth, she thought her knees might give out.

He pulled the other side down, repeating his heated kisses until she was whimpering in his arms. His lips worked their way back up her neck, finding her mouth again. They drank of each other like two people dying of thirst, their moans mixing as she ran her palm over his hardness. He stiffened, pushing his hips into the pressure she offered.

"Burke, I want you," she whined, rubbing her hand over his cock. "No more chivalry. I want to give you such pleasure. Please—"

His lips chased hers until she was arched backwards over the piano. One hand came down for support and the *plink, plink* of the disrupted keys made a discordant sound that echoed around the room. He pulled away, trembling and hungry for more. His hand dropped between her legs, and she rocked into his touch, heart fluttering as he raised her chemise.

"Are you wet for me?"

"Yes," she panted. "Aching for you, dreaming of you, want you inside me—*ah*—"

He pressed a finger inside her. "I'm going to claim this sweet cunt. Only me." His voice was a growl in her ear that had her clenching around his finger. "I want to taste you again. Then we'll see what your tongue can do."

She forgot to breathe as he lowered to his knees, rucking her chemise up over her hips.

"Hold this," he said, taking her hands off his shoulders and making her hold the chemise around her waist. Her hands were barely settled before he was plunging two fingers insider her. Burke kissed up her thigh, spreading her sex open until she felt his mouth against her. He lapped with quick strokes. When he sucked, humming against her, she dropped her head back.

"Spread your legs," he murmured.

She tried to shift, gasping as he lifted one of her legs, draping it over his shoulder. Now she was reliant on the piano for support, the sharp edge of it cutting into her back, but she didn't care. Her knees trembled as he pressed his face back to her sex. The new angle was divine. "Burke—*oh*—god—"

Words lost all meaning as he worked her with fingers and tongue. She shuddered once . . . twice . . . nearly falling on him, but Burke caught her. Her core clenched around his fingers. A cry escaped her lips as she felt herself break apart. She clung to his shoulders as her body curled around him, needing his support.

He stumbled to his feet. "Rosalie," he breathed her name like a prayer. "You taste divine. God, I want more. I want everything."

"Take it," she replied on a breath.

He lifted her chin to meet his eyes. "Say it again. Say what you want."

"I want your cock." Both hands went to his waist. "I want you inside me. Use me and love me and don't hold back. I want you, Burke. No more holding back."

"Rosalie—"

"Claim me, ruin me, own me—"

He snapped. One moment, she was half-leaning against

425

the piano with her hands on the fastenings of his breeches, the next she was in his arms being carried to the sofa. He kissed her as he set her down, and then his hands were working fast, shedding himself of his evening coat and waistcoat. He untied his cravat, tossing it aside.

Rosalie watched, eyes wide with hunger.

"Stand up," he directed, jerking his shirt off.

She rose on shaky legs, still not quite recovered from his attentions. She could feel the wetness pooling between her thighs as he stepped into her, his hands at his waist as he opened his breeches. He took her hand in his and slipped it inside.

"Touch me," he rasped, dropping his forehead to hers. "Touch—*fuck*—"

She wrapped her hand around his cock, squeezing it softly as she slid her palm up the length to the tip of him and back down. Heavens, she knew he was big, but this was . . . she swallowed with nervous anticipation.

He groaned, his hands cupping her breasts as he fought against her stays. With a frustrated growl, he tugged at the laces, loosening them until she could breathe, and he could better access her breasts. As her hand stroked to his tip, he tweaked her nipple and she gasped.

"Want you so badly," he murmured, kissing her neck, her shoulder. "So beautiful. You're mine. My sweet siren."

She kissed his lips, teasing him with her tongue as she gently pulled him out of his breeches. "Your siren is aching, Burke. Tend to me."

He put both his hands on her shoulders and spun them around. Then he sank down onto the sofa, his cock still out. He leaned back slightly, a wicked smile on his face. "My siren is going to drop to her knees and take me in her mouth. Show me what that tongue can do."

Her stomach flipped as she eagerly complied. He spread his legs, and she sank to the carpet, placing her hands on his thighs. He looked like a god, stretched shirtless before her, that sweep of black hair over his brow. He was fisting his cock slowly. She'd never done this before, but the method seemed easy enough to intuit.

Licking her lips, she reached out, taking over his slow stroking action. He groaned the moment her hand brushed his sensitive flesh. The length intimidated her, but she enjoyed a challenge. She bent forward and offered a teasing lick to the head.

He hissed and dropped both hands to her shoulders.

She licked him again, once, twice, enjoying his every reaction. Slowly, she let her mouth experiment with sucking on the tip, while her hand kept stroking his length.

"Don't tease me," he panted, lowering his hands to grip the cushion of the sofa as his body tensed.

Was he holding back again? That simply wouldn't do. She opened her mouth and sank deep onto him, only stopping when she felt him hit the back of her throat.

"Holy hell—"

She did it again.

"Don't stop—"

When she grazed him ever so slightly with her teeth, he stiffened, his strong hands grabbing her by the arms. He lifted her up, sinking his tongue into her mouth for a deep kiss as they both groaned. He wrapped his hands around her waist, dragging her onto his lap, and tugged on her chemise, disentangling it from her legs. She still wore her stays like an open vest.

"Have you ever taken a cock like this?" he murmured,

lowering his mouth over her breast while he cupped the other one.

"No," she said on a gasp, loving the feel of his lips on her. Her hands smoothed over his bare shoulders.

"You'll be the one in control of how much of me you take," he explained. "I'm large, I don't want to hurt you. Take your time and stop if it hurts. I'll not come inside you."

She nodded, her body a basket of butterflies as he tugged on her chemise, lifting her by the hips until she felt her hot, aching sex rubbing against his cock.

"Christ, you'll be the death of me," he groaned. "Your cunt is so wet."

"Wait to die until after I finish you," she said playfully, masking her nerves as she reached between her legs to angle his cock towards her soaking entrance. He braced her by the hips as she lifted up. How could he possibly fit inside her?

"Go easy," he murmured.

She sank down until his cock was pressing at her entrance and they both groaned. She was too tight . . . or he was too large. It took her a few attempts and the position was awkward, but on the fourth time, something inside her gave and he sank in deeper.

"*Ahh*—Burke—" She said his name like an endearment and a curse, for to give him pleasure required her pain.

He held still, hardly breathing as she teased his tip inside her. She sank down a little more, feeling the fullness of him everywhere, stretching her out, calming the ache. "So good," he muttered. "So tight. Want more—*Christ*—"

She smiled, triumphant as she took him another inch. Her core was adjusting to his size, and she wanted more too. She wanted him feral. She took his hands and put them on her breasts. "Burke . . . look at me."

His palms squeezed her softly as he met her gaze.

Giving her best attempt at a siren's smile, she took a breath and sank down hard, sheathing him. They both cried out, falling against each other's mouths as she moved her hips, adjusting to this impossible fullness. He filled every part of her. She rocked her hips, learning how to move with him.

Burke's hands went back to her hips, and he lifted her, keeping himself notched as he pulled her down hard. The sound of her wetness was obscene as he did it again. They both moaned, and Rosalie began to shake. With one hand, Burke lifted her chemise. "Do it again," he muttered, leaning back.

She panted as she arched up, sliding off him several inches, then she sank back down.

"Look at how you take my cock. So beautiful." He watched in the half light of the moon as she did it twice more, his wet length disappearing inside her. While he watched her, she watched him. His look of longing pierced her soul.

"I love you, Burke," she whispered, letting herself feel each word. "I've never said those words to any man. I thought I couldn't feel them. But from the moment we met, I—"

He swallowed her words, kissing her deeply. She gasped as he wrapped his arms around her and sank off the sofa. He dropped to his knees and turned, laying her down on the carpet. He pressed between her legs, the weight of his hips making her sigh with contentment. This is where he was always meant to be. She wanted—

"Oh god," she cried out as he sheathed himself with a brutal thrust.

His hips held her in place as he moved again, sinking so deep, cracking her open. Tears slipped from the corners of her eyes as he dropped his body over hers, his hot breath on her cheek, and slammed his hips into her again and again.

"Yes," she moaned. "Don't stop—"

"Come for me again, love. I feel you close. Come with me inside you. Have to feel it—" He lifted up enough to snake his hand between them. As he gave a few shallow thrusts, his fingers found that spot that made her melt. "Come again," he growled, his voice a command.

She felt herself winding up tighter. The release she craved was so close. She shut her eyes, focusing on the points of joint pleasure—his cock buried so deep, his fingers stroking her. Burke. *Her* Burke. Loving her, claiming her.

She shattered. Her core clenched tight, aching to keep him buried deep forever. Warmth rolled through her that she felt all the way to her toes.

With a strangled groan, Burke pulled out. Warmth pooled over her stomach as he chased his own release. He sat back on his heels and looked down at her. She was splayed before him, her chemise rucked up around her ribs, stays open, his release on her stomach. She wanted to feel self-conscious, but the hungry look on his face erased her doubt.

"You're mine." He kissed her deeply. "I love you and I'm not going anywhere. I accept any terms you offer. I'll take any piece of you."

She pushed him back as she sat up. "You have all of me. Can you still doubt it?"

"No," he replied, cupping her cheek. "Whatever else happens with James or Renley is your own business. I won't stand

in the way. I won't help them either," he added. "But this . . .
you and me . . . this is settled."

She breathed a sigh of relief. Burke was hers. Burke loved her.

His eye fell down her again. "Now we've got to figure out
how we make you presentable again. You look well and truly
fucked, love."

She glanced down. Oh, heaven help her, how was she
going to face a house full of high-society guests looking
like this? Burke chuckled, a grin of satisfaction on his face
knowing he was to blame. There was only one solution. She
shimmied out of her chemise and used it to clean herself off.

Burke dressed quickly, using the mirror above the mantel
to tie his cravat. He caught her reflection and his eyes heated.
She had abandoned the soiled chemise, replacing her stays
without it. She stood next to him in nothing but her stockings
and stays. "Don't you dare laugh," she muttered.

"Wouldn't dream of it," he replied, his large hand stroking
over her bare bottom. He dropped his mouth to her ear and
whispered, "Seeing you like this makes me want to keep you
in here. I'd bend you over the piano, just like I wanted to do
the night we sang our duet."

Her core quickened again, but she gave him a hard look.
"That's quite enough. We have to rejoin the party."

He groaned. "Wouldn't want to miss George's big
announcement."

She checked her hair in the mirror. It wasn't as bad as she
thought. A few curls had come loose, but that could have happened while dancing.

"Help me with this." She snatched her gown off the carpet
and stepped into the blue satin, shimmying it up her body.

With deft fingers, Burke sealed her in. He kissed the back of her neck, his lips lingering as his warm breath fanned over her skin.

"What are you doing?" she whispered, feeling the goose-flesh rise down her arms.

"Memorizing you," he murmured. "I dream of this floral scent. It haunts me. Now go back through the morning room. I'll pop out the window and circle 'round to the front of the house."

"Take this with you." She stuffed the wadded-up chemise in his hands. "Bury it in the yard, shove it in a bush. Anything." She gave him one last kiss, which turned into two, then three.

He groaned, his hands tightening, until he reluctantly let her go.

She moved over to the piano to fetch her discarded gloves. She slipped them on as he watched. Remembering how they came to be in this room, she dropped her smile. "You're mine, Burke. And since you are such a fan of my jealous nature, let me say this: If you so much as look at another woman tonight, I'll cut off those traitorous fingers and feed them to the feral swans in the lake."

His smile turned positively devilish. "Christ, get out of here before I bend you over this piano and fuck you till you scream."

The image sent a thrill through her, and she smiled too. Then she turned away, flitting for the door. She paused with her hand on the knob and glanced over her shoulder. Burke stood next to the piano, watching her leave. "I love you, Burke."

His smile softened. "Rosalie Harrow, I love you to distraction. Now, go."

59

Burke

BURKE CAME AROUND the side of the house, emerging from the shadows with a spring in his step. Light from three dozen blazing torches lit the sweeping front drive of Alcott Hall. Several carriages stood in the lineup as late stragglers arrived in time for dinner.

He slipped behind a group of coachmen to drop Rosalie's ruined chemise on a brazier. It wasn't a terribly cool night, so the brazier was little more than embers. When he dropped the chemise on top, the fire sparked back to life. He grinned, watching it go up in flames. Now, the next time he saw Rosalie, he got to picture her in nothing but stockings and stays.

Perfection.

He nodded to a few more footmen as he trotted up the stairs. If they questioned why he was coming out of the darkness, they tactfully said nothing. Neither did anyone ask him for an invitation as he wove through the crowd into the entry hall. If he played his cards right, he could fix it so he sat next to Rosalie at dinner. It wouldn't be the first time he ruined the duchess' carefully planned seating chart to sit next to a pretty girl.

He made his way through the grand gallery, head turning as he looked for her. There would be a few more dances before dinner. He could hold her in his arms again. Maybe a waltz. No blasted reels. He'd keep her dancing waltzes all night if it meant no one else touched her.

He slipped into the ballroom, eyes scanning the crowd. A large set danced a quadrille. He spied George dancing with one of the Nash twins—*Christ*—he'd almost forgotten about all that. Burke thought James might shit kittens when he told him George's plan. Twins as wives. George Corbin was nothing if not original.

Before he could find Rosalie in the crowd, Reed approached, weaving between the guests like a solemn black crow. "Her Grace is asking for you, sir."

Burke glanced around until his eyes locked on the far side of the room. The duchess stood surrounded by her ladies, each stirring the air with a feathered fan. A king's fortune in jewels sparkled from every wrist, neck, and ear. Tiaras signifying rank sat perched atop piles of curls and powdered wigs. The duchess ruled as queen over them all.

"She asks for you to meet her in the music room," Reed said, standing at his shoulder.

It was all Burke could do to keep his cool. Christ, how did the woman always know everything? Was it so easy for him to forget that the walls of Alcott had eyes and ears? All whispers eventually made their way back to her. No doubt it was a nosy footman listening at keyholes. If Burke figured out who it was, he'd pummel the man into the dirt. His moment with Rosalie was not something he wanted shared.

Damn it. One thought of her, and he wanted her again. He could feel himself aching with it. Another stern look from the duchess was all it took to cool the fire in his blood.

"She's quite insistent, sir," said Reed.

"Yes, fine." Burke wove his way through the throngs of people. His eyes locked on Rosalie, who now stood with little Madeline. Her cheeks were still flushed, those dark eyes bright with excitement. He wanted to go to her, to whisper something in her ear—anything, to keep that bloom in her cheeks. But he couldn't stop. The duchess might already know about his activities tonight, but he could hope that perhaps she didn't know who was with him.

Rosalie raised a brow as he moved closer. With a subtle shake of his head, he tried to warn her, trusting in that unspoken ability she had to read his every look. At first, he found it vexing, but now it was a gift. *Don't worry*, he said. *I'll handle this.* She looked crestfallen for a moment, and he fought every urge to kiss away that frown.

He pushed his way through the crowded ballroom and retraced his steps back to the music room. The room glowed with warmth. He much preferred the darkness of his stolen moment with Rosalie. James and George stood in the middle of the carpet, watching as the duchess prowled between the piano and the sofa. It didn't seem likely she would chastise him in front of the others. Perhaps he was mistaken in intuiting her purpose. He raised a wondering brow at James, who just shrugged.

"Finally. Burke, shut the door," the duchess called. "I don't want us disturbed."

For the second time that night, Burke shut the door to the music room. He had a feeling this conversation would end much differently than the last one. Schooling his expression, he crossed the room to where George and James stood.

The duchess continued to pace as her gown fluttered across the carpet. Each turn made the diamonds at her throat twinkle in the candlelight.

"Mother . . . our guests will surely notice we've—"

"They can entertain themselves for ten minutes," she snapped. "We need to talk."

"Shall I get you a brandy, Mama?" George asked. "A glass of ratafia—"

"Don't you dare 'mama' me." She slapped her feathered fan down atop the piano. "I told you I wanted the matter of George's marriage settled." She glared at Burke and James each in turn. "I expected the two of you to guide him in making a sensible choice. Instead, you've spent the month helping Tom Renley!"

James scowled. "Renley is our friend—"

"George is your brother! He needs you, James. You've disappointed me. Both of you."

Burke allowed himself to feel a moment of guilt. Nothing she said was untrue. He'd done nothing to lift a finger to help George.

"I'm not a child," George whined. "I can handle my own affairs—"

"And I could not have picked a better word," she replied. "I see I shall have to handle this myself. For you three are either too deep in your own pleasure to make a sensible choice"— she glared at George—"or you're wasting all your time helping Renley flirt with the only unsuitable girl in the house." Her eye landed on Burke again. "Don't think I haven't noticed your inappropriate attachment to Miss Harrow too."

He clenched his jaw but said nothing. So, she didn't know how far he'd already taken things with Rosalie. How inappropriate they'd been together in this very room . . . right where the duchess currently stood.

"And *you*," she said, glaring at James. "If you weren't so preoccupied with trying to be a duke when you're not—"

"Thank you," George cried with a wave of his hand.

"Shut up, George!" She leveled a gloved finger in his face. "If you were half the duke you ought to be, we none of us would even be in this position. If you knew anything of duty, you'd be married already with an heir and a spare."

"But I made my choice, Mama. I'm marrying one of the Nash twins—"

Burke heard rather than saw the slap that sent George reeling. The duchess stood before George, hand raised, chest heaving with emotion. For a moment, George stood, wholly surprised by the affront. The moment shattered, and he lunged forward as if he meant to return the favor. James and Burke grabbed him by the arms, wrestling him still.

"You *dare* hit me," George grunted, cheeks pink with embarrassment "I am a duke! You will not hit me in my own *fucking* house. I don't care if you're my mother, the Queen, or the Virgin Mary!"

But the duchess wasn't backing down. "Did you really think I wouldn't discover your ridiculous plan? As long as you dare insult the honor of this family by claiming to take *both* those women, you will see nothing but the palm of my hand against your worthless face!"

George pulled on the others, trying to free his arms.

"Touch our mother in anger, and I'll kill you myself,"

James grunted in his ear. "Then I'll throw you a funeral worthy of a *fucking* duke."

Burke held George tighter, keeping one arm wrapped around his middle while the other held his arm pinned behind his back. James kept the other pinned too, twisting it until George hissed in pain.

"Enough," George whined. "Let me go. I won't touch her."

James relaxed his grip slightly, but neither man let go.

The duchess squared her shoulders at her eldest son. "George, you will marry Piety Nash. You'll propose to her tonight." She took a step closer. "And if I hear even one *peep* out of you regarding Prudence, I shall hunt down a pair of sheep shearers and castrate you myself!" Surprising all three men, she shot out her hand and grabbed George by the bollocks, squeezing until he squirmed. "Do you understand me?"

He pulled against the arms that held him. "*Ungh*—ouch—fine," he barked. "Yes, fine. I'll marry Piety Nash, just let go."

She held on a moment longer before releasing him and stepping away in disgust.

George panted, leaning against Burke. He chanced a look at James and whispered, "Which one is Piety?"

"Christ alive," James muttered, giving his brother a shove as he let him go.

Assuming it was safe to do the same, Burke did too.

George centered the tie of his cravat. "Why isn't Renley in here getting castigated? Is he not also supposed to be announcing an engagement too?"

"I don't care about the marriage prospects of Tom Renley. Hang Tom Renley! He is not my son. You three *are*." She narrowed her eyes at each of them in turn.

While Burke's immediate reaction was to feel a sort of warm relief, he also felt it important to say, "Well, technically—"

"Don't you dare." She rounded on him. "You are my son if I say you are." She raised an imperious brow. "And though you've all made your best attempts to bungle this, I am happy to say I've found a way to salvage the situation that will be to everybody's benefit."

An ominous feeling prickled the back of Burke's neck.

"Mother, what are you talking about?" James asked.

"I'm saying I know about Lady Olivia too," she snapped. "I know what happened the other night, though you all tried your best to keep it from me."

"She came on to me, Mama," George hedged.

"Be quiet," she snapped again. "I'll not hear a word about it from you. James should have been the one to tell me, rather than me hearing whispers from a footman. Then I had to drag the rest of the sordid story out of a maid. So, the lady is set on hunting husbands like a common whore, is she?"

"I think she was just feeling desperate," James said with a frown.

George scoffed. "Not desperate enough, apparently—"

"I said be *quiet*, George," the duchess hissed.

"Since James is so talkative, did he tell you who was in the stairwell with him?" George said, eyes flashing.

The duchess seethed. "What are you on about?"

"Only the fact that James wasn't the *only* one to come to Olivia's aid," George said with a sneer.

"George, you're a fool. Nothing happened," James barked.

"Ahh . . . so Miss Harrow wasn't hidden in the stairwell with you?" said George. "She wasn't deliciously disheveled—those dark curls tumbling loose over her shoulders, those pink cheeks and kissable lips—"

James lunged, and it was all Burke could do to hold him back, even as he fought the urge to turn his bracing arm into a stranglehold. Was it true? Why would James keep it from him? Why would Rosalie?

George darted away like a cheeky fox, laughing as James fought to get free.

"Nothing happened," James shouted. "Do not impugn the lady's honor or mine!"

"Then why was she with you?" George teased.

Yes, Burke very much wanted to know the answer to that question as well . . .

"If you remember, she dropped her sketchbook when she found *you* in the stairwell fucking a maid into the bloody wall!" James replied.

"Enough!" the duchess shrieked. "Burke, let him go. Speak out of turn again, and I shall have you both horse whipped."

Burke let James go and the duchess took a deep breath, closing her eyes.

"Here is how it shall be," she intoned. "George will propose to Piety Nash. It's settled. I've also spent the better part of an hour tonight negotiating with the Marchioness of Deal. She has agreed to my terms. Burke, tonight *you* will propose to Lady Olivia. Now, we won't announce it tonight, obviously, but—"

"What?" Burke barked at the same time James said, "Not a chance."

"Congratulations," George jeered. "A double wedding, how fun!"

Burke's heart had stopped. He blinked slowly, glancing

from a horrified James to the duchess, who looked supremely self-satisfied. "And . . . do I get any say in this?"

"I'm afraid not," the duchess replied. "You shall take the Corbin name, we will settle on you thirty thousand pounds, and on your wedding day you'll earn your title. You'll marry from this house and settle in London by the New Year. Now, come and kiss me, for I've just made you a baron."

60

Rosalie

ROSALIE WATCHED BURKE leave the ballroom with butterflies in her stomach. Their moment together was . . . everything. She was still riding the high of her release. She wanted him again. Soon. She was holding Madeline's fan and her glass of punch, watching with a smile as Madeline danced a waltz with Mr. Bray.

Through the crowd, a lady caught her eye, waving at her with her fan with a wide smile on her face. In this sea of faces, it took Rosalie a moment to place her, but she realized with a jolt it was the same beauty who had been speaking to Renley earlier. The woman who leaned in so intimately, laughing and touching his arm. Now she wove between a few lords and ladies as she came to Rosalie's side.

"Are you Miss Harrow?" she said, her voice sweet and musical. "Oh, you must be, for you're just as Tom described you."

Rosalie felt her heart stop. She knew *exactly* who this woman was . . . but it wasn't possible. She saw all the invitations and her name had decidedly *not* been on the list. "I'm sorry, have we met?"

"No, of course not," the woman replied with an airy laugh.

"I'm being too forward. I should have waited for Tom to introduce us. Though I feel I know you already from how he has carried on. I'm Marianne Young . . . Tom's Marianne," she added.

Rosalie's heart clenched in her chest, even as she forced the smile to stay on her lips. The way Marianne said Tom's name—so informally, so possessively—she was clearly trying to send a message. "Oh, I . . . I had not known you would be attending tonight."

"I know it was last minute, but Tom invited me," Marianne replied with a smile. "And my family is seated here as well, as I'm sure you know."

"Of course," Rosalie replied.

Marianne took a step closer. "May I call you Rosalie? You see, I had a notion that you and I would be fast friends."

Rosalie just nodded, using her cup of punch as an excuse to say nothing. Across the crowded hall, she spotted Renley. He was standing between his brother and Mr. Selby, deep in conversation. The men laughed as he told an excessively diverting sailing story, complete with hand gestures.

As if he could feel her eyes on him, Renley caught her eye in return. His immediate response was to smile. Her heart flipped at the look, but she didn't dare return it. When his eye landed on Marianne, his smile fell. Rosalie watched as his face fluttered—fear, frustration, resolve. He didn't want her talking to Marianne. Why?

Rosalie glanced to her right and knew she was caught. Marianne was watching her too. Those soft blue eyes missed nothing.

"He came to me in London, you know," Marianne said in a conspiratorial whisper. "I curled my little finger at him,

443

and he came running. But then, he's always been so devoted. I don't know how I got so lucky as to deserve him."

Rosalie said nothing, doing her best to keep her features schooled. She knew he'd gone to London. She even knew he went to speak with Marianne, though she'd carefully asked for no details. And Renley offered none.

Marianne inched closer, dropping her voice to a whisper. "I won't tell you what passed between us, for it would be . . . indelicate," she said. "And you are such an innocent. Such a sweet flower." She had the audacity to raise a gloved hand and stroke Rosalie's cheek.

If Marianne was telling the truth, Tom went from her bed to Rosalie's arms. For was it not the day after his return from London that they shared their first kiss in the forest? What about what happened after? Every day since, his every look, touch, and stolen word told Rosalie he wanted more from her.

But he does not love you. He loves Marianne. It's always been Marianne.

"Fate has been unkind," Marianne went on. "I've lived eight years without my Tom, trapped in an unhappy marriage. But we've been given a second chance. He came to me in London and forgave me. He said such beautiful words. It taught me to hope that perhaps he had not completely hardened his heart to me. I braved the journey here, and we find ourselves as much in love as ever. And I want to thank you."

Rosalie felt ready to scream. "Thank me?"

"Tom told me you've been such a good friend. Was it not you who urged him to come to me? You reminded him about what really matters." Condescension dripped from the lady's tone. It was enough to have Rosalie fisting her gown to keep from raising a hand to smack the smug look off her face.

"And what matters, Mrs. Young?"

"Love," Marianne replied. "Honoring *first* love. Building on strong foundations." She leveled a look at Rosalie. "Tom knows what he has with me: a passionate, abiding love. Thank you for reminding him, for being such a friend to us both."

If this woman didn't get out of Rosalie's face, she was going to slam her head into the mirrored wall. Renley must have noticed something was wrong because his eye kept darting across the room. In moments, he was excusing himself.

"Ahh, you see?" Marianne cooed. "See how he comes to my side. He makes such a dutiful fiancé."

Rosalie's heart sank out of her chest. Had Renley proposed? When?

Perhaps while you had Burke on his knees.

Rosalie blamed herself, for had she not encouraged him to forgive this conniving creature?

"I hope we'll be married in Town . . ." Marianne went on.

Rosalie couldn't listen to another word, and Renley was almost upon them. "I'm sure you'll be very happy together," she forced out, her breath nearly choking on the words.

"I plan on it," Marianne replied. "He is my only concern."

Before Renley could squeeze his way past the last barrier of bodies, Rosalie spun on her heel and darted away.

"Miss Harrow, wait—"

"Let the poor thing go, Tom," came Marianne's ringing words of triumph.

Rosalie chanced a look over her shoulder to see Renley standing in the spot she'd just vacated with Marianne's hand curled around his upper arm in a natural gesture of possession.

61

Burke

BURKE STOOD STILL as stone. This couldn't be real. He wouldn't let himself believe it. To have Rosalie in his grasp, only to lose her . . . and lose her like this? Christ, she was going to do more than cut off his fingers. He'd be lucky to walk away with legs.

"Mother, you can't be serious," said James from his side.

"When am I ever *not* serious, James?" she replied.

"But Lady Olivia is . . ."

"The absolute fucking worst," George provided, still smiling like an imp.

"I never agree with George on principle," James added, "but in this instance I do. Mother, she's far too impressed with her own opinion of herself to ever accept Burke."

"Well, she's already agreed, so your point is moot, James," the duchess replied.

"And if I say no?" Burke asked, finding his voice at last.

The duchess turned an imperious glare on him. "Why on earth would you refuse? In one fell swoop, I have secured for you wealth, respectability, a title, and a wife."

"But I don't love Olivia—"

"Oh, pish tosh," the duchess scoffed. "What is love in a

marriage? Absolutely worthless. Besides, just because there is no feeling of love now, doesn't mean you cannot win her over. You are just what a husband ought to be. Why should she have cause to complain?"

"Perhaps because I am the bastard son of a nobody with a literal whore for a mother," Burke replied.

"I thought your mother retired," said George, brow raised in curiosity.

"Not the point, George," James growled. He turned on his mother. "How did you even manage it? Why would Olivia ever agree to this?"

When the duchess made no immediate reply, Burke's heart sank with foreboding.

James shared his anxiety. "Christ, Mother . . . what did you do?"

The duchess just sniffed. "It is enough that the deal is struck."

"Oh, fuck . . ." James whispered.

Burke had already worked it out too. He exchanged a look of horror with James.

"You're blackmailing her," said James. "You're using the mess with George as leverage."

Burke felt sick.

"Oh James, don't be such a ninny," she said. "Olivia knew exactly what she was doing. This is hardly the first time a woman has played the game of politics and lost. Now, she must pay the price."

Burke was beyond horrified. "And I am to be her punishment for the rest of her life?"

"That remains for you to decide," she replied. "If you are the gentleman I raised, you will manage to charm your new wife—"

"I won't do it. I thank you for your pain and trouble, but I refuse."

The duchess' eyes flashed with some hidden fire, even as they remained deeply blue. "You don't get to refuse me. The deal is struck. The marchioness is waiting for you even now to shake hands on the matter."

"Mother, surely we can delay," James hedged. "Let this be George's night. We can return to the matter of Burke's engagement in a fortnight—"

"Don't you *dare* try to handle me," she snarled. "If we let this worm slip the hook, we shall never find Burke such another brilliant match—"

"Christ's sake, let her slip the hook," James cried. "Would you see him trapped?"

"A fair question," George said with a raise of his hand. "One I echo for myself—"

"Enough!" The duchess squared her shoulders at the three of them. "George, Burke, you will *both* do your duty." She narrowed her eyes on Burke. "I secured you this match, and you will cease your whining and see it through . . . or you will leave."

Burke stepped back as if hit.

"Mother," James said, a warning note in his tone. "You cannot kick him out. He is here at my pleasure, not yours."

"And you are here at *my* pleasure," she hissed. "You are not the duke, James. You are a guest in your brother's home. In *my* home, for I am still Duchess of Norland. Test me on this, and you will see how little power you truly wield. If you choose to side with Burke, you can pack your bags and be out with him at morning light."

James rounded his shoulders, ready to fight back, but Burke grabbed him by the arm. "James, don't. *Please.* Not on my account."

The duchess raised her chin. "George, go now and propose.

We'll announce it at dinner. Burke, if I see you leave this room and do anything but walk straight over to the marchioness and shake her hand, I'll instruct Reed to begin packing."

"Mother—"

She raised a hand. "This is what I want, James, and I *always* get what I want."

"He will hate you for this," James said. "And so will I."

"He can hate me," she replied. "But that won't stop me from caring for him the only way I know how. The way I have *always* cared for him . . . for all of you." With that, she turned and left.

George gave them both a sympathetic look. "That was ghastly unpleasant."

"George," James begged. "You are the duke; she is merely the dowager. You can countermand her with a word."

"I don't know . . . she seems set on her course," George said, rubbing his neck. "And it's hardly the first political marriage. You're both too principled for your own good."

"George, please," Burke murmured. "I've never asked you for anything."

George gave him a curious look and sighed. "You're in love with the Harrow girl too, aren't you?"

Too? Burke flinched. Christ's sake, George knew. Of course, he did.

"I don't get it," George muttered. "I mean, I see the attraction, obviously. But she's so . . ." He mimed an oddly strained face. "What do you both see in her?"

"Leave it alone, George," James warned.

"You're asking for my help. I assume it's so you can snare Miss Harrow instead—"

"No," James replied.

"She doesn't want to be snared," Burke added under his

breath. "And this isn't about Rosalie. It's about doing right by Olivia and not trapping her in a marriage that will make us both miserable."

"Will you help us?" James pressed.

George groaned. "You know how I hate to take sides. You heard Mama . . . she put in all that work. And it would make you a baron, Burke."

"I don't care about being a fucking baron," he replied. "I'm happy with my life. I'm happy here."

George raised a brow. "Here, where you can fuck Mama's ward and live free of responsibility?"

Burke tensed. "It's not like that."

"It seems exactly like that from where I'm standing," George replied. "I think if I have to grow up, we all must. It might do you good to marry—"

"Please, George," he said again. "Not like this."

"I'll think on it," George replied at last. "I make no promises, mind. I don't want you thinking you can just push me around and get your way. I'm my own man," he finished with a determined glare.

"Of course, you are," James replied.

George tossed him a scowl. "Fuck off, James. I don't need you patronizing me."

"I only meant—"

"You're not part of this. This is between me and Burke. I'll make up my own mind and thank you to keep your mouth shut. You heard Mama—you're a guest here."

James bristled, but said nothing. That alone was proof for Burke what James was willing to do to help him. In any other situation, if George talked to James that way, they'd already be brawling on the floor.

George left, closing the door with a snap.

"This won't happen," James said as soon as they were alone. "I won't let this happen."

Burke just stood there, staring at the spot by the piano where, not an hour ago, he had been on his knees before Rosalie. "I need to talk to her," he muttered.

"Olivia? I don't know if that's a good idea. We need a plan first—"

"Not Olivia. Rosalie. I have to tell her. Have to warn her."

James tensed. "I don't think—"

"I have to tell her. Now."

James' eyes searched his face. "Something happened. What did you do?"

Burke growled. "Do you really want to stand here talking about where and how I touched her, or do you want to go get her for me, so I can warn her that I'm about to shatter her happiness into a million fucking pieces? And all because fucking George had to go dragging Olivia into his bed, and *you* had to go dragging Rosalie into stairwells."

James bristled, eyes murderous. "I had *nothing* to do with that—"

"You didn't tell me!"

"And you didn't tell me about tonight—"

"Because it just fucking happened!" Burke roared. "Just now, in this very room. She told me she loved me, and I shoved my tongue in her cunt right next to the goddamned piano. That was before I fucked her where you're standing." His shoulders sagged as he turned away. "She told me she loved me and that I was hers . . . and now I get to go tell her that Olivia Rutledge is going to be mine . . . unless I want to leave the only home I've ever known."

451

"Burke—"

"Don't fucking pity me," he snarled. "Just go get Rosalie so I can tell her that she's lost me before she even had me."

After a few moments of silence, James spoke. "Here's what we'll do. You will go now and shake the marchioness' hand—"

"But—"

"They don't want this marriage to happen any more than you do," James reasoned. "They're being blackmailed, remember? If anything, Olivia can be a useful ally in our quest to stop my mother from waging war on the marquess."

Burke saw the sense in this strategy.

"Go to the marchioness and let her know you intend to break the engagement. Mother won't announce it tonight. She won't want to detract from George. We still have time."

"But Rosalie—"

"I'll go find Rosalie and bring her back here. Come as soon as you can."

Burke nodded, feeling the pieces of the plan fall into place. He turned to leave.

"And Burke," James called.

Burke glanced over his shoulder.

"If it all falls apart, if Mother kicks us out . . . I'm still a viscount. I have my own accounts and holdings separate from the estate. We'll move to Town. We'll be fine."

Burke's heart swelled at James' use of the collective "we." It was the olive branch he needed. Despite it all, James was still resolutely on his side. He nodded and went in search of Lady Gorgon.

62

Rosalie

ROSALIE SLIPPED IN with the crowd of people moving into the dining rooms. Her emotions were in utter turmoil. The high of her moment with Burke was so perfectly shattered by meeting Marianne. She knew it was wrong to think of keeping Renley for herself . . . but for a few shining moments, she let herself dream she could have everything—Burke's love, Renley's intimate friendship, a life of purpose here at Alcott. It was more than she ever expected or deserved.

But in the same moment she gained Burke, she lost Renley. And what of James? His cruel words rattled around in her mind, daring to shred her confidence. Worthless. Inferior. Passing fancy. Loose whore. Then he kissed her. The heat of those kisses still burned on her lips, confusing her all over again. Was Burke right? Did James want her too? Renley seemed to think James was fighting himself as much as her . . .

But she couldn't think about James Corbin now. Or Renley, who she must bid adieu. She needed to survive the rest of this night. She'd stay below only long enough to see the duke's engagement announced, then she could retire upstairs.

Perhaps Burke would come find her. She could sleep in the comfort of his arms, knowing he, at least, was hers.

The main dining room typically had a table large enough to seat forty. But that table was exchanged for several smaller round tables, and now nearly eighty people could squeeze in. The smaller drawing room and a parlor had been fashioned into additional dining rooms.

Rosalie quickly found her table and took a seat next to Lady Oswald. The Nashes were already seated, with the duke standing over the back of Piety's chair. Piety looked up at him, batting her lashes. Next to her, Prudence was doing her best to smile and nod along. Rosalie helped herself to a few biscuits. A clatter and a shriek had her glancing up.

The duke dropped to one knee next to Piety's chair. "Dearest Piety, make me the happiest man in all of England, and consent to be my wife!"

There was a collective intake of breath as all eyes turned their way.

"Yes! A thousand times yes, *yes!*" Piety threw her arms around his neck. He dragged her to her feet, twirling her around. The room erupted with cheers.

Rosalie's heart thumped in her chest. She glanced first to Prudence, who was now crying into her napkin, and then Blanche, who seemed too stunned for emotion.

"Well, that's that, then," muttered Sir Andrew, returning his attention to his soup.

The duke put Piety back on her feet and pulled a box from his pocket with a flourish. He opened it for Piety, and she squealed. She held out a hand as he took out a massive glittering ring and slipped it on her finger. The crowd clapped again.

It was then Rosalie realized the duchess was in the room.

She caught Rosalie's eye and gave her a little wink. After all, in a roundabout way, this was all Rosalie's doing. Rosalie sighed. Life at Alcott was about to get a lot more interesting when Piety Nash took up residence.

"Come, we must celebrate!" the duke called to the room. "Everyone, be up standing! Piety, my love, come. We shall lead them all in a merry jig!"

The crowd cheered again, and there was a great scraping of chairs as the happy couple led the way out of the room. Rosalie gave a wistful look at her uneaten biscuits before she got to her feet, following the Oswalds.

News spread quickly, and cheers erupted all through the house as the party surged into the ballroom. The duke and Piety floated to the middle of the room, followed closely by a supremely sullen-looking James.

Rosalie found a place along the wall. Her heart fluttered as she caught sight of Burke. He was speaking quietly with the marchioness. Olivia glared at Burke like she hoped he would turn to stone. Rosalie watched as the marchioness said something through tight lips and offered out her hand. He took it in both of his, while Olivia looked away in disgust. The whole scene was . . . odd.

Rosalie peered about the room and realized with a jolt that Renley had caught sight of her. He was moving her way, entreating her with a look to stay put. Marianne followed close behind. Before she could decide whether and how to move away, Rosalie felt another chill. She followed the sensation to see James' green eyes locked on her too. His expression was grave as he jutted his chin at her, as if trying to say without words that he needed to speak with her in private.

Not likely.

She couldn't take another one-on-one session with James tonight. Not if it would include a repeat of any of his earlier sentiments. It was one thing to know all your own faults . . . it was quite another to have a gentleman list them out for you in order of most offensive. She looked pointedly away.

Before Renley could get any closer, the music stopped.

"My Lords, Ladies, and Gentlemen, your attention, if you please!" called the duke. "I beg your indulgence for one moment. You see, just moments ago, I asked this beautiful woman if she would make me the happiest of men and consent to be my wife." He paused for dramatic effect as Piety glimmered like a diamond. "She said yes."

The ballroom erupted with cheers. Rosalie glanced around to see the stricken faces of the Swindon sisters and Blanche. Only Madeline seemed unfazed by the news, smiling next to Mr. Bray and clapping with the others.

Footmen moved through the room, trying to get glasses of champagne into guests' hands as quickly as possible. Rosalie took a flute from a passing tray. She glanced across the room to catch Burke's eye. The intensity of his gaze warmed her as she remembered his touch, the feel of his breath against her skin.

Even from this distance she could tell his grey eyes were swirling with storms. He was furious. With her? What happened? She raised a brow, asking a silent question. His glower softened as he jerked his head in the exact same way James did moments before. He wanted her to slip out of the room. Could she get to a door without being noticed?

As soon as the duke had a glass in hand, he raised it in the air. "I call for a toast!"

All the guests raised their glasses.

"To a woman of unparalleled charm and grace, to my intended, Miss Piety Nash, the future Duchess of Norland!"

"The future Duchess of Norland!"

Rosalie took a deep sip of the dry champagne, letting the bubbles fizzle on her tongue. Then she moved towards the closest door.

"And where is Miss Harrow? Miss . . . *ah*! Miss Harrow, come forward!"

Rosalie slid to a stop as the crowd around her parted.

The duke smiled at her, that teasing twinkle in his eye. "Our engagement would not have been possible were it not for Miss Harrow, our family's delightful new ward."

Rosalie stilled. First the duchess announced it to all her closest friends, now the duke had declared it to the entire county.

"To Miss Harrow!"

"Miss Harrow!" the crowd cheered.

Rosalie was mortified. What had the duchess told him? Did he know she'd called him an entertainer who must be entertained? That he was a man who craved spectacle? She was immobilized as everyone around her gave her smiles and well-wishes.

Apparently, the duke wasn't done. He waved a hand for silence. "There is one more very special announcement—"

James stepped forward to whisper something in his ear, and Rosalie felt a sudden sense of foreboding. The duke waved him back, almost sloshing the champagne out of his glass. He cleared his throat. "Long before Miss Harrow joined our household, we had another foundling call Alcott home. This man is as close to me as a brother could be, except for you, James, of course," he added.

A few people around the room chuckled, but Rosalie felt suddenly ill. What was happening, and why did James look so upset?

"I am pleased to announce that, as of tonight, our dear Burke has accepted my generous offer to formally join our family."

All around the room were whispers and gasps of surprise.

Rosalie gasped too, eyes wide, as she looked at Burke.

"Hereafter, let all of society recognize him as a Corbin of Alcott Hall!" called the duke.

"Mr. Corbin!"

"Alcott Hall!"

Rosalie's heart raced. They could have offered him use of the name at any point in his long years here. Why change his identity now? Why tonight?

"Oh god . . ." she whispered, tears burning her eyes. She looked desperately at Burke, but he was blocked from view now. Her eye shot over to James, who was looking right at her. He gave a shake of his head, and her heart sank.

The duke cleared his throat again. "And as of tonight, my dear adopted brother is engaged to Lady Olivia Rutledge, eldest daughter of the Marquess of Deal."

Surprised gasps swept through the room.

"To the future Right Honorable Baron and Baroness Margate!" he called, raising his glass aloft for a third time.

"Baron Margate!"

"The Baroness!"

Rosalie's glass of champagne slipped through her fingers, cracking into pieces on the floor. Burke was surrounded by people pressing in to congratulate him and Olivia. They both wore plastered-on smiles that didn't meet their eyes. When did he agree to this? *Oh god* . . . was he engaged when he came to her in the music room?

The music struck up and the floor cleared. "Come," the duke laughed, waving a hand at Burke and Olivia. The crowd urged the other couple forward. Rosalie watched as Burke offered Olivia his hand and led her onto the floor.

This was real. It didn't matter how it began or when he agreed. He was going through with it, and so was Olivia. The crowd clapped as the two new couples took to the floor.

Rosalie used the distraction to make her escape. She couldn't stay in this room and watch Burke dance with a woman who would become his bride. She had one hour of happiness. One hour where she felt like he was hers and she was his and they could make their own way in the world.

It was already over. She was alone again.

She stumbled out of the ballroom, clutching at her chest as she heaved, her lungs desperate for air. Her vision was spinning. The grand gallery seemed to tilt as she did the only thing she could think to do, the only thing her body would allow. Rosalie lifted the hem of her gown, and she ran.

63

James

GEORGE WAS A fucking dead man. Announcing Burke's engagement to the whole county was *not* in the plan. James watched Rosalie's face as George prattled on, each careless word striking her like a physical blow. She fell apart when the crowded ballroom shouted their cheers to the future Baron and Baroness Margate.

One thing was certain: She loved Burke. Whatever else she said about marriage, she loved him. James felt an inexplicable ache. Of course, he understood the appeal, for he loved the idiot too . . . if not quite in the same way.

But James was also jealous. He was jealous of Rosalie that she could so easily earn another's love and devotion, especially a devotion as hard won as Burke's. But he was jealous of Burke too. Burke who wasn't afraid to let himself want her.

James' own passing infatuation wasn't going away. All his usual tricks were failing him. He tried minimizing her charms, focusing on her flaws. He tried avoidance. Christ, he'd even been a total arse, lost his temper, and said all those callous things in the library . . . right before he kissed her.

He was always so in control, so careful. But with one look from her, he fell apart. He hated feeling so unraveled.

Where is she?

As soon as this dance was over, Burke would be tracking her down. James could already see the tension spilling off his friend's shoulders as he led Olivia into the set to begin the dance.

"Hey, what the hell is happening?"

James turned sharply to see Renley striding over. He dragged a hand through his hair. "It's a goddamn disaster."

"What's going on? Is this real or just for show?"

"It's real enough," James muttered. "But we're going to get him out of it." Renley raised a curious brow, but James said, "Not here and not now. I'll fill you in later."

Renley frowned. His eye was also roving around the ballroom. "Is that Marianne I saw you with earlier? I thought she would still be in mourning."

"Not here, not now," Renley echoed. "Have you seen Rosalie? She took off."

"I know, and we need to find her." James skirted around the edge of the ballroom, Renley following just behind.

"She seemed pretty upset . . ."

"That's an understatement," James growled. "Look, let's split up and find her. When you do, bring her to the music room. As soon as the dance is over, Burke's going to be on the hunt too. Don't get in his way. He's out for blood."

"Christ, because of Rosalie? What—"

"No, not her," James clarified. "The blood Burke craves is decidedly Corbin flavored."

As soon as they were in the grand gallery, Renley raised his voice to a normal volume. "Where would she go?"

"I'm not sure—you there!" James waved at a footman. "Billings, right?"

The footman nodded. "Yes, my lord."

"Have you seen Miss Harrow?"

"No, my lord."

James shouted down the length of the gallery to the other footmen lining the way. "Have any of you seen Miss Harrow?"

No one replied in the affirmative.

"Keep both eyes open," he called. "Any sign of her is reported directly to me." He turned to Renley. "I'll get her maid to search her room. You cover the ground floor here. Check the large and small library. Get a footman to open my mother's study if you have to."

"And if she's run off?" Renley called after his already retreating form.

James slid to a stop. "It's one in the morning. Where the hell would she go?"

Renley shrugged. "She's a wild thing, James. She may not have wings, but I wouldn't put it past her to fly off."

"Just . . . find her," he said with a sigh. "Or Burke's going to have a first course of Renley before he feasts on us Corbins."

Rosalie wasn't anywhere to be found, and not one of the dozens of servants seemed to have seen her. James checked the whole of the new wing, finally resorting to calling her name in an increasingly angry and desperate tone.

A sudden thought occurred to him, fragile as mist. Something Renley said . . . something about flying . . .

"Goddamn it." James turned on his heel and swept down the deserted hallway. Music from the ballroom filtered down to this far end of the house. The dance was still going strong.

It must be a massive set, or a long reel . . . or both. Good, because James needed more time.

He shoved his way out the back door, trotting down the dark stairs and across the garden towards the stables. Renley said she might fly off. Well, the little bird didn't have wings, but she could ride well enough. If James felt his world crashing down, if everything was being ripped from his arms, he'd be fighting the urge to flee too.

Hell . . . he *was* fighting that urge.

Alcott was doubling its pork production because of James' investments. The south barley fields were yielding better crops. The mine was producing again. Leases were up, taxes were being collected with consistency. But all his hard work was for naught. He was nothing but the second son. He lived at the whims of his ridiculous brother and scheming mother.

He stomped his way over to the stable. The yard was busy, as all the coachmen and footmen busied about, laughing and gaming and smoking pipes.

"Wallace," he called to the groom. "Has Miss Harrow passed through here?"

The young lad looked lovestruck, which was answer enough. Did she ever *not* turn a man's head? Fucking hell.

"She's inside, m'lord," young Wallace chirped.

James swept into the stable. It was dark, the only real light coming from the torches in the courtyard. He knew without asking where she'd be. He moved down the row of stalls, stopping at the one on the end for little Magellan.

Rosalie stood there in the straw in her ballgown and pearls, back turned, brush in hand, currying the pony. She was singing softly to it, a tune James didn't recognize. Little Magellan perked up his ears.

"Planning to run away?"

She gasped, dropping the brush to the straw, and spun around, dark eyes wide. Her hair looked so different all done up in those curls. It showed off the arc of her neck, but he preferred it down, all wild and tumbling about. And his mother's pearls were the first thing he noticed when she came floating down the stairs. He recognized the necklace as a gift from his father. He liked seeing her in Corbin family jewels—

Fuck, don't start. Keep it together. Do not let her unravel you.

"How did you find me?" she whispered.

"I was told you would fly away given half a chance," he replied. "I thought you might seek help from a surefooted accomplice."

"Did he send you?"

He frowned. "I should ask you to be more specific . . . but in either case, the answer is no. I sent myself. Look, about what happened earlier—"

"Don't." She held back a sob as she spun around. "Please, I can't discuss it now. Not now . . . not with you."

James fell silent. He'd lost her trust with his outburst in the library. First with that horrid verbal assault . . . then that bloody kiss. He ought to apologize for both, but it would probably only make her cry, and that he couldn't bear, not when he already felt so frayed. She didn't want comfort from him, and it pained him deeper than he'd have thought possible.

If James wanted to fix what was broken between them, he'd have to make the first attempt. "What do you need?"

She stilled, holding the brush. "What?"

He leaned over the top of the stall door. "I'm asking what you need. Tell me, and I'll make it happen if I can."

She took a few shaky breaths before turning slowly around

again. "I want to go home. I want to go to London to see my aunt. I want—I need to be with my family. I need to think and . . . can you do that?"

A buzzing feeling vibrated inside him. "Right now? You want to go to London at one o'clock in the morning?"

"Well . . . if we leave now, we could be there by breakfast," she said with a shrug.

This was quite possibly the worst idea James had ever indulged. But this little bird wanted to fly free, and James found himself wanting the same thing. "I'll see it done."

Her lips parted in surprise. "Wait—really? Right now?"

"Why would we wait?"

"I . . . have no things. My trunk . . . my bonnet and dresses," she gestured at her ballgown.

"They sell clothes in London, do they not?"

"Of course, but—"

"I'll buy you a replacement wardrobe. Here—" He shrugged out of his evening coat and handed it over the stall door. "Put this on for now. I'll go see the carriage prepared."

Their fingers brushed as she took the coat. The sleeves were too long, and it hung off her at the shoulders, but James couldn't deny she looked edible all the same. Seeing her in his coat, the Corbin jewels, those wide eyes . . . it made his cock twitch.

This was a terrible idea. He smiled anyway.

"Will we . . . tell anyone?" she whispered.

He met her excited gaze. "You tell me. This is your plan. I'm just setting it in motion."

She considered for a minute before she shook her head. "No . . . tell no one."

James took a breath. This was madness. As much as he

wanted to abide by her wishes to ask no questions and offer no excuses, he couldn't stay silent. "Burke's engagement was not his idea. They are both under duress. He's in love with you. The second he realizes where we've gone, he will come after us."

She took a shaky breath, eyes welling with tears. "What do you mean duress?"

"My mother found out about Olivia and George," he explained. "She's blackmailing the marquess to buy Burke a respectable wife and a title, threatening to ruin Olivia if she doesn't agree."

Rosalie raised a hand to her mouth. "How despicable."

"It's her love language," James replied with a shrug.

She scowled. "Ruination and misery as a language of love?"

He nodded. "But they will be rich and titled . . . which will make it all worth it in her eyes."

Heat burned across Rosalie's face. "No, it won't. And we're going to stop it. We're going to London, and we'll make a plan, and then you and I are going to get Burke and Olivia free of this mess."

He raised a brow. "You still want to go?"

She gave a curt nod.

"Why?"

She put her hands on her hips, her eyes dancing with hidden fire. "Because your mother seeks to add me to her collection too, and I will not be used by her or anyone. Leaving sends a message she needs to hear: Rosalie Harrow cannot be bought."

The story continues in

His Grace, the Duke

coming from Kensington Books in
October 2025

THANK YOU

BEAUTIFUL THINGS HOLDS such a special place in my heart. It's the first book I ever self-published. At the time, I was a poor graduate student working two jobs, finishing a dissertation, and raising a two-year-old child. With no budget, I taught myself Photoshop so I could design the cover. I did all my own editing. I sent out eARCs, built out my social media accounts, and designed merchandise. Overnight, I became a one-woman publishing house.

All the while, I was told no one would read this book. It was too niche. No one was looking for a "why choose" Regency romance, and I was wasting my time writing it.

I published it anyway. Then I wrote and published the next book. This series helped me secure my literary agent. Within a week of signing with Susan, we sold the audio rights to the series. And we haven't looked back since. Together, we've now sold rights to all my books in multiple formats and languages.

It's customary with a "thank you" section to thank all the people who helped bring a book to life. I hope you'll all forgive me, but just this one time (in this one very special book), I'm thanking only one person. It's the one person I never publicly thank. I'm thanking me.

Emily, you've worked so damn hard for this. Keep writing. Don't let anyone dim your light.

BEAUTIFUL THINGS
PLAYLIST

She | Harry Styles
bad guy | Vitamin String Quartet
Falling | Paravi
Lieder ohne Worte, Op. 19, No. 1 | Felix Mendelssohn
Mind Games | BANKS
Mercy | Shawn Mendes
Nocturne for Piano No. 1 in E-Flat Major, H 24: Molto
Moderato | John Fields
Words | Birdy
I Want Your Love | Charlotte OC
I Feel Like I'm Drowning | Two Feet
Treacherous | Taylor Swift
Symphony No. 1 in B-Flat Major: Allegro | William Boyce
GOMF (feat. BRIDGE) | DVBBS
Riptide | Duomo
Violin Sonata No. 21 in E Minor, K. 304: II Tempo di
Minuetto | Wolfgang Amadeus Mozart
thank u, next | Vitamin String Quartet
Cold Front | Laura Welsh
Suite No. 5 in E Major, HWV 430: IV. Air con Variazioni
(Andantino) | George Frideric Handel
Heathens | Midnite String Quartet
Watermelon Sugar | Harry Styles

ABOUT THE AUTHOR

EMILY RATH is a *New York Times* and internation-
ally bestselling author whose chart-topping, sex-positive,
queer-inclusive fantasy and romance novels include the
Second Sons Regency romances, the Tuonela Duet fantasy
novels, and the "why choose" sensation, the Jacksonville Rays
Hockey Romances. A former university professor, she holds
PhDs in Political Science and Peace Studies. Emily was
born in Florida, raised in Kentucky, and now lives in the
Pacific Northwest.

Visit her at: EmilyRathBooks.com
Instagram: @emilyrathauthor
TikTok: @emilyrathbooks